Marianne Fredriksson was born in 1927 in Gothenburg, Sweden. She has two children and was a well-known journalist before she wrote her first book in 1980. She is the author of eleven novels, including *Hanna's Daughters*, for which she was awarded the Author of the Year award and Book of the Year award in 1994. *Hanna's Daughters* has been translated into 37 languages and has been on the World Top Ten Bestseller list for three years in a row. *Simon & the Oaks* was Number 7 on the same list in 1999.

Simon & the Oaks

MARIANNE FREDRIKSSON

Translated by Joan Tate

PHŒNIX

A PHOENIX PAPERBACK

First published in Great Britain by Orion in 1999
This paperback edition published in 2000 by Phoenix,
an imprint of Orion Books Ltd,
Orion House, 5 Upper St Martin's Lane,
London WC2H 9EA

Original title: *Simon och ekarna*
Published by Wahlström & Widstrand, Stockholm, 1985

Published by agreement with
Bengt Nordin Agency, Värmdö, Sweden

A CIP catalogue record for this book
is available from the British Library.

ISBN: 0 75381 075 1

Printed in Great Britain by
Clays Ltd, St Ives plc

Part One

Chapter 1

'An ordinary bloody oak,' the boy said to the tree. 'Hardly fifteen metres high. That's nothing much to boast about. And you're not a hundred thousand metres either.' He thought of his grandmother, now nearly ninety and nothing but an ordinary, shrill old woman.

Named, measured and compared, the tree retreated from the boy. But he could still hear the singing in the treetops, melancholy and reproachful. He resorted to violence and crashed the stone he had kept for so long in his pocket against the trunk. 'That'll shut you up,' he said.

The great tree fell silent and the boy knew something important had happened. He swallowed the lump in his throat, disowning his grief.

That was the day he said farewell to his childhood. He did so at a definite moment and in a definite place, so was always to remember it. For many years he was to ponder over what he had relinquished that day. At twenty he was to have some idea, and would spend the rest of his life trying to recapture it.

But, at that moment, he was on the hillside above Äppelgren's garden, looking over the sea, at the fog gathering round the skerries before rolling in towards the coast. In the land of his childhood the fog had many voices and, on a day like this, was singing from Vinga to Älvsborg.

Behind him were the mountains and the meadow, the land that is but doesn't exist. At the end of the meadow

3

were the oak woods, the trees that had spoken to him over the years.

In their shade, he had met the little man with the strange round hat. No, he thought, that's not true. He had always known the man, but it was in the shade of these trees that he had actually seen him.

But it no longer mattered. 'It's just a load of shit,' the boy said aloud as he crawled under the barbed wire of Äppelgren's fence.

He managed to avoid Edit Äppelgren, the old woman who tore out the couch grass in her straight flower beds on early spring days like this. The foghorns had frightened her indoors. She couldn't stand fogs.

The boy understood that. Fog was the grief of the sea, as infinite as the sea, and not really bearable . . . 'Oh, shit,' he said again for, although he knew better, he had decided to look at the world as other people saw it. The fog was the warmth of the Gulf Stream rising when the air grew cold. Nothing more than that.

But he couldn't deny the sorrow in the long drawn-out wail of foghorns over the harbour entrance as he slanted across Äppelgren's lawn and slipped into his kitchen where he was given hot cocoa.

The boy's name was Simon Larsson. He was eleven, small, thin, dark-complexioned. His hair was coarse, brown, almost black, his eyes so dark that sometimes it was hard to distinguish the pupils.

His appearance had not bothered him before for, until now, he had never compared himself with others. He thought about Edit Äppelgren and her difficulties with the fog. Mostly he thought about Aron, her husband. Simon had always liked Aron.

The boy was a runaway, one of those children who, like cheerful puppies, followed the temptations of the road. It could begin with a colourful toffee paper in the ditch outside the gate, continue with an empty box of Tiger Brand and a little further away a bottle, then another, a red flower, further on a white stone, then perhaps a glimpse of a cat.

In that way he ended up further and further away from home, and he remembered clearly the day he realised he was lost. He saw the tram, large and blue, as it rattled out of town. It frightened him terribly. But just as he opened his mouth to bawl, Aron was there.

Aron bent his tall figure over Simon and his voice seemed to come from the sky. 'Good gracious, boy. Running away again, eh?'

He heaved him up on to the carrier of his black bicycle and started walking home, talking all the time about the birds, the fat chaffinches, the cheeky great tits, and the grey sparrows hopping around them in the dust on the road. He said he had nothing but contempt for them – the flying rats.

In spring, Aron and Simon cut across the field and the boy learned to distinguish the song of the lark. Then, in his tremendous voice, Aron sang a song that went rolling down the slopes and echoed against the cliffs: 'When in spri-i-i-ing among the mountai-ai-ains . . .'

Best was when Aron whistled. He could imitate any bird and Simon almost burst with excitement when Aron got the female blackbird to respond lustily and willingly to him. Then Aron grinned his good big grin.

The song that surpassed all other birds in the hills and at the mouth of the river was the skrieking of gulls. Aron could imitate them too, and could tease them into such rage that they would dive-bomb them as they stood in the road.

Then Simon laughed so much he almost wet himself, and the neighbours, hastening past on their constant errands, would stop and smile at the tall man enjoying himself as much as the little boy.

'Aron will never grow up,' they said.

But Simon didn't hear this. To him Aron was the king of his world.

Now, Simon sat at the table with his cocoa, seeing Aron as other people saw him, realising for the first time that Aron's amazing ability to rescue him coincided with his working hours. Simon had run away after his midday meal. Aron often finished work early and had just caught the tram when he reached the tram stop. Aron picked up his bicycle there, and had thus come across the strange little boy who was always getting lost.

Simon could see the contempt, the sly grins and half-words that gathered around Aron. He was the bouncer at a disreputable pub in the harbour and had a nickname Simon didn't understand, but which was so foul that it made his mother turn scarlet with indignation.

As Simon swallowed the last bit of bun and scraped round the cup with his spoon, he reckoned Aron had never taken the step he had taken that day. Aron Äpplegren had never stood up on a hillside and said goodbye to his childhood.

Sleeping on the wooden sofa in the kitchen turned Simon into a socialist.

His was a spacious, sunny kitchen, with large mullioned windows facing west and south, white curtains, flowering pot plants and old apple trees outside. Below the south window was a zinc-covered bench with a cold-water tap in the angle and a double-burner Primus stove. Against the long wall below the window was the kitchen sofa, painted blue like the chairs. The big kitchen table was covered with oilcloth for everyday and an embroidered cotton tablecloth on Sundays.

Slow cooking, often meat soup. Coffee. Baking: a good smell on Wednesdays, baking day. Gossip. If you made yourself small and invisible, you could absorb it from the wood-box: who was expecting and whom to be sorry for.

There were many people to be sorry for and Simon learned never to think ill of them. In that way, he lost his rage early. In fact, he never really found it again, shouting only occasionally throughout his life, always too late and often in the wrong place. He also learned that he must never talk about feeling sorry for himself.

There was Hansson who was unemployed and who beat his wife on Saturdays when he'd bought strong liquor from the store. There was Hilma who had two daughters at the sanatorium and whose youngest had died of consumption. And then there was Andersson's beautiful girl who always had new clothes and walked the streets in town. But, when they came to what she did on the streets, they sent the boy out.

The women noticed Simon, but the men didn't. That was what was so good about sleeping on the sofa. The men sat in the kitchen in the evenings, drinking beer instead of coffee, discussing politics and talking about that damned vehicle that had packed up yet again.

Simon's father and his uncle had a haulage business which meant they owned a truck. In the daytime it took timber and materials to the building sites around the city and food to the houses. At night they mended it for the bearings were worn, the valves had to be re-ground and the gearbox was shot to pieces.

They were skilful, his father and uncle. The day they came across a six-cylinder engine instead of the worn-out old four-cylinder one, they were happy. But the change forced them to lengthen the truck's driveshaft and give it an extra coupling. Having decided to retain the sturdy cog-wheel transmission, they soon had a vehicle that could crawl up the steepest of all the steep hills in the city, even when they were icy.

Gradually their truck became a piece of craftsmanship in almost every detail. It said Dodge on the front, but in the end the question was whether there was all that much left but the red shell from Detroit.

Simon's father and uncle took a break at ten o'clock every evening to listen to the late news bulletin on the radio perched on a stool at the foot of the kitchen sofa. At the other end of the sofa Simon lay under a piece of red and white check cloth which was fixed like a tent between the seat and back, and hooked up when he was considered to be asleep.

That was how he heard about the terror creeping out of the heart of Europe; a terror called Hitler. Sometimes Hitler bellowed on the radio and Germans yelled their 'heils'. Afterwards his father said that sooner or later their world would go to hell and everything the workers and Per Albin had built up would be smashed to smithereens.

One day a man came with specially forged bolts – bolts he had made out of the goodness of his heart, the boy's mother said, after his father had thrown him out.

'Goodness of his heart?' raged his father. 'A Jew-hater, a Nazi in my kitchen. Are you mad, woman?'

'Don't shout like that! You'll wake the boy.'

'Worse things could happen to him,' said his father. But then his mother started to cry and the harsh words faded into silence.

Lying under the tent on the sofa, Simon was frightened. He remembered the words that had been flung at him at school. His father had turned pale when he had told him and, one improbable but wonderful evening, had taught him how to fight. Hour after hour they practised in the basement, straight right, swift left hook and then an uppercut if the occasion arose.

The next day the boy practised his new skills at school and had never heard those words again.

Until that evening.

Chapter 2

Simon's mother Karin was a good woman.

She was also beautiful, tall and blonde with a large, sensitive mouth and surprisingly brown eyes. Her goodness was always present and shaped the world in which Simon grew up. But it was never cloying. She was strong in herself and not threatened by change in other people. Karin was simply one of those rare people who knew that, given sufficient nourishment and encouragement, love would always flourish.

She also understood that nothing could be done about the fear running through people's lives and that no one could help another person internally. So she became the person everyone turned to. There was no ill-treated woman or man who was not given coffee and redress in her kitchen, and every child for whom things went wrong was allowed to cry his or her sorrows out over cocoa.

She neither dried their tears nor found any solutions. But she would listen.

Like most good people, Karin did not believe in evil. It existed, of course, but was generally a symptom of injustice and unhappiness. People will only treat each other like animals if they are treated like animals themselves, she said.

Mrs Ågren had eight children and hated them all. Simon was probably the only person in the village drawn to her, even going so far as to make friends with one of her sons. It was no easy friendship for, like all the Ågrens, the boy was sly and suspicious. But his friendship gave Simon entry to the Ågren kitchen and as he was good at making himself invisible, he was able to see and hear that hatred, so forceful that it boiled over and enveloped them all.

'Bloody cow!' she would yell at her eldest daughter who was doing her hair at the kitchen mirror. 'That's no use. You're like some wretched heifer, so skinny you wouldn't be worth even the butcher's fee. Don't you go thinking anyone'll cover you.'

She was worst towards her daughters, simply scolding the boys as if in passing.

'I've got you for my sins,' she would cry. 'Get out of my kitchen so I don't have to look at you.'

One day she spotted Simon and suddenly he became the focus of her hatred.

'Little bastard, you,' she said slowly, quietly, drawing it out. 'Just you go to hell and take your damned sanctimonious mother with you. But don't forget to ask her where she got *you* from.'

Simon drew a deep breath as he felt her rage arousing his own. He could find no words, but rushed out and ran down to the shore and the rocks by the bathing place. It was autumn, the sea grey and angry. 'Bitch,' he said. 'Evil bitch.'

But that didn't go far enough and soon he had to take some action. So he cut off her breasts, gouged out her eyes, then kicked her to death. Afterwards he felt strangely pleased.

Mrs Ågren was not old. But she had had four miscarriages and eight children in thirteen years, and she had hated every single one of them as soon as they were inside her. She felt they devoured her, swallowing her life, breaking up her nights and filling her days with bilious resentment. They robbed her of her self-esteem and her joy. Only anger kept her going, putting food on the table and providing clean clothes for her man and children.

'She's an over-fertile woman,' Karin said. 'That's her misfortune.'

Mrs Ågren blamed her husband – the lecherous bastard – yet he came home every Friday with his wages so she didn't dare start on him.

She had married early, a kind man in good circumstances, a crown servant, a customs officer. Many considered she had been lucky in life, while she had once had dreams of life in the new house by the sea.

One spring the eldest daughter walked into the sea. She was only sixteen years old but when the police found her body she turned out to be pregnant. At the grocer's, Mrs Ågren said it was just as well the girl had had the sense to do away with herself or she, her mother, would have strangled the damned little whore.

Then she went home and had a miscarriage.

By winter, her belly was swollen again, but this time there was no baby. In her thirty-seventh year, Ågren's wife died of a cancer raging through her just like her hatred.

Simon grieved for her and when Ågren married again, an ordinary submissive woman who kept the house clean and baked cakes, he stopped going there.

It was the evening after the day he had decided to be grown-up. The fog had lifted towards afternoon, and the light May sky looked as if it was dyed pink by the red and white check cloth over the kitchen sofa. He lay thinking about his decision.

He had done it for his mother's sake, that was clear. But he couldn't find the words that would explain it to her. So he had lost his reward, that of seeing the sorrow disappearing from her brown eyes.

This sorrow was the only truly alarming thing in Simon's life, the only unbearable thing. He always thought he was the cause of her sadness. He was not to understand until much later, when he was an adult and she was dead, that it had little to do with him.

He could make her happy. Over the years he had thought of a great many tricks to get that laughing glint in her brown eyes. A few days earlier, they had learned that Simon had got into high school, the first in the family to be allowed to study. Although only eleven, he had filled in the application form himself and cycled along the long road to that stuck-up school, as his parents called it, when the time came for the entrance test.

Simon had seen the glint in his mother's eye when he had returned with the news that he had passed.

The light went out the moment his father spoke.

'So you're going to *be* something, are you? And I'll have to pay, of course. Are you sure we can afford it?'

'The money'll probably work out,' his mother said. 'But the rest you'll have to do yourself. You thought it all up.'

A few years afterwards, in puberty, he was to hate them for the words spoken in the kitchen that evening. And for the loneliness that followed. Later in life, he came to understand his parents and their divided attitude to the middle-class school which devoured the bookish children and ate the working classes from within. He was also to have some idea of their feelings as they sat over dinner and considered how their son would outgrow them.

But they also wanted him to have the very best.

So when Karin cleared the table and wiped the oilcloth clean, Erik took out his account book and asked about school fees, calculating the cost of books and tram money, and looking worried. It was all largely ritual for there was no real shortage of cash. Only the eternal terror of poverty.

His mother was not in a good mood and her eyes darkened with the weight of her words. 'Then all these dreams'll have to come to an end.'

Perhaps her anxiety was nothing to do with Simon not coping with school. Maybe she was thinking her boy would now become one of the kind who was neither one thing nor the other, people who had to be someone in themselves or go under.

But Simon only heard the words and lay on the kitchen sofa thinking how pleased she would be if he could somehow tell her that he would be like other children, but more so and better. For he had noticed she was proud of his good marks and the teacher's words at the end of term last year. 'Simon is very gifted.'

His father had grunted, then been embarrassed. Saying things like that when the boy could hear, was crazy. 'The lad could get uppish,' he said as they walked slowly home. 'Gifted,' he went on, savouring the word, spitting it out.

'He's clever,' said Karin.

'Of course he's clever,' said Erik. 'He takes after us.'

'And you talk about being uppish,' Karin said, but her laugh was happy.

Simon had always been bookish. It was a quality that was accepted, like his smallness and his black hair. He had devoured all the books in the house the previous summer holiday. He remembered when one woman found him on the sofa in the parlour with *Gösta Berlings*

Saga. 'Is the lad reading Lagerlöf?' she said in a disapproving voice.

'You can't stop him,' said Karin.

'But he can't understand a book like that.'

'He must understand something or he'd stop reading it.'

His mother had ceased apologising, but the woman had the last word. 'Believe you me, nothing good can come of it.'

Did a shadow of disquiet come over Karin? Perhaps, for she must had told his father.

'Don't you go thinking the world consists of upper-class misses and mad priests,' he commented. 'Read Jack London.'

Simon read the collected works of Jack London, brown marbled editions with red borders on the spines. Some characters were still close to him from that time: Wolf-Larsen, the priest who ate human flesh, a mad violin player. And some images: a long leafy lake in the sun and the East End slums.

At the age of eleven he found his way to the public library in Majorna, his thirst less urgent now, as happens in someone who knows he always has access to water. He had also become more cautious, seeing the anxiety flitting over his mother's face as she asked herself whether there might be something different about her boy.

'Get on outside and run around before the blood rots in your veins,' Karin would say. It was a joke, but beneath it lay an unease.

Then she found him in the attic, deep in Joan Grant's book on the Queen of Egypt. His eyes stared at Karin from Pharaonic heights and he had not heard what she had said. Not until she shook him back through the centuries did he realise she was frightened. 'You mustn't lose your grasp on life,' she told him.

That evening on the kitchen sofa, he made her question his own. Was there something seriously wrong with him?

He had taken the step into the world of comparisons.

But the next day he had forgotten it completely. He and his cousin took a canoe out towards the harbour mouth, lay there with the paddle, waiting for the ferry from Denmark. It came so regularly, you could set your watch by it and it was nowhere near the largest vessel on its way into the harbour. But unlike the American ships and the white ships from the Far East, the ferry had to pass the river mouth at full speed. She made a great wash and the boys had become skilled at steering the canoe up on to the first wave and riding with it into the shore.

There she came, swift and handsome. Simon heard his cousin shout with excitement as they balanced on the crest of the wave. But they were out of line, the canoe tipped over, flinging them out, and they slid with the wave down into the depths.

For a moment, Simon felt a stab of fear, but he was a good swimmer, as was his cousin. He knew what he had to do to prevent himself from being sucked under by the next wave and he floated with it, unresisting, and the next, and the next.

As the sea calmed, the boys swam over to the canoe and towed it ashore to where the gang was waiting, scared as well as scornful. But his cousin boasted about the enormous wave – higher than any other – and honour was saved.

But Simon had something else on his mind: the image of the man he had met on his way down into the depths. The little man had been there, the old man he had said goodbye to for ever the day before.

Back at home he was scolded and given dry clothes. Then he climbed the hill and ran across the meadow towards the oak woods. He found his great trees, silent, just as they should be. Their agreement held. This was good. This was all he wanted to know.

But in his sleep that night he met his little man again and sat on the seabed carrying on a long conversation with him. When he woke in the morning he felt strangely strengthened.

Later on in the day, after he had handed in his maths test at school and had a free moment, he remembered he had forgotten to ask who the man was. Nor did he remember a single word that had been said.

It was an unusually hot summer, heavy with unease. The adults in the kitchen listened to every news bulletin.

'It's getting darker,' said his father.

'We need rain,' said his mother. 'The potatoes are shrivelling and the well is drying up.'

But the rain didn't come and, in the end, they had to buy water and have the well filled from a tanker.

Chapter 3

Simon started school that autumn, the same day Ribbentrop went to Moscow.

He was the smallest in the class and the only pupil from a working-class home. He didn't know how to behave, failed to stand up when the teachers spoke to him and said yes and no without saying thank you.

'Thank you, thank you, thank you, sir,' his classmates

16

said. Simon thought that silly, but realised he had to learn, learn for school, and keep things apart.

At home, they would have laughed their heads off. You were grateful at home, but you didn't say thank you.

Although he was the only pupil to apply for a reduction of the school fees, he was, like all the others, given a German reader and a German grammar textbook.

Home was nearly four miles away. Simon was unused to city traffic, heavy lorries and large trams and, once back in his kitchen, was in need of some comforting.

But Karin was worried about Erik who was sitting in front of the radio in the kitchen, his world shattered. The pact in Moscow was a betrayal of the workers of the world, he declared. Simon didn't understand how upset he was until Karin fetched the schnapps bottle from the larder on a perfectly ordinary weekday.

By the evening the liquor and Karin's calming words had done the trick. The ground that Erik stood on was firmer and he decided that the Russians had signed the pact to give themselves time to arm for the great and decisive battle against the Nazis.

Karin breathed a sigh of relief and looked at her son. 'Well now, how was the new school?'

'Good,' Simon said. And, throughout the years of middle, high school and university, nothing more was really said.

That evening, he didn't take the German textbooks out of his backpack.

'Little Jew-bastard, you,' said the tallest and fairest boy in the class the next day during the first break; a boy with such a grand surname that a murmur rose when it was read out at register.

Simon struck out, his right arm shooting swiftly and

unexpectedly straight from the shoulder, just as he had been taught. The tall boy fell, blood spurting from his nose.

Nothing else happened before the bell went. And it never became any worse for Simon had acquired respect and knew now that the great loneliness was to be his – here, as in his junior school.

But he was wrong for as they ran up the stairs to the physics lab, an arm was put round his shoulders and he looked into a pair of sorrowful brown eyes.

'My name's Isak,' the boy said. 'And I'm Jewish.'

They sat next to each other in the lab just as they were to sit next to each other throughout their school years. Simon had a friend.

But he didn't understand that all at once. His surprise was much greater than his delight. A real Jew! Simon looked at Isak during the lesson and simply couldn't understand. The boy was tall, thin, had brown hair and looked kind.

Just like an ordinary person, in fact.

In the long break, Isak took Simon home with him and offered him sandwiches. They had a maid rather like Mrs Ågren and she put thick slices of liver pâté on the bread and pressed tomatoes on them.

Simon had never seen a maid before and had rarely eaten tomatoes, but that wasn't what struck him. No, it was the large dark rooms, the heavy velvet curtains at the windows, the red plush sofas, the endless rows of bookshelves – and the smell, the fine odour of wax polish, perfume and wealth.

Simon absorbed it all and, as he cycled home that afternoon, he thought he knew what happiness was. He had met Isak's cousin, as grand as a princess with long painted nails. Simon wondered whether she ever needed to piss. Then it occurred to him that Karin would ask questions if he came back with his sandwiches uneaten, so he made a detour to the oak trees and ate them there.

The trees were silent.

As he walked down the slope to Äppelgren's garden, he met one of his cousins, the backward one, and felt ashamed. How dirty the boy was, Simon thought. How unbearable his ingratiating grin.

I hate him. I've always hated him, he decided. And he felt even more ashamed.

They were the same age and had started school at the same time. But soon his cousin had been put in the special class and by now the school had given up on him. He spent most of his time in the cowshed at the Dahls, the people who still had a smallholding among the houses in the growing suburb. The Dahls thus acquired a labourer who was simple-minded, but he was a good boy and strong enough for the hard work on their holding.

At home, Karin brought a folding bed down from the attic and showed Simon how he should unfold it every evening and make up his bed in the parlour. She cleared a shelf in the oak sideboard for his bedclothes. Then she took the cloth off the big table by the window and arranged a box and a shelf for his books. He was to move out of the kitchen into the parlour. All this was an acceptance of the seriousness of school.

So that first long week came to an end and Sunday arrived: the Sunday the world would never forget. Hitler's troops marched into Poland, Warsaw was bombed, Britain declared war and all of it was somehow a relief.

This was most noticeable in Erik who straightened up. 'At last,' he said. Simon also observed it in the voices of the people gathered round the radio in the kitchen.

Only Karin was more sorrowful than usual as she helped Simon make his bed that evening. 'If I had a

God,' she said. 'I would thank him on my knees that you're only eleven.'

Simon didn't know what she meant and felt nothing but the guilt he always experienced when his mother was sadder than usual.

Something had also changed at school the next day. It was as if the air had cleared and a simplification had occurred. For they lived in Sweden's major port in the west of the country, facing the sea and England. There were very few Nazis.

They had history first lesson, but there was a delay before they opened their books. The teacher was young and despairing, and considered it his task to explain to the boys what had happened. Nearly all of them, he assumed, came from homes where children were protected from reality.

To Simon, his words were familiar: fascism, Nazism, the persecution of the Jews, Spain, Czechoslovakia, Austria, Munich. His time spent on the kitchen sofa had been of some use. He was the one who knew, who faced the teacher and soon found himself in a dialogue.

'It's good to know there is at least one of you who understands what this is all about,' the teacher said finally. His words were a challenge to the others, to the middle-class boys whose world map had been given its first realistic contours.

Isak didn't say much but the teacher's eyes rested on him occasionally, as if he knew that the person with the greatest insight had remained silent.

Simon sat at his desk and thought that perhaps there were bridges between his two worlds. That much of what Erik and Karin stood for also had some value here in this grand school. That everything doesn't have to be denied, or be shameful. For he had realised that what was worst for him in his new world was that he was ashamed of his family.

That afternoon he felt confident enough to ask Isak whether he would like to come home with him one day.

At that moment, the teacher spoke: 'Whatever happens in the world, everyone has to play his part. Open your books. Now then, history begins with the Sumerians.'

Simon was no longer in the classroom. Never could he have dreamed of anything so amazing.

They read Grimberg: 'In our day, Mesopotamia is a land of the dead and great silence. Heavily weighs the Lord's restraining hand over the centuries on this unhappy land. The words of the prophet Isaiah, "How hast thou fallen from the heavens, thou destroyer of peoples", ring like a lament of the dead throughout the fallen walls . . .'

Simon didn't understand, but was caught up by the torrent of words. Then Grimberg came to the Sumerians, those broad-browed, squat people, reminiscent of the Mongols.

'They discovered written characters,' the teacher said and told them about the innumerable hieroglyphics in the great temples. For the first time the huge ziggurats rose before the boy's eyes and he followed the teacher down into the tombs of Ur and found the dead.

Many years later, Simon came to believe that his interest in prehistory was born at that moment, and that it was nourished by the success he had felt during the first half of the lesson. Perhaps he also remembered it so clearly because this was such a historic occasion, the first day of the war.

But Simon understood too that the world now opening to him had something to do with the meadow back at home.

★

He weighed the heavy knife in his hand and the blue stones of the lapis lazuli spoke their secret language to him, giving strength to his hand. His gaze was fixed on the long golden blade.

The tool was good.

But it wouldn't help him if he couldn't stay in the approaching moment and make himself timeless. He walked towards the great temple hall, sensing rather than seeing the upturned faces of the thousand people united in prayer for him.

But the bull was massive and, in the decisive moment, time caught up with him, as did that great ally of time, fear. As the bull raced towards him he knew he was going to die and he screamed . . .

Screamed so that he woke Karin, soon there and shaking him awake. 'You've had a nightmare,' she said. 'Get up and drink some water. You always have to make sure you wake up properly after you've had a nightmare.'

Simon sat at Isak's dinner table together with him and his father, his mother and the cousin with the painted nails. He had trouble with all the different knives and forks, but he watched the others and hoped that no one had noticed his uncertainty.

He had been invited to dinner. At home, people were never invited to dinner. If people came at the time of their midday meal, they just joined in. Invitations were to a party.

Isak's father was one of those rare people who lived intensely in the present. There was a suppleness in his body and his finely chiselled features were lively, always shifting. He had a quick smile, light and friendly. His eyes were brown and sparkling, and held a curiosity – and something else. Fear? Simon could see it but didn't want to, rejecting the idea as inappropriate.

Ruben Lentov had created a life for himself in Sweden based on books. His bookshop in the city centre was the largest in town and he had branches in Majorna, Redbergslid and Örgryte. He was known all over the world, with contacts in London, Berlin, Paris and New York.

In his youth he had been a seeker, lured to Sweden by Strindberg and Swedenborg, but he had been cold and gone without before his business had found a secure base for growth.

His departure for Sweden had been a matter of rebellion against too much maternal love and too strong ties to his father. This had made him clear-sighted: the one who, long before 1933, had realised what was going to happen. His family supported him with money and bank contacts and, in his absence, looked after his wife and their little son.

In the mid-1930s, Ruben's wife had followed him, by which time he was well-established and she was frightened to death. During the early years of their marriage he had never really known what to make of her tendency to put the worst interpretation on things or her terrible visions.

The doctors she went to in Sweden talked about persecution mania. These were words that could be used in the daytime, but never after dark for a many-thousands-of-years-old ghost was ever present.

Simon was having dinner with them. Simon, this Swedish boy, his son's friend. Ruben was grateful for every hand that could be clasped in this new country, and he had listened with great attention when Isak had told him about the history lesson and about the boy who was so politically aware and hated the Nazis.

But he was also disappointed and ashamed of it. For he

had not expected this dark little boy but a tall, fair-haired Swede. That would have felt better.

His miscalculation was banished during their conversation as Simon relaxed. Ruben realised the boy was Swedish working class and, although his voice was that of a child, its source was an increasingly powerful social democracy. They disagreed on the communists and Simon lost his foothold for a while when Ruben maintained that the Soviet Union was a slave state of the same ilk as Hitler's Germany. Then Ruben stopped, understanding he had no right to destroy anybody's illusions. Ashamed, he offered Simon more ice-cream.

Simon would never forget that evening, not just because of what he heard, but because of what he saw of the anxiety and unhappiness in the middle of all this wealth. And because he was so frightened of Isak's mother.

Simon had never before come across anyone so contradictory. Her mouth and her fragrance tempted him, but her eyes and the sounds she made scared him. Her bangles tinkled, necklaces rustled and her gaze burned with anxiety. She clutched him to her. Hugged, kissed him, then pushed him away and said uncomprehendingly, 'Larsson, but it can't be true?'

Then she forgot him and Simon realised she had banished him from the moment and from her mind. And he understood the sorrow in his friend's eyes, the sadness he had noticed that very first day.

The next weekend, on the Saturday, Simon made an attempt to build a bridge between his old world and the new, and at the kitchen table he told his parents about the grand family who had invited him to dinner. 'They were so . . . nervous,' he said, fumbling for words that would explain the unease in the big apartment in town.

24

But Karin found them for him. 'They live in terror,' she explained. 'They're Jews and if the Germans come . . .'

But autumn went by and the Germans didn't come. Something else happened, something that from Erik's point of view was almost worse. On the thirtieth of November, the Soviet Union bombed Helsinki.

The Winter War had begun.

God, how cold it was that winter when the earth nearly died of the wickedness of man. There were days when children were kept indoors, when the radio announced that the schools were closed. Simon sat in the parlour, where Karin had lit the stove and the anthracite smelled anthracite-dry, and Erik came home with frozen ears and said that if this went on they would soon be able to drive across the ice to Vinga.

The next Sunday they did just that and it was an adventure never to be repeated. The ever lively, ever present, unconquered and immense sea was clapped in irons by the hideous wind from the east, which at twenty metres per second was blowing thirty degrees below zero out in the islands.

Russians and Finns died like flies of cold and bullets. Death took about two hundred and twenty-five thousand lives, they found out later, once circumstances made it possible to start counting.

In Simon's home city, the great shipyard worked overtime and the workers gave their earnings to Finland. In Luleå up north, houses were blown up and five committed Communists lost their lives.

By February it was all over and Karelia lost its domiciliary rights in Scandinavia. That was when Karin said that in the spring they must try to rent a field from the Dahls and grow more potatoes and vegetables.

The shortage of food had started.

Chapter 4

It was the ninth of April 1940 and, for a long time afterwards, Simon was to wonder whether, that morning, he had felt anything special. He had woken at dawn and heard his mother weeping in her sleep.

Karin had premonitions.

But he felt much the same as he normally did as he cycled off to school. The city had woken to what seemed to be an ordinary day and, from the top of the hill at the city boundary, Simon could see all four cranes in the harbour moving like long-legged spiders dancing. As usual, he cycled past the tram taking his better-off friends to school and, as always, he felt a certain triumph. The sun was out above Majorna and there were streaks of warmth in Karl Johansgatan.

He did his German homework during morning prayers in the hall. He had still not been able to bring himself to take his German textbooks home so he did not do well in lessons. On Tuesdays they had chemistry in the morning and, as ever, Simon was not very interested. But in the third lesson, in the middle of history, the caretaker, his face blank, went from door to door saying curtly that they were all to assemble in the school hall.

What Simon remembered best afterwards was not what the headmaster had said, but the terror he induced when the boys were told they were being sent home. He said they were all to go straight to their parents as the school could not take any responsibility for them that day.

Simon's legs went like pistons as he cycled back to Karin, only to find her weeping at the kitchen window. But, as she lifted him up and put him on the sofa, her arms round him, he felt the reassurance of a child. Nothing really bad could happen as long as she existed.

An excited voice on the wireless announced the sinking of the battleship *Blücher* by the Norwegians in the harbour entrance to Oslo. Karin said it would have been better if the Norwegians had done what the Danes had and capitulated immediately.

Erik came home with the truck. The Prime Minister spoke to the nation, saying that the defence of their land was in good hands. In many households his safe south-country voice inspired a little confidence. But not in the Larssons' kitchen. 'He's lying. He has to lie,' Erik declared.

A few days later Erik was called up for military service and disappeared to an unknown place. Karin and Simon dug up the field they had rented and planted potatoes.

In Simon's dreams, wild mountain people with drawn swords raced down from mountain peaks, spreading like locusts over great fields of crops, burning, killing and flinging dead bodies into canals and rivers. The images of the night had little to do with the war raging round in the world. He knew what that looked like from newspapers and newsreels. In the daytime his terror contained swastikas, jack-boots and black SS uniforms, but at night they took on the form of colourful, fat madmen cutting his throat and flinging him into the river where he floated about among thousands of other dead, the water turning red. He saw Karin with her head smashed in floating beside him. He knew it was her, although it didn't look like her.

As an adult, he often wondered what the war did to children, what effect this terror had on them. What he remembered most was his longing every morning for the day to come to an end without anything happening, that day, and the next, and the next: an ever present painful desire. Five years is an eternity when you are a child.

School reopened and Simon, like many of the other boys, no longer had a father at home. Only for Isak was it different, for in his home it was his mother who had disappeared. On the night of the tenth of April she had tried to poison the children and set fire to their apartment in Kvarnsgatan. Isak and his cousin had been taken to a clinic and had their stomachs pumped. When they returned home, their mother had gone, admitted to the mental hospital on the other side of the river, where injections were given to her to make her sleep. Gradually she became an addict. Isak never had his mother back again.

At night Ruben Lentov paced through the big silent apartment from the bookshelves in the library to the hall, through the row of four rooms, back and forth across the thick carpets. He had always been a man of action and now he found himself powerless. A caged animal. But there was still one door to flee through. Jewish friends had kept the flight open to London and, from there, on to America. He could sell his business, take the children and his money and escape.

He thought about his brother in Denmark, the one who had delayed too long. But most of all he thought about Olga, locked up in the mental hospital in Hisingen, nothing but a shell, drugged, beyond all contact, but still his wife and Isak's mother.

The door of his cage had slammed shut and he knew it.

For Simon, the terror now had names so could be controlled a little more: the bombs, the Gestapo, Möllergatan 19. Isak knew these words too but they were no use to him. His terror was all-embracing and wordless, as terror is when we have had it within us very early on and are unable, or cannot bear, to remember.

Karin understood this the very first time she saw Isak. 'We can do no more than die, any of us,' she told him.

It was a simple truth, but it helped Isak. Karin, her kitchen, her food, her sorrow and her anger were things he could rely on. Through Karin, he had order and she made life acceptable.

All that spring term, Isak had brooded in her kitchen while his mother was becoming more and more confused and frightened at home. That Sunday in May when the Norwegians capitulated and the King and his government left Norway, Isak went out to help Karin and Simon with the weeding.

He had been to visit his mother in hospital and she hadn't recognised him.

The next day Karin put on her best clothes, the pale-blue coat she had made herself and the big white hat with blue roses on the brim, and took the tram to Ruben Lentov's office.

They sat in silence for a long time, looking at each other, and Ruben thought that if she didn't soon turn away her eyes he might begin to weep.

Then she looked away and gave him time to say something about the weather before she came out with her message. 'I thought Isak might come and live at our place,' she said. 'With Simon and me, for a while.'

At last Ruben returned to the thought he had been rejecting for weeks now: that the terror in Isak's eyes was like Olga's and that things could go very wrong for the boy if nothing were done. 'I'm so grateful.'

Nothing much more was said. As he went with her through the office to the outer door, he thought he had never seen a more beautiful woman. Later in the afternoon it occurred to him that he must pay for the boy. Larsson was a working man and couldn't be all that well off.

But there had been no trace of lower class in Karin Larsson and, when he phoned her in the afternoon to take up the question of payment, he could find no words. He was glad about this, once he had realised that what Karin was offering couldn't be paid for.

So he produced gifts instead; coffee and preserves, books for Simon and presents for Karin which he took with him once a week out to the little house at the mouth of the river by the hollow mountain where the military stored their oil. Like everyone else, he was welcomed into the big kitchen and if he was looking particularly miserable he was offered a drink. He didn't like schnapps, but had to admit Karin was right. It helped against melancholy.

As it turned out, Isak was able to pay his own way, for he liked physical work and was a practical, patient friend of the axe, spade, spanner and hard toil. Gradually he took over Erik's tasks which meant that he contributed a major share to the home, more than Simon and his bookishness.

'It's as if we've exchanged boys,' Karin said to Ruben one Sunday when Erik was home on leave and Ruben had come out to see him.

Erik was thinner, though just as voluble, and he was disturbed about the state of Sweden's defences. 'We've vehicles and no petrol,' he told them. 'On the other hand we've got ammunition but no guns.'

A look from Karin, who had noticed the anxiety in Ruben's eyes increasing, stopped him.

That evening Ruben told them what he knew from secret sources about the fate of the Jews in Germany. The boys were sent out of the kitchen, but Simon never forgot the expression in Erik's eyes when he crept back in for a drink of water. His father was frightened. And Karin was very pale as she made up the boys' beds in the parlour.

That night, Simon happened to overhear a telephone conversation. Erik was in a hurry as he had to catch a train back to his unit. It was not his haste that sharpened his voice, but the note of something immensely important.

'You must burn the letter . . .' he instructed '. . . Yes, I know I promised, but I had no idea then that . . . You must see that if the Germans come, then it concerns his life.'

Simon listened, sitting up in bed to hear better, though he had no real need for the telephone was in the hall just outside the parlour and every syllable came quite clearly through the wall. Questions swirled in his head. Who was Erik talking to? What letter? Whose life was in danger?

He felt a knot tighten in his stomach as he realised he knew the answer to the last question. It was his life they were talking about.

Isak was asleep in the bed next to him. That was good, for he wasn't to be upset. But Simon felt very lonely as he tried to make it all out. He heard Erik saying goodbye to Karin, then picking up his pack. ''Bye then, Karin, take care of yourself and the boys.'

''Bye Erik, take care of yourself.'

He could imagine them standing together, rather clumsily holding hands.

'Did you get her to understand?' he heard Karin asking just before the door closed.

'I think so.'

Simon was angry, as children are when they don't comprehend. His fury gave him confusing dreams. He met Mrs Ågren, now even more horrible dead than she had been alive. She chased him along the shore screaming at him, 'Go home and ask your mother.' But he had forgotten the question, dropped it, couldn't find it and searched in despair as if his life depended on it.

Simon woke crying and stayed in the twilight realm between sleep and waking. He went to the trees, his oaks, and managed in the end to find the land that is, but doesn't exist, and met his man, the little man with the peculiar hat and the mysterious smile. They sat together for a while talking, as they had over the years, without words and beyond time.

In the morning Simon stood for a long time in front of the kitchen mirror above the cold-water tap, gazing at those alien eyes, his but unlike everyone else's, darker than Karin's, darker even than Ruben's.

But he asked the image no questions. Neither did he ask Karin.

Daily life developed around him. In the rush of porridge to be eaten, his packed lunch to be made, his homework books to be assembled and socks to be found, the previous evening's telephone call faded away, lost contours and seemed to him unreal: a dream.

That day, Simon failed his German test. Isak was worried. 'Do you think Karin'll be miserable?' he asked.

Simon looked surprised. School was his responsibility. Karin wouldn't even ask. 'No,' he said. 'She doesn't bother about school.'

Isak nodded with relief, remembering that when Ruben had asked her about Isak's homework he had heard her say that you should trust your children.

'I could help you with your German. After all, it is my mother tongue.'

Simon was so astonished he almost choked over the toffee he had bought to console himself after the test.

Isak didn't go to German lessons. Simon had assumed

that he was excused them, just as he was excused scripture lessons because he was Jewish. Now he realised for the first time that Isak had no need to learn German as he already knew that frightening language with all its harsh commands: *Achtung, heil, halt, verboten* . . .

And so the kitchen walls which, over the years, had become familiar with Hitler's bellows began to absorb another tongue, a German spoken in a softly rounded Berlin dialect. Even Karin was surprised how deft the Nazis' language could sound. Simon learned quickly, passed the next test and, on the day the Germans marched into Paris, got a good term report.

Then there was an outbreak of meningitis. The same night that the British shipped three hundred thousand men in small boats out of Dunkirk, one of Simon's playmates died, a girl he had always found difficult. This small death became more real than all the dead of the big war. Simon felt guilty.

Only two weeks earlier he had called the girl a silly bum in a furious and unnecessary squabble. She had been red-haired and clever like him, the middle child in a big family, where the bricklayer father drank and the mother wept.

'She was caught in the middle. She didn't want to be part of it any longer,' Karin said. But she kept a watchful eye on the boys for the next few days and was very worried one evening when she thought Isak had a temperature.

Simon remembered very clearly yet another event of that spring. Karin woke one morning recalling a vivid dream, and told the boys how she had been in a bomb shelter and had seen the crucifix hanging on the wall. As the bombs fell, the figure came alive, raised his arm and pointed with a palm branch at the roof, and it opened up. And Karin saw the sky was blue and endless beyond the little planes. 'Both the planes and the bombs were toys,' she said and added that the sight had comforted her.

The boys felt strengthened too, especially when Edit Äppelgren came into the kitchen to fetch some scissors Karin had borrowed, and was given coffee and a share of the dream. She was a devout Christian and knew about Whitsun, which they had just celebrated with the first daffodils on the table, a reminder of the outpouring of the Holy Spirit in the human world.

They had had coffee when they heard the anti-aircraft guns up on Käringberget firing. They rushed out just in time to see the German plane with the swastika on it and the German pilot in flames, like a torch, before he and his machine disappeared into the cool of the sea.

Simon cried, but Isak appeared excited and strangely pleased.

Despite everything, it was a good summer for the boys out in the meadows between the hills where the river flowed out into the sea. Light summer nights, tents on the shore, girls to tease, boys to fight with, canoes and sailing dinghies.

Erik came home and told them how in secret they had helped Norwegian Jews cross the border.

One Sunday, he took the truck to go to see Inga, one of Erik's cousins. She had a smallholding several miles north of the city. Did Simon want to come too?

No, he disliked Inga. She was fat and slow, smelled of the cowshed and never looked at him. Isak said the outing must be important as Erik had used his precious petrol ration and that made Simon uneasy.

Then he forgot all about it, as he and Isak stood on stands round the house and painted it white with paint Ruben had bought. The paint was a present to Erik, and

Isak sang as he worked: *cold is the wind, cold the storm from the sea.*

Simon hated it when Isak sang but he had to agree: nothing much seemed to be going to happen that summer of 1940.

Chapter 5

The house was no bigger than a cottage and lay on the slope with mountains behind. It was south-facing and the view was still magnificent, although less so now than it had been when there were able-bodied men to keep down the undergrowth and the view to the sea was clear. The sea could still be glimpsed from the bedroom in the autumn when all the leaves had fallen, and also in the spring when it could be heard breaking free of the ice.

A few meadows, some fields, potatoes, no cereals any longer, four cows in the cowshed, two pigs and twenty or so hens, and then, in the cottage, two very old, confused and feeble people. Of the family in the city, all except Karin avoided thinking about how lonely Inga was.

Like everyone else, Inga had made her way into town in her youth, taken a job with a family, then later in a shop. They had been interesting years, full of people, impressions and events.

Inga was good-looking, fair-skinned and plump in a soft attractive way, and could probably have found a man as her sisters had. But she had been the eldest of seven children, and had seen too much of love and what that could do to a woman.

So when the old people could no longer manage to

keep up the holding, she was the one who had to go back and care for them. This meant that they wouldn't have to go to the poor house – nowadays called the old people's home but still considered worse than death.

It would perhaps have been easier if there had at least been some affection, a possible means of talking to her mother. But life had not given Inga even that. She had been regarded with disfavour since birth, having arrived too early, barely a month or so after her parents' marriage. The shame stuck to her throughout her youth.

After her return, and during those long first winters, Inga had wanted to poison her parents and set fire to their farm. She knew where the henbane grew and remembered how Ida, the witch in the village, had extracted the poison from the capsules. Then she realised she was going insane. She had to learn that you can go mad from thinking and that her thoughts would only lead to the Lillhagen lunatic asylum in Hisingen. So she decided to stop and, after a few years, she managed quite well.

When her father went blind, the newspaper was cancelled. The family were not letter writers so only holiday postcards came. And, although this was the late 1920s, electricity had still not been brought over the hill to the cottage, so there was no question of a radio.

Her brothers and sisters sent money, but there were long gaps between their visits which was good, for when they did come, especially her brothers, Inga's mother grew more uneasy than ever and that had an effect for days afterwards.

Erik was the one who came most, as he had his truck, and Karin who had helped Inga find a job in the bazaar in town and was so kind – kind and strong at the same time. That had always amazed Inga.

They came because they felt sorry for her, Inga knew.

Karin once said straight out to her parents that Inga had a right to a life of her own and folk nowadays were well cared for in old people's homes. But Inga's mother's heart started to pain her and Erik had to go for the doctor who found nothing wrong, but told them nevertheless that you had to be very careful when people were so delicate. No more was said on the matter. Inga could see Erik was angry and realised Karin would be reproached for what she had said.

That spring a fiddler was sitting by the stream.

It couldn't be true, Inga thought afterwards. He must have sprung from her dreams. But that evening he was quite real, and the next, and the next, right up until the light midsummer nights, when he vanished.

The stream was a fairly modest one that had a long way to go through the forests and much trouble making its way among the hills to reach the sea. At the end it hurtled over the last rocks and down the slope to the shore. For such a small stream, the waterfall was quite an achievement, particularly in the spring when it was forceful and noisy.

To Inga, the waterfall was a joy and a liberation.

She looked after her parents, struggled with the potatoes, milked the cows and kept all the creatures in good condition. But she didn't talk to the animals nor see what was individual in each of them, so her work did not give her much pleasure.

Thus she went from mute animals to mute human beings. Her father had said not a word for years, and her mother would occasionally burst into long and increasingly incomprehensible harangues. She was bad-tempered and had always been, Inga decided.

Mostly Inga thought about the waterfall to which she would go to wash herself after her parents had gone to bed and the animals had been shut in. She used to go there every evening, and would undress and stand in the water, feeling cleansed and trouble-free.

The fiddler appeared again one evening in the spring. He sat and looked at her as if she were a creature from a Nordic saga.

Inga wasn't frightened. It was all too unreal. She walked straight over to him, naked as she was, and lay down with her head in his lap. He took out his violin and played for her, and his music was wild and beautiful.

It could be argued that it would have been better for Inga if her lover had been the man from the dairy who came to fetch the milk every other day in a tanker. But he was ugly and gruff, and married.

Perhaps the fiddler also had a wife, but she never found out for they couldn't speak to each other. He was a foreigner. Later on, Erik discovered that he was Jewish and a music teacher at a college on the other side of the lake. When the term came to an end, he went back to Germany leaving a name and address in Berlin.

But no one ever wrote to him. Inga knew that he had never really been of this world and she stuck to her *Father Unknown*.

All that happened much later, long into the winter when she finally had to admit she was with child and that the man by the waterfall had been of flesh and blood.

They made love – made love half the nights that spring – and Inga understood at last why people were able to give up everything, dignity and prosperity, for its sake. She had had no inkling of what her body could experience when caressed by practised hands, nor had she realised how beautiful a man could be. He was slender, finely built, but his member was large and stiff, and she could never have enough of it. Nor of his eyes, which were as dark as the forest mere.

He talked and his voice was full of tenderness. But as

she couldn't understand the words he had to express his feelings with his violin. He played to her every evening, driving her almost insane with desire.

She remembered that he was very sad on the last evening and that his violin had been full of pain. So she wasn't surprised when he didn't come the next night. Only infinitely sad.

She told herself that she had known all the time that this would happen, that it had been a dream and that, sooner or later, people like her had to wake up and get on with life.

That autumn, she was clumsy and ungainly as she lifted the potatoes yet gave no thought to there being a child inside her.

Erik and Karin came at the time of the first snow to help her get the sacks of potatoes into the earth cellar, and immediately Karin saw what the situation was. 'Inga,' she said. 'You're going to have a child.'

'What the hell have you been up to?' Erik's voice was so sharp it struck Inga like a whiplash.

But Karin intervened, swiftly and harshly. 'Hold your tongue just for once, Erik Larsson.'

Then she went up with Inga to the attic bedroom and, slowly and tentatively, Inga began to tell her about the dark-eyed fiddler by the waterfall. If that great belly hadn't been there Karin would have thought that, in her loneliness, Inga had become crazed.

'It'll be the death of Mother.' Inga wept and Karin kept quiet, although she thought perhaps that would be for the best.

Karin and Erik were practical people and promised Inga that no one would know of her shame: no one in the village, none of the family, and never, ever, her parents.

So Erik informed Inga's parents that she had a serious stomach complaint and that she would have to go to hospital in town. He didn't know how much they had understood. But Inga's middle sister understood all right when he appeared in her kitchen and told her that, as her child was big enough to manage on her own, she, Märta, would have to go home and look after her parents while Inga had her operation.

Märta objected, but in the end gave in as people always did to Erik. She believed him too when he said that Inga would die if she wasn't cared for, so she packed her bags and went back to the old ones.

But she couldn't stand the loneliness in the cottage for more than a few months so, in early spring her parents went into the old people's home, where what happened was just what they had predicted: both of them died within the course of a month.

By that stage, of course, the child had been born and was adopted by Karin and Erik. Inga returned to the farm, although she no longer had to as Karin had offered to help her find a job in the bazaar again.

'She's become unsociable,' said Erik. 'She no longer dares go back into ordinary life.'

Karin nodded, thinking things were probably not that simple.

As Karin held the new-born babe in her arms, the nurse saying that the mother hadn't even wanted to look at the boy, she felt in the depths of her heart that she had no right to the child. She hadn't borne him in bliss and anguish, nor given birth in pain.

She gazed into the boy's eyes and found that the melancholy from the long twilights over the lake was there and also something else: a great loneliness, a non-being.

That's from Inga denying him, Karin thought. And she thought too about Inga's words in the attic: that she had believed the man with the violin had been a water sprite.

But the man had clearly existed. And Karin, absorbing what she had already seen, perceived that here was a very Jewish child. A stranger's child that was to be hers. Not that she was concerned about the difficulties over his difference. For she loved the boy already and knew beyond all doubt that her love would move mountains and change the skies if it became necessary to make him feel secure.

Children are of the earth, she thought, with the ancient history of the earth in their cells and the entire wisdom of nature in the circulation of their blood.

She also saw that he possessed the truth as all children do. For a brief time children *know*, she thought. Perhaps every new child is the earth's attempt to give expression to what cannot be understood.

Inga decided on his name. After her parents' funeral she went up to Erik in the churchyard. 'He's to be called Simon,' she said.

Karin realised they had to comply and, as she stood there with the child in her arms, she thought that after all, he had been given a good name, the name of the water sprite.

Chapter 6

Karin had been an afterthought, the youngest of a family of six, the others all boys, the smallest already at school. When it was clear that yet another babe was coming to

Master Tailor Lundström's cottage opposite the railway in the Värmland industrial community, her mother wept, and cursed her fate and the child growing inside her. She was over forty and had thought she was free.

Driving the child out of her was a long three-day struggle and she nearly died. As she lay there with the new-born infant at her breast she still had tears in her eyes but this time she was weeping because her baby was a girl, another poor thing condemned to slavery and painful births.

All through her childhood Karin was to hear how unwanted she had been and how she had nearly cost her mother her life. It was an oft-repeated story which she perceived to be natural, as she understood her mother. On the other hand, she never understood the sorrow that had struck deep roots in her heart and which grew and branched out with such force that she never managed to tear it out.

Perhaps she should have given up early on, as did other unwanted children who were afflicted by tuberculosis in that area. But Karin survived, and grew large and strong. This was because she had a father.

Petter Lundström was over sixty when his daughter was born. He had been married twice and had two batches of children. The first lot, all sons, had long since grown up. But he had had one daughter, a little one who had died of consumption at the age of seven. What was amazing was that this dead little girl was Petter's link with life, to what was alive within him. He had loved her. His sons from his second marriage had also heard a great many stories about how strangely sweet she was and how exceedingly fond he had been of her. It had therefore been a great joy to him when another daughter had been born towards the end of his life. God alone knows if he didn't start imagining that his little darling had come back to him as a comfort and new light in his increasingly grey existence.

Petter Lundström worked from home and, from the very first day, he made the child his own. She lay in a box on the big table in his workshop and he prattled to her, smiled at her and sang for her. People came and went, and Petter sat among them with his angel child Karin, the sweetness of his life, the apple of his eye. True, some laughed at him and his boundless love, but this was Värmland where there was room for oddities. And the child was pretty, troubling no one nor getting in the way when people came for fittings.

He knew a hundred songs, a thousand sagas and even more crazy stories. All this, he gave Karin and she floated on a wave of warmth and subtle wisdom, learning early most things about the foolishnesses and sagacities of people, about how nearly everyone wished to be good and ended by going to the bad.

Petter had always been very neat. His workshop was now so clean and tidy that people said you could eat straight off the floor. He got hold of a book from Karlstad and learned what small children needed. It contained a great deal about cleanliness, nourishment and fresh air. There was nothing about about tenderness and love but, as far as Petter Lundström was concerned, this didn't matter at all.

This was how Karin acquired her strength and insight into the mysteries of life and how sometimes they may be grasped. By the time she started school she had long learned to read and write and, much to Petter's immeasurable pride, was put up a class.

Her mother? Well, she was there, coming and going in the workshop, weighed down by the image of herself as a patient beast of burden, prematurely worn out from too many childbirths and all the hard cooking and cleaning work. She was the guilt in Petter's life. He would never escape the fact that it was he who had given her all those children and, as she so often said, he who had sent his first wife to an early grave.

All Petter could do was submit to his wife's complaints, but these had come in useful since Karin had been born. For his wife had to admit that he did what he could to lift this last burden off her shoulders. He no longer touched her in bed and she realised that there was a connection, that his need for closeness was satisfied as long as he was allowed to be with his daughter.

The discord grew worse as Karin grew older and her mother thought she should help with the household chores. Petter could not deny her this and loaned Karin out, but only for short spells. She never became domestic and was often clumsy at the stove. Her mother once struck her across the back with the poker. No one in the tailor's house was ever to forget this event for the kind-hearted Petter went straight for his wife with the same poker and struck her too.

'Now you know what it feels like,' he shouted, white with fury.

Her mother never forgot, neither the humiliation nor the pain, both of which went deep.

When Karin was nine Petter died, seated there on his table, falling forward like an open clasp-knife.

Karin did not understand. This couldn't have happened. She ran into the forest and stayed there all night. She woke in the morning under a spruce tree and remembered. She went deeper into the forest and found a clearing where there was a stream. Slowly she realised what had occurred and saw that the stream was too shallow to drown herself in.

In the dawn light, a flock of waxwings appeared on

their long journey from the high mountains in the north to the warm southern rivers. They settled round the child, who had never seen these strange shimmering birds before, nor heard their calls, halfway between rejoicing and sorrow.

Karin sat very still, knowing her father had sent her a message, that he was still there around her and always would be. She decided she would be able to live after all.

Her mother sold the tailor's business and moved to Göteborg with two almost grown sons and this little girl whom she scarcely knew. There, she found a new use for the image of herself as a tormented beast of burden at a factory that took all her strength but provided her with money for her tiny one-room apartment in Majorna and food for her and the children.

Then came the First World War, with shortages of food and people with a fading desire to live dying like flies from Spanish flu. Thanks to the waxwings, Karin survived. One or two teachers had taken to this unusual and gifted girl and, when Karin was to be confirmed, the priest came to see her mother to say her daughter ought to be allowed to go on to the high school.

'Whims and fancies,' her mother said after the priest had left. 'Your silly father made you think you were someone.'

When her sons came home she told them about the crazy priest and they laughed loudly. Spend money on a girl? They'd never heard of anything so stupid. But the quiet son said that if Dad had been alive . . .

That was when Karin realised why they hated her.

At thirteen, Karin took a job with a family. At fifteen, she worked in a dressmaking workshop and at sixteen in a shop in the bazaar. The waxwings followed her everywhere. When she was eighteen she met Erik, saw that he resembled her father and, like Erik, became a socialist. After a while she even dared to believe what he said to her: that she was beautiful.

Erik was the only boy in the one-room apartment in a great block in Stigeberg. He was his mother's hope and the support of his younger sister who was delicate, having been forced to live with a punctured lung after the ravages of tuberculosis at the age of six. Denied personality and a life of her own, she grew slowly and crookedly in the shadow of her mother.

Erik's mother was strong, handsome, bitter and very religious. She had married late and hated love with such fury that she had driven her shadowy husband out of their marriage bed as soon as she had given birth to her children. She acquired an outlet for her desire by smacking her son on his bare red backside with the carpet-beater and, when she could no longer rule him with this, she got him to obey by threatening him, as he reached puberty, with a heart attack.

Erik's childhood was not easy but there was a respect for his sex and for the man in the boy who had inherited his mother's intelligence and strength, and who was to realise her dreams. This respect eventually gave him the confidence to take a stand against her, her opinions and her dark Christianity.

Much worse were the influences he had absorbed early on, and which were invisible. All his life, he perceived physical love to be linked with sin and no one helped him to understand the strange and, in his mind shameful, connection between desire and cruelty in his fantasies.

As a fifteen-year-old, Erik started work at Götaverken and came home every evening after a ten-hour day to evening classes and his books. There he found the tools which were to help him eventually to understand the cruel world he had grown up in. He also learned how oppression functions when it seeks an outlet against those even weaker than itself.

Sometimes he understood his mother. Just as he understood the dreadful sense of humiliation attached to the shoes which, every Christmas, he had had to accept from the parish priest who, in his turn, had received them from a charitable organisation that called itself the Älvsborg Christmas Gnomes.

At sixteen he told his mother that God didn't exist and that her church was no better than liquor when it came to keeping the working man down. She clutched her heart and threatened to die but that failed to have any effect, as Erik was already out of the door on his way to his next meeting.

But he was much more defenceless when it came to love and his mother, terrified her son would desert her, quickly blew the girls he fell in love with out of his life.

When he met Karin he was nearly thirty. As soon as he looked into her gentle brown eyes he realised this was serious and his longing for her was so great, his fear so immense, that he was going to need a heavenly power to pray to.

Dear Lord, help me with Mother.

But he had been mistaken about her gentle eyes and he soon found that behind Karin's meekness was a strength that matched his mother's.

'Erik and I are to marry,' she announced on her first visit to his home.

'You'll be the death of me.' The old woman turned pale as if she were about to have the threatened heart attack there and then at the kitchen table.

But Karin laughed in her face and said that was the point of life: the old were to die and leave room for the young on this earth. Then she left and took Erik with her.

His mother survived and remained a great affliction to them both for many years.

Erik never quite knew what a fate Karin had saved him from. But he did realise that evening that his woman was as strong as his mother. Frightened, he brushed aside the thought that he had escaped one female trap only to fall into another. His challenge now was to maintain his manhood so as not to become a shadow like his father.

They married that spring, both mothers weeping, Karin's because her daughter was now moving into the inevitable fate of constant pregnancies and awful births.

They set up house and were childless. Erik made their furniture himself – armchairs, sideboard, dining table and linen cupboard – and Karin sewed.

The home they made was different and beautiful. And, much to the delight of the mothers-in-law, they remained childless.

At a birthday gathering his mother mocked Karin openly and, for once, Erik lost his temper and told his mother that their lack of children could be blamed on him. He had had a shameful disease, the kind you get when you are not allowed to have a girl of your own, but had to go to whores. It was all her fault.

As they went home that evening, Karin took Erik's hand and said that as his mother hadn't died on the spot that evening, she would certainly live to be a hundred. In fact, she lived until she was ninety-six.

Karin never dared ask whether there was any truth in the story Erik had told. He'd been magnificent. He was a man to be trusted. Not like Petter, she now realised, who was much less secure, more pugnacious and vulnerable. But that was good too. Petter still lived his life in her heart and no one could threaten him there.

So they received their son and what did it matter that their longed-for child was not of their own blood? Erik was as proud as a king, drew out his savings and bought a plot of land at the river mouth, where their boy would have fresh air and open space.

He built his house with his own hands, its dimensions decided by the scraps of material he could acquire cheaply as he drove his truck around town. He knew all the builders and demolition sites, and returned to his plot with slatted windows and fancy carpentry, handsome tiled stoves from patrician houses being modernised in the Allé, and beautifully made doors from an old manor house being rebuilt in Landvetter.

Gradually, it became a delightful home, full of surprises and warmth, and he and Karin were never happier than that summer as they trudged in the mud outside, and slept through the hot nights in a great crate Erik had found in the harbour and which was no more reliable than a tent.

Neither mother-in-law knew where the child had come from and moaned about bad blood and poor heritage, but Erik frightened them into silence, and he and Karin found security in their socialist faith in the importance of the environment to human development.

Sometimes Erik felt a twinge when he looked into the dark eyes of his baby son, but he pushed aside the pain and made the boy his own. Soon he no longer saw the darkness in his eyes or the coarse hair. Simon was his and therefore good — first class in every respect.

Erik had a strong singing voice, trained early in church and later in the labour movement, and as he couldn't bring himself to prattle as Karin constantly did to their child, he used to sing the 'Red Flag' so that it rolled round the hills. He almost burst with pride when Simon gurgled with delight. When he ran out of campaign songs, Erik went over to the old hymns, not the words, of course, but the tunes, weighty with tranquillity and force. This time there was no mistaking the boy's delight. Even Karin saw it and was surprised.

Karin nearly always had Simon in her arms but, in the spring when the garden began to take shape, she had to sow and plant. So Erik made a cradle and hung it up in the big pear tree that had been there long before they had arrived. The boy slept there and woke to the hum of bees and the rustle of leaves, white blossom falling like snowflakes on to his bed.

Chapter 7

The sea was always present in Simon's childhood, flavouring the air with salt, filling it with its song from its depths and wide expanses, and colouring all light between the houses and hills. Grey days became impenetrably grey. Blue ones were bluer than the sky, days when the sea became its mirror, multiplying the light and reflecting it back over the land.

Simon carried this light with him all through his life. It penetrated his skin, filtering through flesh and bone and entering his soul where his longing was born: a blue yearning for freedom and infinity.

Whenever his yearning sought for a fixed point in reality, Simon was drawn to the huge ships making their way past Oljeberget towards great harbours. Despite the war, nearly all his friends went to sea, many of them before he was halfway through high school. They signed up on the safe-conduct ships with their yellow and blue flags painted on their plating. Some of the boys never returned, vanishing into the depths with their neutral ships and their longings for freedom. Others came home with a hardness in their eyes and, in Karin's kitchen, their mothers talked of the nightmares their sons had at night.

Simon and Isak were also attracted to the ships in the harbour where life had fallen silent, for Sweden was blockaded. And so were the quays, now guarded by the police.

Yet the harbour had never contained so many ships, so many giants shackled to buoys and anchors, condemned to inactivity. Despite the closed quays, they couldn't be hidden and the boys soon found the best way to see them at close quarters was to take the ferry across the river.

They started at Sänkverket. Then they found their way to Fiskhamnen, took the ferry to Sannegården and stood on deck gazing at the huge hulls looming like ghostly mountains.

Many of them were Norwegian merchant ships, some brand new. They had sailed straight from the Swedish shipyards to their anchorages, having never tested the assignment that was to be theirs. Others had sailed the oceans of the world and, worn out, had been approaching their home country the spring the Nazis raped Norway. In despair, the ships had altered course and headed for their still free neighbouring country. There they remained, lying silent, unemployed, impounded.

But early that spring rumours flew round town that the Norwegian ships were being loaded with ball-bearings and arms; that they were preparing for departure and that explosives were being taken on board so the ships could sink themselves if necessary.

On the night of the thirty-first of March the city by the river held its breath while ten Norwegian ships slipped past the fortress and out towards Rivöfjorden. It was foggy, but this was to be no help to them. On board were hundreds of men who were never to see the dawn for German naval forces were waiting at sea by Måseskär.

Three of the ships were sunk by their own crews according to the suicide plan, three went to the bottom after being hit by German torpedoes, and two managed to turn and make their way back to safe harbour in Sweden. Only two broke through and reached England, a small tanker and the swift, sixteen-thousand-ton *B. P. Newton* which, on the third of April, entered a harbour in Scotland, escorted by HMS *Valorous*.

It was a grim day for all sea-minded people in town, one of the blackest days of the war. There were whispers of treachery.

Simon sat through his lessons, like the others not really listening. The teachers were equally despairing, but no one spoke of what had happened. The hours crept by and the usual rituals were observed. 'Open your books on page ninety-eight,' they intoned.

At the end of the day, the weight inside Simon floated free and he was the first to slump over his desk and weep. They were having a Swedish lesson and their woman teacher on the podium also gave up and wept silently at her desk.

No one said a word.

The bell went and the boys rose slowly and silently dispersed, snivelling and blank-eyed. When they got out into the corridor and put on their jackets, Simon noticed that Isak hadn't wept and there was something he found difficult to grasp in his eyes.

They should have gone to the library but Simon saw they had to get home as quickly as possible, to Karin and her kitchen. As they crossed the school yard on their way to the bike shed, Isak was walking like a mechanical doll and Simon knew suddenly that they should take the tram.

Isak followed him like a dog but his eyes never met Simon's. It was as if he didn't recognise his friend. When they came to the stop, he couldn't find the familiar route and Simon was so frightened he felt a knot in his stomach. He wanted to run. Instead, he took Isak's arm and they walked up and down the hills along the route Aron Äppelgren had taught him to love.

They arrived home and Karin was there. At once she saw what was wrong and as he heard Karin's voice sliding and saw the flickering darkness in her brown eyes as she spoke, the cramp left Simon's stomach.

'Outside with you.'

He flew out of the door and ran to his oak trees, to the land where everything is simple.

Gently and cautiously, as if there were a risk of Isak bleeding to death, Karin took off his jersey and shoes. Then she sat down in the rocking chair with the big boy on her lap, rocking slowly and stroking his head as she prattled.

He grew a little warmer, but his rigidity remained and it was obvious that he didn't recognise her. She sang an old nursery rhyme. He grew a little less rigid, but when she tried to meet his gaze it was clear that Isak Lentov no longer knew where he was.

I ought to phone Ruben, Karin thought, but every attempt to get up and loosen the boy's grip seemed to increase his terror. So things had to remain as they were until Helen came with the milk and Karin could give her Ruben's number. 'For God's sake, hurry,' she whispered.

Ruben Lentov managed to find a taxi, but his arrival changed nothing. Isak did not even recognise his own father.

*

When Isak was four, Ruben told Karin later, his mother had loved him in the way one loves something that is intended to give meaning and dignity to an anguished life. This love forced Isak to respond to her needs and stopped him feeling his own emotions, the emotions he required to evaluate and understand.

He became a good boy, a quiet child. But sometimes he had incomprehensible outbursts of rage and ran screaming around their large Berlin apartment.

His father was in a far-away country, his mother told him and she spoke with a longing that was to colour the boy's image of Sweden throughout his life. But he had a grandfather, Ruben's father, and he was God. Isak understood this for Grandfather had a voice that thundered like the Lord's and, on Saturdays, when he walked to the synagogue holding the little boy by the hand, he was clad in majesty and dignity. Just like Job's Lord.

He punished just as God did too, raining his blows on the righteous and unrighteous. Isak accepted this for he had learned at the synagogue that the counsels of the Lord were not to be questioned. And he buried deep within him those moments when he raced round the apartment screaming, tormenting his mother who appealed to the Lord who, in his turn, punished him with a heavy heart and hard hand.

One afternoon when he was four or five, and sunshine and spring were in Berlin, Isak hurt his mother again with his screams. He was sitting under the dining-room table with its thick cloth embroidered in red and gold, surrounded by the faint smell of wax polish and stale wine, listening to his mother crying in her room and waiting for the Lord who was coming to beat him.

On this particular day he experienced a new emotion. For he was aware of his anger and this gave him hope.

54

He could think, and he decided that he would run away and go to his father in that distant country.

He would ask his way there. He knew the address.

Isak took off his shoes and crept out into the hall, then stood there for a moment looking at the coat stand, thinking that perhaps he would need an overcoat on the long walk to this new country where it was said to be so cold. But he couldn't reach it.

He managed to open the door and close it behind him without making a sound. Then he made his way down the stairs and out on to the street, where the sun was shining and people's faces were alight with the sound of military music and the regular tramp of Hitler Youth boots.

He forgot how they caught him, those tall men in brown shirts and swastika armbands. But he remembered their nostrils quivering with delight and how they laughed as they sat him up on the counter in the nearest beer hall and pulled his trousers off to see if he had been circumcised. He was a little Jewish swine, they told him, sent their way by friendly forces on this sunny day, so full of hope for all those who had seen the birth of the Third Reich.

They pulled his little penis until it turned blue. Isak lost consciousness in the middle of it all and this lessened their pleasure. Nevertheless, they did not stop until blood spurted and the barmaid intervened, picking up the child and putting him behind the bar counter.

She was tall and blonde like Karin. Recognising him, she waited until the cheerful marching had ceased and, in the evening, took him back to the Lentov apartment.

When Isak regained his senses he realised that his grandfather was not God for he was weeping with terror and despair. A doctor came with bandages and medicine, but the boy would have no future, the doctor – himself a Jew – said. He was so frightened that the calming syringe was trembling in his hand.

While Isak slept his drugged sleep, his grandfather and his mother sat hating each other, striving to place the blame beyond themselves.

It's you, you damned stupid goose, with your tears and your behaviour. You made me beat him, his grandfather accused.

It was you, you old devil, frightening the life out of him, his mother replied silently.

But they said nothing and the old grandmother crept around with wine and consolation. 'Children forget so easily,' she said.

Gradually they overcame their shock and became allies in an agreement: Ruben Lentov was never to know what his son had endured.

They must have been slightly uneasy, as they went off to their rooms to try to sleep, that the boy might speak of what had happened. But they could have saved themselves that worry for when Isak woke he was mute.

He neither spoke nor cried and only whimpered a little when the doctor came to rebandage his injury.

'He's in shock,' he told them.

Isak was still in shock a month later, when Ruben Lentov came to see them and, raging with misery, demanded to know what had occurred. The two conspirators stuck to their agreement. But they hadn't reckoned on the doctor who was still coming and going, and was increasingly worried about the state of his patient.

For many years afterwards, Ruben was to make a conscious effort to blot out his conversation with the doctor that night, to forget his horror and guilt. He never thought to ask why the boy had run away. In this drama, there was only one accused: himself.

When the day dawned, with all the strength of despair, Ruben did what he should have done long ago, as he wore out the stony streets and waiting-room chairs of Berlin. Insulted and humiliated, he was able to rely on his Swedish credentials.

Some time later, he stood in his son's room with the stamped documents. 'You're coming with me to the new country now,' he said and lifted Isak up.

The strength in his father's voice and the warmth of his arms were forceful enough to penetrate the boy's paralysis. Isak revived and was able to think at last. What he thought was that he had succeeded after all, that running away had led him to his goal.

Isak wept quietly all day, refusing to let Ruben go. In the evening he began to speak but only to his father, screaming loudly from the darkness within him as soon as his mother appeared in his room. Ruben understood and reckoned his burdensome duty in future would be to protect the child from his mother.

As they stood with their suitcases in the hall of their old home in Berlin the next morning, Ruben told his parents that he hoped they would soon follow him. But he felt an immense and guilty relief when his father said that they would stay in the Germany they loved and that this Nazi business would soon be over.

Isak didn't look at his grandfather, having already obliterated him from his mind.

The Lentovs' other son made his way to Denmark, and their only daughter went to America with her husband and children. But the old people stayed and, in the very spring the sequestered ships were sunk and Isak fell ill, they went to their deaths in one of the huge camps in the east of the country.

Ruben sat on the train, listening to the thump of wheels over the joints and looking at his wife. Perhaps it would have been better if she had stayed behind in Berlin, he thought. But Isak's cousin, an eleven-year-old girl he had promised to look after, was sitting beside her and despite his wife's self-absorption, she would care for both children.

They were lucky with the weather and, after changing trains at Helsingborg, the early summer countryside opened out before Isak's eyes, light and beautiful.

A maple was flowering outside the window of his room in his new home and he would stand for hours, almost inside the great crown of the tree, listening to the buzz of bees and smelling the scent of honey from the thousands of pale-green flowers.

This distant country smelled good. And, best of all, they spoke another language, he thought.

There was a large girl in the bookshop called Ulla. She had been to a high school for girls and could speak German. She was too grand to be a nursemaid but, when Ruben saw how fond she was of his son, he increased her wages and called her a governess. Ulla loved songs, poems and fairy tales. For three years she devoted herself to Isak and soon he was singing Bellman and Taube. He loved the new language with such passion that he made it his own at furious speed. After only a few months he had a larger vocabulary and was more voluble than he had ever been in German.

Ruben was astonished and pleased that Isak was not as untalented as his mother and grandfather had feared. He realised too that, through his new language, his son had found the way to his own emotions and had been given a history and coherence.

Isak never spoke Swedish to his mother.

Chapter 8

Isak fell asleep at last in Karin's arms in the rocking chair.

Simon and Ruben helped to pull the bed out from beneath the ottoman and put Isak into Erik's bed. Ruben slept as best he could in the kitchen on Simon's old sofa, but it was not discomfort that kept him awake that night.

Karin lay beside Isak with his hand in hers. He slept so soundly that he didn't wake when Simon went to school the next morning, or when Ruben went into town to see to what was most urgent at the office. He was to be back about twelve and Karin whispered about food he was to buy and other practical details. He nodded from the kitchen door and muttered that if Isak ended up beside Olga . . .

Karin forgot to whisper. Isak was not going to any madhouse as long as she, Karin, had any say in the matter. 'I'm strong, Ruben,' she told him. 'Go on, now.'

But at heart she was much more frightened than she cared to admit.

Then, quite undramatically, Isak woke up, looked at Karin and recognised her. But he was frightened and gazed around the room as if expecting to find someone else there.

'Who are you looking for, Isak?'

'Grandfather,' said Isak, just as surprised as she was, almost smiling at his own foolishness.

'Why are you afraid of your grandfather?'

'He used to beat me when I had been away like this and couldn't remember.'

Fragile, oh, how fragile was the ice Karin had to walk on; don't be afraid, don't hesitate for too long, or think too much. Take the next step calmly and have faith, she told herself. 'What happened yesterday?'

'In the lunch hour we cycled to, you know, the railway station in Olskroken and looked at them.'

His eyes widened as the terror took hold of him. Karin's mind worked quickly and clearly for she knew what the boy had seen, the German trains rolling through Sweden. At Olskroken, they stopped so that the soldiers could stretch their legs.

'It hurts,' cried Isak, his hand over his crotch.

'You probably need to go,' said Karin, knowing instinctively that she had made a mistake.

But he accepted her diversion and went out to the privy in the backyard. When he came back, she had cocoa and a honey sandwich ready for him. She knew he liked that, but his eyes were flickering and she worried that he was about to glide away from her again.

'What happened next, Isak? After you'd been to Olskroken?'

'I don't remember.'

The ice was brittle, but her voice warm and safe. 'Of course you remember, Isak.'

'We got to school and there they told us . . .'

'Told you what? Isak!'

'I don't remember. Bloody hell, I don't remember.'

'Yes, you do, Isak. They told you about the ships.'

'Yes,' he shouted. 'But shut up now, for God's sake.'

But Karin wouldn't let him go. The ice was safer now and would hold. 'About the ships trying to break out and the Germans waiting for them?'

He threw himself backwards on the sofa, clutching at his crotch and crying out. 'It hurts. Help me, Karin, help!'

'Does your willie hurt?'

'Yes, yes.'

'What happened to you, Isak?'

'I don't remember.'

'But you can see in front of you, Isak. Open your eyes – look.'

Isak realised that he had to go down into the depths of his horror. He had to see and experience it yet again. He clung to her, changed languages, cried out in German, the words pouring from him, the tears and the terror.

It was perhaps just as well that Karin could not understand it all because, if she had been able to see the event being relived in her kitchen that morning, her terrible wrath would have overtaken both her and the boy. As it was, she understood the main facts and managed to keep calm, as she took a sequence of deliberately careful steps over the thin ice.

When Ruben came back most of it was over, and Isak and Karin were sitting on the kitchen sofa holding hands. Both of them were crying, their tears sorrowful but healthy.

Without more ado, Karin told Ruben what Isak had told her. She asked about what she hadn't understood and Ruben, scarlet with shame when not pale with guilt, filled her in. Isak's gaze went from one to the other. There were words for everything and everything could be told.

It was all a great relief to him, not least when Karin said that the Nazis were indeed swine, but she reckoned both his mother and his grandfather were damned monsters.

Isak stayed away from school for the whole of the spring term because this was what Karin wanted. But that same evening he went with Simon to the oak trees and Simon told him how the trees had spoken to him when he was small.

Isak thought he understood and said it was a pity Simon had forced them into silence.

'Oh,' said Simon. 'Trees can't talk. It's just something you get in your head when you're a child.'

But Isak said he knew trees could speak and that the maple outside his window had had a lot to say to him the spring he had come to Sweden.

'What?' Simon asked eagerly.

'I suppose it was about nothing being really harmful,' Isak replied, and Simon knew that something important had been given to his friend.

Karin needed some air so she went with Ruben to the tram. She could also see he could do with comforting, but her energy seemed to have run out. 'Did you know his grandfather beat him?'

'I should have realised.'

'It's your wife who makes me so angry,' Karin said. 'What kind of mother informs on her own child, then looks on when he is abused?'

'I had a mother like that myself,' Ruben told her.

Then Karin was ashamed, but he didn't notice for, in the March twilight on the road, he saw his mother through Karin's eyes and knew that he hated her. And he imagined the extermination camps.

It was a long and difficult spring for Isak. Most of all he wanted to sleep and, every time Karin woke him, he wept.

Sometimes he thought the grief in him had no end. He had no desire to live any longer and no energy.

Then Erik came home and the two of them, Erik and Isak, started building a boat.

Chapter 9

A boat was being built out in Norden.

Isak sang as the frame was stretched under the great tarpaulin Erik had erected over a skeleton of demolition timber. She was to be carvel-built with mahogany cabin tables, the finest double-ender in the river mouth. How Erik had acquired the mahogany in the blockade year of 1942 only he and God knew. But it had been off-loaded into the backyard between the house and the hillside, and lovingly covered over.

Erik had returned from military service and, like so many others, was now unemployed. His truck ran on industrial gas, but brought in little more money than what his brother-in-law's family needed to live. Yet Erik was pleased. 'We'll be all right, you'll see,' he said. 'Those bastards have got their hands full and old Sweden is a hard nut to crack.'

The Larssons held a party in their garden that night in early summer, and friends and neighbours raised their glasses to drink to Hitler's death, the courage of the Russians and the American Flying Fortresses.

Strengthened and comforted, Ruben Lentov drank deeply. The year before, he had realised that Erik had political sense.

Erik had been on leave at midsummer and, one evening, had rung the bell of his apartment. 'I thought I'd look in and tell you things are turning now. The whole damned war's turning,' he stated.

Ruben had been more pleased by the visit than the news. He had taken out a treasured bottle of French brandy and tried to keep his voice steady. 'What in the name of God makes you believe that?' he asked. For there had been little hope at the time, only that the British had repulsed Hitler in the Battle of Britain.

'England's never lost a war,' Erik said. 'And it looks as if something's going to happen soon in the East.'

Ruben couldn't remember how much of the brandy they had consumed by the time they turned on the news. But he remembered staggering slightly in the middle of the library floor as the excited radio voice announced Operation Barbarossa, Hitler's invasion of Russia. He would never forget Erik's yell of delight and how he had almost hugged his breath away.

'You've got a cruel, just old god, haven't you? Pray now, Ruben Lentov, for a hellish winter of snowstorms and temperatures of forty below!'

Then they had laughed like madmen and finished off the brandy while talking about Napoleon and King Karl XII.

As the ice piled up round the coasts that winter and the two men met, they had joked about it. And when Erik read in the paper that the ice-breakers in the Baltic had had to work hard right into June, he had said to Ruben, 'See, what a bastard you are for getting your prayers answered!'

For a while the building of the boat had been a sensitive issue. Ruben had commissioned the boat, which was to give his son new courage. He drew up an all-embracing contract which included a decent wage for Erik, but when he brought the papers, silent angels started moving through the Larsson kitchen. Or perhaps they were Christmas gnomes, the Älvsborg gnomes – the charity which had presented Erik with a pair of shoes throughout his childhood.

'Go to hell and take your money with you,' Erik shouted.

Ruben bowed his head, as his people had done through the ages. Then bitterness turned to anger and he said he had earned the money honestly and it was clean, even if it did come from the pockets of a Jew.

'You must be damned crazy,' Erik said. 'This has nothing to do with Jews.' But he was ashamed and, afraid Karin would come, suggested they should go fishing.

They took the dinghy, set sail, and anchored in the Rivö channel where they fished for mackerel and drank home-brewed brandy. Erik told Ruben about the Älvsborg gnomes and his dream of a boatyard of his own. 'Times might be good after the war,' he said.

During the following week they formed a company at Ruben's lawyer's office, laying the foundations to an organisation which would eventually make Erik a respected employer in the town.

The keel was laid for the first double-ender that summer. Simon was left out, preferring to pore over his books rather than work on the boat. He hated Isak for the collaboration between him and Erik, and himself for hating him, for things had been terrible for Isak. And, besides, they should all be pleased about his interest in the boat and his friendship with Erik.

Karin explained this to Simon. But she didn't take much interest in him. He was just her own secure boy. Things had always been good for him. Her thoughts were with Isak as she watched for signs of him sliding away again into no man's land. And Isak, whose mother had never really loved him, basked in Karin's concern.

Karin did notice Simon when she found he had shot up and was growing out of his clothes. She sewed some trousers for him out of an old pair of Isak's, not noticing the rage in his eyes as she made him try them on.

Simon ran to the oak trees and cried like a child. Then he went down to the sea and murdered Isak. He was not all that successful at that either, as it gave him no relief and the little man of his childhood had long since disappeared. Perhaps he should run away? Thinking about how miserable Karin would be, and how she would have regrets and wring her hands in despair and cry out that she had driven her son to his death, gave him some pleasure. For she would find him, killed by his own hand.

There was only one snag to this plan: Simon didn't want to die. Then he was ashamed for Isak had had a bad time and Karin was an angel – Ruben said so and Simon had always known it.

He went home with his tail between his legs and was pleased Karin no longer noticed him for if she had seen his black thoughts he really would have died. He was sure of it.

That night he dreamed about the forest and a far-flung lake. He recognised it all, knew he had been there and that its melancholy was to become his own anguish. He existed, but no one could see him. Desperate, he cried out, wept, kicked and found himself in a cave. With furious determination he forced a way out, narrow though it was, his whole body paining him as he pushed his way through. But the person who had to see him to enable him to live wasn't there, and his rage ebbed into a huge weariness. Then somebody picked him up. It was Karin, and her eyes were brown and full of love. But his misery over the one who had not been aware of him continued to haunt him long after he awoke.

No one noticed next morning that Simon was pale as they sat over breakfast with paper and pens among the coffee cups and porridge plates, making new sketches of how to solve this or that detail inside the cabin. Karin as usual was worrying about food for dinner. She had used up all her meat coupons, last year's potatoes were poor and her imagination blank.

She noticed Simon wasn't eating much. 'Finish up your porridge, boy,' she said. 'You need it, growing so fast as you are.'

Simon looked at his mother and hated her.

He was saved by his cousins who came into the Larssons' kitchen to ask Simon to go fishing with them. It was a grey day, the clouds low and heavy with rain, so Karin made him put on his oilskins, sou'wester and boots. But he was free from her and the boat-builders and their constant nagging for him to come with them to fetch and carry.

For once, Simon and his cousins had land wind. They headed towards Danska Liljan, found lee behind Böttö Island and dropped the small anchor. Simon usually didn't enjoy fishing, but today the long wait in the dinghy suited him.

He was frightened by his thoughts about Karin at breakfast and, as he stared at his line on the surface of the water, he told himself he hadn't meant it. He had meant Mrs Ågren, and Isak's bloody mother, and Mrs Jönsson at the grocer's who had once caught him nicking sweets, and crazy Mrs Äppelgren, who did nothing but house-work and had once accused him of stealing apples from her garden. That bitch, he thought, remembering that the apples had tasted sweet and forbidden.

Then he recollected Aunt Inga and felt he hated her most of all, although she had never done anything to him. He could see her fat face in front of him, her eyes always evading his. A slut, he mumbled to himself, and was surprised by how fierce his loathing was whenever he thought about her in that filthy smallholding. Then he saw the long lake and heard the soughing in the trees, and the next moment his heart beat faster and he knew he was touching on something very dangerous.

The pull on his fishing line was so strong that Simon almost fell off the thwart. He hauled in hard, as he knew he had to for cod, and realised he had hooked a giant of at least five kilos. His line held and eventually the boys got the whopper over the railing and killed it jubilantly.

The sun came out as they were on their way home and a friendly wind blew up, drying the sail and coming from the right direction, from the sea, enabling them to sail free all the way in to the harbour. Simon looked with gratitude at the cod that had saved him and had given him a good day. Karin would be pleased and he would be welcomed in a manner fitting for a man bringing food home in bad times.

It turned out just the way he hoped. Karin hugged the cod and the boy, and dug up some new potatoes overcoming her fears that this was a wicked waste for the potatoes were still very small and could have grown twice as big if she had waited a month or so.

They phoned Ruben and told him that, thanks to Simon, there was to be a party in the kitchen. Could he come and had he a dab of butter they could melt?

Ruben came, bringing with him butter and a bottle of wine. He also had news for Isak. He was to start extra lessons next week to make up for what he had missed when he had been ill during the spring term. He had already spoken to the teacher: Isak was to have lessons for three hours a day for the rest of the summer.

Erik looked surprised, but said nothing. Karin was silent as she too thought it unnecessary. What was important now was that Isak was enjoying himself.

Isak himself was scarlet with anger but didn't dare say anything either.

Only Simon was pleased. Then Erik said that he

would have to help with the boat when Isak was away, and Simon knew what would happen. He would be all thumbs and his father would be impatient with him.

Chapter 10

Ruben Lentov went to concerts. Occasionally, he tried to get the Larssons to come with him, but Erik looked embarrassed and Karin said they were probably not for the likes of them.

'To me it's a way of surviving,' Ruben said.

'Well, everyone has some way of doing that,' Karin replied and Ruben hadn't the courage to ask her what hers was. But he knew her so well by now that he could see her sorrow and realised that it was always there.

One Saturday evening when he had to leave the Larssons and their boat-building early because Berlioz's *Symphonie Fantastique* was being performed, he took Simon with him.

No one thought much about this. Perhaps Ruben sensed that Simon was lonely and wanted to comfort him. Maybe Simon accepted to challenge Karin, or because he was flattered. Possibly it was just chance. Or perhaps destiny moved the determining counter in the game of Simon Larsson's life.

At first, Simon didn't like it. The great concert hall, the grand people with their dignified expressions and the solemn men on the platform scraping away on their instruments and looking like magpies – it all gave him a sense of alienation. If he'd dared, Simon would have fled.

Then one of the black-and-white figures raised a baton. And Simon heard the grass singing in another country and in another epoch, when the world was still young and full of hope. The sky was rent asunder by the wild cries of birds, endless like the grass, and each bird in that blue expanse had its individual character just like the grass on the ground. The wind moved over the plain touching everything, challenging fiercely one moment, gentle and tender the next.

But there was also pain and a great yearning, an impatience and a dream. And a man who carried all this within him. He sat by the great river, but he was also the water of the river, eternally the same and forever new. And he searched the shores as if he could never have enough of their beauty and gentle footholds.

Others came, people with expectations of him, and he knew that his destiny was to give shape to their dreams. Then the wind grew into a storm and drove him to a decision, his agony increasing almost to madness for, like the river, his disposition was gentle and he had no desire for violence.

But the storm had drawn swords, coming from the mountains in the east, and blood washed over the fields.

When the storm moved on across the plain the survivors flocked round him and put their dreams and longings in his hands. He spoke to them of the god whose temple had been destroyed and whose name could no longer be mentioned. But most amazing was the language he spoke, the ancient language that had slept for centuries.

The language and the temple: his mission was to restore them both. The weighty language that had been the home of these people for thousands of years but had been trampled over and forbidden, and the old god, exiled from his fatherland in the people's hearts.

As the man stood on the shore and spoke, he felt that the old language was also the language of the river and the grass, the language of peasants and peace, heavy with earth and toil. He looked across the plain, saw the canals patterning the landscape with their silver threads and carrying the water out over the fields. Like the language, they were now under alien domination. And, although it was forbidden, he sang the old hymns to the people, songs of the sanctity of the earth and the love of the water, of the river which gave life to the great mother earth.

The old men and the women still knew the words and they too began to sing. The young, perceiving that they had gained the right to their mother tongue, sensed that this language had the power to touch their hearts. Their joy rose to the sky, sounding like a dance, a game from vanished times when everything was simple and people's hearts were open to the fundamental earth, to the colour and strength of the endless sea of grass and the yellow waters of the river.

He resurrected forgotten images, the man who was speaking and singing by the river, and his beautiful words aroused a sorrow so great it had had to be denied for hundreds of years. The wrath, that mindless rage, that had slumbered during the sorrow, now awoke. 'Death to Akkad,' the people cried.

But the man walked alone and his fear was great, although far greater was his grief for he knew the price of this action of his. And he prayed to the forbidden god in the blue sky to be released from his task and the god answered him with bird-song full of freedom. And the man realised that he could reject great actions and live a small life in restraint and peace.

When dusk fell he was still by the river, resting under the great tree in whose branches birds were settling for the night. He spoke of his doubts to the birds. But all the birds could tell him was that life was good as it was and people's actions were madness. The tree spoke to him of the mysterious bond beyond good and evil. This gave him strength and he took it to mean that he must go beyond the border guarded by guilt and shame. But the river sang through the night of a change, of a movement that is independent of man. You are nothing but a guest of reality, it told him. So you do not see it. You see nothing but the parts, never the connection from which grows the whole.

This was the river's message and the man was greatly perplexed. But when dawn came with the first glint of sun on the river and the first bird call from the sky, he had made up his mind. Defiantly, he replied to them all, the trees, the river and the birds. He was a human being and had to go the way of human beings – the way of action and the mind.

The new war was as grim as the first and the waters of the river turned red with the blood of the many who lost their lives for his sake. On the day of victory, he laid the foundation stone of the temple while his tired soldiers returned home. Their footsteps were as heavy as death's and the grass died wherever they trod.

The man saw this, but banished the sight from his memory. For he was alone with the god whose honour he had restored and whose temple was the largest in the world. It rose in its stunning beauty to the sky and contained fifty lesser temples, one for every one of the great god's sons and daughters. Hall after hall was clad in gold and was intended to give lustre to the hymns and the old language. So great was the man's victory, so vast, that all that was unobtrusive and providential was obliterated. The walls of the temple were so massive that the wind dashed itself to oblivion against the stones, so well made that no bird could find foothold there.

The drums thundered their weighty rhythms over the

town in the evenings, carrying the news of peace to the people who spoke their own language at last. But the people could find no peace in their hearts because of the dead, the divisions and the fratricides, the treacheries and betrayals that followed this war of liberation. In every home, shame stamped on the threshold and guilt stood watching over their beds at night. The days were no easier to bear for sorrow wept in the wind and everyone heard it except the man in the huge temple, the man who had killed his memory.

In town it was whispered that the divine king could not sleep, that he bore their guilt as he walked endlessly round the walls of the new temple. And it was true that he walked night after night as he struggled with the question of what stood between him and the god whose realm he had restored to earth.

He received no answer and he trembled at the thought that his god was dead.

But his astrologers were full of hope for the new kingdom and songs were written in his honour. And the people's sorrow was subdued by great ceremonies, spectacles of unimaginable magnificence.

He had two mothers, Ke-Ba, the priestess of the goddess Gatumdus who had given birth to him in secret. She was still beautiful and her reputation among the people was great. But of Lia, who had brought him up, he knew nothing for she had disappeared into the grey, faceless multitude.

In burdened moments, he considered returning to the river, to the trees and the birds, but he had come so far from the truth now, he thought they would no longer listen to him. And that he could not endure.

Then finally his sacrifice came, the night in spring when he was to meet the long-horned bull and thrust the golden knife into the great animal's heart. He knew the action was dependent on freedom from fear and had to be pure of every thought. He had had a long training. He had done it year after year at the time when the bird-song rose again over the reborn grass and over the fields, where the first seeds were already shooting out of the red soil.

But in this, his last moment on earth, the guilt rose out of his memory, burst open the door he had sealed and, as the horns of the bull ripped his body in two, his heart fell out and shattered.

Then all the people saw that only the surface of the heart was of stone, and that this was as thin as an eggshell. Inside was dark sorrow, so overwhelming that it could, at any moment, have broken the fragile shell.

Chapter 11

Ruben observed Simon during the concert, at first with delight, then with wonder and finally with anxiety. The boy was as white as a sheet and, towards its end, seemed to have difficulty breathing.

It had been decided that they should stay overnight in town at his apartment. Neither of them said a word as the tram rattled them out to Majorna. A plate of sandwiches covered with a white cloth had been left on the dining-room table, but Simon shook his head and went straight into Isak's room and fell into bed. Ruben had never seen a person fall asleep so immediately – the boy only just had time to get his clothes off. But Simon had smiled at Ruben as he went to bed and, a few hours later, after he had digested the impressions of the evening with a cognac, Ruben could hear Simon laughing in his sleep and crying at the same time.

'Why did he have to die?' Simon asked at breakfast the next morning.

'Who?' Ruben said from behind the newspaper.

'The one in the music, the king or the priest, or whatever he was called.'

'Simon.' Ruben looked at him. 'I saw no priest. The music isn't about anything special. Different people experience it in different ways.'

Simon was astonished. 'So that, what's his name, the man who made it up . . .'

'Berlioz.'

'Yes, Berlioz, him. He never saw the priest?'

'No.' Ruben sensed the seriousness over the breakfast table, folded up his paper and chose his words carefully. 'Art, Simon, comes to people who listen or read or look at a picture. It arouses something – emotions there are no words for.'

Simon made an effort, screwing up his eyes as he always did when he was intensely preoccupied with trying to understand and, as he had done before, Ruben thought that there was a fire within the boy. 'So it's not real then?'

'That depends on what you mean by real. You read a lot, so you must have realised that people in books aren't real in the same way as you and I are, and what happens to them hasn't happened in what you call reality.'

Simon had never thought about this and had taken for granted that the worlds he stepped into and the people he met in books existed and looked just as he saw them. Things seemed to be sliding round his head. He screwed up his face again and bit his lower lip as he tried to put his thoughts into some kind of order.

'Don't use your head, Simon. Use your heart,' Ruben told him.

Simon's face smoothed out and his eyes opened wide as he stared into the unknowable, and he remembered the trees that had talked to him in his childhood, so clearly and yet so impossible to remember afterwards. He thought about the man and their conversations under the oaks, about how much strength he had been given, without ever remembering what had been said.

Ruben saw the change and finally risked a question. 'Can you tell me?'

'I recognised the man in the music, the priest or king. He was with me when I was small.'

Ruben nodded and smiled. 'I see. He once existed for you and the music reminded you.'

'But he truly did exist.'

'I believe you. He was once part of your essence, your inner world. It's common for children to create fantasy figures as a solace against loneliness.'

Simon felt relieved and cheated, for something was wrong with what Ruben had said. He felt it.

Then the maid cleared the table and Ruben had to go to visit Olga in the asylum. It was one of those rare days when hot water was allowed, and Ruben urged Simon to take a bath before catching the tram back to Erik and Karin. Simon nodded and washed as skimpily as he usually did.

After Ruben had left the house, the boy went round the apartment to look at everything. There were large paintings there which Erik used to joke about, daubs representing nothing. Simon stood looking at them for a long time, thinking perhaps something would come into his heart – but nothing did.

Then he went home and everything was as usual. There was the boat, no one had time for him, nor did anyone ask what he had thought of the concert, a fact for which he was grateful.

But Ruben couldn't get the way Simon had disappeared into the music out of his mind. On Sunday evening he phoned Karin and told her he had reason to believe that Simon was musical and that he would very much like to see the boy develop his talent. He, Ruben, had a friend who was a music teacher and Simon could go for a test. 'I may be wrong,' he concluded. 'But it wouldn't surprise me if perhaps there were a violin player in Simon.'

It was just as well Ruben Lentov was unable to see Karin's expression. All he could hear was her voice quavering as she replied that Simon would have to decide for himself. They certainly couldn't afford music lessons.

Simon was lying in the attic with his nose in a book. But despite Lord Jim having just made his fateful leap from the rusty deck of the steamer *Patna* in Conrad's novel, Simon was not with him in the entrance to the Persian Gulf. His mind was roaming in the country where the grass sang and the river spoke its gentle wisdom to people. The priest–king had talked about resurrecting a language that had been forbidden and forgotten.

Simon made an effort to understand. He recollected what Ruben had said about remembering with your heart, and he could hear the river and the people's voices. Then his head took over. What had they called out? What was the secret of the forgotten language?

Karin came up the creaking wooden stairs. 'Uncle Ruben has got it into his head that you're musical and wants you to learn the violin.'

For once he didn't hear the reproach that usually went

straight into the marrow of his bones. The idea exploded in his mind. If he could play, then he would be able to re-create the miracle himself.

As always, the boys went to bed in the attic during the summer. Isak slept heavily from exhaustion, so only Simon was woken by the quarrel in the kitchen as Erik shouted at Karin that she was bloody crazy and that he had had quite enough of that mysterious fiddler.

As usual when they quarrelled, Simon's guilt increased and this time he was quite certain it was his fault. He sat up in bed feeling sick and, as the voices rose and the abuse grew worse, everything became unbearable. He went downstairs, opened the kitchen door and stood there crying, saying he didn't want to have violin lessons.

Karin felt as if the boy had struck her in the heart and Erik was so ashamed he continued to shout. 'Go back to sleep, you damned good-for-nothing!'

But Simon did not hear. He was in Karin's arms and four years old, and she minded only about him as she dried his tears and comforted him, assuring him that all she and Erik wanted in life was that he should be happy.

'But you only care about Isak,' Simon said. The next moment he was asleep.

It was a difficult moment for Erik who went down to the basement, resolving to take a week off working on the boat and go fishing with Simon. As she tucked the boy up in his bed, Karin too looked back on the spring and summer, and everything that had happened since Isak had gone mad.

The next morning, after Simon had gone for his music test and Isak to his extra lessons, Erik and Karin were able to speak to each other again. Not about their unpleasant quarrel, nor their fear of the hurtful words, nor their mutual guilt over the boy feeling left out. And least of all about why Ruben's suggestion had upset them so much. What they did talk about was what was strange about Ruben's proposal.

'Simon has never liked music.' Karin remembered how they had laughed when Simon had come home from junior school and said that he couldn't stand the song they had to sing every morning. 'Do you remember he said it made him feel sick when the kids sang at the end of term and the teacher played the organ?'

'Mm.' Erik nodded. He also remembered the way the teacher had played, what the children had sounded like and that Simon had curled up in misery even when he was small whenever Karin had sung to him. Karin was tone deaf.

'He never liked the portable gramophone either,' Karin continued, and Erik thought about those warped records and awful ditties, how he himself had found it hard to bear when some singer was wailing even worse than usual because Karin had forgotten to wind up the gramophone.

Then he remembered the time when he had been making a wooden truck for the boy – Simon could have been no more than three at the time. He had been perched on the work-bench as Erik chiselled away whistling the Toreador aria from *Carmen*. Suddenly Simon had taken up the tune and sung it. As clear as a bell.

Even then the thought of his son's origins had disturbed Erik.

Hair flattened with water, in a newly ironed shirt, tram money in his pocket, Simon walked the old way to the tram stop. He was feeling as light-hearted as long ago when he had sat on Uncle Aron's bicycle carrier and had just been saved from getting lost.

He changed trams at Järntorget and found his way to his destination, a large, strange apartment in Park-Viktoria where an irascible and impatient man was expecting him.

Simon was not scared that day. Yet the visit was a disappointment. The man had long hair, shouted in broken Swedish and did nothing but tinkle on his piano, wanting Simon to imitate the notes. There was no violin to be seen. The long-haired man was a little nicer towards the end and muttered something about being intrigued. 'Very interesting,' he commented.

'Not much,' Simon said when he got home and Karin asked him whether he had enjoyed it.

'So you're not going to continue?'

Simon noticed her concern and answered no, he probably wasn't.

An hour or so later, Ruben phoned and told them that the man at Park-Viktoria had said that Simon had something called perfect pitch and that was very unusual.

'But he doesn't want to take lessons.'

Ruben could hear that Karin was relieved. 'Can't be true,' he said. 'I'll come and talk to him myself.'

They sat in the parlour that evening alone, Ruben and Simon.

'You'll have a new language,' Ruben told him.

Simon thought about English which was fun, and German which had been hard going. He couldn't understand why he had to learn another one. 'What use would that be?'

Ruben looked downcast and said he'd had an idea that Simon had a natural talent for music and this would enable him to express a lot of what he had inside him.

The boy vanished so quickly that Ruben never had time to see the surprise and pain in his dark eyes.

Chapter 12

This was when Simon began lying. He found it so easy that it was as if he had had a natural talent for that as well.

It was like running, like the time he had run sixty metres at the Nya Varvet athletics ground faster than anyone else, won a prize and was the centre of interest.

He was soon quite masterly at it. Lies ran off his tongue, the first providing the next and that giving birth to the third, which in its turn spawned the next and the next. He couldn't stop. His lies gave him a place in the sun, at school, in the gang at home, in Karin's interest and Erik's appreciation.

Simon was lonelier than ever.

He was a liar, and the realisation caused guilt to fasten its claws into him. And fear. He thought that if Karin caught him out a single time, her love for him would come to an end. With growing anxiety, he trained his mind to remember what he had said and tried never to contradict himself. The effort caused his insides to tie themselves into knots.

It began with Dolly, the girl on the upper floor of the neighbouring house, the girl he had loved for as long as he could remember. She had eyes like forget-me-nots and a cloud of fair curls, carefully set once a week by her hairdresser father.

Dolly was an only child and as stuck-up as her mother and father. When they moved into the Gustafssons' apartment next door, the walls were decorated with flowered wallpaper, the floors covered with colourful oriental rugs. Period furniture was lined up in dead straight rows and chandeliers tinkled from the ceilings.

Dolly had a room of her own. This alone was so remarkable it gave her a special appeal.

Her father had gone round the houses, holding his daughter by the hand and pointing out the ones in which she was allowed to get to know the children and play in their kitchens. Not at Olivia's, because gypsies lived there, nor at Helene's, because they had had consumption. The houses had women's names like ships.

Fortunately for Dolly, the Larssons' house was approved of because that meant access to Karin's kitchen and her wholesome food.

Ten years later, Dolly was to become the district's elegant whore, but no one could imagine that when she and Simon were fourteen and loved each other.

Simon never really knew whether Dolly really loved him but he went to a posh school and his father's boatyard was growing in influence and grandeur. He had also grown tall and good-looking, the darkness that had marked him out when little now attractive. From the half-moon window in the Larssons' attic, he could see right into Dolly's room. Neither of them ever said anything to anyone about it but, slowly and voluptuously, Dolly undressed every evening with the ceiling light on and without drawing the black-out curtain.

Simon stood in the attic with his hand round his penis. Their enjoyment was mutual and soon they managed to co-ordinate their activities. Once Dolly had at last got her knickers off, she would put one foot up on the window-sill, thrust her hand into her crevice and push her backside back and forth at an increasing pace. Then Simon came, desire straining in him and exploding for one dizzying second, his hand filling with warm sperm and his heart with gratitude to the girl for so generously offering herself to him.

Whenever they met they avoided each other's eyes. Not a word was uttered for Simon was tongue-tied. Then, one Sunday, he told the local boys that he had done it with Dolly in the winter-empty kiosk down by the bathing place. He hadn't really expected the interest this aroused. They wanted to know more and he obliged. Lie spawned lie as he painted exciting and colourful pictures. Yes, she had hair on her cunt. And a birthmark on one buttock which she wanted you to bite. No, she hadn't bled much. That virginity business was not all that great to make a fuss about. Yes, you could suck her breast.

Simon's own surprise at what he said was so great he didn't really notice the murmur in the air. But he soon came to enjoy the admiration apparent in the wide-open eyes all round him.

One Monday he tried it out again at school, with the same result. Even Isak was struck dumb with surprise and pride in his friend. In the long break, they walked round the girls' school in the cold, looking at the tittering bunches of girls inside, hating them because they had everything boys needed, those holes that all their dreams were about, those soft, moist, secret places.

'Imagine having a hole that you could do what you liked with,' Isak said, and Simon was scared and worried. They had never put this into words before. Now, after his story about Dolly, he realised anything was possible.

'Did you stick it in her?' Isak asked.

'No. Just a finger.'

Then he cursed himself, sensing a wall rising between them and wishing he could knock it down. But there was no going back.

One early spring morning when the weather was

stormy, he took the sea way along the shore and sat on the cliff, hoping the storm would blow him clean of all this falseness. He was late for his first lesson and had to knock on the door and apologise. This had happened before and he never usually made any excuses, accepting the bad-conduct mark which Karin would sign without reproaches.

'I was involved in an accident,' he announced this time.

He described the squealing brakes of the lorry, the woman who had been run over and the blood pouring down the gutter in Karl Johansgatan, and how he had only just managed to stop his bicycle and had been questioned by the police as a witness.

They had Rubbet for maths, a big man in his fifties used to decades of seeing through boys. He didn't join in the murmur of surprise which ran round the class, just told Simon to sit down and do his square roots. There was distrust in his cold eyes and Simon felt his stomach contracting. His story could be checked and Rubbet looked as if that was what he was going to do.

But Simon was to learn that the wickedness in him had allies. For the next day there was a report on the accident in Karl Johansgatan in the newspaper and Rubbet took the matter up again. 'You were wrong, Larsson,' he said. 'It wasn't a woman who got run over, but an elderly man.' He expounded on the psychology of witnesses, on how the agitation when witnessing an accident distorts your vision. 'Witnesses are often wrong and rarely to be relied on,' he concluded.

At first, Simon felt only relief and a touch of triumph, but later his terror came creeping back, fastening in his midriff this time, not in his stomach.

The devil sees to his own, Erik used to say. And now Simon knew that to be true. The devil had helped him, again and again. He told Erik that he was the only one in the class who had dared climb the rope right up to the ceiling and the gym master had been astonished. 'The devil you did,' the gym master had said. Erik was delighted.

The next day Simon, who was generally afraid of heights, climbed right up to the ceiling and the gym master, a ridiculous bow-legged old cavalry officer, exclaimed 'The devil you did!'

He told Karin he had been to see his grandmother and Karin was pleased. The next day he realised he would have to go and see the old bat. He took flowers with him, flowers he'd bought with money borrowed from Isak, to whom he said he had lost a bet he'd made with Abrahamsson in scripture. He didn't have to safeguard that story, because Isak never went to scripture lessons, so had never met Abrahamsson. Simon's flowers were much appreciated and this touched his mother's heart.

One afternoon as he was walking home from the tram stop, someone had chalked Simon loves Dolly with a heart and an arrow on the baker's wall. Simon felt the back of his neck stiffen with the effort of keeping his head so that he couldn't look at it.

As he sauntered along the road to the garage, he saw her sitting there below the hedge. Dolly. Her cheeks red, her eyes blank. 'Did you read it?' she said.

He nodded.

'Is it true?' she asked and he wanted to die, or at least for the earth to open and swallow him. He thought of Nordenskjöld's voyage through the North-east Passage and the great expanses of ice in the arctic night. His mouth was dry and he didn't dare meet those forget-me-not eyes.

'Is it true?' she persisted.

Afraid Karin might hear, Simon nodded and said almost inaudibly, 'I suppose so.'

You're not supposed to hit girls, he thought. Supposing she leaped on him and scratched? But she looked extremely content and said that if they met after dinner down by the bathing place where no one could see them, he could kiss her.

Simon had no desire to go, but didn't dare stay away. So it happened that when he kissed a girl for the very first time it tasted of lies and yellow terror.

All his love ceased with that kiss. He detested the girl he had dreamed about. When he realised she would soon be making demands on him and he would have to do all the things he had already said he had done he was panic-stricken. Then, as usual, the lies came leaping out of his mouth to rescue him. He screwed up his eyes. 'I'm going to die soon,' he told her. 'You see, I've got TB, though no one knows yet. I cough up blood all night.'

Dolly fled.

Fear of consumption had proved stronger than the desire to conquer, stronger than lust, stronger even than vanity. When the ten o'clock news was switched on in the kitchen and he went upstairs to watch Dolly undress, as usual, he saw that she had drawn the black-out curtain.

Simon was relieved.

A week later, Karin said, 'Aunt Jenny was in and said you had a bad cough. I hadn't noticed anything but she looked so frightened, I was almost worried.'

'Oh,' said Simon. 'I had a bit of cold one day and happened to cough on the same tram as Dolly.'

Karin smiled then sighed at the thought of their grand neighbours in those neat rooms with bacteria crawling all over the walls.

Spring came with strong west winds blowing clean

between the mountains. The grass grew green and people's voices rang more clearly than they had for many years, full of hope.

When the apple blossom was out they launched Isak's boat and it was just as Erik had imagined, the finest double-ender in the river mouth. She was moored to a buoy and anchored inside Oljeberget, and given a ballast of granite while waiting for the lead that could not be bought for money. They were delayed by the sailmaker, but eventually one day, at the end of May, they were able to test sail her.

She flew, cleaving the sea as if dancing, and Isak forgot his dreams of that moist hole in his happiness to get her close to the wind. They named her *Kajsa*, after Karin and the west wind.

On D-Day, when the Allied invasion force established its bridgehead in Normandy, Isak and Simon took their exams, and Simon was awarded the Premium, the school's literary prize. He had written an essay on the peasant who farmed the fields inside the Oljeberget, a sour-eyed old man of whom Simon had always been afraid. But in his essay he made the old farmer into a man with great gifts, a man who was a master at runes, who knew the influence of the old signs, who was friends with the powers and who put the evil eye on people but also cured them of serious and rare diseases.

His teacher read the essay aloud in class and said it was a wonderful story. 'Is there any truth in it? Or is there a writer hidden there inside you, Larsson?'

Her words flashed like lightning through Simon's head and with one relieved breath, he said, 'I made it all up.'

For a while he acquired the nickname the Poet, but he ignored it. He thought a lot about Uncle Ruben and what he had said at the concert about there being a reality based on lies yet which possessed the truth. Before he fell asleep, he decided to write down all his lies. All summer, he would write stories about women and breasts and holes, and about Arctic explorers and death down there in Europe. He would write about Karin as one of the Fates sitting by her spinning wheel in her kitchen, spinning people's destinies into a thread, and about the little man in his dreams, the man who had such a strange hat and fought wars in the realm of high grass, and died when he was to sacrifice a bull in the temple. And he would write about Dolly, the faithless slut, betraying the man who loved her, and about Aunt Inga up there in the lonely smallholding by the blue lake. The latter surprised him. What the hell could he invent about Inga?

But he didn't worry about it. Tomorrow he would ask Uncle Ruben for exercise books, a whole stack of them.

Summer came with its free delights, enveloping the two boys, now no longer inseparable.

Isak sailed and Simon wrote. Karin worked in the garden, Erik sang, laid the keel of his third double-ender, and the Americans and British liberated Paris.

When summer was at its best, the lies stopped running off Simon Larsson's tongue. Perhaps his writing helped, although there weren't as many stories as he had imagined. Maybe he found writing much more difficult than lying. But something happened in all that reality, something so astounding that it went beyond all Simon's fantasies.

Her name was Maj-Britt and she was the kind of woman who swells over all limits, like dough set to rise when you've been mean with the flour and generous with the yeast: lush, creamy, overflowing.

She was nineteen, the daughter of a widowed rock-blaster who had built his house at the top of the hill out on the city boundary. She was suffering from a broken heart because she had loved one of the seamen who had met his death in the metal innards of the *Ulven*.

Isak and Simon were sent to her one warm afternoon to have their hair cut. She was employed by Dolly's father, the hairdresser, and cut and fondled their hair, unable to find enough words for how fine Isak's hair was, what quality, and what a mane of hair Simon had been blessed with. The boys were as scarlet as the peonies growing outside the window in the buzzing hot afternoon. Both had a hard-on.

She noticed and her laughter rolled round the hairdresser's salon and out into the garden, where astonished bumble-bees fell silent in the blowsy flowers.

'Come to my place this evening. At six. You know, the rock-blaster's house. Use the basement entrance,' she told them once she had collected herself.

The hairdresser, his wife and Dolly were away on holiday, so they were alone in the salon.

Back at home, Karin said their haircuts weren't up to much and that girl should have taken more off, considering she was paid to do it. Karin reckoned she could have done better herself, the way they looked now.

Fortunately, they were eating early that day, and just before six the boys raced on their bikes to the city boundary and up the hill with its stunning view over the sea and the city. The hill was steep and hard work, but their thumping hearts and the sweat pouring off them were not only from their exertions. They slipped down the side of the house and found the basement door at the back.

Maj-Britt was expecting them. She had a room in the basement, and a big bed which the seaman had bought cheaply at a sale and humped up there. And she laughed just as hugely as she had at the hairdresser's salon and was

89

so unembarrassed that the boys soon found they had to laugh with her.

It was a dream, a crazy wonderful dream, as she pulled off her dress. She hadn't a stitch on underneath. Then she lay down on the bed and spread out her arms and her legs. 'Come on now, little ones,' she said. 'Let's have some rejoicing. I'll teach you.'

She did. Soon they were there, one on each female arm, as she guided their hands to her secret places and showed them how to practise the right grips, hard and soft alternately. They sucked and bit at a large breast each and Maj-Britt moaned and groaned with lust and delight as Simon thrust into her.

When she came, she shrieked so loudly that the basement ceiling bulged. A moment later she came again and Isak had to learn how to find that slippery pea in her moistly dripping crevice.

'More, that's the best,' she moaned. Her desire exploded again and she collapsed and laughed her huge laugh, then milked Isak off, for he still had a hard-on.

This can't be true, thought Simon, but it was.

Then suddenly Maj-Britt saw the time. 'My God, he'll be back soon. Off you go, little billy goats.'

Her laughter followed then as they swished down the hill feeling like gods. At the bathing place they threw themselves into the sea, cleaving the water with long strokes. They had never known before that they could swim so fast. When they reached Isak's boat, they were still hot and excited, but noticed the line was sticky with jellyfish and knew they had to get on board as quickly as possible. Simon was stung, but there was fresh water on board and they washed off the salt and jellyfish threads. Then Isak lifted up the floorboard and extracted beer from under the keelson, secret beer stolen from Ruben.

They drank and tried to calm down.

'Did you hear what she said when we left?'

Oh yes, Simon had heard. 'Come back tomorrow at the same time.'

Every evening that hot summer when thirty thousand Balts were fleeing across the Baltic in small boats, they went back and rejoiced, as Maj-Britt put it, learning everything boys needed to know about making love. Both of them were to have good times with girls in their lives to come and they were often to send grateful thanks back to the wonderful Maj-Britt on the mountain.

One evening, as they slipped round the corner of the house as usual and knocked on the basement door, a sailor in nothing but his jaunty bell-bottoms opened up, a man as broad as a hatch cover and tall as a flagpole.

'What the hell do the kids want?' he said to the just visible Maj-Britt on the bed in the cool of the basement.

Simon had not forgotten his skills from the previous winter. 'We're selling Älvsborg Christmas gnomes,' he said.

'In the middle of the summer?' the sailor asked, then forgot them as Maj-Britt's laughter came rolling off the bed.

On their way home they tried to hate the sailor. But they were grateful for what they had been given, almost satiated, in fact, and both had always known that this incredible business could not go on.

Chapter 13

Then it came, the longest spring of all. Never before had time been so dilatory, the days creeping towards evenings, as nothing happened.

Wallenberg disappeared in Budapest. In Germany, twelve-year-olds were conscripted into war service. And in Yalta, important men met to carve up the world between them. Roosevelt died, and Karin said with fierce resentment that it was not fair.

Then Hitler shot himself in a Berlin bunker and for a while time stood still for peace had not yet come. The radio ticked over in its corner, the old kitchen clock refused to budge and Karin found herself shaking it. There was nothing wrong. Time itself seemed to have stopped, driving the waiting people mad.

Eventually, just as the birches began to come out, the seventh of May came to an end. There was a smell of wet earth from the garden and the birds should have sung in people's hearts. But no one had the energy. They gathered round the radio in the Larssons' kitchen and listened to the jubilation in Oslo, London and Stockholm. They couldn't take in their joy.

Wallin sat on the kitchen sofa staring at his huge working man's hands lying so still in his lap as if they would never come to life again. Ågren had feverish red patches on his cheeks. Damn and blast the bloody bastards, he kept swearing.

For once, Erik was silent. He looked with envy at Äppelgren stalking like an awkward crane across the kitchen floor, tripping on the rag rug, not attempting to hide the fact that he was crying like a baby.

Karin was also crying quietly.

Simon and Isak had squeezed together on the wood-box as usual, and Simon was thinking that tonight no one was killing anyone else down there in Europe. He wanted to cry too, but he was too old for that now. The excitement went to his legs and feet, now drumming on the wood-box until Karin begged him to cease. 'For God's sake, Simon, stop it. Be quiet!' she said.

Isak was beside him, as strangely still as Wallin was. His heart was burning but his head was cold and empty, his body so rigid it could have been frozen. Not until Johansson the postman, a fisherman by birth and as large as a house, said they should now boil all the Nazi bastards in oil and make sure they stayed alive and were tormented as long as possible, did the tension in Isak's body give way. He drew a deep breath, and realised that what had been knotting his muscles was hatred, what was burning in his heart was the knowledge that revenge was possible and sweet.

In the middle of it all, Helen arrived with the milk. She looked round at them. 'I think you should all come to the chapel and thank God for peace,' she announced solemnly.

At that, Erik leaped to his feet. 'And who the hell do we have to thank for the war and all the dead?'

'War is the work of man,' said Helen, without losing an ounce of her gravity.

'You're crazy,' said Ågren. Karin interrupted and said that at least in her kitchen, people should show consideration for other people's views. Her words were familiar, but her voice lacked force.

Towards evening, Ruben appeared, something inscrutable in his eyes, great relief mixed with unbearable pain. When Karin's eyes met his, she took out the schnapps bottle and the footless glasses, and poured out a full measure for everyone.

'Let's drink to peace then, shall we?' she said in a voice as thin as paper.

They drank, Karin too, swallowing the horrible drink in one go. If it hadn't been such a momentous moment, the others would have noticed Karen's action and been surprised and a little shocked. As it was, they were all absorbed in themselves.

Karin went out to the old privy in the backyard and threw up. She stood leaning against the plastered wall, white in the face and sweating as the nausea kept washing over her. But worst of all was the pain in her chest.

She felt annoyed with herself. Why should she have pain now it was all over, and the earth and people could breathe out again? The pain churned inside her, as if someone were twisting a knife round in there. She tried to think about Petter and the waxwings. But at that moment her mother and her bitter eyes and sharp tongue were in Petter's place. Something was being dislodged in Karin's heart. The old, safe sorrow was moving, tearing at its roots. She was afraid that the war had taken the lives of her waxwings.

Karin stayed outside until dusk. Then she realised that time had reverted to its usual pace and she had to go back in, get the men out of her kitchen and begin on dinner. Her hand clenched beneath her left breast, she set about her ordinary everyday chores.

Over the winter they had altered the house, raising walls on the upper floor and abolishing the attic. Simon had a room of his own now, and there was plenty of space for Isak too. They had made a guest room with a view over the sea for Ruben, who stayed increasingly often with them, tired as he was of the refugees and his brother's family to whom he had given house room in his apartment in Majorna.

The Larssons had a bathroom and an indoor lavatory.

They had raised the sink unit in the kitchen and replaced the zinc with stainless steel. They had central heating and two kinds of water. Karin could hardly believe that the end had now come to heaving wood and anthracite about, and to smoking tiled stoves. Or that she

94

only had to turn on a tap for hot water to come rushing out, warming her hands and making things clean. A handsome refrigerator had been put in the place where they used to stand and wash themselves in the kitchen.

Karin had a great deal to be pleased about. She thought about it when, late that night, they were on their own and dinner was on the table. As she put some potato into her mouth, she was at last able to admit that she detested them – fried, grated, baked or boiled, especially boiled. It was over. Her worries about food were soon to be as dismal a memory as the anthracite and the cold privy in the backyard.

Rationing would cease and there would be fruit again. Bananas, thought Karin, remembering that Simon had loved bananas when he was small. He had probably forgotten what they tasted like.

She looked at Erik and saw how pride had grown in him like a cock's crest. Things were going well for him and his boatyard, the list of orders for his double-enders was long and he employed four men. They supported four families now, as Karin liked to put it. She liked the money too, the money that nowadays was there when needed.

As always when Karin ran through all the things she had to be grateful for, she missed Ruben out and saved Simon till last. The boy who had brought her so much joy.

He'll soon be an adult, she thought. How he had changed! He was almost handsome, like a strange bird which by some wonderful chance had settled in her kitchen.

But still she was uneasy, and again she felt that stab in her chest.

Simon noticed the pain flitting over her face. 'You're tired, Mum,' he said. 'You go to bed. I'll do the dishes.'

She nodded, but when she met his anxious eyes, she knew that all her gratitude had not helped her this evening. Her abundance of riches was no use as a defence when it came to what was tearing at her inside. What is the matter with me, she wondered?

Erik had gone to the boatyard so Karin had the bedroom to herself. She stood among the roses on the new wallpaper and looked at herself in the mirror. She had always been content with her appearance, liking the firm and fine features of her face, its big mouth and straight nose. She studied her features for a long time, wondering whether they had anything new to tell her. An answer? She could see that those brown eyes, always surprising in her fairness, had acquired new depths.

What was it in those depths? Fear?

No! I've got a few wrinkles, Karin told herself, and my hair's faded to straw colour. I'm not yet fat, but heavier, sturdier. It'll have gone by tomorrow. As long as I can get some sleep.

Next morning, as they tore down the black-out curtains and cleaned the windows in the spring warmth, Karin was almost happy.

But one evening, Ruben brought the first English newspapers with eyewitness accounts of the liberated concentration camps in Poland and Germany back with him. He sat at the kitchen table and read from them. Isak's eyes rolled up at the ceiling as he translated. Erik was white in the face and the blue in his eyes darkened. Simon's eyes sought Karin's, as always when he was afraid.

The next moment he snatched the newspaper out of Ruben's hands and cried out that that was enough.

Through his great weariness, Ruben looked from Simon to Karin and saw that she was close to fainting.

He was deeply ashamed, then frightened.

Karin protested that if his relatives had had to experience it, then she had to cope with hearing about it. Yet, from that evening on, it was clear even to the others that there was something wrong with Karin. They tried to spare her. Erik took the radio to the workshop and Simon smuggled the newspaper out in the mornings. But Karin was drawn to what was terrible and went into town to buy magazines with pictures of corpses stacked up in piles.

Then the white buses came to Malmö, and Karin went by herself to fetch the morning papers with photographs of people who had seen evil and should have been dead, not staring at her with lifeless eyes. And Karin realised she was to die, she, too. And she welcomed that insight.

A few days later Ruben said to Erik that this would no longer do and they took her to a heart specialist Ruben knew. He listened for a long time and, troubled by the ragged clatter in her chest, said that she must rest completely if things weren't to go badly wrong.

Karin was admitted to his private clinic, so tired she hadn't the energy to protest. She was given medicine and sleep. In her sleep, she faced her mother again and realised that she had hated her from the day she was born. Just as her mother had hated Petter.

Like a huge black crow, her mother came tearing towards Karin, croaking and shrieking, swastikas flashing round her, flying in and out between them. Suddenly they were in the tailor's workshop at home. Karin saw Petter crouching below the swastikas. He was like the people pouring off the white buses in Malmö, who should be dead. The horrible croaking went into his heart and hurt so badly that in the end it broke and he died at his tailor's table.

Her dreams came and went, and Karin let them, let the images speak their clear language without resisting or seeking explanations. Her mind would have to be washed clean before she could leave. That hurt but was good, necessary somehow.

In waking moments she carried on a conversation with her mother. 'How did you come to be like you were?' she asked.

But her mother croaked 'poor me, poor me' and Karin turned her head away with distaste, seeing that she had always denied evil because she had grown up in its shadow.

Then, half asleep, she heard herself croaking over Simon, poor me, poor me, and saw those anxious eyes of his that always followed her. She cried out and the doctor came, told her she must not worry so, and gave her tablets to banish her fears.

The next night Petter came to her, and her sleep was deep and peaceful. She thought perhaps it was all over, and she would be allowed to follow him and escape having to wake to another day. He was there all night, cradling her in his arms, singing to her, and there was no evil, and Karin was as safe as a child. She knew there was something he wanted to tell her, but she was too tired to listen.

Dawn came and when Karin became aware of the sunlight coming through the crack between the blind and the window frame she realised it wasn't all over. She was still there, and alone. While they washed her and persuaded her to eat some gruel, she thought about what Petter had wanted to tell her. But not for long, for she couldn't collect her thoughts.

Then suddenly, Simon was there and it was night again, and difficult to understand. But Simon was quite real and holding her hand so hard it almost hurt. She heard the anger in his voice as he spoke. 'Don't leave me, Mum.'

When Karin next woke it was light again. He was sitting by her bed and she realised he was right. She mustn't leave, not yet. 'Simon,' she whispered. 'I promise to get better.'

His delight was so great that it went straight into her soul, warmed her and gave her life.

After he had left, Karin wept quietly for a long time. She had no idea she had so many tears in her, or where they came from, but she sensed where they went, straight into her heart, warm and relieving.

Simon cycled wildly through town, the slanting morning rays of sun glittering in the harbour and out at sea as he raced on to the boatyard and Erik. 'Dad, she's going to get better. She promised.'

Ordinarily, Erik would have taken little notice of such a statement, but he was in such a state of fear that he took Simon's words as the absolute truth. They were almost of equal height now, Erik and Simon, as they stood facing each other across the half-finished double-ender. They were crying, both of them, the same kind of healing tears as Karin's.

Then Erik went inside, washed the sawdust off his neck and hands, shaved and put on his best suit, wintery and dark blue. There was no ironed shirt for him, but Simon picked all the tulips from the garden into a huge bunch.

Erik felt slightly foolish as he stood in the corridor of the clinic with all those flowers. Karin could see it and his uncertainty, that worker's fear, the unironed shirt, and her tenderness was great as she saw she had to stay for the sake of this fragile creature.

Chapter 14

Karin's days of recovery were peaceful.

Ruben brought roses. 'I had decided to go,' she told him.

'I've long seen you weighed down with some great sorrow,' was all he replied.

Karin was surprised, as she had never seen it like that, but it struck her as the truth, and she told him about Petter and the waxwings, and about her mother and the evil she had always had to deny.

'Nothing is ever simple,' was Ruben's only response.

Much later, Karin found herself thinking about this. She wanted to ask him about the God he went to every Saturday at the synagogue. This belief must, after all, have given him some strength to live through his misfortunes. But she could find no words.

'You really must try to live, Karin. For my sake, so that I can cope,' he told her as he was leaving.

She could see it had been difficult for him to say this.

Then he had gone and she lay there, watching the sun trickling through the dark spruce outside. A tram rattled round the corner and, when the nurse came with dinner, Karin noticed she had brilliant blue eyes.

The veal smelled of dill sauce, strong and good, and the apple purée afterwards freshened her mouth. The world seemed to have acquired a new tangibility.

For a while that afternoon she tried to feel ashamed of burdening Ruben with her sorrows, for he had quite enough of his own. But there was no strength in the feeling so she gave up. Perhaps I've lost my conscience, she thought.

When Simon came that evening and she saw how pale and thin he was, she realised this was not true. 'I hope you're all eating properly,' she said, guilt stabbing at her in the same old way. 'And where's Isak? Give him my love and tell him to come tomorrow.' Her voice now contained all the old weight of responsibility.

Simon nodded, but his expression was so odd that she saw she had been neglecting something important.

Simon cycled through town, strengthened by Karin being herself again, as forceful and demanding as ever. But he was also worried. And angry. Bloody Isak, he thought.

Simon knew where to find him, down in the harbour out at Långedrag, where Ruben had rented a mooring and Isak had become king in the glory of handsome double-enders. Simon could hear the racket from the cabin from far away and his anger reached boiling point when he saw beer bottles bobbing about in the water round the boat.

They were smoking and the air was thick as Simon opened the hatch into the cabin. 'Get to hell out of here, you lot,' he shouted. 'I want to talk to Isak on his own.'

They didn't leave at once and there was some jeering, but a quarter of an hour later, Simon and Isak were alone. Simon took the net, fixed it to the boathook and fished up the empty bottles that hadn't already sunk, emptied ashtrays, swilled down the cockpit and deck, then turned to Isak hunched up on the bunk. 'You're to go and see Karin tomorrow.'

'I daren't.'

'She's better now. Well. Do you understand?'

'Because of the beer.'

'For Christ's sake, she doesn't drink beer,' Simon said in astonishment. 'Are you crazy? Or just drunk, you bastard?'

They stood there staring at each other. Deep in Isak's

eyes there was an emptiness Simon recognised from the war, from when those Norwegian ships had disappeared into the depths. Simon's anger evaporated and he was truly frightened as he thought that this time there was no Karin to cope with what was unfathomable and he would have to do it himself.

He flung his arms round Isak. 'For God's sake, Isak. Karin's illness has nothing to do with you.'

Simon had no idea where these words came from but he could see he had said the right thing, for Isak relaxed and when their eyes met, the frightening emptiness had gone.

The next day Isak was at the hospital and could see with his own eyes that Karin was almost herself again. As always, he could talk to her. 'I was going to boil them in oil, twist their pricks off, you see. I was going to sail up Oslo Fjord because the papers said that a lot of Germans were still there, and I was going to find them and –'

'And what?'

'Well, then you fell ill.'

In a few words, Karin managed to explain that what had made her ill was her grief over everything that had happened, and what had been disclosed by peace, and that his wicked thoughts were just a breeze in a world of evil deeds.

'Perhaps it was good for you, Isak, to fantasise about revenge,' she said.

He told her about the beer, the boys on the boat and how they laced it with brandy Isak filched from Ruben's cupboard.

That put an end to her gentleness. Karin sat up in bed and looked him straight in the eye. 'Isak Lentov, you must put a stop to that kind of thing. Swear you will now, at once –'

Scarlet with shame, Isak hunched up at her fury.

'You must learn to distinguish between fantasy and what actually goes on, Isak. Maybe you have to have horrible ideas of revenge, but if you caught some terrified German boy running away from Norway, you would cry with pity. Revenge is only sweet in your imagination, don't you see?'

Isak said nothing. He did not believe her.

'Stealing drink tempts other people to ruin, that's the truth. And you must stop doing it.'

Isak promised solemnly and left her, ashamed and happy.

Karin lay there thinking how stupid and selfish she had been. It was obvious she had to go on living and make life comprehensible for the people she was responsible for. The thought pleased her so much, she fell asleep and slept all night without pills. Strangely enough, she thought least about Erik, who was the worst of them all.

He came one day for a talk with the consultant, weighty words on the importance of sparing Karin. Strong emotions had to be avoided, the doctor said. The responsibility for Karin's life being calm rested with Erik. 'If she gets angry or frightened, the result could be disastrous,' the heart specialist told him.

Erik was dispirited. His shirt button stuck into his larynx and class hatred rose within him as he thought, here we go again, that old sense of inferiority. Bloody hell!

When he at last got away and slunk in to see Karin, he was distraught and scarcely present. He had been going to tell her about the car he had bought, expecting her protests with some pleasure, her arguments about extravagance, then her delight when he would finally say he had bought it so that she could get out and about in the world. But nothing came of that.

Nor did he take any pleasure in the handy Fiat Balilla

as he cruised home through the Avenue and along the quays, where the cranes were dancing as they had done in the old days. He drove up towards Karl Johansgatan and went in to buy a whole bottle of spirits.

That afternoon at the boatyard he was curt and restless, and he noticed he was upsetting people.

The kitchen at home looked terrible and smelled of rubbish and dirty dishes. Simon was going sailing with Isak, and came and went.

'You go on out.' Erik's tone was more friendly than he intended. Just why he didn't really know until he had locked the door and taken out the bottle.

As he had his third drink, he thought about his mother, how she had threatened and frightened him with her heart over the years. He was back there again and now it was for real. The trap had slammed shut and there was no way out. He hated Karin because of her heart, then felt bitterly ashamed. Of course, Karin was nothing like his mother. She never threatened. Then he felt angry. Karin was more cunning than his mother. She didn't frighten, didn't give any warning, just hit out.

No quarrelling, the doctor had said. Nothing to upset her. Go with it, agree with her. God Almighty!

What hadn't his rebellion cost when he'd left the congregation and joined the union? But his mother hadn't died as he'd thought she would. She was still alive and kicking even today. Whereas Karin – she might die at any moment.

Erik had strange thoughts as he sat there on his own, drink eliminating the boundaries between sense and insanity. An old curse would be fulfilled, a penance demanded. He tried to pull himself together and heated up some coffee. But he could see things would be just the same as when he was a child. He had always known that the weak heart inside his mother was his doing and he had had to behave so that it kept on beating. Oh God!

The next day he spoke to Anton, the carpenter at the boatyard, about Lisa. Erik considered he was humiliating himself, but the wages he was offering were better than usual, and Anton was pleased and said he would speak to her. They needed the money and his wife hadn't so much to do now the children had left. She was good at cleaning and at keeping a place tidy, and she wasn't a bad cook, either.

Thus Erik built ramparts against the darkness ahead. He went to the hospital and was so nice he could have spewed at the thought, while Lisa meticulously cleaned every corner of the white house and made it shine. But nothing helped Erik with his anger, that great wrath burning in his chest which he only understood when he drank.

Soon that would come to an end too, for Karin would be back from the clinic and he knew what her eyes looked like when he drank. Oh hell!

It was a trap and he was racing round in it like a mad rat.

Chapter 15

Karin came home for midsummer and Erik paid a bill corresponding to half the profit on a double-ender. He did so with bitter satisfaction, as if he had bought his freedom.

They had a festive meal with new potatoes and smoked salmon. Ruben brought wine, and friends and neighbours came with flowers. Karin was happy, deeply and quietly happy.

She was also happy about the car Erik had fetched her in. And, naturally, the spotless house. But when life returned to normal, she had to come to terms with Lisa who was so nice. But Karin found her rather difficult, although she had to admit the house had never been so tidy and she was also happy to find the cupboards cleaned out, neat piles of linen, the men's shirts all ironed, the windows cleaned and the pot plants cared for.

Karin had once been a domestic servant and had learned from that how to be a housewife. So now she felt inferior.

But she was tired and couldn't really cope with the house, and Erik was kind to have engaged Lisa, she knew that. And, when she realised that Anton and Lisa, who had always lived on the poverty line, had already adjusted their dreams to the level Lisa's new wages brought them, she soon accepted the new state of affairs.

As she grew stronger, Karin found a solution and told Lisa she thought she could cope with hourly help. So it was settled that Lisa would come at eleven in the morning and finish every day at three after having cleaned, done a quick wash and prepared dinner. Thus Karin had the mornings to herself in the kitchen, with coffee within reach and neighbours dropping in, just as it had always been. The afternoons were hers too, when she took a nap, did a little sewing and read a lot. In the evenings she was even heard to joke about having become an upper-class wife.

Best about the new system was her walks. When Lisa came at eleven and took over the house, Karin went out along the river, on to the rickety jetties creeping through the reeds, stopping to listen to the water and gazing at the funny little grey bells of the knawel. Then she walked on round the hill, through the overgrown wild garden and out towards the sea, the sea which made everything grandiose and easy to comprehend.

On her way home she roamed the hills, sat on smooth warm rocks and spoke to the wind and the harebells. She also found her way to Simon's old oaks. Soon, she went there every day, greeted them and made friends with the great trees.

For the first time in her life Karin had time and space for many thoughts, difficult ones as well; thoughts that could no longer be chased away with household tasks. They were mostly about her mother. She talked to the oaks a great deal about the old people and her childhood. The oaks listened gravely and taught her that she did not have to understand, that it was part of the human condition that she had to explain everything and thus came to misunderstand all. And she remembered Ruben's words: 'It's not that simple.'

The sloes were angrier and reminded her of the malevolence and injustices of her bitter childhood. Then Karin went to the sea and sat looking at its endless expanse and listening to its message about life being so much greater and with many more flavours than the bitterness of sloes.

In Andersson's meadows the hay had been stacked and the strong scent tickled her nipples and loins, making her flush like a seventeen-year-old, unfamiliar as she was with her desire. But she picked a bunch of summer flowers, cornflowers, ox-eye daises and swaying lacy cow-parsley, put them in a vase in the bedroom and tempted Erik into bed when evening came. Afterwards she couldn't avoid seeing he was anxious. They tried to talk.

'You know, the doctor warned –'

Karin laughed her forceful old laugh. 'Oh, to hell with the doctor.'

Erik laughed too, daring to believe that at last there would be excursions into the open air. He fell asleep like a comforted child, his hand on her heart which was now beating calmly and steadily.

The next day, Karin dressed up to take the tram into town to go and see her mother and, unusually for her, having put on her new white summer coat, her gloves and the big hat with blue roses, she stood in front of the mirror. She thought her new thinness suited her. She even took out a lipstick and reddened her lips.

Then she went to the boatyard to tell Erik where she was going. He climbed down from the mast of the boat he was rigging. 'You're not to go to see her by yourself. Wait a minute, and I'll change and drive you in.'

As Karin sat on the bench outside the porch, she realised with some astonishment that Erik understood a lot more than she had imagined.

Things went better than expected at her mother's. She was genuinely please to see Karin and fussed over how thin she was. 'Goodness me, you do look wretched!' she exclaimed.

Karin could hear her anxiety and forced herself to eat the horrible pork sandwiches her mother made to ensure she would put on a bit of weight.

Erik talked more than usual and Karin noticed how pleased her mother was. She remembered her mother had always liked her son-in-law. He talked about the home for pensioners being built in Masthugget and the old lady seemed interested. Suddenly Karin realised that her nightmare that her mother would have to live with them when no longer able to cope on her own, was not going to happen.

Her eldest brother appeared and Karin rather liked

him. This was new too, for she had been estranged from her brothers for many years. They left together as her brother wanted to see Erik's new car.

On the stairs, Karin said, 'Mother was really quite nice today, wasn't she?'

'She's been worried about you, you must see that.'

Karin didn't believe this. 'I've never known her care about me.'

Her brother looked embarrassed, as men do when women get emotional. 'You took Dad away from both her and us,' he said heatedly. 'So it wasn't all her fault.'

Karin stopped on the stairs, her heart beating fast. Erik intervened. 'Now shut up. Karin's not to be upset.'

The men went on down, but Karin heard her brother speak as he got to the entrance. 'Then things can't be all that easy for you.'

In the car, Karin put her hand on Erik's shoulder, Ruben's words swirling round in her head.

Nothing is that simple.

Chapter 16

They dropped the bomb on the eighteenth of August.

Hiroshima, a lovely name. It must have been a lovely city, thought Karin. She heard that about three hundred thousand people died. The number was too great for her to take in. Heads couldn't take it in and hearts, her heart, had had enough.

Erik read aloud from the newspaper that the world would never be the same. Man now knew that he could exterminate himself as well as everything else on earth.

Karin couldn't take that in either. Her world had

already changed, but the boys, sitting in the kitchen listening to Erik, froze in the warmth of summer. Isak thought about Hitler and knew that you had to watch early on for lunatics in the world. Simon reckoned that his universe had already shifted from trust to unpredictability that night in the hospital when he had sat with Karin, terrified she was going to die.

School started again, first year at senior high, everything the same. No war, no atom bombs could change that world. Boredom permeated the walls, thick layers of it, dripping into corners where it collected, flowing inexorably along the rows of desks, burbling from the Latin master's mouth, crashing between the maths master's teeth. It smelled of chalk and sweat. It was there in German and in their own language which dried up as boys examined its source.

Simon was frightened. Soon he would be as dead as the old men at the master's desk. Boredom would fill his lungs, poison his blood and turn his body rigid. It's a disease, he thought, and the worst of it is, you die without knowing it. You go on as before, your legs moving and your mouth declining irregular French verbs.

'It would help if you had something in your head, Svensson,' the language teacher would shout. 'As it is, the verbs are rattling around in a vacuum.'

Svensson, Dahlberg and Axelsson belonged in Stretered, the maths master told them, the city's institute for the mentally retarded.

Larsson did not, for he found everything easy. Too easy. All he had to do was to learn and regurgitate as required. Chew, swallow, regurgitate, chew again, swallow, regurgitate.

Boredom crept out of the classroom along the corridor

into the science labs. It stopped at the library door, then crept on towards the school hall. It was a handsome hall, but boredom found nourishment in edifying speeches on peace and God, who had to be particularly thanked for sparing their country. The priest had the best of it, coming to morning prayers once a week and spouting astounding stupidities to four hundred boys trying to memorise words slipped inside their hymn books.

The boredom might have broken Simon in the end if he had not had the good fortune to find a book in the Dickson Library about yoga. From it, he learned how to get your mind to leave your body. You had to concentrate on a point in the upper part of the brain, the imaginary breaking-point in a straight line drawn from the right eye to another drawn from the right ear. With a little practice, it wasn't difficult to find that point. Then you sat still for two minutes and focused your mind on it.

Soon Simon was able to project his mind through the seam between his temple bone and his skull out into the world. He flew across the Atlantic to the skyscrapers of New York and whirled with astonishment round the Empire State Building. He went west across the prairies, turned sharply up the Pacific coast, then back to Europe. Across the Mediterranean he went, to the Sultan's harem in Istanbul where he realised with delight that he could also move freely in time. For now it was the seventeenth century and the harem was wonderful to behold, and he fell in love with a belly dancer wriggling like a snake in golden veils. He was forced to put his school textbook on his lap so no one should see he had a hard-on.

On the rocks by the bathing place at home, Karin sat gazing at the river flowing into the sea, wondering whether it grieved for its waters now lost irretrievably.

She thought not. In fact, it was probably a fulfilment and a liberation.

Karin thought about the spring when she, too, had been about to join what was infinite and how she had stopped herself when Simon had sat at her bedside. She was not like the river water for she had not completed her task.

Simon had a right to know, she thought.

She thought about it again and again that summer, and it was so obvious and threatening that it appeared like a mountain wall in front of her: steep, with no hand- or foot-holds.

He had to be told.

Guilt assailed her. They should have talked to him long ago, Karin scolded herself. To begin with, they had meant to tell him as soon as he was old enough to understand. But then, in the 1930s, anti-Semitism had taken root in Sweden, poisoning the air and frightening her and Erik into silence.

She remembered a pedlar, one of a number of tramps and hawkers to whom, over the years, she had given coffee and a sandwich in her kitchen. This one had been superior to the others as he had a niece who was a film star. Karin had bought a packet of needles, not noticing that the man was mad until Simon, rosy-cheeked and dark-eyed, had run into the kitchen for a drink of water. He had always been thirsty as a child, as if he was on fire and needing cooling.

She could see it all before her like a play at the theatre, scene by scene, as Simon stopped, bowed and greeted the man politely.

The man's face had twisted with hatred. 'A bastard Jew,' he had said. 'Christ, woman, why have you got a Jew-boy in your kitchen?'

The scene blurred and Karin couldn't remember how

she got the man out of the house, only that she had flung the packet of needles at him and threatened him with the police if he came back. But the picture of Simon's pale questioning face remained as clear as the memory of her sitting at the kitchen table, her son on her lap, trying to explain the inexplicable.

She also remembered the evening that followed. Erik had driven the truck into the garage and she hadn't managed to tell him what had happened.

'Dad, what's a bastard Jew?' Simon had asked.

Erik had stiffened, then collected his wits. 'There's no such thing.'

But Karin knew Simon had seen the fear in Erik's eyes.

That evening they made the decision that it would best if Simon didn't know about his true parentage.

There were whispers, and Karin remembered her anxiety over Mrs Ågren's poisonous tongue, and how Simon had come home one day to say that Mrs Ågren wanted to know where she, Karin, had found him. Then war came, it was the spring of 1940 and the insidious ill will changed to threats. Karin recalled those warm April nights when the Germans invaded Norway and she thought they would be at her door at any moment, pointing at her boy.

My heart ached then, she thought, surprised she hadn't remembered before. She had also understood Ruben's anguish, and Olga, the mother she had never seen, the woman who had chosen madness as her refuge. I should have talked to Ruben too, she realised.

The sea beyond the fortress was turning grey. They would have rain before evening Karin knew as she rose. It was past three o'clock, Lisa would have gone home and Helen would have been with the milk. She would have time for a sleep before Simon came back from school.

But Karin got no sleep. As she lay on her bed with a blanket round her, the mountain wall appeared again before her.

He had to be told.

Her memory went back to the war years once more. Inga had received a letter from the violin player, a letter in German which none of them could read. But they had decided that she should keep it and give it eventually to Simon. Then, she remembered the telephone call and Erik's voice urging Inga to burn the letter. Afterwards, fear of the parish register had haunted Karin: what was in it and whom had Inga given as father of the child?

Karin had hoped Erik would reassure her when he came on leave, tell her she was blowing it up out of proportion. But her fear had aroused his and, using his precious petrol coupons, he had driven all the way to the hamlet where Simon had been registered. This had made things worse. Erik had told the whole story to the priest, a middle-aged man who had licked his lips.

'The damned priest was a fascist,' Erik told her when he returned. 'I didn't realise it until he started gabbling on about keeping the Aryan race pure.'

They had quarrelled. 'I could have killed him,' he admitted later.

In the parish register, Inga had written *Father Unknown*.

Karin opened her eyes. There was to be no afternoon nap. Her gaze fell on the rocking chair where she had sat with Isak when the Norwegian ships had been lost and Isak too had lost his mind. Everything had combined at the time to keep her fears alive. The memory of Isak gave her strength nevertheless. I managed, she thought.

Then Simon came in, flinging his school books on the

stairs. He stood there, intense, full of life. 'Hi, Mum. How's things? What's for dinner?'

Karin laughed. 'Meat loaf,' she said. 'Are you in a hurry?'

'Yes. I'm going to a dance at Långedrag.'

Karin looked at the handsome youth. I would like to be young, she thought, and going out to dance with him.

Perhaps it's been good for him not to know, she reflected as she set about getting dinner ready. 'Is Isak going with you?'

'Yes. Ruben's driving him here. He sent his regards and said he'd like to come in for some coffee.'

After dinner, when Simon went up to his room to change, she said to Erik, 'We must tell him. He's seventeen and has the right to know.'

Erik looked ten years older suddenly. He nodded. 'I've been thinking that too.'

'It's so difficult,' Karin said. 'Perhaps we should consult Ruben?' But she could see that Erik disagreed.

When Ruben came she served coffee in the parlour so that he would know it was going to be no ordinary evening. They talked, sluggishly, feeling their way at first, then more and more eagerly, Karin and Erik almost at the same time. Karin had always known Ruben was a listener, but she hadn't realised how good it was to be able to tell the whole story.

The October dark closed in on them and, when Erik finally got up to light the lamp, Karin noticed Ruben's eyes were glistening. 'So it was no chance that you were able to help Isak,' he observed.

'We were in the same damned boat,' Erik said.

There was a long silence, then Ruben spoke again: 'I did wonder a little at first. He didn't look particularly Swedish.' He remembered Olga saying, 'Larsson, but this is not possible.'

'But he's got the same temperament as you, Karin, the same purity, if you see what I mean. And he's like Erik too, eager and intense.'

This helped a little. But how did Ruben think Simon would take it, Karin asked.

Ruben sighed. 'It won't be easy. But I don't think it will do him any real harm. He's got such good foundations.'

Ruben told them they should be natural, not throw the truth into the boy's face, and wait for a suitable moment.

'When will that be?' Karin was surprised.

'You'll know when the moment comes,' Ruben said so confidently they had to believe him.

When the boys came back from the dance, they sat in the kitchen as usual over a beer and a late sandwich.

Ruben embraced Simon and thumped him on the back. 'Oh, my goodness, boy. If you only knew what I've ordered you for Christmas from America.'

The next morning the fog was like cotton wool round the houses. Simon woke to the wail of foghorns and thought they sounded more ominous than usual. Karin too seemed burdened by the fog as she put out breakfast and told him she had to go over to Edit Äppelgren's before the fog drove the woman mad. Simon was to leave his bicycle behind and take the tram.

'You can hardly see your hand in front of your face,' she said.

Simon had to run the last bit to the stop as the blue tram appeared like a phantom out of the fog, its warm interior receiving him with its friendly incandescent lights.

The parish minister, the stupidest of all the priests, was on the platform in the school hall saying morning prayers. Boredom soon crept up on Simon. At the beginning of the Lord's Prayer, he managed to leave his physical self, but found to his disappointment that his mind went straight home. He found the kitchen empty. Karin had already gone to her neighbour's, so he went to the boatyard but halfway there he stopped. They were having a break, Erik and his men, and Simon could hear Erik bragging over his coffee, talking about the bomb and the changed world, the men all listening respectfully.

He's happy, Simon thought. He's at his worst and best and greatest. He hated and despised his father, just as his father despised him, the boy who was all thumbs, his head full of useless whims and fancies. He would never make an honest worker!

God, how tired Simon was of the house. And the boatyard. And the bragging about boats. And politics. And everything sterling and reliable.

His mind turned to the garden path, where he met Karin coming towards him in the fog, and he saw her with new eyes, from the outside. She wasn't particularly beautiful and the expression round her mouth of complacent self-satisfaction was detestable. She, the angel, had done her good deed for the day. He hated her too. He could never carry on a sensible conversation with her. She was uneducated and stupid, and had never understood him.

'Thanks be to you, oh Lord, for what . . .' It had started again.

As always, Simon felt sick as the loud and out-of-tune singing went on all around him. He never sang a note.

Then his stomach started to ache and, in the physics lab where his teacher was droning on about some idiotic experiment and there was plenty of time to think, he remembered the previous evening when he and Isak had come back from the dance. Something strange had been going on and, even more peculiar, Erik had looked tired.

But the memory of Erik fired his anger and, once again, Simon started to hate his father with his coarse hands and simple truths.

Karin was also thinking about Erik as, later in the day, the fog lifted and she went for her usual walk.

Erik had not had an easy evening. The decision they had made during the war not to tell Simon that he was adopted had become an excuse not to think about it. And Erik was good at not thinking about things.

He had always been more sensitive than Karin about Simon's background. And he had been the one to react badly when they were reminded of it, such as the time when Ruben had thought Simon should become a violinist.

Erik was a man who created his own reality, Karin thought. He constructed it himself, stone by stone. Anything that did not fit in with what he built was thrown away. Other people had to re-create themselves so that they could be fitted in. And Simon was fitting in less and less well.

There was trouble in the air. Karin knew that, even if both Simon and Erik were saying nothing. And this time it wasn't just about Simon being impractical. Erik had to be superior, the marvellous son of his mother. And if he wasn't that?

'Well, then he'd die,' Karin said aloud, irritated as usual when she glimpsed this inheritance from her mother-in-law.

Now Simon had surpassed him in many ways, in acuteness, in knowledge, in swiftness. Erik felt threatened and angry, and was taking it out on his son. 'Give us a hand here, boy,' he would say, 'unless you're afraid of dirtying your hands, of course.'

Simon was upper class and was suffering for it. School

had something to do with it, of course. Perhaps he'd been born upper class? But the next moment Karin knew this was foolish.

Could it have anything to do with race, she wondered. With the fact that Simon was Jewish? But no. Isak was both upper class and Jewish, and in him was everything Erik demanded: cleverness, a good hand with nails and screws and, most important of all, a great admiration for Erik and an obvious admission of his leadership.

The sun came out, the light shining silvery white from the fog, and Karin went to her oak trees. There, beneath the largest tree which was heavy and golden in the early autumn, she realised that she was protecting herself with her concerns for Erik. She didn't dare examine her own fears in the light of day.

When Simon is told he will be free, she thought. She wasn't his mother, so he could discard her. She knew that there were moments when he despised her.

She felt a pain in her chest and no tears came to heal it.

In the mirror at home, Karin saw that her lips had turned blue, but she took her pills and slept. She dreamed that she was in great pain giving birth to a son and it was Simon who came out of her womb. She swaddled him and took him to his father.

It was a long way to the man waiting for her on the hill, but with great dignity she went to him and held out the child. He took it in his arms, and only then did she look at him, up into his face, and recognise Ruben.

Part Two

Chapter 17

'Is that Mr Ruben Lentov?'

'Yes, speaking.'

'My name's Kerstin Andersson. I'm the welfare officer at Söråsen Sanatorium.'

She named the town and Ruben was able to place it somewhere in the uplands of Småland.

'Oh yes. Good morning.'

The voice on the telephone appeared to be doing everything to seem assured, but not succeeding. 'Is it possible that your wife's name was Leonardt. I mean, her maiden name, before she married you?'

'Yes.' Now Ruben was feeling threatened.

'Olga Leonardt?'

'Yes. What do you want?' His tone was so formal that the other voice seemed to lose confidence.

'Perhaps I could phone her?'

'No,' said Ruben. 'My wife is ill.'

'Oh, I'm sorry.'

What the hell's this all about, Ruben wondered.

'We have a girl here, one of those rescued from Bergen-Belsen. Her name is Iza von Schentz and she says she is your wife's niece, the daughter of your wife's sister.'

The walls of the spacious office began to close in on Ruben, the room growing smaller as images raced through his head. Iza, a lively five-year-old. She had been bridesmaid at his wedding once upon a time in another world. Oh God, he thought, God of Israel, help me, and he put the receiver down on the desk and managed to get to the window facing Norra Hamngatan and open it. He drew a deep breath and noticed the sea was white right up to the harbour channel. Stormy weather over Göteborg.

Then, as if from another universe, he heard the voice on the telephone. 'Hello, hello. Are you still there, Mr Lentov?'

He pulled himself together, picked up the receiver intending to ask questions, but found he could only say, 'Iza? Little Iza?'

Kerstin Andersson's voice had regained strength now. 'I realise you need time to think,' she said. 'Perhaps you could ring me back a little later?'

She gave him her number, he noted it and as he put down the receiver he found he was very cold.

The room had reverted to its usual size as he closed the window and told his office that he didn't want to be disturbed for the next half-hour. Then he lay down on the black leather couch, a newspaper over his head.

He tried to remember the child, see her. And couldn't.

One of the dead millions had returned, but she had no face. Was she like her mother? Suddenly Ruben remembered what it had cost him not to think about Rebecca throughout his years in Sweden, to forget the girl in Berlin he had once loved.

Rebecca Leonardt.

She had married a German officer. Ruben couldn't locate an image of von Schentz either, but he recalled very clearly a conversation in a café in Paris, when Rebecca had tried to explain her engagement to the German.

'He's kind, von Schentz,' she had said. With his help she was going to get herself out of the Judaism that was ensnaring, imprisoning her. 'I can't breathe in the women's gallery at the synagogue.'

Ruben had not shown his despair but had been generous and understanding. So the marriage hadn't helped her, he thought.

He got up and fetched some mineral water to quench his sudden thirst.

Rebecca had been a writer and, up to the end of the 1930s, had sent letters and signed copies of her books to Olga. Ruben had never been able to bring himself to read her work, but he knew she had a good reputation.

I married Olga to be near her, he reflected.

The two daughters of wealthy Dr Leonardt, one of whom had had everything: talent, beauty and a large open mind. While the other . . . Ruben felt an almost wild tenderness for Olga, the younger sister now in a mental hospital playing with dolls.

The image of his wife and her dolls brought him back to reality, to the late autumn of 1945 in Göteborg, to his responsibilities.

I never even asked how the girl was, he thought. He sat down at his desk to phone, but his finger dialled Karin's number and when he heard her voice he realised what he had always known: that Karin was like Rebecca in every respect.

'But Ruben,' Karin exclaimed. 'How wonderful. We must get her better and make her feel at home here in Sweden.'

This was just what he needed to hear.

'First of all you must find out how ill she is. She's presumably got tuberculosis as she's in a sanatorium. Talk to the doctors. You must go there.'

'Yes.'

'And you must ask about her family, her mother.'

'Yes.'

'Ask the welfare officer, not the girl. Oh, goodness, Ruben, it's a miracle.'

He could hear Karin was upset and wanted to say something calming. But he could still not get over the fact that he had recognised Rebecca in Karin the very first time he had met her.

'Ruben . . .'

'Yes.'

'We'll make her glad to be alive again. How old is she?'

He worked it out. He had married in 1927, so she must have been born in 1923. 'She's twenty-two.'

'Oh, good,' said Karin. 'I think the young mend more easily.'

He still had some of Karin's confidence left when he spoke to Kerstin Andersson again.

'A few patches on her lungs and they healed well,' she told him. 'Iza is a survivor. She went to school here, learned the language and was tremendously inquisitive about her new country. But this business with you will be difficult,' she added.

'What do you mean?'

Kerstin told him that some of her patients found it hard to cope with joy. She spoke of a woman who had had a good prognosis but had died when she got a letter from a surviving sister, now in Palestine.

Ruben attempted to understand. 'Is that why you haven't tried to contact me before?'

'No. Iza has been talking all summer about an aunt in Sweden, but she couldn't remember her married name and we didn't really take it all that seriously.'

She didn't know what my name was, thought Ruben. Rebecca obliterated me just as I obliterated her.

'Then one day she saw an advertisement for your books in the paper.'

Ruben remembered the column, autumn news from England and America, books that had once again reached his shops.

'She recognised the name and became very excited. Her temperature shot up and she scared the doctors. I didn't really believe her story, but the specialist thought I should check it out. Mostly to calm her down, you see. So I phoned you.'

'Does she know anything about our conversation?'

'No. I will try to talk to her this afternoon.'

'I thought I'd come at the weekend.'

'Good, but wait until you hear from me.'

'Is there anything she'd like to have, do you think?'

A laugh came over the phone. 'She wants everything,' the voice said. 'Clothes, shoes, make-up, sweets, books, handbags, stockings. They all want everything.'

Ruben couldn't laugh. He collected himself for the most difficult question. 'Is anything known about her mother?'

'Yes, she was gassed in Auschwitz. Both children saw her being taken to the gas chambers. The brother died in Bergen-Belsen a week after it was liberated.'

'Oh, no.'

'That was hard for Iza. Many gave up at that stage. There was a lot of disease too, typhus and so on.'

Kerstin sounded tired. There was a brief silence. 'Your wife, is she very ill?'

'She has no contact with the outside world. She's in a mental hospital. But you needn't worry, I have a son and friends. I'll take good care of Iza.'

'I didn't ask because of that. I just wanted to know what to tell her.'

Erik rang later to say he'd be glad to drive Ruben to the hospital on Saturday. Train services to upland

Småland were poor and he knew Ruben didn't like long journeys in the country.

'I can find the way,' Erik said. 'I was admitted there once myself when I was young.'

Ruben thanked him. This was a relief, but he was also surprised. 'Did you have consumption?'

'Yes, for a spell in my youth after a broken heart.'

Broken heart sounded odd coming from Erik, but presumably he couldn't think of another way of putting it. How well they knew each other, Ruben thought, and how little they knew about each other.

Kerstin Andersson put down the receiver with a bang and stayed seated. She knew that the women's ward was simmering with excitement over Iza having relatives in Sweden, rich ones, too. Everyone's hopes had been ignited by Iza's.

She's as fragile as a reed, Kerstin thought, but she won't die. Despite everything, this was no personal link. Iza couldn't remember her uncle.

Kerstin got up, went over to the bookcase and took out the file she had kept after her talk with Iza. She read again that her father had been a German officer and had shot himself with his service revolver when the Gestapo had come to arrest his wife and children.

She recalled Iza's astonishment: 'He died, you see, right in front of us.'

The girl seemed to have forgotten, then suddenly remembered this first death of the thousands she had seen. There had been a younger sister as well who had died on the way to the camp.

'It was best for her,' Iza had said. 'But Mama couldn't take it. They had to wrench my sister away from her.'

Through all that hell, Iza and her brother had managed to stay together. But when he died after the liberation, Iza had fallen ill and had hovered between life and death.

Kerstin sighed, put the file back and wondered, as she had many times before, whether she could go on with this job. There were tensions over Iza. She was perceived to be superior. At the sanatorium the patients were mostly Polish people who had grown up in the ghettos of Lodz and Warsaw, and she challenged them with her good German, her grand name, her manner. And her ruthlessness, Kerstin thought with some reluctance.

But she looked as awful as the others. I must prepare Lentov for her increased weight and loss of hair, Kerstin decided.

She went off to look for Iza and found her in the schoolroom with a book, a Swedish novel, Moberg's *Ride This Night*.

'Isn't that a bit difficult for you?'

'No, it's exciting.'

Kerstin considered the strange eagerness with which the girl tackled the language, in fact everything that was Swedish. She remembered Iza reading newspapers, starting on the front page and devouring everything, advertisements, death announcements, radio programmes, reports of lost dogs, lost wallets and young and old people seeking companions for eventual marriage. Everything surprised her, delighted her. She asked about each word she didn't understand, making the nurses, the assistants, Kerstin and even the doctor himself, explain. They had been as surprised as she was at the oddballs in Swedish society.

'I am a cheerful girl of twenty-two who loves muesli and long walks. Where is the person who can tame me? Reply to Wild Cat,' Iza read. 'But that's crazy.' Her eyes gleamed. And it was.

Kerstin asked Iza to come with her to her office and

gave her a chair. She stood as, briefly and factually, she told her about Ruben Lentov, that he had remembered Iza and her mother, and would be glad to look after her.

Iza's triumph was boundless. 'I knew it,' she cried. 'I knew it, but you didn't believe me.' She flew down the corridor, from ward to ward, calling out, 'I've got an uncle in Sweden, a rich uncle and he's going to look after me.'

Excitement erupted. Iza's companions forgot she was so grand. A miracle had happened to her, so miracles could happen to them all.

Now I'll be in trouble again, Kerstin thought as she saw Sister coming towards her, dignified as usual but more forbidding than friendly.

'I told you the patients mustn't be upset. They'll all have temperatures tonight and it'll be your fault.'

Kerstin hurried after Iza. 'Come with me. Put your coat on and we'll go out in the grounds.'

'Your aunt is sick, mentally ill,' Kerstin told her as they stepped outside.

'Why?' Iza stopped in midstep.

'What do you mean? No one knows that kind of thing.'

'But how silly,' said Iza. 'Here, in peace, with food and with a rich husband, and then to go mad.'

She was angry and afraid, for she realised that this changed her position. Ruben Lentov was no blood relative and she was only his wife's niece. 'You said he was going to look after me?'

'Yes. He's sure to be a man to be trusted.'

Iza calmed down, her voice less sharp. 'Is it true he's rich?'

Kerstin thought back to her poverty-stricken student years at the Institute of Social Studies in Göteborg when she and her friends had slipped into the elegant bookshop in the city centre with its soft carpets and smell of fine books. 'I should think so,' she said.

Ruben and Erik set off early on Saturday morning in Ruben's old Chevrolet which had been laid up during the war and was now purring like a contented cat along the narrow winding road to Borås, growling with delight up the hills and generally enjoying being able to go out into the world again.

'Quite a car,' said Erik. 'They don't make them like this any longer.'

But the car gobbled petrol and it began to snow in Borås. Erik filled her up and, when told the weather would be worse towards Ulricehamn, bought some chains.

Simon was in the back with Isak who, after some hesitation, had decided to go with them to meet this cousin returned from the kingdom of the dead. In the boot was Olga's fur coat, a new handbag of the finest patent leather, a bag of cosmetics Karin had bought, bars of chocolate and a heap of books.

'She reads everything she can get hold of,' Kerstin had told them.

They wriggled out of Borås and began the climb into the uplands of Småland and into the kingdom of snow, with its blue mountains, miles and miles of forest and white spruces.

'It's lovely here,' said Ruben. He was always surprised by how magnificent Sweden was whenever he got out of town.

But Erik muttered about worn tyres, changed into second gear and crawled along, eventually stopping to fix the chains. Isak helped him while Ruben and Simon went into the forest to relieve themselves. Then Ruben stamped his feet to keep warm and watched while Erik quickly and skilfully put on the last chain.

Ruben remembered suddenly what Otto von Schentz had looked like. As they drove on, he thought about the German, Iza's father. He might be still alive he realised, in a Russian prisoner-of-war camp, perhaps.

It grew quiet in the car as all four of them, ill at ease as they thought about the accounts they had read and the photographs they had seen of the camps, recognised that none of it had truly meant anything to them until now.

Then they were there, driving into the courtyard, the sun shining, the snow sparkling and perfectly real people swarming round the car, fat, amused, inquisitive. Livelier than ordinary people in Sweden, yes, more childish, more openly affectionate.

'Have you any food with you? Bread?' they cried.

'Why are they hungry? Don't they get enough to eat?' Erik felt his anger rising. Then Kerstin Andersson arrived, a tall, grey-eyed girl who explained that everyone got double rations of everything, but nothing was ever enough for them. 'You can see how fat they've got.'

Simon thought she was horrible, but the patients laughed and said that this was the worst thing of all, that they could never get enough food. They spoke a mixture of German and Swedish.

Erik didn't find them difficult to understand and was soon sitting with a pot of coffee and a bun among ten fat women. He felt pleased, in a good mood.

Iza was waiting for Ruben in Kerstin Andersson's room. The last few days had changed her. She had become quiet, tried to eat less, had washed her hair and wept in despair when it kept coming out in chunks. Alone in the schoolroom, she spent hours trying to remember how to speak and behave in polite society.

She had borrowed some nail varnish from a nurse and that strengthened her, for she had lovely hands. But she didn't dare look in the long mirror in the gym.

Her temperature had been high that morning and Sister had looked cross, but Iza was pleased because in her pocket mirror she could see this had put colour in her cheeks and a gleam in her eye.

She's like Olga, Ruben thought. Not like Rebecca, like Olga. She has the same nervous craving round her mouth, the identical curved nose and high narrow forehead. Even the fine, slightly bluish network at her temples was there. And the restless eagerness, the hunger which nothing could satisfy. 'Iza, my dear,' he said.

Iza saw in a flash that she wouldn't have to make an effort, that his guilt was so great that he would accept her as she was. 'I want to get out of here. Now, at once.'

'I understand,' said Ruben. 'But the doctor decides that.'

'I loathe him.' He was astonished at the intensity in her voice, and the hatred. 'He's a Nazi, the same kind of bastard as the Germans in the camp.'

She may be right, Ruben thought, and he was frightened. 'Kerstin Andersson told me about Rebecca,' he said, changing the subject.

'I don't want to remember.'

'I can understand that.'

Her reply came like lightning. 'No! You understand nothing.'

Ruben lowered his head. 'Do you know anything about your father?' His question was tentative, but he had to know.

It went right into Iza, making her open and genuine and surprised, like a child. 'He shot himself,' she answered. 'Right in front of our noses. We just stood there, and then he shot himself.' Her eyes looked back in time to that moment when all those incomprehensible things had begun.

'Why?' whispered Ruben.

'When the Gestapo came to fetch us, Mama and us.' Her eyes turned back into the room and on to him. She laughed. 'Can you imagine being such a coward? The bastard.'

Ruben didn't dare look at her.

A little later he opened the door and called to Isak, asking the boys to bring the presents.

She barely glanced at either her cousin or Simon. She had eyes only for the gifts. 'God, what a wonderful fur.' She tore it out of the bag and tried to squeeze into it, only just managing though it would not button. 'I'll get slim again,' she said. 'I shall, I shall.'

As Simon helped her take the coat off, he saw the clumsily tattooed numbers on her arm. It was a moment outside time, a second containing everything anyone ever needed to know. He read the number, saw the dead and knew they could not hold the living responsible. They had ceased to whisper in the wind.

As he took his gaze from Iza's arm and met her eyes, he saw she was angry, and knew that her anger would make his life real.

Isak had also seen those numbers. 'Why do you go bare-armed in winter?' he asked.

But Iza wasn't listening. She was busy with the marvellous patent-leather handbag, the lipstick and the perfume.

Kerstin Andersson came to tell them that the doctor would like to speak to Ruben. A Nazi, Ruben thought uneasily, as he followed the tall girl along corridors, knocked on a door and found himself eye to eye with a very old Jewish friend.

Olof Hirtz!

They were equally astonished.

'I've just been told about a rich uncle,' Hirtz exclaimed.

'And I about a Nazi doctor!'

They hugged each other.

Hirtz was a leading doctor specialising in tuberculosis. He was married to a psychiatrist and Ruben remembered that he had always been interested in the psychology of tuberculosis, the connection between the disease and grief, and the lack of a will to live.

'What are you doing here?' Ruben asked.

'I took a sabbatical from the Sahlgrenska Hospital,' Olof said. 'You know, you want to do something. And this is very interesting study material.' His words were deliberatly cynical and he spoke with a grimace.

'But these cases are hardly representative.' Ruben was feeling his way. 'They've contracted the disease in terrible circumstances.'

'That's what I thought too at first,' said Olof. 'But I'm beginning to wonder. These were ordinary people. They were brought up, loved, hated, had good and bad mothers, cold homes, warm homes, siblings, poor parents, rich ones.'

'Yes, of course, but . . . but then —'

'They landed in hell and, regardless of background or any strength they had been given in childhood, they were humiliated and abused in extreme ways, and reacted variously.'

'They're similar to each other. Is that what you mean?'

'Their circumstances are similar, yes. But they're different from us because they've been tested. They have an unconscious knowledge of what is solid and what semblance. We ordinary mortals are seldom allowed to know that.'

'That's true,' Ruben agreed.

'Maybe we'll be allowed to experience it when we're *in extremis* or near death, if we're not so drugged that we miss out on it.'

Olof sounded angry, so Ruben didn't say what was on the tip of his tongue – that by then it wouldn't matter. He also remembered that Hirtz was deeply religious and Ruben had no desire for a discussion about extremes.

'Iza,' he said instead. 'I came to talk about Iza . . .'

'She'll be all right. It surprises me that she contracted TB. She's hungry for life, one of the ones who survived because of their will to live. Perhaps that's why the disease made such a late appearance and was in the early stages when it was spotted in the quarantine ward in Malmö.'

'I still don't understand.'

'She had strength as long as the battle lasted. When it was over she gave way to her weariness. Then her brother died and she could no longer hold back her sense of being abandoned in childhood.'

'What do you mean?'

'Iza didn't have an easy childhood.'

Ruben felt as if something had attacked his heart. 'But her mother was a wonderful person.'

'Possibly. But to a great extent Iza was her father's daughter and he . . .'

'And he?'

'Well, he was a Prussian officer.'

The words hung in the air and Ruben reckoned Olof knew more than he wished to tell.

'Anyhow, she must stay here this winter,' Olof continued. 'We'll make another assessment in the spring. There's a risk we'll have to operate. One lung is gassed. Perhaps you knew that?'

Ruben knew nothing about the treatment of tuberculosis, but he reacted to the word. Gas!

'You can have complete faith in us. She couldn't have better care than she gets here.'

'I'm quite sure of that.' His words restored the warmth between them. They talked for a while longer about mutual friends and the books Olof wanted and Ruben said he would get hold of.

'You would help Iza if you could bring yourself to say no occasionally,' Olof told him. 'You probably have a touch of the Christian veneration for suffering and that's no help to survivors of concentration camps.'

Ruben had expected a scene when he told Iza that she had to stay in hospital for some time. But there was none. She shrugged. Perhaps she already knew.

Trying to sound firm, he continued, 'The doctor is an old friend of mine, a famous medical man and a humanist. He is no Nazi. He's Jewish.'

'I know more about Nazis than you do,' said Iza. 'And I despise Jews.'

'Just as the Nazis did.' Isak's voice was like the crack of a whip. She looked frightened and said she hadn't really meant it, that she was so tired of all the talk and she had a temperature.

There was not much talk in the car on the way home. Erik was the only one to speak at first about how strong people's will to survive was and how surprising it was to find sick people with so much joy in them. 'They really do believe in the future,' he said.

Ruben nodded. He was thinking that a life directed only at survival would probably find strength in great simplicity.

Simon sat in the back feeling ashamed of Erik. Isak wasn't listening.

They drove to the house by the river where Karin was

waiting for them with dinner: veal with pickled gerkins and compote of strawberries. 'How was she?' she asked.

'Full of life,' answered Erik. 'And anger.'

'Frayed,' said Ruben. 'Hectic and frayed.'

'She's a bloody cow.' Isak dropped his fork on the floor.

Karin looked from one to the other and thought about those spectres getting off the white buses and how she had felt they should be dead, just as she herself ought to die, and how she had decided to survive just as Iza had. But she said nothing.

Ruben was thinking how like Olga Iza was, and he too said nothing.

Later, when Karin was alone with Simon, she took up the question again. 'But what was she like, Simon?'

Simon looked at Karin for a while, thinking she would never understand. 'Lively,' he said, hunting for words. 'Affected. Open. She's open to everything, hungry. And sometimes she's got those eyes, you know, like Isak had that time.'

Karin nodded. Empty, she thought. Perhaps eyes that have seen too much were always empty.

Chapter 18

Two days before Christmas Eve, totally surprisingly and in the middle of the morning, Ruben turned up in a hired truck at the house by the river mouth. He was so pleased, he was glowing.

'What on earth?' Karin exclaimed and she could hear from his laugh that she had said the right thing.

The driver helped him ease off a large heavy wooden

crate, stamped *Handle with Care*. Ruben had spent all morning at the customs, but now he was here with it – his Christmas present to Simon.

After the truck had gone, Ruben went to the boatyard to ask Erik for some help.

'What in heaven's name is it?' Erik demanded.

'I'm so nervous. I'll put the coffee on,' Karin said. But Lisa had already set about it.

They had coffee while Ruben continued to crow over his surprise. 'Upstairs with you, women,' he ordered. 'Go and tidy Simon's room.'

'It's already been tidied, I'll have you know,' Lisa said.

'No,' Ruben explained. 'I mean the long wall opposite the bed has to be cleared.'

Karin laughed, infected by his delight. 'All right, we'll do as you say, Ruben.' And she and Lisa went upstairs to move things.

'We'll never get that up the stairs,' Erik objected. But then he measured, calculating angles and got around to saying yes, they probably could.

'Have you any electricians at the yard?'

'No, I do that myself,' said Erik. 'Is it a machine?'

'Well, yes, you could say that.'

It took a lot of sweat and half an hour to get the crate up the stairs, which was just as well, for Lisa and Karin needed the time to move the bookcase over to the short wall in Simon's room.

The men were given a beer each as they stood panting on the top landing before they set about opening the crate, levering the lid off with a jemmy.

'Careful,' warned Ruben.

Wood shavings and paper scattered everywhere and Lisa grumbled that she would have waited with the cleaning had she known about this. Finally it was revealed: a terrifying radiogram in fiery shiny walnut with garish gilt mouldings and silvery material in front of the loudspeaker.

'It's not beautiful,' Ruben said.

'It certainly is,' Karin replied. 'It's handsome. But what is it for?'

Erik's smile ran from ear to ear as he plugged it in. Was this what Ruben had wanted an electrician for?

'Wait,' Ruben instructed. He pressed a button, then twisted a knob. A symphony orchestra thundered out as if the players were in the room with them.

The house held its breath. It had never heard anything like it. Erik screwed up his face. Karin sat down on Simon's bed with a gasp of surprise and Lisa almost dropped the vacuum cleaner on her way up the stairs.

'That's not the most important part,' said Ruben. 'Where in heaven's name is the gramophone?'

None of them could hear what he said because of the noise. Ruben turned it down and looked at them with satisfaction. 'Now, listen, Erik Larsson. You're a technical genius. Please find the gramophone and connect it up.'

Erik nodded. 'You must be able to open it somehow.' He fumbled round the piece of furniture which they now knew was called a Victorola.

'Switch if off!' Karin cried. 'It might explode!'

This was a remark that was to provoke a great deal of laughter for some time to come.

'You're crazy, woman,' Erik said and Ruben laughed so much that he had to sit down on the bed. He hadn't had so much fun for ages.

Erik was a good hand with things, even the new and unfamiliar, and it wasn't long before he found the button that made one half of the top rise like a lid. The turntable, heavy and sturdy, was in place. But the pick-up had been removed and lay there neatly in pieces in a carton, with instructions on how to assemble it.

Ruben started to translate, but Erik took the leaflet away from him impatiently and, glancing at the drawings, put the pick-up together.

'Now.' Ruben took out a record. 'This is for you and the other two are for Simon.'

Jussi Björling sang about Sweden through the hideous loudspeaker and the atmosphere in the room grew quite solemn.

'Christ, that's good,' said Erik, and Ruben could see his eyes glistening. Again he thought how little people really knew about each other.

After a while they went down to the kitchen, and Ruben said they would wait for the boys and, as soon as they saw them coming up the drive, he would go upstairs and put on the Berlioz.

'What's that?' Karin asked.

They laughed at her again and she laughed with them, saying it was just as well she wasn't easily offended.

'I brought some smoked salmon and wine with me,' Ruben said. 'But what did I do with it?'

'I expect you left it in the truck,' suggested Karin and they all laughed again.

'We'll go and get some more,' insisted Ruben. 'We must have a party.'

While Karin was laying the table, he told her that he and Isak were going to his brother in Copenhagen for Christmas. They were to fly from Torslanda in the morning of Christmas Eve, taking Iza with them. She was on leave from the sanatorium.

'We used to talk about it when they were staying with me during the war,' Ruben said. 'About celebrating Christmas in Copenhagen. A dream my brother had.'

Karin nodded. It made sense. Ruben couldn't look

after the girl on his own and he needed help from his family. He was trying to get Iza to become a joint Jewish affair. That won't be easy, she thought, remembering Ruben's brother's family.

'Isak was pleased,' Ruben told them. 'He finds his Danish family difficult, not to mention Iza. But he was persuaded, largely, I think, because he wants to fly so much.'

Silent angels went through the kitchen as Karin thought about Iza whom she had now met. Karin had seen her unnaturally large eyes and thought Simon was wrong. Iza's eyes were not empty, but filled with everything they had seen, degradation and horrors. In their depths, they were burning with a hunger no one and nothing could satisfy which would devour anyone who got in her way.

She doesn't know it herself, Karin reflected. She thinks she is going to take back everything she has been robbed of.

'And what did you do during the war?' Iza had asked Karin. 'Grow potatoes and worry about dinner?'

'Yes. What would you have done in my place?'

Karin had not been dismayed, but had sensed that the girl was making divisions, and when Karin looked at Simon and saw how bewitched by her he was she was frightened.

But Ruben and Karin put their thoughts of Iza aside for this was a happy day.

The truck came back again and the driver knocked on the door. 'You forgot this.' He handed over the salmon and wine.

An hour or two later they heard the boys coming up the drive on their bikes and Ruben shot upstairs, found the record and turned the sound up at full volume.

Then Simon was in the hall, the music rolling down

the stairs. He stood stock still, a shimmer of happiness round him, then slowly went up to his room and lay on his bed, still in his outdoor clothes.

Little was said in the kitchen as the music filled the house. They recognised that Simon had gone into another world, a world that was his and to which he had always longed to go.

Ruben understands, Erik thought, ashamed of the time when Ruben had wanted Simon to learn the violin. And now I understand Simon too. And he listened to the strange, unfamiliar music pouring through the house.

Silence fell eventually, and Simon came down and stood in the kitchen door looking at Ruben. 'You're crazy, Uncle Ruben,' he said.

Everything lay in his words, not only gratitude, and Ruben felt honoured, touched as so many times before by the forbidden thought: if only this boy were mine.

Later that evening after Erik had driven Ruben and Isak home, Erik and Karin sat in the kitchen, listening to the music upstairs, pondering the question they had wanted to ask all day. What had the radiogram cost?

'The freight from America alone,' Erik began. 'You know, the freight and customs . . .'

'But he's rich,' Karin said, and Erik thought about the profit Ruben made from his investment in the boatyard. In this way they overcame their concern about how much the radiogram had cost.

Neither Erik nor Karin saw much of Simon that Christmas. He made brief excursions into their world for food and to give Karin a hand in the kitchen, and he was physically present on Christmas Eve, opening parcels from his two grandmothers, knitted socks and other things he didn't want. But he didn't dislike the old people quite as much as usual.

Christmas morning dawned, not sparkling, but grey everywhere, and Simon washed the dishes while Erik demonstrated the radiogram to the neighbours who all said it was as if Jussi Björling himself were in the room. But he wasn't angry with Erik for boasting, nor did he hate the piles of plates with sticky remains on them. Everything was as it should be and, when Erik had finished with the neighbours and the kitchen was clean and tidy, Simon went back to Berlioz's *Fantastique*.

The first time he played his record he was back in the great grassy realm and saw the man speaking the forbidden language, the war, the building of the temple and death on the great bull's horns. But gradually those images faded and Simon was able to sense the great sorrow in the long notes at the beginning, and the painful beauty when the first movement started in all its splendour. In the middle of the liberating storm he became aware of the thumping darkness in the back-ground, its solemnity giving order to the world, and the power, frightening and wonderful. He experienced space and the heavens, the vast heavens which were like light flowing in from the west, white and liberating, followed by the sun playing with the wind in the sea of grass, where the images appeared again, coloured by brittle joy.

He was filled with melancholy. He put on the first movement over and over again and made a strange discovery: if he let his mind go free, let it roam where it wanted to go, at the same time experiencing emotions without naming them, a fusion occurred. Eternity, he thought. The Kingdom of Heaven. But as soon as he started thinking it was all lost.

He put on the first movement again, projected his mind into the unknown, and returned again to the floor where he had been lying, knowing what he had seen, remembering the oaks, the land that is but doesn't exist.

Simon thought about his philosophy teacher, one of the few at school who managed to dispel his boredom. He had talked about thought, the mind. Was it unlimited, he had asked? And what is it that sets the limits? Simon had thought this a stupid question at the time as it was obvious that the universe could be conquered by the mind.

His teacher had talked about Einstein and Bohr and explained the theory of what is not manifest. He had said something amusing, something they had laughed at, but what? Simon rummaged in his notebooks, remembering he had written it down because it was so contradictory.

He found the quotes, but discovered that he hadn't bothered to note down who had said it. '*Every attempt to understand what is not manifest leads to self-deception. You think about it and the next moment you have formed an idea of it, and thus you have lost it.*'

A little further on was another quote, carelessly written and hard to read. '*The mind can ask all the questions on the meaning of life. But it cannot answer one of them, for the answers are beyond the mind.*'

'That's true,' Simon said aloud, astonished. He put on the first movement again.

It took him nearly the whole of the Christmas holidays to conquer the symphony and make it familiar, make it his own.

Before he fell asleep at night, he thought with secret delight about the other record, the one he hadn't heard yet. Mahler's second symphony. 'It's easy, more earthy,' Ruben had said. 'I think you'll like it.'

He would listen to it on Twelfth Night when Karin and Erik were going to a party.

For a while that evening Simon thought he would go crazy with his delight in the music, the humour, what was young and untamed, the freedom flying through the great forest. It was easier to let the images go this time, but he did so with a sense of loss for they were full of joy.

When he went beyond the content in Mahler, in the afternoon of Twelfth Night, he felt like a king, splendid and victorious. He felt anger too, was filled with wrath. But no guilt, no fear.

By the next evening, Erik had had enough and, closing his eyes to the appeal in Karin's, yelled up the stairs. 'Can't we have a moment's peace from that damned music?'

Simon switched off the gramophone, gathered himself and went downstairs. Now, he thought. Now.

He stood in the kitchen doorway, looking at them, tall and slim, his eyes burning, as if the music had darkened them even further. As he turned to Karin, there was more sorrow in his voice than anger. 'What the hell's wrong with the music? What are you afraid of?'

Tears came into his eyes as he remembered the time when they had stopped him having music lessons. 'What were you quarrelling about that evening when Ruben wanted me to learn the violin?' he asked. 'What was so awful about it?'

It was snowing outside, the flakes as big a child's hand and, as always when it snowed, the house was bathed in a vast silence. Karin knew the moment Ruben had mentioned had come. She could see that Erik knew it too, but was reluctant and would soon escape to the boatyard if she didn't nail him down in the kitchen.

'We must talk about it, Simon,' she said. 'Let's take our coffee into the parlour.'

Simon realised something tremendous was on its way. He was so frightened that he felt sick and he, too, tried to get away. 'Can't we go for a run in the car?' he asked Erik.

But they both went into the parlour and sat down on

the uncomfortable armchairs, listening to Karin clattering with the coffee tray.

Erik did not meet Simon's eyes, but spoke when Karin came in with the coffee. 'Make sure you take your heart pills before we start.'

Chapter 19

It was all so momentous, there was no room for small or palliative words.

The thing is, Karin told him, she and Erik couldn't have children. They had never been able to. Simon was adopted and had come to them when he was three days old.

Simon's gaze wandered from Karin's face to the window. It was still snowing, the light going. Everything that was happening was beyond reality.

I've always known, he thought, I've somehow always known. I've never belonged. 'But who am I?' he asked.

Karin took a gulp of her coffee, swallowing noisily, and Simon felt he had always loathed them: Erik and his boasting, Karin and her simplicity. But that feeling was also part of his dreams, that secret world he created when he was angry and miserable.

Karin started to tell him about the fiddler, the Jewish violin player they knew so little about.

She's talking about my daydreams, Simon thought. This is crazy, shameful somehow.

'Inga believed your father was a water sprite,' Karin said.

'Inga!' This didn't fit. This didn't match his dreams. Simon turned icy cold and looked round the parlour, trying to come to terms with what was actual amid all this unreality.

No.

'She was young and lovely then,' Erik said.

'They fell in love in the forest by the waterfall,' Karin continued. 'But they couldn't speak to each other.'

The preposterous story calmed him. It simply couldn't be true! He gave Karin an appealing look, then heard himself ask the question: 'Doesn't Inga know his name?'

'No,' said Erik.

'It's probably Simon,' Karin told him. 'He was a music teacher at the college on the other side of the lake, but he came from Berlin and was Jewish.'

'A Jewish bastard,' said Simon. So it was true. The words made sense now.

The snow kept falling, but the silence between Karin and Erik continued until Simon broke it again. 'But I'm not like Inga.'

'No, you're like your father. At least, if one can believe Inga.'

'So we're related – you and me?'

'Yes,' said Erik.

'Dad.' Simon felt desperate. He wanted them to say to hell with all this, let's go back to the essence to everything being the same again. 'Why have you never told me?'

They both began to talk at once about the creeping anti-Semitism, the Nazism, the Germans in Norway hunting out Jews in second and third generations.

'I remember a telephone conversation, in the spring of 1940. I heard you say that someone should burn a letter?' Oh God, he thought, I've always known it was about me.

'We were so frightened.' Karin spoke, but Simon felt no pity for her.

'There was a letter?'

'Yes.' This time it was Erik. 'Inga had a letter from Berlin, but none of us could read it. We decided to keep it to give to you when you were older.'

'Someone could have translated it.' Simon was almost shouting.

'Yes, but it was all so shameful, out there in the country, and we had promised Inga we would tell no one.'

'Was the letter burned?'

'As far as we know.'

Erik told him about the parish register and the Nazi priest.

But Simon just heard the words parish register. 'What did it say?' he asked.

'*Father Unknown,*' said Erik, his old bitterness washing over him. 'You see, I had to save you from that Nazi bastard.'

More silence, like the snow. Simon was so cold that he was shaking. But he looked at them, from one to the other. 'So I'm supposed to be grateful, even more grateful?'

Karin could find no words. Her mouth was like sandpaper.

'To us you were a gift from God.' Erik had spoken again.

Simon was so surprised that, for a moment, he was shocked out of the present for his father's words were so unlike him, and because of the great truth the words contained. 'Sorry, Dad,' he managed to say.

Karin took another gulp of coffee. She wanted to tell him about her nights with him when he was a baby, the thoughts she had had, those strange ideas about all children being children of the earth. 'You were only three days old,' was all she could say.

Another silence. Then Simon spoke once more. 'Does anyone else know?'

'Yes, Ruben. We've talked to him.'

'What did he say?'

Karin's thin voice stopped fluttering. 'He said children belong to those who love them and care for them.'

'He said something else, too,' Erik told him. 'That you're like Karin, that you have the same temperament as she has.'

Simon was so cold now that his teeth were chattering so Karin went to fetch a sweater. As she started to drape it over his shoulders, he shied away from her touch and she had to put it on the arm of the chair.

He pulled it on and looked at Erik. 'So that's why I'm not as clever as you are.'

'Good God, Simon, you're much cleverer.'

Simon could see his surprise was genuine.

In the end, they didn't have anything more to say. Simon seemed collected, but was still shaking with cold. Must be this damned parlour, thought Erik.

Simon went into the kitchen for some water and drank glass after glass, then stood in the doorway looking at them. 'In a way, I've always known,' he said.

A moment later they heard the gramophone again, the incomprehensible music filling the house. But it soon stopped and, when Karin slipped upstairs to look in on him, he was fast asleep.

'It went well, didn't it?' Erik asked.

Both of them were so tired that they went straight to bed without supper.

There was school the next day and the usual scrum in the kitchen over breakfast. Term report. Simon found it and Karin wrote *Have read* on it and signed it. This was not true really as she never looked at Simon's marks. 'You all right?' she asked.

'Of course, Mum. Don't worry.'

But he came home a few hours later with a fever. There was nothing odd about this. Half the city had flu. Karin tucked him up in bed, made a honey drink and took his temperature. It was high and this scared her. 'Does the back of your neck hurt?'

He managed to shake his head and smile at her. Then he fell asleep.

At this time, all mothers had a terror of paralysis which hovered over everyone with a high temperature and a stiff neck. So Karin rang their old doctor, who said it sounded like influenza and she should phone again the next day if his temperature hadn't gone down.

A girl was running alongside Simon in the kingdom of long grass. Birds were making a nest in her hair and she said, 'Nice, isn't it?'

He desired her and knew he could do anything with her as long as he was careful about the bird's nest. He undressed her, sucked on her nipples, kissed everything that was her. Her appetite was as wild as the spring and seeing she was more beautiful than any earthly woman, he couldn't have enough of her. The grass played the second movement of Mahler's first symphony, the rhythm striking its waves with theirs, and when he stepped towards the unknown the drums beat as if obsessed and he was obliterated, crossing the border into the land where nothing has shape and everything is comprehensible and perfect.

Then he saw there was an egg in her bird's nest, shimmering white and almost luminous, and he knew that the chick soon to leap out of the shell would take on his shape. He loved the egg – it was as precious as his life.

Karin came with clear soup, saying it was important to drink and, if he didn't improve soon, she would have to get the doctor to come. He swallowed obediently, hearing her tell him how good it was for him and thinking it was good for the egg, for the chick that was soon to be hatched.

He wanted to return to the grass, to the endless sea of grass and the girl with the bird's nest in her hair. But he couldn't find her and his fear was as great as the sea of grass as he ran, crying out her name. Yet he knew she had no name, although he could hear it rolling over the plains and echoing in the mountains far away.

He was almost mad with fear. Didn't she understand that he had to get back to her and the egg if life, his chance of life, was to be saved?

Now Simon was standing at the foot of a cliff and could see, high in the sky, a large bird and he knew it was the bird of wisdom and that it would know where the girl and the egg were. Using the last of his strength, he climbed the mountain and prayed 'Dear Lord, don't let me frighten the bird away.'

But the bird had settled on the cliff and when he got close, he saw she was sitting on an egg and realised the egg she was keeping alive with her warmth was his egg, his life.

Then he heard a violin playing a strange tune, full of melancholy, and when he turned to look down the mountainside he saw the girl, saw that she was a man now, a young fiddler with his violin, and the loneliness round his figure was great.

The big bird looked at Simon with Karin's eyes and he saw it was the bird of sorrow, not of wisdom, and he could be sure of his egg, of the life inside its fragile shell and those thin membranes. The bird of sorrow was faithful, loving, and strong – no harm would come to her chick.

'Simon, you must calm down,' the bird cried. It gave him an aspirin and his temperature faded into a great sweat, then it put cool clothes on him and wiped his body and his forehead.

Karin was really frightened and called out the doctor although it was ten o'clock at night. He felt, probed and shone his torch, listening and calming Karin down. It was an unusually severe bout of influenza, nothing more, he told her.

'Has anything happened to him?' he asked as he was leaving. 'He's showing some signs of shock.'

Karin put her hand to her forehead and thought what an idiot she was not to have thought of it.

Erik carried the old camp bed into Simon's room and Karin lay down beside her son. Simon slept all night and woke before she did. He lay, looking at the bird of sorrow who had watched over his life. Then he must have fallen asleep again, because when he woke the next time Erik was there with tea and sandwiches. As Simon ate and drank, Erik and Karin sighed with relief. A little later, he was able to walk unsteadily to the bathroom and when he came back, Karin had changed his sheets.

'I can hardly remember how many times I've done this now,' she said, and looked forward to Lisa who would soon come and do the washing and clean the house. She found an old bedspread for the camp bed and a blanket, and lay down again as if she had always known that she and Simon would be able to talk. The words were there, forming perfectly natural sentences. She told him about the winter when she had got up in the night to give him an extra feed, how she had sat in the kitchen with him in her arms and had so many strange thoughts.

'I was terribly presumptuous,' she admitted. 'I was sure

153

I could give you everything you needed to become a strong and happy person.'

'But you were right,' Simon found he was able to say.

Karin cried as she told him of the happiness he had brought them, how he had given them the strength to escape from their mothers-in-law and the world of the poor, to buy a plot of land and build their house. 'They thought we were conceited and reckoned it would all end badly,' she said. 'But we both knew we had to have a house in the country for you.'

A nest by the sea, Simon thought.

She told him about the pedlar, the Jew-hater with his packet of needles, the way he had looked at Simon and hissed at him. 'He frightened me to death,' explained Karin. 'Do you remember?'

Simon remembered the tramps coming and going round the houses, but recalled only that there was something strange, something frightening about them. But he remembered them shouting at him at school, *Jew bastard*! And how Erik had turned white and taught him to fight.

'Well, I didn't really approve,' Karin said. 'But it did help you. It was a useful lesson to me, too, for I was made to see I couldn't protect you all the time, that you would have to be strong enough to manage on your own.'

They talked over several days as they reclaimed his childhood.

On the morning of the sixth day the sun shone over the snow and Simon returned to his music, while Karin went for a walk along the river and out towards the sea. She stood for a long time, watching the Vinga shimmering like a mirage in the crystal clarity of winter. 'I've done my bit,' she said to the sea.

When she went home, she was tired but not in the

hopeless old way. Her heart was beating calmly and regularly.

A few days later Ruben came to see them. Isak went to the boatyard and Karin told Ruben they had talked it through, that no one had died of it, but that Simon had been delirious with flu. 'It'd probably be good if you spoke to him,' she said.

Ruben nodded and went up to Simon's room.

At dinner, all five of them were able to talk about Simon's background. What had been concealed for so long, hidden carefully and perceived as terribly dangerous, was now out in the open. It was a relief.

Only Erik clenched his teeth when Karin said: 'I thought perhaps we ought to try to find out if Simon's father is still alive.'

'He was a musician,' Ruben said. 'A lot of artists left Germany before it was too late.' He was thinking about the Jewish organisations still working to reunite scattered families.

But Simon saw the back of the young fiddler walking below the mountain with his violin and knew that he was heading straight for the gas chambers, their chimneys just visible on the horizon. 'He's dead,' he stated. 'He's one of those numbers on Iza's arm.'

He was so definite that no one protested, although Isak thought, how the hell can he know that?

'He was probably a good man.' Karin took up the conversation again.

Good! Simon smiled at her. 'He was lonely and miserable.'

Isak couldn't stand it any longer. 'How do you know? Perhaps he was wild and happy?'

Simon laughed. 'That too, perhaps.'

'I was thinking about inheritance,' Karin pointed out

and Ruben talked for some time about the influence of the environment in which you grew up on your personality.

'We inherit certain physical features and a talent or two, like Simon's musicality,' he said. 'But goodness isn't in the genes, Karin. It depends on how much security a child has.'

Simon wasn't really listening. He was thinking about what Ruben had told him upstairs, that all young people dream about being changelings, and that they often despise their parents and rebel. 'I used to wonder sometimes why I was not as practical as Erik. But you're saying that I might not have inherited it from him anyway.'

Ruben had laughed. 'What about Inga, then? Your biological mother. I've always heard she ran the small-holding as well as any man.'

Simon felt uncomfortable about this, but he had to smile with the others.

'Didn't you ever wonder why Isak isn't as well read or interested in books as I am?'

'No,' Simon answered.

'Perhaps every son has to vanquish his father,' said Ruben. 'He's likely to to choose a field in which the father does not excel so that he can defeat him by a wide margin.'

Throughout that long spring Simon sometimes found the fear hurt as it crept from his stomach up his throat, making it hard for him to breathe.

He thought about Inga, but pushed away the decision to go to see her. He thought about roots – that he had none. He also thought about the girl waiting for him at the sanatorium, like the spider for the fly. He felt calm in the knowledge that he would let himself be caught, that it was only a matter of time.

Chapter 20

They would always remember that last school summer holiday: Simon because he was cheated and Isak because he fell in love.

Iza had been discharged from the sanatorium and was living with Ruben. She found the apartment cramped, the city dull and Ruben as hopeless as all of his middle-aged and bookish friends. She also refused to go with him and Isak to Karin's and Erik's. 'Karin's an old cow, just like Mamma,' she said, oblivious to Ruben's feelings.

Ruben tried to put her in touch with other Jewish families in the city, appealing to mothers and daughters for help. But despite their attempts, no one could cope with her and, as Iza went in and out of shops in the Avenue and Kungsgatan, buying things to get relief, her anguish grew. Isak was so frightened of her that, before term finished, he moved out to the Larssons and the boatyard.

'We have to understand. Iza reminds him of what happened,' Karin appealed to Ruben.

She reminds me of someone else too, Ruben thought. With her restless trotting round the apartment in high heels, the tinkle of bracelets and necklaces, the heavy perfume in the air, and most of all the unease reverberating through every room, she makes me think of Olga.

Only one thing truly interested Iza and that was Simon. 'There's something mysterious about him,' she said. Ruben tried to be dismissive. 'He's just a kid who hasn't left school yet.'

'I've nothing against little boys,' Iza responded.

She had become as slim and pretty as she had intended, and she talked to Simon about the horrors of the camp.

'She needs to talk it out,' Simon said to Ruben when Ruben interrupted them.

'No, she doesn't. She wallows in it, and now she is tying you up. Watch out, for God's sake, Simon. Just watch out.' Ruben had found Simon in Iza's room one afternoon after school, driven him out and followed him down to the street.

Simon hung over his bicycle and stared at the man he admired more than anyone else, his eyes dark with misery. 'I can't escape, Uncle Ruben.'

But as he cycled home he had forgotten Ruben's and his own fears. All he could think of was how attracted he was to Iza, to her red lips and her delicious, tantalising body.

A week later Iza was sent to convalesce at a spa in Switzerland. Ruben's friend Olof Hirtz had arranged it, plus therapy from a famous psychoanalyst in Zurich. Iza was pleased for she wanted to go out into the world. Simon could grow up after all, she thought, remembering Ruben's admonishment.

'Was that necessary?' Karin asked when she heard about it.

'You know as well as I do that it was damned necessary,' Ruben answered.

Simon felt cheated, but there was also some relief mixed with his disappointment. The air around him seemed fresher since Iza had gone.

After midsummer, Simon and Isak went sailing for almost a month, cruising along the Bohus coast and into the Oslo Fjord. At last they came to the city where the Nazi boots had tramped.

'I can almost hear them,' Isak said. Simon stopped and listened for the rhythmical tramp of boots on the stone-laid streets. 'Let's go, Isak.'

They didn't see much of Oslo, nor the Oseberg ship that Isak had dreamed of, nor the Nansen Museum which Simon had longed to see.

They returned home, proud of their sparse beards, brown as Indians, dirty, bleached by winds and salt water.

Karin laughed at them and sent them packing to the bathroom with razors. 'If you want beards, you'll have to wait until they grow more evenly,' she told them. When they saw themselves in the mirror they knew she was right.

They took up the boat, scaled her and cleaned her interior, for Erik and Ruben were now off on a long trip. They had wanted Karin to come too, but she had declined. Ruben thought she was afraid on account of her heart, while Erik was sure she didn't want to leave the boys on their own.

But Karin didn't want to be at such close quarters with Ruben.

So one evening in high summer the boys went to a dance on a quay down by Särö island. And Isak met Mona.

Isak saw immediately that she was one of those rare people who make the world comprehensible. She was pear-shaped, all her weight below the waist, and she had straight, rather sturdy legs which always, wherever she was, kept her centred, close to the earth.

No one had noticed she was beautiful until Isak saw it. She looked at him with Karin's eyes, although strangely enough hers were blue. And she loved him too, from the very first moment.

Mona had been deeply hurt the day her mother had died, but she had been fourteen by then, stable, secure and straightforward. And there was no time to grieve or brood over her fate. She was forced to be mother to two small siblings and little children had to have what they needed, every day and every moment.

If it hadn't been for her aunt, her mother's sister, things might have been more difficult for Mona, but her aunt had insisted that Mona had a right to a life of her own too. So the fish dealer's daughter had gone to the girls' high school after all and, the summer that she met Isak, she was going to Sahlgrenska Hospital to train as a nurse.

She brought with her a slight contempt for men. She had never considered they were worth taking seriously. Perhaps she had read about love in some magazine or other, but she hadn't really believed in it and it had never occurred to her that she might be afflicted by it. So she was tremendously surprised.

So was Simon. He had come across love in a thousand books, passions sweeping people with them, driving them mad with despair or happiness. But he hadn't really believed in it either and he had never seen it in actuality. Now he saw it happening in front of his very eyes. It filled him with astonishment, jealousy and something else he gradually had to accept as envy. 'They're nuts, Mum,' he said to Karin. 'They seem to be in a trance and see nothing but each other.'

'I hope he'll bring her here soon so I can see this miracle,' she replied.

But Karin and Simon had disappeared from Isak's world. He slept in town, in Ruben's apartment, got up every morning and took the old Chevrolet out of the garage and drove, without a driving licence, to Axelsson's grocery store on a crossroads in Askim where Mona was waiting. She was even more beautiful than the day before and the car took them to the woods in the south, the rocks at Gottskär, the freshwaters of the Del lakes and the thick spruce forests of Hindås. They found soft mossy banks to lie on, new meadows to wander across, fresh flowers to pick.

She gave herself to him simply and without fuss, and he was gentle and tender, blessing the stone-blaster's daughter whenever Mona was with him. She was a virgin, of course, but that was neither difficult nor painful. The next day she went to a doctor and learned how to use a cap.

Isak did not remember there was anyone else in the world until the end of the brilliant week after their meeting on Särö island. Then he said to Mona, 'We must go and see, well, not exactly my family, but those closest to me.'

She nodded. 'I don't even know your surname.'

Isak was overcome with shame, his head empty of thoughts, his mouth of words. 'Lentov,' he said. 'Isak Lentov.'

She closed in on herself and he sensed it, fear shuddering through him.

'I'm Jewish,' he admitted.

She laughed. 'I'm not an idiot and I've read all about circumcision.'

His fears left him and he stopped the car and kissed her. But there was still a stiffness, a surprise, an absence. 'What's wrong then?'

'Lentov?' she asked. 'The rich Lentov with all those bookshops?'

'Yes. Anything wrong with that?'

'No.' But she was still rigid. 'It's all so impossible to

believe.' Then she added in a voice thin with unease, 'What'll your father say?'

'My dad'll love you,' said Isak.

'Don't be silly! You must know he'll want a rich Jewish girl for you.'

'You don't know my father,' Isak contradicted. 'He'll dance for joy at our wedding.'

Mona wasn't surprised that marriage had been mentioned. That had been obvious from the start. But she didn't believe in the father Isak had painted for her.

Now she was being taken to meet Karin and Simon who were really only a quarter of an hour's car journey away, but it took several hours. There was so much to tell each other. Isak knew he couldn't explain who Karin really was if he didn't pluck up the courage to tell Mona about his time in Berlin when the Hitler Youth were on the march.

Mona cried, good child that she was, hugged him and comforted him, good mother that she also was. I'll never abandon him, she thought. Not even if Ruben Lentov disinherits him. Then she told him about her mother, how death had come one night and wrung all her blood from her, about all those sheets stained red and her own peculiar thoughts.

'You don't believe it,' Mona continued. 'Dying – it goes on there in front of your nose, and yet you don't believe it. Isn't that strange?'

Isak didn't think so. Then he remembered Olga and knew that he had to tell Mona about her too. 'My mum's in the loony-bin,' he said. 'She went mad the night the Germans took Norway. It could be hereditary.' Isak hadn't dared think this before, but he knew he couldn't hide *anything*. 'And I've also got a cousin who seems mad. But she's been in a concentration camp.'

Mona was crying again. 'We'll have four happy kids,' she promised.

Finally they were on the sofa in Karin's kitchen, not saying very much but lighting up the whole room. They're like sunlight, Karin thought, looking out of the window at the pouring rain. 'You'll stay to dinner, won't you?' she asked.

'Yes, please.'

When it stopped raining they went out into the garden to pick strawberries for dessert.

Simon came back from the lake where he'd been fishing from the rowing-boat. He was pleased to see them. 'You two are the most amazing thing I've ever known,' he said after watching them for a while. Then they all had to laugh.

Karin took Simon with her back to the kitchen while the two lovers went on picking strawberries. 'Do you see how bright it is around them, Simon?'

'Yes. Is it wise, Mum?'

'Wise?' asked Karin. 'I have to tell you that not even in my wildest imagination when I tried to find something great for Isak, could I have created that girl.'

'I like her,' said Mona to Isak out in the strawberry bed.

'Of course.'

'But Simon's jealous.'

Isak laughed. 'Serves him right.' He put a strawberry in her mouth and kissed her.

They slept in the guest room in Ruben's narrow bed and Karin lent Mona her very best nightdress.

I've got a daughter, she thought as she went to bed.

She heard Mona phoning home. 'I'm staying overnight with a girlfriend in town. Tell Dad, will you?'

They must be a good family to have such a nice girl, Karin said to herself before falling asleep.

★

163

They still had a few days to get to know each other before Ruben and Erik came home and Karin kept Isak busy so that she would have time with Mona on her own.

The first morning she sent Isak home with the car. 'Put it into the garage, but clean it first. And not a word to Ruben about you driving without a licence.'

He obeyed and Karin said just what Mona's own mother always used to say. 'Oh, men!'

As the boys took the car into town, Karin and Mona went to the bathing place. Karin took a cautious dip, but Mona swam like a seal. She seemed to have nothing to hide. She told Karin about her mother dying and how difficult that had been, then about her younger brothers and sisters, now old enough to look after themselves. And her father, the fish dealer.

'He's not up to much,' Mona said. 'He's troublesome and easily offended, lots of toes to be trodden on. Stupid, too, and mean. But you have to accept it. He's the father I've got.'

Karin laughed. 'How will he react to Isak?'

'Well, there'll be a row, of course.'

'Because he's Jewish?'

'That too, but mostly because Dad'll lose me, his slavey.'

'Is he religious, a nonconformist? They usually live out on the islands.'

'Yes. There'll be a lot of shouting about anti-Christs and so on. But like a lot of religious people, it will be mostly for show.' Her eyes glittered. 'Of course, that'll soon pass when he stops to consider the money.'

Not even my own daughter could have been so like me, Karin thought, amazed and pleased.

Mona frowned. 'But I'm worried about Isak's dad. About what he'll say.'

'He'll like you.'

'How do you know that?'

'He's a good man.'

'That's a strange thing to say,' Mona said. 'Will that help me?'

'You'll see,' Karin promised.

Erik rang from Marstrand on the Saturday to say all was well on board. 'We'll be there tomorrow as arranged,' he told Karin. 'I'll go to the boatyard to take the provisions ashore. Are you well?'

'Yes,' Karin answered. 'Love to Ruben and tell him we have a big surprise for him here.'

'None for me?'

'I'm afraid not,' she said, thinking about Simon and Iza. 'But we have to take life as it comes.'

She sounded just the same as ever – a weird sister spinning destinies in her kitchen, looking out for broken threads or tangles, accepting that the weft of life was complicated, not easily sorted through. 'Your heart? I hope you've been taking your medicine?'

'Erik, I'm fine. I haven't even thought about my heart lately.'

She sounded happy to Erik. They had spoken a bit, he and Ruben, about Karin getting so much better after their talk to Simon last winter and the doctor had been pleased with her on his last visit.

As the handsome double-ender rounded Oljenäset at full sail, Mona, who knew about boats, drew a deep breath of admiration.

'That's my boat,' said Isak, his eyes full of pride.

Erik let the big sail go, but the foresail flapped in the wind as they dropped anchor and lowered the dinghy.

Erik stayed on board while Ruben rowed to the jetty. 'Where's my surprise?' he called out to Karin.

'I'll come down,' said Karin.

He is so young, thought Mona, and handsome. And every inch is upper class. Her heart thumped and her hand clutched Isak's.

They couldn't hear what Karin was saying to Ruben on the jetty, but Isak knew that he couldn't have a better messenger.

'They're so much in love, Ruben,' Karin told him. 'And she's everything you need.'

Ruben was sufficiently taken aback to have to sit down on one of the piles of ropes. Over the years, he had come to rely on Karin's judgement, so he was already convinced about Mona before he went up to meet her. It was a grey day, but he was aware of the light around the young couple at once.

He looked at Mona, took in her essence in one single look. 'Heavens! What does one say?'

Then he embraced her and laughed. 'You're a wonderful surprise.'

He gave Isak a long look and they all sensed the tenderness in his gaze. 'My boy,' he said.

Things went much as Mona had predicted with her father. He was furious. She was too young. A Jew! Was she crazy? What would people say?

But when he heard Isak's surname and thought about his father's money, the gold glowed in his mind and he calmed down. 'The Jews have been punished for two thousand years,' he said. 'Maybe the debt has now been paid.'

Isak and Mona became engaged formally at the Gardening Society's restaurant on the Sunday before they went back to school. On the morning before the party, Ruben took Mona to meet Olga. It was the first time for years he had not made that weary journey on his own. He was moved when he saw how naturally and fearlessly Mona faced Olga, the way she made contact through the dolls. And he thought he saw a glint of life in Olga's eyes.

On the way home in the car, Mona said, 'She's not unhappy. In a way, that's what's most important.'

Ruben nodded. He had thought the same himself, that Olga was now happier than during the years when she had been well and exposed to her fears. 'It's true. But that doesn't console me much.'

'I can understand that,' Mona said.

When Ruben met Mona's father for a drink at the restaurant before they went in to eat, he thought that one's journey through life was more mysterious than any psychology could ever explain. How in heaven's name had Mona managed to grow up in the shadow of this man?

Erik made a speech, stating the essential. 'You've found a Karin,' he told Isak. 'Take care of her. She is very rare.'

Chapter 21

The Göteborg Symphony Orchestra was playing Gösta Nystroem's *Sinfonia del mare*.

Simon listened as gentle Indian women washed their children at the source of the river where the wave was born, the wave that would go out to sea, taking with it the smell of their children. The wave would also remember the scent of mud and the moss of the trees that could halt the course of the river with their heavy roots and calm the eager water for a moment before it continued its journey.

At the outlet of the river, the wave met salmon full of energy on their way upstream. Yet it soon forgot the fish because of its fear, its terror of losing itself in what was limitless. But the wave was not obliterated. It froze and its imprisonment in the ice almost took away its lust for life.

Spring came and the wave broke free of the ice and knew that it had survived, that it was on its own while, at the same time, being a part of the great whole that was the sea. It began to flow east, huge ships dividing it and great winds playing on its surface.

On the southern tip of Greenland the wave met icebergs, swung round in surprise, stopped and murmured round the transparent green of the smooth precipices. It continued, taking on the colour of the melt-water and the knowledge that sorrow existed in everything that allowed itself to be shaped.

Between Iceland and the Shetlands it became heavy with salt and learned to hiss, enjoying the constant exchange between white crests and its green base. It raced across Skagerrak in heavy breakers and rounded Lister, slow and mighty, aware of its strength.

In the autumn it was smashed to pieces on the rocks of the Bohus country. But it found it could not die; that its memories had become part of the sea once more. Reborn, it headed north again towards that great coastline of deep fjords and heavy granite, of ice and tremendous winds.

Simon stayed in the concert hall as the audience left. Finally Ruben put his hand on his shoulder. 'I think we must go too.'

Olof Hirtz came up to speak to Ruben as Simon managed to put his new insight into words. 'The wave

168

doesn't die,' he said to the strange man. 'It can't be obliterated because it can never be separated from the sea.'

Olof Hirtz was pleased and interested. 'Come back with me for a late snack,' he said to Ruben and Simon.

There were only a few blocks to walk and soon they were in the spacious kitchen of an old apartment. This can't be happening, Simon thought as he met Maria, one of the Indian women from the source of the great river. She had a strong curved nose, wide cheerful mouth, black eyes that were far too large for her triangular face and a boyish haircut like a black helmet. Then he realised that Maria was Olof's wife and that she was a doctor.

'They're both psychoanalysts,' Ruben said as he introduced them to Simon. But what was just as astonishing was the fact that Maria was wearing trousers and a red velvet top, her handshake firm and her broad smile inquisitive.

While Simon was helping her take smoked salmon, cheese, bread, butter and beer from the larder and refrigerator, he could hear Ruben phoning Karin. 'We'll be late,' he was saying. 'So don't wait up for Simon. He'll probably stay overnight at my place.'

Olof was working at the Sahlgrenska Hospital again, doing research and teaching after his years at the sanatorium in Småland. His knowledge of suffering in the concentration camps had marked and absorbed him. He and Ruben often met to talk about Iza, and their acquaintance had matured into a firm friendship.

Ruben had told him about the Larssons, how Karin and Erik had helped Isak, and about Simon, the boy who was lonely amid his happy family.

'He's attracted to Iza,' Ruben had also told him.

'If his mother is as good as you say, perhaps he needs to singe his wings,' Olof had replied, adding the usual wise words about young people having to have their own bitter experiences. 'All we can do is to hope that they have the strength to endure their fate.'

As they sat at the table in the old-fashioned kitchen, Olof told Maria what Simon had said at the concert. He also said that he had come to believe lately that a lot of misery could be traced to people striving to create a personality that distinguishes them from others.

'But that's necessary,' Maria objected.

'It just makes us lonelier.'

'But we are alone,' Ruben protested. 'We're born alone and we die alone. We're not waves in the sea. Anyway, there's great satisfaction in having a personality.'

'Not on a deeper level,' Olof said. 'If you have a distinct personality, you may never find the meaning of life, or have any peace of mind.'

Simon looked at him in surprise, but Ruben didn't give in. 'But other things can make you happy. The struggle, the joy of striving for a goal and winning. All these things require you to have a personality.'

'And power and money?'

'Those too.' Olof laughed, so Ruben added, 'Well, they keep the fear at bay. And help a bit against the guilt.'

Olof became serious, and told them about his patients, the camp people with lung troubles and how they still felt guilty in spite of all they had had to endure.

'But that's crazy,' Simon exclaimed.

'No, it strengthens their sense of destiny and gives them a feeling of difference, of separation from their executioners.'

Ruben's face turned red with anger. 'If it's guilt that allows me to feel different from the Nazis at Buchenwald, then I'll pay that price. God, Olof, we *are* separate.'

Maria laughed. She had a way of tossing back her head. Her laughter was as dark as the primaeval forest,

Simon thought. 'I know you don't like talking about the Fall of Man,' she said. 'But it did happen, Olof. You know as well as I do that all children must have an identity, a sense of selfhood or things will go wrong. You can lament that the identity or the personality, as you call it, is so vulnerable that we defend it with feelings of fear and guilt. But that doesn't change the fact that the experience of self is the destiny of human kind.'

Ruben smiled this time. 'Eve,' he said. 'The eternal Eve, an earthly woman who keeps our feet firmly on the ground.'

'I think the Fall of Man is a delusion,' Olof persisted. 'And the perception of the importance of a separate identity is a defence mechanism against threats that don't exist.'

As always when Simon had to make an effort to understand, he screwed up his eyes and tightened his face muscles. He felt he wanted to write down what they were saying so that he could think about it later. Afraid of being left out, he started to tell them about the wave in the symphony he had just heard.

Olof and Maria listened with interest. Encouraged, Simon began to describe the kingdom of grass. 'I feel as if I've always been in that country. I was there all through my childhood and now I'm there in my dreams.' And he told them about the girl with the bird's nest, the precious egg and the bird of sorrow.

Maria was taken with his story. 'When did you dream that?'

'When I was ill, after I'd been told I was adopted.'

Maria said he was one of those people who have thin walls against the subconscious mind and he should be pleased that this was so.

Simon didn't know what she meant. He told her about his gramophone, how he played movements over and over again in order to free himself of the images and, finally, of the content of the music.

'Where are you then?' Olof asked.

'Why, I'm in reality.' Simon was surprised and looked straight at Olof.

Olof nodded. 'That's a good expression. Others call it God.' Seeing Simon's astonishment, he continued, 'I'm not one to go to church or synagogue. On the contrary, I try to think as little as possible about God, but I constantly want to be in Him.'

'Like the wave in the sea?'

'Yes, that's a good image. That's why I was so interested when you said the wave couldn't die because it avoided separating itself from the sea. I think the same condition applies to human beings when they are able to relinquish the self.'

'But they have to do their bit on earth first,' Maria said. 'Everyone must take responsibility for their lives and their world, cope with their relationships, be good parents and decent citizens.'

Simon turned to Olof. 'How do you get rid of the self?' he asked. 'What do you do?'

'Well,' said Olof. 'How do you obey the will of God? It's the same question, isn't it?'

It wasn't to Simon, but he made no objection.

'One way is to do what you did and go beyond the images,' Olof went on. 'But that's not easy, for anyone with a strong ego has a great many images to overcome.'

Ruben could see the boy was on fire with enthusiasm. 'Many people have described the experiences you have, Simon,' he said. 'Seekers and mystics have gone the same way. They've used prayer or meditation, whereas you've used music.'

Simon had never been so surprised in his life. He thought about his endless lessons in religion, the morning

172

prayers at school and how he used to ask himself how anyone could be so stupid as the priest up there in the pulpit. Was it possible that he was the one who hadn't understood?

He told them about the priests at school. 'So I'm the idiot then?' he asked.

They laughed again.

'No,' said Ruben. 'You're probably not the stupid one. Religions create a system that makes people stupid.'

'All answers make people a little stupid,' Maria added.

'Yet you have to ask questions,' Olof told him. 'I think everyone seeking answers to questions on the meaning of life is religious. You are too, Simon.'

There was a long silence.

'But many people never get as far as asking questions,' Simon said. He was thinking of Karin and Erik who went through life as though everything was self-evident.

'Many more than you think do,' Ruben countered.

'But Uncle Ruben, think about Mum!'

Ruben smiled so brightly it lit up the table. 'Karin's one of those who don't have to question. She lives in the answers.'

Maria smiled. 'There are people like that. A very few.'

As they were leaving, Maria turned to Simon. 'Don't take too much notice of these old men. You're welcome to come again. It's been nice meeting you.'

Ruben phoned for a taxi and asked Simon whether he'd like to come back with him, but Simon had left his bicycle outside the concert hall and needed to be alone.

He flew through the sleeping city, out towards the sea, to the furthest quay at Långedrag. The wind had risen and he could hear the sea roaring among the skerries. Storm clouds were racing past the moon, and the scents of the sea blew around him. He stood and let what had been said that evening run back and forth through his head until he was certain he would remember it.

Then he got back on his bicycle and set off home with the wind behind him, thinking he would write a poem about the sea. He crept up the stairs, found a pen and paper in his room, and tried to describe the wave born of the Indian women at the source of the river.

What does the sea smell of?
Turn your face to the storm
Out there, bringing to you all the scents of sea,
Filling your nose, your lungs.
Start with sturdy words.
Seaweed. Salt.
There is no answer to the words.

What does the sea smell of?
Try the other words, the harder ones:
Force, freedom, adventure.
They fall to the ground, limit the unlimited.
Ask the question yet again:
What does the sea smell of?
And you realise that the question has no meaning.
When you have stopped asking,
Then perhaps
You can experience the sea.

It was past two in the morning, but Simon wasn't tired. When he went to the bathroom he must have woken Mona and Isak. He could hear them laughing in the spare room, softly, then passionately, and he listened in the hall until he heard Mona's half-suppressed bird cry.

He was ashamed, but only for a moment and, as he crawled finally into his lonely bed, he felt how damnably he hated Isak.

Then he remembered his poem and thought about

how he could make it acquire strength through the music, the rhythm in the symphony.

Simon went on writing his poem about the sea all through the whole of his last year at school. And hating Isak.

Chapter 22

Simon and Isak left school in the spring of 1947. The end of term was no great day for them. The only important thing was that they were going to be free.

No more compulsion, thought Isak.

No more boredom, thought Simon.

Ruben threw a party in his apartment in town, which pleased Karin for a student celebration in her house at the river mouth was challenging. It was enough that for a few days Simon tore round the roads in his grand new cap which seemed to be glued to his head, then it was forgotten.

Isak was going on to Chalmers Poly. This was no problem as his marks were good enough. And Simon wanted to read history at college.

Erik and Karin were not pleased with Simon's choice. What use would that be and what kind of profession would it lead to, they asked? But Ruben talked to them about research, and said that in a few years Simon could be a teacher.

This comforted Karin, but Erik thought Isak had made a better choice. He would become a civil engineer which was what he had always wanted to be.

'Just as I wanted to be a historian,' Ruben responded,

which made them laugh at their old joke about their reversed sons.

But first the boys had to do their military service.

Karin was secretly pleased as this meant Simon would be out of Iza's reach for another nine months. For Iza had returned from Switzerland and had been given an apartment in Stockholm where she was to go to art school.

Erik was worried about the army. They were still only kids for heaven's sake! 'Remember to look on it as a game,' he told them. 'Don't take it seriously, just obey, and it'll soon be over.'

Simon nodded. He understood what Erik was trying to say.

But Isak stated solemnly that he thought it was important and anyhow he wanted to learn how to defend Sweden.

Karin and Mona smiled, Karin gently, Mona proudly. As they sat over coffee at the table outside, no one noticed Erik's uneasiness.

The moment passed, Isak started singing the battalion song and, as always when he sang, Simon winced. 'It's a miracle I've put up with you all these years,' he said and told the others about being woken from his dreams at school by Isak bawling away at the top of his voice.

They laughed again. Mona sang the old song, Erik joined in and they sang it as a part song. Simon approved and told them that it should sound like that.

'I can't hear any difference,' Isak protested.

But, aware of Erik's unease, Karin also felt uncomfortable.

Forwaaaaard march! Halt! About . . . turn!

The unmentionable was out to get Isak. It crept through his body from neck to midriff where it hurt, spread to his arms and down into his hands which prickled as if from a thousand pins, reached his legs which refused to obey.

'Lentov, for Christ's sake, keep time . . .'

'Preseeeeent . . . arms! Left. Right. Left. Right.'

The unmentionable was in the air Isak breathed, in the measured tramp of the straight ranks. It clung to him, conquered him and when it reached his head he knew he was going to die.

Simon was close by. 'For God's sake, Isak, you'll get used to it. You'll soon get over it.'

This might have been possible if Lance-Corporal Nilsson's mother hadn't died. His place was taken by a sergeant called Bylund who hadn't chosen this occupation by chance for his great delight was in tormenting boys. He stood before them, a large tall man, not bad-looking, with a quick and peculiar smile.

Like a wolf, Simon thought, who had never seen one. It came and went, that smile. Bylund was pleased. Two bloody Jew-boys in his platoon. Bliss!

'You there.'

'Who, me?'

'Yes, *sergeant*, for Christ's sake.'

'Yes, sergeant.'

Then it started. 'Crawl, up, down, crawl, left turn, halt! Lentov, you put us all to shame. But that's to be expected.' And always that dry rattling laugh.

Bylund was happy. This was going be a jollier summer than he had reckoned on when Nilsson's damned mother had gone and died. Hilly terrain, sheltering rocky slopes between him and the lieutenant who didn't like Jews either, so would no doubt look the other way. Bylund smiled his wolf-smile. He smelled, sniffed, the scent of weakness, of corpses, in the air. I know him, I recognise him, he thought.

But Isak stuck with it. He got through each day, crawled, wriggled, was humiliated, shouted at. Simon was almost mad with rage and fear for, when they were in the canteen in the evening, he noticed Isak was becoming more and more mechanical.

Inaccessible. Like that day in the school yard.

That night he got Isak to bed in the hut among six others who didn't meet his eyes, then he went to the lieutenant. He stood to attention. 'Isak Lentov . . .'

'Number and name.' The lieutenant didn't shout, but his voice was icy cold.

'Isak Lentov was badly damaged by the Nazis in Berlin when he was a child. He was ill later, mentally ill. He isn't able to stand the kind of treatment he's getting from Sergeant Bylund.'

The lieutenant's blue eyes narrowed.

'Are you reporting him?'

'I just wanted to – to tell someone. It could be harmful.'

'Didn't you understand my question, man?'

'Yes –'

'Yes, *sir* . . .'

'Yes, sir.'

'So you're not reporting him.'

Simon saw the derision in those blue slits. The bloody man was amused. Despair washed over him as he turned on his heel and left.

Damned unpleasant story, Lieutenant Fahlén thought. Bylund was known, his methods notorious. Why do the hell did they have Jews in the service?

Larsson was hardly Swedish either. More Jewish than the other one, in fact. And Lentov, he was the son of that rich book Jew, of course.

The next day he kept Bylund's platoon in sight and

made sure the sergeant was aware of his presence. Then he forgot all about it.

Bylund took it out on Simon when they were next out on exercise and Simon went along with it. He was careless, messed things up, drew Bylund's hatred, absorbed his rage, crawled, wriggled, let himself be humiliated, conscious that he was sparing Isak. Bylund knew in his guts that he couldn't break Larsson, but he comforted himself: the summer was long and he had plenty of time for Lentov.

That evening in the barracks, Simon saw the emptiness had crept into Isak's eyes. It was no easier for him to see his friend being tormented. God, Simon thought. What shall I do?

There was a telephone down on the jetty. Simon had seen it when they had come, an ordinary public telephone. But he was locked in. The fence? The guards were good shots, he had been told. But he had to get a message out.

The next morning Isak went on parade like a puppet, was shouted at, took nothing in. They were due to go out on exercise again, and, suddenly, Simon had an idea.

At their first break he made sure he was alone with Isak behind a stony hillock. Bylund was out of sight for a second so Simon picked up a stone and struck Isak's lower arm as hard as he could.

'I'm so sorry Isak,' he said. 'But I can't see any other way out.'

Isak smiled at Simon. It was almost as if the pain had brought him back to himself.

'You'll end up in the sick bay now,' Simon told him. But Isak wasn't listening any longer. He had gone away again.

Simon ran across to Bylund. 'Sergeant!' He stood to

attention, remembered his name and number, everything. 'Lentov, 378 has broken his arm.'

'What the hell?'

Bylund looked anxious and perhaps a little disappointed that the mouse had slipped through his hands. Then he gave orders: stretcher, transport, sick bay.

Simon went with Isak.

'Stay here, Larsson!' Bylund yelled.

Simon continued to walk beside the stretcher.

'Halt!'

Simon walked on.

'Halt or I'll fire!'

But Bylund didn't fire for he was suddenly aware that the other six in his platoon would jump on him if he drew his gun.

Isak was unconscious. The doctor was a captain, a man called Ivarsson. Simon went into the treatment room with Isak and, while the arm was being examined – yes, it was fractured – and plastered, Simon told him about Bylund, Isak's childhood in Berlin and the risk of psychosis.

'But why didn't you say something before?' Ivarsson was more of a doctor than a captain and was very upset.

'I reported it to the lieutenant.'

'Oh, God,' said the doctor and Simon realised the man was frightened. 'Larsson, leave the hospital immediately,' he barked.

Simon went out into the sunny parade ground and saw that they had forgotten him. Now was his chance. He got his wallet out of his locker in the barracks, prayed to God that there were some coins in it, flew over the fence, down to the jetty and the telephone.

'Uncle Ruben, it's me, Simon.' His voice was shrill and sliced through Ruben.

'You must get Isak out of here. They're killing him. I've broken his arm, so he's in the sick bay now, but he's gone away, you know, like he did during the war.' He managed to tell Ruben the doctor's name before his money ran out and the line went dead.

Ruben's blood pounded in his head as he dialled the number of the Sahlgrenska Hospital.

'Professor Hirtz. It's urgent.'

'One moment, please.'

'Olof, it's me, Ruben. You know what happened to Isak in Berlin?' Briefly he related what Simon had told him.

'Have you the phone number?'

Ruben had it in his pocket diary.

'I'll ring you back.'

A minute later, Olof got through. 'Dr Ivarsson, this is Professor Hirtz at the Sahlgrenska. I'm a friend of Ruben Lentov who's just had a worrying message about his son.'

Ivarsson had been to Hirtz's lectures and admired him. 'An uncomplicated arm fracture. There's no danger.'

'I want a psychiatric assessment.'

'Not so good, I'm afraid. He's fairly distant, preoccupied.'

'He's to be sent here immediately. He needs special care.'

'Yes, Professor Hirtz.'

Ivarsson supervised procedings as Isak was put into the ambulance, Simon beside him. Lieutenant Fahlén, who seemed about to protest, stood watching.

As the ambulance left the barrack square the doctor looked at the lieutenant. He's a fascist too, he thought. Both men sensed the silence of the parade ground and both realised that every man there knew what had happened.

The doctor walked across to the regimental commander's office.

'Lentov's rich,' said the commanding officer.

'And influential.'

The regimental commander groaned. That sevenfold damned Bylund – why the hell was he on duty again?

Fahlén was ordered into the office. 'Larsson didn't report anything, not formally. He stammered something about Nazis and that the boy couldn't stand Bylund. I didn't take it all that seriously.'

'Lieutenant Sixten Fahlén,' said the regimental commander slowly. 'If there's a court martial on this and a scandal, and there probably will be, then you'll be the one, Lieutenant, to hang for it. You've brought shame to the regiment.'

Fahlén clicked his heels and left in search of Bylund. But the sergeant had vanished.

The ambulance climbed through the twilight up the hill to the hospital, Simon holding Isak's hand, Isak far away.

At the entrance the driver asked for Professor Hirtz and was given directions. Ruben was there too but Isak didn't recognise him. He was taken straight to the psychiatric department.

While Olof examined him, Ruben, Simon and the driver waited outside in the corridor.

'I did what I could.' Simon's voice was breaking.

'I know, Simon.'

'There was a sergeant,' Simon began, but couldn't go on.

The driver took over and Ruben was given a detailed account of what had happened, of Bylund, of how Simon had tried to protect his friend and of his report to the lieutenant.

'He's a fascist, that Bylund, notorious.' The driver was

so agitated that he was trembling. 'Crack down on him. Crack down on all those bloody bastards! He almost fired at Larsson. The boy in hut eighteen said he almost fired his gun just because Larsson was with Lentov when the accident happened.'

'Accident?' Ruben glanced at Simon.

'Broken arm,' the driver replied.

At that moment Olof came back. 'Shock. Impossible to make a diagnosis, possibly pre-psychosis. He must stay here.'

'Phone for Mum,' Simon suggested. Olof nodded.

Ruben thought of Karin, of how she had once said that Isak was not going into any loony-bin, she would see to that. 'Can she stay here tonight?'

'Yes. We'll put him in a single room.'

Ruben went to telephone and stood holding the receiver for a long time trying to find the right words.

'You'd better come back with me,' the driver said to Simon. 'Otherwise you'll be charged with desertion.'

When Ruben came back, Simon was already by the door. 'I don't know how to thank you.'

Simon shrugged and left hurriedly.

An hour later, Karin was at the hospital, Mona beside her. She had also been in the house when Ruben had phoned. Karin was pale, but calm and collected as she sat down by the bed and exchanged a few words with Olof.

As soon he had left the room she told Mona to get into bed with Isak.

In the corridor, Olof shook hands with Erik who was as white as a sheet and was saying to Ruben that it was all his fault. 'I knew what it was like. I ought to have realised.'

'But he wanted to go,' said Ruben.

Erik was inconsolable. 'I've no damned imagination when it comes to people. Will he recover?'

'I don't know yet,' Olof said. 'We'll see when he wakes. Karin's managed to put him back together before.'

Erik sighed. 'Shall I drive you back, or are you staying the night too?'

'Thanks,' said Olof. 'I think we should all go home and try to get some sleep. Karin'll ring me when the boy wakes.'

'As long as those bastards don't take it out on Simon,' Erik muttered on the way home.

Ruben felt his stomach contract. He was tired and frightened.

'I'll ring Ivarsson in the morning,' Olof said.

But it was too late by then. Hours and hours too late.

Chapter 23

Simon was so tired in the ambulance that his whole body ached. He had been unable to think from the moment he had handed Isak over to Ruben.

'Lie down and have a kip, boy,' the driver advised.

Simon stretched out on the stretcher bed and fell asleep immediately. When the driver woke him an hour or so later he was feeling sick. The barracks square was deserted and his one thought as he jumped out of the ambulance was bed.

But as he stood in the dark corridor of the hut – and God how dark it was – he caught the scent. Fear collected in every muscle in his body and before he saw the shadow of Bylund, just visible in the light from the door, he knew that his life was now at stake.

Don't let on you've sensed the danger. Go straight in and hit him. His mind worked like lightning, Erik's old instructions still there. His straight right was precise, swift and strong, and so was the smashing left jab which hurt his knuckles. He ducked the blow that came towards him and, as he rose again, his mind said, kick him in the crotch, Simon, as hard as you can. He kicked and was almost happy to hear the roar of pain. He struck again, into the man's stomach this time, horribly and effectively. Bylund bent double, Simon lashed out at his head and the sergeant fell.

At least fifty pairs of eyes stared at him in the light that poured into the corridor suddenly. But all Simon could see was Bylund's front teeth in a pool of blood on the floor. He's dead, he thought, and he felt a wild joy.

The ambulance driver had seen the light go on and took control. 'Put the lights out!' he yelled.

They obeyed. The driver's voice came out of the dark. 'Two men take Bylund to the wash-room and give him a shower. The rest of you get back to bed. Not a single bloody one of you has seen anything, understood?'

The whispered yes was enthusiastic. The two men who had been to the showers returned to say that Bylund was alive.

'Is he the duty officer here?'

'He changed with Fahlén.'

The driver helped Simon put a plaster on his damaged knuckles. 'Put Bylund in the duty officer's bed,' he instructed. 'Remember, no one's heard or seen anything.'

As Simon got into bed, he added, 'You injured your hand when you jumped out of the ambulance. I can testify to that. Got it?'

It'll never work, Simon thought, but he was much more preoccupied with his own pleasure in having killed Bylund. I'm crazy too, he thought. 'Is he dead?' he whispered.

'Not bloody likely. He'll go on plaguing the life out of the new rookies.'

At reveille the next morning, Simon was ordered to report to the sick bay where he found the driver at the entrance.

'Not a word,' the man whispered. 'This is the man who injured his hand when he fell out of the ambulance yesterday,' he said to the nurse.

She was pretty and asked no questions as she bandaged Simon's hand.

Ivarsson came in for a moment. 'Arm in a sling,' he said. 'Off sick for a week.' His eyes did not meet Simon's.

This is crazy, Simon thought. They haven't found out about Bylund yet.

'They stitched up Bylund as well as they could this morning and took him to the nearest hospital. Suspected concussion', the driver told him.

'But they must know?'

'They haven't set up an inquiry. They seem to be going to hush it up.'

In his office two floors up the regimental commander was striding back and forth like an angry tiger.

'Lieutenant Fahlén, did you not realise Bylund's intentions in taking over your guard duty?'

'No, sir.'

The old man gazed at the lieutenant. 'You're no fool, Fahlén. You're something much worse.'

Fahlén left and the commander sat down at his desk and dialled Ruben Lentov's number.

'I need hardly say how sorry I am about what happened to your son. How is he?'

'He's in the psychiatric department at the Sahlgrenska Hospital.'

'I'm sorry.'

'Did you phone just to say that?'

'No.'

A long pause. Simon, thought Ruben. It's about Simon.

'Simon Larsson almost killed Sergeant Bylund last night.'

Ruben found it difficult to breathe. 'It must have been in self-defence.'

'Possibly. But there wasn't a scratch on him so he must have used much more violence than was necessary. Bylund's in hospital with teeth knocked out and concussion.'

Ruben could say nothing.

'You understand, Mr Lentov, that this might mean prison for Larsson, and for quite a stretch too, if we don't hush it up?'

'What price did you have in mind?' Ruben asked, although he already knew.

They settled the matter in a business-like manner. There was to be silence on everything on both sides.

'I'll arrange for Larsson to go on patrol duty out on the coast,' the commander concluded.

Ruben phoned the boatyard to speak to Erik.

'Christ Almighty,' said Erik. 'What a lad.' There was no mistaking the pride in his voice. They agreed not to say a word about what had happened to Karin, Isak or Mona.

'He's being sent on patrol duty to the islands,' Ruben told him. 'So he won't get any leave for a while.'

In the commander's office, Captain Viktor Sjövall of the patrol service was listening to the old man's story with increasing displeasure. 'Good Christ,' he exclaimed.

'You can look after the boy?'

'Yes. Must be a fine fellow.'

'Devil of a fighter.' The commander spoke with admiration as he took out Simon's papers. 'An A student,' he went on. 'Highest marks we've ever had in the IQ test when he came. He ought to have been an officer.'

Sjövall laughed. 'No doubt we've got rid of any such desire now. If he ever had any.'

The old man sighed.

Simon was asleep in the sick bay, but was woken in the afternoon, discharged and sent off to a patrol boat down at the quay. In the boat was a captain. Simon noticed some warmth and understanding in his eyes as he told him to sit down.

'I'm Viktor Sjövall and you're to spend the rest of your military service with me out in the archipelago.'

Simon had heard about the patrol service and knew it was much coveted.

'I know what happened, Larsson.'

He's almost human, thought Simon in surprise. 'Yes, sir.'

'That is, I know what happened to Bylund last night but no one else does and neither do you. Understood?'

'Yes, sir.' He saw the corners of Sjövall's mouth twitching and added, 'Perhaps I may tell you some dark night at sea?'

Sjövall laughed and Simon relaxed. 'Sir, do you know how Isak Lentov is?'

'No, but you can phone home by radio as soon as we're at sea.'

'Thank you, sir.' He felt a sudden lump in his throat

and swallowed hard to hold back his tears. Viktor Sjövall noticed. 'This has all been a bit much, hasn't it, Larsson?'

'It was worse for Isak, sir.'

'I understand that.'

'I don't think anyone can understand.' As the boat made its way through the islands, Simon told the captain about the sequestered ships, and about Isak and the Hitler Youth waiting for a four-year-old one May morning in Berlin.

When he had finished, he looked up at the other man and saw that he was moved, and that he resembled Erik.

An hour later, the telegraphist called him. 'Your mum's on the line, Larsson.'

Karin had never had a radio phone call before and thought that with no lines she had to shout. 'Isak's all right. He's coming home tomorrow.'

'Oh, Mum,' Simon said.

'He's going for treatment with Maria Hirtz.'

The Indian woman, Simon thought, and shouted back, 'Great, Mum.' For the first time in ages, Simon felt a heavy weight roll from his shoulders.

'How are you?' Karin asked.

'Fine,' he said. 'I'm at sea.'

And he wondered what she would say if she knew, if she ever got to know, he had nearly killed a man and that he had enjoyed it . . .

Simon's life became simple, a jetty, a few huts, boats for patrolling, guard duty. But his unease gnawed away at him.

Sjövall noticed. 'How are the nerves, Larsson?'

'I need to talk to my father,' Simon said to him at last.

The next day, Simon was put on a transport with an assignment at Nya Varvet. The skipper had been told to put him ashore at Rivö Huvud for two hours' leave.

Simon phoned his father and told him the plan. 'Bring Ruben with you if you can, but not Karin, do you hear, Dad? Not Karin.'

'Understood,' said Erik.

They were there in good time, and anchored the double-bender on the wind side so that she was fully visible from the sea. The wind was fresh, pulling on the grapnel.

'We'll have to keep an eye on her,' Erik said.

He and Ruben sat staring out towards Vinga, waiting for a torpedo boat. Instead, a fishing smack sailed past and there was some delay before they saw she was flying the three-tongued flag. She yawed up, crept up against the cliff and Simon jumped out. He had become an adult, all of his soft boyishness had gone and there was a new and bitter awareness in his eyes, which Erik and Ruben both noticed.

They shook hands as if they were strangers, then Erik spoke formally and in a mawkish way Simon detested: 'Bloody proud of you, I am, boy.'

Simon's eyes darkened and his mouth twitched. 'Steady on, Dad. You don't know the worst yet. I almost killed the sergeant.'

'Yes, Simon. We know.'

Ruben told him about the telephone call with the commander and the settlement they had reached.

'Christ,' Simon said. 'Christ Almighty, Uncle Ruben, if you'd been a poor old bastard, Isak would be in the bin now and I'd be in prison. It's nuts!'

'Yes,' Ruben agreed. 'It's nuts.'

All three of them sat down in the lee of the wind.

'Does Mum know?'

'No, we're keeping her out of it, you know – her heart.'

Her heart, thought Simon, nothing else . . .

A moment later, he put his head on Erik's lap and covered his eyes with his bandaged hand.

'Does it hurt?'

'No, it's getting better. It stings like hell in salt water though.'

He looked at Erik, his brown eyes boring into Erik's blue ones. 'Just think, Dad, every punch went exactly where it should've.'

Erik thrust his fingers through Simon's hair, as he had when the boy was small.

Ruben went over to the boat. 'I'll get the coffee and sandwiches.'

As they ate, Simon told them what had happened in the corridor when Bylund had been waiting for him. 'He'll have false teeth as a souvenir for the rest of his life. And by Christ, that thought pleases me.'

He looked at them, as if expecting protests, but they laughed, the same satisfied laugh as his own. 'Later,' he went on, 'when the ambulance driver had got me into bed, I thought Bylund was dead, that I'd killed him. I was so happy. Then I realised I wasn't all that different from Bylund.'

'We've probably all got a little sergeant in us,' said Erik.

It was so easy, Simon thought. Even for Ruben it was simple, a matter of course.

When the fishing smack appeared again, they shook hands. 'See you soon,' they said and Simon went on board feeling he was now adult, on an equal footing with both men.

'He never asked about Isak,' Erik remarked as they set sail once more.

'No. Thank God for that,' said Ruben.

Chapter 24

Isak had woken at about four in the morning in his hospital bed, warm from Mona's body. He had felt her presence and hadn't dared believe it.

Then he'd heard Karin's voice. 'Time to come back now, Isak.'

'Explain it to me, Karin,' he had said without opening his eyes.

'Well, Simon broke your arm to get you away from the sergeant.'

Isak remembered, the stone, Simon's eyes. Then Bylund's voice intruded and everything went empty again.

'Simon managed to get hold of a telephone and rang Ruben,' Karin continued.

'He got over the fence then? Bloody brave of him.'

Karin had been keen that he should understand the entire context and then she had started asking questions, trying to drag the whole wretched story out of him, bit by bit, over and over again. 'Who was he like?'

'Don't know.'

'Isak, you do.'

But the Nazis in Isak's childhood merged and he couldn't distinguish one face from another. 'It was something about his nose, Karin. He sniffed. Then laughed. Oh, God.'

He had screamed with terror, wept, begged them not to send him back to the regiment and Bylund.

Ruben arrived and Olof Hirtz with Maria. Isak had looked at her and thought of Simon. Simon was fond of her.

He must have fallen asleep, because when he woke

only Maria was with him. His tears had gone, for the terror inside him was far too great for tears.

'Am I going mad?'

She hadn't snorted like Karin, or consoled him. 'There's always a risk of that Isak,' she had said.

But Maria's face wasn't like Bylund's and she couldn't frighten him over the edge.

'You must stop running away, Isak. I think I can help, but you must stay put in your anguish,' she had told him.

'But I'll die,' he had shouted.

All that was many weeks ago. He had been discharged, gone to Karin's and Erik's although the strength from them and their house no longer had any effect on him. Sometimes he got rid of the terror for a few hours, mostly when he was needed at the boatyard and his hands obeyed him. But usually he didn't know what to do and would sit looking out of the window for hours.

Mona came and went. He could see she was growing more and more frightened, and in a moment of clarity he thought that the least he could do was to release her.

He gave her back his gold ring and told her to go. But she disobeyed and he hated her, just as he hated Karin for the dark anxiety in her eyes and Ruben who had aged so, shrinking every day that passed.

Maria came out in the evenings. They sat in Simon's room and occasionally he would make an effort to find a thread in the tangle that was the terror inside him. But when they pulled at the thread, it all became even more tangled, more unendurable.

One day he ran away. He ended up on the Onsala peninsula on the smooth rocks where he and Mona had made love only a year ago. He thought the boy who had made love to the girl had never known himself. It had been someone else who had been so happy, so full of hope. He thought about putting an end to himself by diving into the water from the rock.

He remembered a cat they had once drowned, he and Simon. They had put it into a sack with some stones and flung it into the river, and even though Erik had said that it was an old wild thing that was hurt and would be better off dead, the cat had howled for a long time in their dreams.

Dreams. Maria kept going on about dreams. I've never dreamed in all my life, Isak thought.

He couldn't remember how he got to the main road, but when he saw a grocer's shop he went inside and phoned Karin.

'Heavens, Isak. Ruben has been talking to the police.'

'The police? Why?'

'You've been missing for three days.'

He was surprised. 'I'll make my way home now.'

He got a lift to Käringberget and walked the rest of the way. They were waiting for him in the kitchen, but he couldn't face them and turned back at the door and went across to the stairs. Then he stopped. 'Perhaps it's best to give up,' he said to Karin. 'And put me in the bin.'

Karin looked straight at him. 'Maria says you'll get better and the worse you are the more certain it is that you'll recover.'

'She's crazy as well,' said Isak.

'How much worse do I have to get?' he asked the next day when Maria came.

'I don't know,' she said. 'But I'd be happier if you trusted me.'

Together they pulled at another thread, the memory of drowning the cat. But the tangle became worse and the thread snapped. 'I can't do it,' he pleaded.

As she was leaving, Maria told him that they might have to admit him again.

'What for?'

So that he didn't run away and harm himself, she told him. He could feel himself going rigid and that night he did have a dream. He was stuffing Maria into a sack and filling it with stones, and she was crying and begging for her life, but he drowned her and as the sack sank, he thought that now he would never have to pull at threads any longer.

This was a great relief.

The next morning he remembered the dream but knew he would never dare tell Maria about it. He stayed in bed while Lisa cleaned the house and Karin went for her walk.

He realised he had to get away again. He would take the boat this time. Right out into the western sea, he decided, and there was freedom in the thought, a moment's respite from his terror. He couldn't find his bicycle so he took Simon's from the garage, stopped to pump up the tyres and was soon down at the jetty in Långedrag. There she was – *Kajsa*, his double-ender.

What an idiot he was not to have thought of her before!

Soon he was cruising westwards, past Vinga, due west towards the sunset. When the summer night that had no darkness crept round him, there was nothing but the sea and the boat. The land was now out of sight.

He must have fallen asleep at the rudder, for suddenly there was a fishing boat and a man shouting, 'D'you want any help, boy?'

The sail was flapping like mad and he couldn't get her into the wind. 'Rudder's failed,' he shouted back.

They flung a rope to him and took him in tow. It must be meant, he thought. He was not to sail to his death either. They towed him between the skerries and he reached Korshamn channel early in the morning. The skipper pointed to the boatyard and its crane on the north side of Brännö, saying he could get help with his rudder if he went there.

Isak untied the rope and shouted his thanks across the water, which was now so still it seemed to be holding its breath. He knew there was nothing wrong with his rudder, but was ashamed they might see so he rowed into the yard and stayed there for an hour or two. There wasn't a living soul there at this time of the morning for which he was grateful.

In the end he set the foresail, slipped along the hillside until he found a bay in the lee, moored, crept down into the cabin and slept. I'm not even any good at taking my own life, he said to himself.

It was late evening when the rain pattering on the deck woke him and he was in a worse mood than ever. There was no grocer's shop here with a telephone to ring home to tell them not to worry. It's the loony-bin for me. It's best for everyone, he thought as he set sail again. He set the course towards Långedrag, but went too far north and at Kopparholmen ran on to the barrier that had been erected to defend Göteborg in 1914. The impact sounded like a pistol shot. There was his *Kajsa* on the stone barrier, shuddering as if he had wounded her. Isak stopped feeling frightened and went into action. He got her afloat with the aid of the boathook and headed for the boatyard and Erik. She was taking in water.

For a moment Isak thought he could turn and sail out to sea again and sink with her. But the boat was expensive, had been built when he was sick and had been his mortgage on life. So he headed for the river mouth.

They were in the kitchen waiting for him as usual, but there were more this evening, Olof and Maria, and

Mona too, strangely hunched up.

But Isak had eyes only for Erik. 'I went aground at Kopparholmen. Smashed the bottom. She's leaking like hell to the fore of the starboard side.'

Erik blew up. 'You damned spoiled good-for-nothing,' he shouted. 'You're the most selfish little bastard that ever walked in a pair of shoes.'

'Erik,' said Karin warningly, but he wasn't listening.

'Who do you think you are, you damned fancy piece? Tearing round the islands like an idiot without a thought for anything except your bad nerves. Bad nerves! For Christ's sake, that's no worse than Karin's bad heart, is it? You'll have to learn to live with your nerves, just as she has to live with her heart.'

Isak raised his hands and held them out towards Erik as if begging for mercy, but nothing was going to stop him.

'What do you think it's like for Karin when she worries about you all the time? And Ruben who'll crack up if this goes on much longer? And Mona?'

'I've finished with Mona,' Isak whispered.

'Shut up!' Erik shouted so loudly that the cups rattled. 'Do you think you're some kind of god, who can finish with anyone? You belong, you two, we all belong and it's only you who's so bloody stupid that you can't take it in and take some responsibility.'

Isak thought it was coming back again, his fear. He was slipping away, but Erik did not take his eyes off him for a second and the rage in them forced him to stay – the rage and something else. Despair?

Isak loved Erik and admired him. 'Please,' he said.

'Please nothing!' Erik yelled. 'I'm damned well going to make a man of you.'

'Erik!' Ruben was shouting now, his voice so loud that for a moment Erik's rage subsided.

Olof intervened. 'Go on, Erik,' he said. 'You're quite right.'

Erik's voice had gone back to normal as he leaned forward towards Isak. 'I'll fix a job for you at Göta-verken, boy. On the factory floor, where your father's money can't buy you out of trouble. You've got to grow up now, Isak Lentov, and I'm going to see you do.'

The kitchen was silent until Karin spoke. 'Have you had anything to eat, Isak?'

'There'll be nothing to eat until the boat's taken up,' said Erik. 'Come on, Isak. We'll get her up before she sinks.'

Five minutes later, the lights were on in the boatyard.

Isak did not sleep much that night. He stood at the window of his old room. He felt just as fearful as before. But at least he was real.

Again and again he came back to what Erik had said, that he would have to live with his nerves just as Karin had to live with her heart.

Hell, he would too.

The next day he phoned Mona. 'Do you dare start again?' he asked.

Erik began to arrange Isak's job at the Götaverken factory at breakfast the next morning. 'School papers are no use,' he said.

'But what if they ask what I did after middle-school exams?'

'You've been working here at the yard, for Christ's sake. You've got a reference from me.'

It was true that Isak had helped Erik at the boatyard during his years at senior high. With Karin's aid they wrote a reference which, without lying, amounted to a year's work.

Isak also started to repair the boat which wasn't as

badly damaged as he had feared. Two boards had to be replaced but there was plenty of mahogany at the yard.

'You'll have to pay for it gradually,' said Erik. 'You'll soon be earning some money.'

Isak wondered whether this was a joke, but Erik didn't look as if he were joking. 'Are you still angry with me?' he asked.

'Not any more. I really wanted to say that you have to take responsibility for your actions, even if everything inside you is bloody awful.'

'You've never thought you were going mad.'

'Yes, I have,' said Erik. 'A lot of people have. But as I said, you have to live with it.'

'I know that now,' Isak said.

Ruben phoned them at the yard. 'How's it going?'

'Better, I think.'

'So it was good you got so furious?'

'Yes, the doctors said so.'

'Eriksberg are advertising for apprentices in the paper today.'

'To hell with that,' said Erik. 'The boy's to go to Götaverken. The yard's known for its good spirit.'

'I didn't know that.'

There's quite a lot you don't know, Mr Lentov, Erik wanted to say, but managed to bite back the words on the tip of his tongue.

'Things are turning now, Ruben,' he said instead. 'I can feel they're turning.'

For the first time in ages he heard Ruben laugh. 'You told me that once before, Erik. Do you remember?'

'No,' Erik answered. 'Was I right?'

'Very much so.'

'Apply to the machine shop,' Erik instructed Isak at dinner. 'The yard's screaming for people and most of all for turners.'

At the appointments office the next day, everything went smoothly. The officials accepted his qualifications, nodded and asked a few questions about Larsson's boatyard.

'They have some fine double-enders there,' they said. 'Things are a bit bigger here, and there's not so much timber.'

Next, Isak had a medical: 'Breathe in, breathe out, never had heart trouble, asthma, TB? Good, fine blood count, next one please.'

Isak found filling in the form the worst. There were several alternatives for religion: Lutheran, Catholic, Jewish, other faiths. He put a cross against Jewish. No lies, Karin had said.

Completed military service? There was only yes or no there. Exempt. Nationality: Swedish, Isak wrote in a firm hand. Place of Birth: Berlin.

A few hours later, his papers had been processed. His name was called in the waiting room and the man behind the counter said that he could start on Monday at seven o'clock as an apprentice to Egon Bergman in Machine Shop Two. He was told the rates of pay and when he looked surprised, the man behind the counter said that depended on the agreement he would be given in a month or so.

Isak had not realised that he was going to be paid.

He was frightened as he left the office, but it was a tangible fear in his knees and stomach. On the ferry back, however, it rose to his throat. If I don't cope with this, it'll be the end of me, he thought.

'Whatever happens, I'll stick with you,' Mona had said the evening before. She was unshakeable. But he couldn't live on her strength alone. You can't rely on women, he thought.

The thought surprised him so much. Was he crazy, he

who had had Karin for so long, as solid as a rock? But she had almost left him when she nearly died.

Isak, he said to himself, a person doesn't let you down because she's ill. And Mona. He knew with his whole being that she was like Karin. He felt ashamed of himself.

Maria was always reminding him that he should tell her his dreams. Well, he didn't dream, but now he had a strange thought to tell her. He cycled away from the ferry towards home, and Erik and Karin, to tell them he'd got the job in the yard.

But when he got to Karl Johansgatan, he turned his bicycle into town. Ruben, he thought. I must tell Dad first. Ruben was pleased, but Isak could see the anxiety in his eyes and knew that he was thinking just what Isak was thinking: would he cope?

'There'll be good men and strict discipline there,' Ruben said, but when he saw the anxiety in Isak's face he wished he hadn't.

'Isak,' he went on, putting his arm round the boy. 'It'll go well. You've always been good with your hands. And if it's too hard for you, we've still got Chalmers waiting for you. Afterwards, you'll easily get a . . . a less demanding job.'

Isak moved away from him.

'Dad,' he said. 'You don't usually tell lies. You know perfectly well that if I don't manage this, then that's the end.'

The pain in Isak's eyes went through Ruben. Isak noticed, turned on his heel and ran through the office and out to his bicycle.

Mona was on duty at the hospital all weekend. Isak was relieved. He wanted to be alone. He took the boat out and sailed close to the wind between Vinga and Nidingen, taking in no sail despite the fresh wind beyond the skerries. He was searching for a boat with a three-tongued flag with Simon on board. But there was nothing military as far as his eye could see and he didn't dare go into the prohibited waters.

I'm childish, he thought. For the first time I'm alone and must sort it out myself.

Bylund's face appeared on the surface of the water astern, that sniffing nose, those quivering nostrils. The next moment, Isak was heading straight for Böttö lighthouse. The wind was too strong to jib and Erik would have shouted at him, but he managed to hold his course and by the time he got the boat up into the wind again he thought he would sort it all out even if Egon Bergman was like Bylund.

The world was perfectly real to him and the salt water pouring down his face was only sea water, he thought as he sailed towards Långedrag and moored. He cleaned every nook and cranny of the boat so that no one could complain that things were not shipshape, neat and tidy.

When he got back he rang Mona at the hospital. Yes, he was fine. No, he wasn't nervous. They had already eaten at home, but Karin heated up some meat balls. He wolfed them down, went to bed early and slept all night.

Chapter 25

At half past five the next morning Erik woke Isak and Karin made sandwiches. He drank half a cup of coffee and packed a rucksack with his lunch, overalls and reinforced shoes. At half past six he put his bicycle among a thousand others at Sänkverket, and at twenty to seven he was one of a hundred sleepy men, packed like sardines in a barge, being hauled over to the great shipyard on the other side of the river. He could feel the quiet friendliness surrounding him, but didn't dare believe it.

The shipyard appeared in front of him, freeing itself from the morning mist. On the right along the shore were the slipways where the ships were built and beyond them the two docks, both enormous, one of them unimaginably huge. Railway tracks, workshops, warehouses, a jungle of larger and smaller buildings swung into view. How would he find his way around.

'I'm to go to Machine Shop Two,' Isak said to the tall man nearest to him.

'Behind the joinery shop and across the tracks,' he was told.

'You can come with me,' another man said. 'I work there. New, are you?'

'Yes. I'm to be apprenticed to Egon Bergman.'

'Onsala,' said the man, who was large and fat.

Isak didn't like to ask what he meant, but he looked into the man's face as the barge reached the quay and met a pair of pale-blue eyes embedded in fat. He seemed inquisitive and slightly amused. 'My name's Tich.'

'Lentov,' Isak replied.

'Turning?'

'Yes.'

Isak trotted after the fat man, past the joinery and into the machine shop, and caught a glimpse of an endless world of steel and machines, before going up some stairs. He was given a locker and changed quickly. As they went down the stairs to the workshop, the hooter went. Over five thousand men started their machines and for a moment Isak thought he would drown in the noise.

'You look almost grown-up,' Egon Bergman, whose nickname was Onsala, said. 'I'm used to little kids.

Fifteen-year-olds who can't control their fingers.' A smile flitted over his face, lighting it up from within.

Onsala was twenty-eight, proud of his skill, famous on the floor for his precision, his ability to maintain even tolerances of thousandths of a millimetre. He was paid extra to train apprentices, but he hadn't chosen the task for the money. He liked teaching and felt a quiet satisfaction when he had a boy with intelligence on his hands as well as that rare talent for being exact.

When Isak was allowed on the lathe after an hour or two, and the machine delivered his first flanges, Onsala knew he was in luck.

Machine Shop Two was an unsurveyable and chaotic landscape. But round Onsala, his lathe and his pupils was a circle of comprehensibility and security.

They had to shout to each other that first morning.

'They're testing a diesel in the assembly shop,' Onsala bawled. 'It'll stop in an hour or so, then we'll be able to speak like human beings.'

Isak nodded.

'What was your name again?'

'Lentov.'

'Lento?'

'No, Lentov,' shouted Isak. He wasn't going to lie about his name, his origins or his wealthy background. 'Tovv,' he shouted so loudly that it cut through the noise to the men on the other lathes.

Someone laughed.

'Hi, Tovv,' someone else shouted.

One of those rare smiles slid across Onsala's face. 'Well, that happened quickly,' he said.

Isak realised that he had a new name. His Jewishness had gone.

A week later, he discovered that being Jewish meant

nothing whatsoever. He understood this, when Onsala told him to go to the moulding shop to fetch a pig-iron.

'It'll be a heavy and filthy job,' he said. 'But you have to learn everything from the bottom, lad.'

'Ask for the Jew,' he called after Isak as he ran off.

Isak managed not to stop but he was pleased he had his back to Onsala.

In the moulding shop was a very tall man with a pink complexion and chalk-white hair above a young face. An albino, thought Isak, like that priest at prayers at school. 'I was told to ask for the Jew,' he said, keeping his voice steady.

'Then you've come to the right place. That's me,' the man acknowledged with a huge grin.

Isak laughed and remembered Tich, the fat giant who had shown him the way on his first day.

Onsala was not much of a one for praise and expressed his satisfaction in grunts. He often grunted at Isak. Gradually terror of defeat began to lose its grip on Isak. It was still inside him and made itself felt occasionally, but in the daytime there was little room for it and at night he slept heavily, exhausted.

Two evenings a week he went to see Maria. They appeared to be getting nowhere, but he was beginning to enjoy their talks.

'You'll be a good turner,' Onsala told him after a fortnight. 'I hope you'll stay.'

I'm going to work here all my life, Isak thought. Then he remembered. 'Dad wants me to go to Chalmers.'

'You need school qualifications for that.'

Isak knew he should tell the truth, that he had been to school. But he was glad he had said nothing when Onsala continued, 'God, lad, I would have liked to have gone there. But you know, there wasn't any money, and now it's too late. If you get the chance, take it. Chalmers . . .'

And there was a world of longing in his voice. Isak felt ashamed.

Otherwise conversation proved to be no problem. As in Karin's kitchen and Erik's yard, there were lively and occasionally heated political discussions, but here the borderline between social democrats and communists was more distinct.

Isak joined the union. He bought books and, to Ruben's surprise, read them.

He also began to understand the importance of money. This started in the lathe shop. In his beginner's eagerness, he found it hard not to work too fast. But knowledge of his fellow workers' negotiated rates of pay was just as important as skill and he soon learned to keep to a more reasonable pace. He knew that there would be a row if the piece rate was poor. But the bosses were reasonably fair and although there were one or two unpopular overseers in dark suits and ties, most of them were respected by the men.

No mistakes were made in the great boring mill where they made cylinder linings a metre and a half in diameter. But at the older lathes, where nuts and bolts were made of every size, disasters could occur.

One morning, Eskilsson wrecked a whole consignment and Isak was astonished by his disappointment and anger that found an outlet in ferocious swearing. But when he was told that Helge Eskilsson had to pay for the damage himself he understood it better. For Helge had four kids at home and a big mortgage on a recently purchased house in Torslanda.

He was walking across the tracks to Onsala with a new drawing one morning when he was stopped by a young man not much older than himself. 'Hi there, aren't you Isak Lentov?'

Isak didn't recognise him. But the man, who worked

for the transport foreman, walked with Isak to the turning shop and told him and Onsala that they had met on national service. He had driven the ambulance when Isak had broken his arm and gone to hospital.

There were a lot of men in the hut at the midday break.

'Then you've done your military service, have you, Tovv?' Onsala asked.

Isak thought the world had stopped, time had ceased, and he remembered Karin's words, *don't lie, don't lie.* 'No,' he said. 'I was called up, but then I was ill.'

'I suppose they're waiting to get their claws into you again, now you're better?'

'No, I was exempted.'

'What was wrong with you?' Onsala sounded more worried than suspicious.

He likes me, Isak realised.

Suddenly and quite voluntarily, Isak found himself telling the whole story, the whole appalling tale: 'You see,' he began. 'I'm Jewish. I grew up in Berlin . . .'

Everyone in the hut fell silent and by the time Isak got to the end, about how he had recognised the Nazi in Bylund and how he had had a nervous breakdown, you could have heard a pin drop.

The silence frightened Isak. Oh God, he thought, Israel's God. Why do I talk so much?

Then he felt it in the air, could experience the compassion which hung, warm and strong, between the walls of the hut.

Tich spoke. 'Damn it, you shall have my sponge cake.'

Usually everyone laughed at Tich, about his packed lunch and his cakes, but this time nobody smiled. It was almost as if they thought that Tich had said and done the only thing possible.

When the hooter went, some of them came over and

shook Isak by the hand. And when they went back to the machine shop, something even more unusual occurred: Onsala put his arm round his best apprentice.

That afternoon at Maria's, Izak told her what had happened and how he had told his friends everything.

She was pleased. 'Good, Isak, that's one step forward.'

'They were so bloody nice.'

'I can see that. People are often nice when you meet them singly. But in groups, they can be much worse, much more afraid.'

'Not in the machine shop.'

'What comes next?' she asked. 'I mean in the promotion stakes?'

'You don't really become anything more than a skilled turner. But that's fine and has great prestige.'

'So they don't compete?'

'No.' Isak told her about the rates of pay and the unwritten laws around them.

When his session was almost over, Isak remembered his strange thought about not being able to trust women. 'It was the day I got the job,' he said. 'I know it's idiotic, but it's been like a thorn in my flesh, this idea that all women are unreliable.'

'What did you think of next?'

'I thought about Karin and Mona, but they're as loyal as rocks.'

'But there has been another woman in your life, before Karin, hasn't there, Isak?'

A wave of heat raced through him and his face flared. 'Mamma . . . But I never think about her.'

'I know that,' Maria said. 'But she's there in your memories.'

'No! I remember nothing.'

Maria leaned over her desk and looked him straight in

the eye. 'Why did your grandfather beat you? Why were you running away that day in Berlin?'

Isak did not turn away. He has asked this himself, Maria thought.

'I don't remember.'

'Something happened to you when you were with your grandparents, often, I suspect. Your terror of madness was there before the assault, I'm sure of that. You realise we have to tackle this together?'

'The thing is, I simply can't remember.'

'Do you ever go to see your mother?'

'No. Mona does, sometimes, and she wants me to go with her.'

'I think you should, Isak.'

Isak said that he didn't want to go.

'You dare not,' Maria stated.

'That's true. It's bad enough with Iza, and I have to see her sometimes.'

'Why?'

'Hasn't Ruben told you that they're like twins, she and my mother?'

'Perhaps he's never seen it.'

'Oh, yes, he has,' said Isak. 'But Dad's the kind of person who thinks everything's his fault. Simon's the same. Sometimes I think he's crazier than I am.'

'Maybe you're right there.' Maria smiled. 'But this is about you. Have you ever considered that your mother can't do you any harm any longer? That she's just a confused old woman, and you are strong and adult?'

Isak started to fumble for a handkerchief. He hadn't got one so he borrowed one from Maria who said nothing, not a word of consolation.

'I'll go with Mona to see my mother,' Isak told Maria as they parted.

'Good. Then come back to me.'
'I promise.'

Isak and Mona said nothing to Ruben or Karin, just slipped away early on Sunday morning and, on trams and buses, went all the way out to the Lillhagen mental hospital in Hisingen.

Isak looked straight ahead as they walked down the corridors, unwilling to see any lunatics. Olga had a room of her own and was perfumed and smart, bracelets tinkling as always as she sat there playing with her dolls. She was dressing them and undressing them.

She recognised neither of them, but Isak was prepared for that. Mona had told him she knew Ruben only in glimpses.

Mona thought Isak would feel pity and tenderness when he saw his mother, and he was relying on Maria's assurance that he would no longer feel fear. But when he met Olga's flickering eyes, he was seized with a rage that took possession of his whole being. 'You bloody witch,' he shouted.

Olga didn't understand the words, but she must have felt the tension in the air for she turned her attention to the doll. Pulling it roughly, she crooned, '*Mein süsser, süsser Knabe.*'

Her mouth was smiling, but she whimpered as she pulled the doll's hair and pinched it as she prattled in her strange voice.

Isak knew he had to get out. He ran through the doorway and into the corridor.

'Wait for me in the grounds. I'll be with you soon.' Mona called.

He sat down on the grass under a tree, aware of the power of his anger. God, he was a shit to behave like that! What would Mona think and what would Ruben say if he ever found out. And as for Karin . . .

But Mona was neither angry nor reproachful. 'We must go straight to Maria,' she said.

Maria was at home, thank goodness. For Isak was heading back into an unreal world as his terror began to take hold and control his mind. Mona related briefly what had happened.

Maria took Isak into her room. 'At last,' she said. 'We're on our way.'

Step by step, holding his gaze in such a grip that he couldn't look away, she took him back to Berlin and his early childhood. Isak could feel her strength and knew he was going to die.

'I recognised her,' he cried. 'I recognised her face, her look, the way her nostrils quivered. She's like Bylund.'

'Yes.'

'I was so angry I went mad. I raced around the apartment screaming, and she couldn't get me to be quiet. She pulled my hair and pinched me and complained, but all the time she was pleased. And then . . .'

'Then?'

'Then I disappeared. I disappeared just as I did in the army. And then . . .'

'Then?'

'Then Grandfather came home and beat me.'

'Your mother was horrid,' said Maria.

'Yes!' He shouted it out, for then it came back again, that great anger that made everything real. He wanted to gouge out her eyes, and cut off her breasts, and stick a pole up her cunt.

'Good, Isak. Just give it to her,' Maria encouraged him.

The pain was intense, but it could be borne and the world seemed perfectly clear.

Isak had begun to see again, at last.

Part Three

Chapter 26

The heat was quivering between the skerries. The men guarding the long coast in this land of darkness, who usually loved the sun, had learned to fear it. They had always sought every ray of light, but now they huddled like flies on a flypaper in the shade of a sail they had slung between themselves and the heat.

Every morning the sun rose and by midday, helped by the mirror of the sea, it increased in strength. It beat down on them, heating up the rocks and jetties so that they burned their feet. There was not a tree, nor a blade of grass to rest their eyes upon.

It was August and there was a heatwave.

'The whole damned Kattegat will boil soon,' the soldiers said. The sea was seething with jellyfish, so they had to clear the bay of slimy monsters for a quick dip, a minute-long cool. But the sea salt made their bodies smart, increasing their pain. The day they shared their last tin of Nivea, two red-haired men were taken ashore to the sick bay.

It was easier for Simon than for the others. He turned dark brown and leathery.

'You look like some bloody desert sheik,' a soldier said one evening, and Simon laughed, his teeth dazzling white. He was thinking about his distant ancestors who had wandered in the Sinai Desert and the leathery skins they developed to survive under a sun even more merciless than this one.

To the surprise of his friends, he read the Bible in the evenings and this gave him an undeserved reputation for being religious. Then a parcel from Ruben had arrived containing Bendixon's *History of Israel* in two volumes. So Simon spent his evenings with Isaiah and Jeremiah, Ezra and Nehemiah in a fruitless attempt to distinguish between myth and history.

But his dreams were of trees, mysterious earthly giants, their tops providing protection and shade. Tall aspens drew lacy patterns against the sky, ancient oaks presented strength and wisdom, and wide-skirted spruces invited rest in bird song and the soughing of forests.

When he was woken by the shrieking gulls and curses from his companions, and saw the sun begin its journey across the sky, he thought that as soon as he got some leave he would walk in the forest by the long lake where Inga's smallholding was wedged on a ledge in the hillside.

The night the thunderstorm came, they ran naked out of their huts on to the smooth rocks and stood letting the rain wash their skin, hair, mouths and eyes, and slake their thirst. They stayed, relishing the downpour until they grew cold.

'Christ how marvellous!' one man said. 'Never again will I complain about the cold and the dark.'

Simon had been on leave once before, to a feast when Karin had cooked all his favourites dishes. He was to have come on the Saturday morning, but had been able to get away on a boat heading for Nya Varvet on the Friday afternoon. He found Karin alone in the kitchen with a bowl of green peas on her lap. He went to her and laid his head on her apron, breathing her scent and feeling her hands running over the back of his neck.

This business of regressing had its delights after all, Simon thought. At least for a while. Then they looked at each other and he saw that a great deal had changed, that she was smaller than he remembered, older and more worn. He was filled with a great tenderness, an almost painful need to look after her and please her. My bird of sorrow, he thought. My good bird of sorrow.

Karin saw the boy in front of her was now an adult, that there was a hardness and a strength in him that made her feel shy. He is man, she realised, and there was alienation and sorrow in the thought. Then she pulled herself together and told herself not to be silly. Wasn't this what she had tried so hard to achieve — that Simon should become grown-up and independent?

The weekend after the thunderstorm, Simon obeyed his dreams about the trees and phoned Karin from the quay. 'Mum, I thought I'd go and see Inga.'

He could hear Karin's fear from the silence that followed. Then her voice came back with her usual confidence. 'Do that, Simon dear.'

'I'm getting a lift with a guy who lives in that direction whose brother's going to meet him by car.'

'That's good.' Another silence. 'Shall I phone and warn her?'

'Yes, perhaps you'd better,' Simon said.

They dropped him off beyond the village store where the forest track to the lake came out on the road. 'Can you find your way?' they asked.

''Course.'

'We'll pick you up about five on Sunday.'

'Great. 'Bye then, and thanks.'

Simon walked beneath the leafy foliage. The tall trees calmed him. Be, he told himself. Don't do.

He saw the trees had been scorched by the heat. Some leaves had already fallen and glowed like fairy gold in the moss. The lengthy preparation for winter had begun and the trees were shutting off their circulation systems as they prepared for their long sleep.

He came to a glade, a clearing in the forest where the woodcutters had spared an oak out of respect for its stature and age. It was hot. Simon took off his jacket, rolled it up into a pillow and lay gazing up into the tree, the top still dark green and impenetrable.

He slept for a while in its shade before going on towards the lake and the house where Inga was waiting for him.

She had had time to clean and everything was neat and tidy. She turned bright red when he appeared on the edge of the forest. 'You'd like some coffee, wouldn't you?' she asked.

All through his childhood Inga had distanced herself from Simon, afraid, glancing out of the corner of her eye at the quicksilver little boy. But when Karin and Erik had been to see her the previous spring and told her that Simon now knew who she was, she had torn all that down, just as you remove boarding when it no longer provides shelter from the wind.

She was grateful for the months between then and now. She had needed the time to think about their meeting, to imagine what would happen next. But she hadn't realised that he would be so adult, so handsome, so like . . .

Over coffee, they talked about the weather, the heatwave and the rain that had come too late. She had got rid of the cows, she told him, and got a job in the school, in the kitchen.

'That's a long way to walk,' said Simon.

'Yes, but I can manage.' She cycled until the snow came and then she took the kick-sled. They snow-ploughed the road nowadays.

Simon saw she was pleased to have the job and enjoyed the people she met, and the company. Like

Karin, there was no bitterness in her, although she possessed more of a sense of wonder.

It started to cloud over and the wind brought with it a touch of autumn chill, so they went in.

'The leaves are turning,' Inga said. 'Did you notice?'

'Yes.' Simon remembered the fairy gold in the moss and smiled his new white smile. When she drew in a sharp breath, he gathered up his courage. 'Am I like him?' he asked.

'Heavens, yes,' said Inga. 'If he were standing there beside you, I'd find it hard to tell you both apart.'

But perhaps that wasn't completely true. Simon was sturdier, taller, had more strength and was less of a dreamer. There was tension in the air, yet Inga was relieved that he had dared to say what he had come to talk about.

She sought an outlet for her unease by busying herself, splitting kindling and lighting the kitchen stove. 'It's cold, don't you think? I've some dough rising, so the heat from the stove'll be just right.'

Simon wasn't cold. He looked around the cottage as if seeing it for the first time, sensing the security and comfort to be found below the low ceilings of old houses. It's beautiful here, he thought, with the light peeping through the mullioned windows and dancing on the rag rugs on the wide floorboards.

Inga lit the tiled stove in the front room too. It was now so hot that Simon had to take off his jacket. He sat in the rocking chair in his shirt-sleeves.

'Did he come in here?' he asked.

'Oh no,' Inga said. 'Father and Mother were both dying in this room. We never came here. We met by the stream. It was such a warm and lovely spring.'

As she said this, her calm returned and she sat down at the table. Words started to flow, and it was as if she had thought about it all through the summer she had been waiting for Simon. Then at last she came to their last evening.

'I realised he was saying goodbye as his violin was so sad. So I wasn't really surprised when he never came back.' The melancholy in her voice was like a thin blue note.

'Weren't you sad?'

'I was,' she said. 'But then I'd known all the time, you see. We were not created for each other. He was too grand for me.'

Simon noticed how she bowed her head to the yoke as peasant women had always done, humble and grateful for the little they were given.

'He wasn't really of this world,' Inga continued. 'Afterwards, I almost believed I'd dreamed it all. But then you began to make yourself felt.'

'Was it some time before you realised you were pregnant?'

'Yes. I didn't dare think about it. I was heavy in November when Karin came, and I suppose I really only took it in when she told me.'

You're with child, Inga, Karin had exclaimed. Even today, Inga could feel her terrible fear as she was forced to confront the shame of the child growing inside her.

I was denied, Simon thought. He could remember it from the dreams of his childhood. Denied, then abandoned between the tiled walls of the hospital far away from the trees, the soughing in the tree-tops and the light over the lake.

'I had a letter afterwards,' Inga said.

'I know, but Erik made you burn it during the war.'

'Erik couldn't make me.' Her voice was as firm as the ground she stood on. 'He phoned in the spring of 1940, sounding quite hysterical. I thought to myself that if the

Germans came I would have plenty of time to hide the letter in the crack in the oak behind the barn. But the Germans didn't come. So it's still in the bureau where it's always been.'

Simon's heart thumped painfully as she got out a key, unlocked the old-fashioned desk, pulled out a drawer and took out a brass container with a lid. 'I put the letter in this when I thought I might have to hide it in the oak.'

Inga couldn't get the lid off so they found a knife to prise it open. German stamps, postmarked 4 March 1929, Berlin. Opened, never read.

'I didn't know the language. We couldn't speak to each other.'

Why is life so incomprehensible, so unfathomably sad, Simon wondered?

'I've got the attic room ready for you, and made the bed,' Inga told him.

What a lot she had done since Karin had phoned, Simon thought. She had cleaned the place, ironed her best blue dress, kneaded the dough for bread and made the bed in the attic.

'Go on up,' she urged. 'You should be alone when you read it. You can read German, can't you?'

'Yes.'

He went up the creaking stairs and lay flat out on the crocheted bedspread, the letter on his stomach. His mouth was dry, so he went down again for a glass of water and stood watching Inga putting the risen dough into the oven. 'You haven't got a beer, have you?'

'No,' Inga said. 'I didn't have time to go to the shop, and I hadn't really thought of you being a man and wanting beer.'

They laughed. Inga found some fruit juice, blackcurrant from this year's crop. So Simon had the taste of

221

childhood in his mouth and the smell of freshly baking bread in his nose as he plucked up his courage and read the letter in his bedroom.

It was a love letter, full of romantic words. 'Siren of the woods, my siren of the woods,' he had called her. He hoped to come back in the autumn and had applied for the job at the college. But he had to know if she was expecting him, that she was longing for him as much as he was for her. Would she write, send some sign of life? A thousand kisses, Simon Haberman, and an address in Berlin.

Disappointment flooded over Simon as he read. What had he expected, what had he hoped for? The Jewish violinist could never have known that his love had borne fruit, that he had had a son.

He covered his face with the pillow and wept.

When he went over to the washstand to wash his face a little later, he found the water in the can was yellow and stale. She had put the room in order a long time ago, he realised. She had been expecting him for ages.

Inga was in the kitchen when he came down. Her cheeks were glowing, but she was pale, very pale. He sat down at the table again and began to translate the letter for her.

'"Siren of the woods . . ." I'm not sure, but I think it's siren of the woods.' Then Haberman's feelings of longing, love, kisses, and begging for a reply.

'But why didn't he come?' Inga's voice was scarcely audible. Her hands covered her face, but Simon could see her shoulders shaking.

'He was waiting for a reply.'

'But he knew I wouldn't understand what he wrote.'

'Perhaps he thought you'd find someone to translate it for you.' Simon's voice was bitter as he went on reading,

'"Write to me, give me a sign of life so that I know you exist, that you're not just a wild and beautiful dream."'

'Heavens,' Inga said. 'Who would I have gone to? I could tell no one. The shame, Simon. I would have died of shame.'

'Because of me?'

'Yes.' When Simon rose and left the cottage, she ran after him. 'You don't understand, Simon,' she cried. 'You'll never understand what it was like in those days.'

He stopped and turned round. 'I don't suppose I will.'

'Things were so good for you. So good for you with Erik and Karin.'

Karin, he thought with wild fury. Karin could have had the letter translated, could have written to Berlin and told him about the child. But he knew she had never wanted to, that she wanted to leave the letter unread while she looked after her baby and tried to think as little as possible about the father of the little boy with those dark eyes.

'I'm going to walk in the forest for a while. I'll be back for dinner.'

His voice was rougher than he had intended, still charged with anger not directed at Inga, but at Karin. He tried to smile to hide it, but Inga had already turned back to the cottage.

He climbed up the hill and sat gazing over the lake, now a dull blue, in perfect harmony with his melancholy. But the trees were silent and he knew their peace was not for him. On the way back, he thought that if Haberman had meant what he said in his letter, he could have asked one of the many Swedes in 1920s Berlin to translate it for Inga.

Inga was waiting with meat soup, which she thought he might like, freshly baked bread and beer. She had cycled to the store and bought a few bottles.

Simon gulped it down, but it was only Pilsner and gave him no relief.

Neither of them slept much that night.

The next morning he told her over coffee that she should keep the letter. 'It's to you. I'll write a translation on the back.'

But she said she too had been thinking about it all night. 'I know you'll laugh. But I want to say that I've come to believe that all this happened for your sake, so that you could be born.'

She's crazy, thought Simon, but he didn't laugh.

'I like to think you chose us. We two, him and me, we were so incompatible. If he could have talked to me and found out what a simple person I was, he would never have fallen in love with me, nor even looked at me. We were from different worlds, Simon.'

Perhaps she's right, Simon thought. They could never have become a family. Then his eyes hardened and he thought that if she had married him, he might have been saved from Hitler and the concentration camps.

But he said nothing. He remembered the man in his dream, the man who had gone down the hill with his violin towards death. He had wanted to die.

'You would've known he didn't really belong on earth if you'd heard him playing,' Inga said as if she'd been listening to his thoughts. 'There were no tunes, Simon, not the kind of fiddler's squeals we used to dance around to. It was music sent from heaven. I'd no idea a violin could sound like that.'

'Do you know what he played?'

'I once heard the music on the radio and I imagined he was there, playing, because it was an orchestra from Berlin. The person who'd written the music was from Finland, but I've forgotten the name now.'

'Sibelius?'

'That was it,' she said. And Simon would have given anything in the world to have a violin so that she could hear the wild yearning music by Sibelius.

But he had no violin, and he couldn't even play an instrument.

Simon gave Inga a hug before he left, then stopped at the edge of the forest and waved. As he ran along the forest track so as not to miss his lift to the main road, he was thinking that what Inga had told him was more comforting than anything else he had heard.

'I think it was for your sake all this happened,' she had said. 'You wanted to come into the world. You chose us.'

Perhaps I'm going nuts, he thought. It was such a crazy, incredible, foolish idea. But it comforted him.

He had a moment at the jetty while he was waiting for the boat to pick him up so he phoned Ruben. 'His name's Simon Haberman,' he said. 'And the address is in Berlin. Can you look into it, Uncle Ruben?'

'Of course. I'll let you know.'

I know it's pointless, that he went to the gas chambers, Simon said to himself. All the same, you have to give what is rational a chance.

Jewish congregations all over the world were constructing a network between the dead and the survivors, and it only took Ruben a week to find the information. Simon Haberman, violinist with the Berlin Philharmonic Orchestra, had been deported with his sister in November 1942 and sent to Auschwitz in May 1944. The sister had died earlier from her privations. He was unmarried and there were no living relatives.

Simon was sixteen when he had died, Ruben thought. For sixteen years the man could have known he had a son in Sweden. Undeniably he had had every right to know. For the first time, Ruben felt a grudge against Karin for she had been a part of that injustice.

There was a letter waiting for Simon when he got back to camp, postmarked Stockholm. He knew it was from Iza. She enclosed a photograph. She was slim, lovely, made up like a film star and she looked at him with eyes burning with hunger.

'Wow, what a bird!' said the boys. 'Where the hell have you been keeping her?'

'In Stockholm.' Simon could see his stock going up in their estimation.

'Going to see her?'

'She wants me to.'

'Getting engaged to her?'

Simon stared at the man who had asked the question. 'I sincerely hope not,' he answered bluntly.

There was much head-shaking.

Bengtsson gave him an embarrassed grin. 'If you escape, perhaps you'd let me know? I'd be glad to step into your shoes.'

Chapter 27

Simon was standing by Ruben's bookcase reading about spiders in his 1935 encyclopaedia.

> ... distinguished by an enlarged, usually undivided
> rear abdomen, connected like a stalk to the thorax and
> equipped with four or six poison glands ... the four
> pairs of legs have comb-like toothed claws (fig.2) on
> the tips of which are the ducts for the poison glands

. . . the main part of the nervous system consists of the brain . . . sexual organs are in pairs, the ducts merging into a passage flowing out at the base of the abdomen . . .

He looked at figure two and shuddered. 'Nocturnal,' he read. 'Predators. Poison of unknown composition. Those indigenous to Sweden are harmless.' But there was a European species, the tarantula, whose bite could injure humans, although the effect of the poison was limited to the immediate area round the bite.

Simon was waiting for Isak, who had taken his driving test and was to drive him back to the barracks in Ruben's car. It was autumn, yellow leaves were swirling off the trees and the light from the sea was bright and crystal clear.

Most of the boys were on harvest leave or having a few extra days for 'domestic reasons'. Simon had gone to Captain Sjövall and stood to attention but there was a slight jokiness over the ritual as he applied for three days' extra holiday.

'What's the Larsson family up to now?' Sjövall asked.

'I have a girl in Stockholm,' Simon told him.

'That won't do.'

'She's ill,' Simon said. It was true in a way.

Sick fiancée, Sjövall wrote and that was that.

Simon said nothing at home and by Wednesday morning was on the express to Stockholm, trying to remember what he had read about spiders.

It's Isak's fault, he thought, remembering the quarrel they'd had in the car when Simon had said almost in passing that he was going to see Iza in Stockholm next weekend.

Isak had been upset and told Simon loudly that he was heading straight for perdition with his eyes wide open.

Simon had been frightened by his outburst and by the speed they were going for, within a few minutes, Isak had Ruben's old Chevrolet tearing along so fast that Simon had shouted at him to calm down for God's sake before he killed them both.

Isak had braked and said nothing more. They had driven into the parking lot in front of the barracks at normal speed with ten minutes to spare. He had then told Simon about Olga, and the conclusion he and Maria had come to. 'You're free to choose if you want the kind of life Ruben has with a mad wife. He had no peace from her until she went to hospital. But you've damned well no right to bring children into the world with a mother of the kind Iza would be.'

He had sounded almost tearful and Simon had sat as if struck by lightning. 'For Christ's sake, I'm not marrying her, am I?'

'If she can get you to give her a kid, she will. Her chances of marrying are few because she frightens the life out of any normal man. If she gets her claws into you she'll never let you go.'

'Claws in which are the ducts of the poison glands,' Simon said aloud.

'Are you going mad as well? Perhaps you should talk to Maria. Maybe she'd get you some sick leave.'

Simon attempted to laugh. 'I'll think about . . . everything you've said. And it was great you wanted to tell me about your mother.' He had realised what it had cost Isak.

Now he was on the train trying to conjure up his old image of Iza as an evil but real person. He felt childish, like someone playing with emotions.

Isak is more adult than I am, he thought as the train stopped at Skövde. For a moment, he considered getting off and waiting for the next train back. But he stayed where he was. I must conquer her, he decided. At least, I must conquer my image of her, and he was so ashamed of his desire that he flushed. A girl opposite him looked surprised, so Simon went to the lavatory to wash his hands, then on to the restaurant car for some coffee. He stayed there, watching the landscape rushing past, being swallowed up by the train.

Iza met him at the Central Station in Stockholm and was the same, the same as ever. The famous psychoanalyst in Switzerland had not touched her. She talked of the city as if she owned it. 'Göteborg's a dump in comparison,' she said. As he stood in her window looking out over the city, Simon had to admit it was magnificent.

Ruben had bought her an apartment on the heights of Södermalm. The sun was shining on Strömmen's waters, the palace and the thousand roofs, although it was well into October. Simon thought how strange it was that no one in Göteborg ever talked about Sweden's capital, or acknowledged that it was beautiful. Although he'd never been here before he reckoned he knew it quite well from Strindberg, Söderberg and several hundred other books he'd read. Most of all he wanted to go on a voyage of discovery, walk along Drottninggatan up to Blå Tornet, stroll along Strandvagen, take the ferry to Djurgården and see those famous oak trees.

'Let's make love now,' Iza said.

Simon looked into her face and thought about spiders. *Come into my parlour said the spider to the fly.* 'I'm hungry,' he said instead. 'Have you any food in the kitchen?'

Iza was furious, stamped her foot and swore. 'Here I am, having waited for months for my lover and all you want is food,' she cried.

But Simon had opened the refrigerator and found a tin of corned beef and a few slices of stale bread. 'Come on.

Let's eat.' He paused. 'And since when did I become your lover?'

Iza burst into tears and Simon found to his surprise that he was quite unmoved.

She noticed his coldness and stopped crying abruptly. 'I've bought a bottle of wine,' she told him.

They ate and drank, quite like old friends until Iza said in her feverish voice, 'So you haven't come to make love to me, then?'

'No. I've come to see the place and find out how things are for you.'

'You're joking?'

'Maybe.'

'How cruel you are,' she said, her eyes narrowing with expectation, her mouth wet with desire.

Simon finished his wine and they went to bed. He was randy after his months in the islands and had plenty to offer her. But Iza didn't want tenderness, just endurance and hard hands.

He couldn't satisfy her. She wanted him to hit her. He thought about the spider's ducts merging into its abdomen, and all he could manage were a few slaps. Wild with frustration she fetched a whip from the wardrobe and Simon lost his erection.

Feeling sick, he went into her bathroom and threw up, blaming the tinned stuff they'd eaten. He could feel his body contracting with loathing. After his stomach had emptied itself of its contents he washed, pulled on his trousers and went back to her.

Iza was lying on her back, staring at the ceiling. 'You're nothing but a little shit, Simon Larsson,' she said.

You may be right, Simon thought, but said nothing because her despair was obvious. He crept back into her bed and lay close to her. Her body caught fire again and soon they were both burning with desire.

They stuck it out for three days, love-hating, weeping, sleeping for a little, getting up occasionally to eat. He went down to the dairy for bread and butter, and she made no attempt to pay for it. He reckoned his money would soon run out.

Iza sucked his blood, cracked his bones, and he let it happen, as if he was paying off an old debt. She hated him for that. She humiliated him, hitting him, tormenting him, and he complied with everything. She screamed out her contempt.

As dusk fell on the city on Saturday afternoon, he fell asleep, away from his and her despair.

She woke him with the whip. 'Hit me,' she shouted.

But he couldn't. He got out of bed and suddenly was free of them: Karin and Inga, Mrs Ågren and Dolly. He had confronted them all and knew they couldn't be conquered.

Just as on the first day, Iza lay in bed. 'Go away,' she said, eyes vacant on the ceiling. 'Go away now. I never want to see you again.'

Simon showered, put on his uniform and walked out into the cold, dark and alien city. He had five kronor, seventy-five öre in his pocket. He knew that, because he had counted it on his last trip to the dairy. Not enough for a hotel room.

He had a return ticket though, so could make his way to the Central Station and take the first train back to Göteborg. But as he walked down Katarinaberget, he decided take a look at Stockholm after all, at least the old part, Gamla Stan. There was no frost yet, so he could probably walk the streets for one night. He crossed Slussen, walked along Skeppsbron and turned into the narrow alleys, icy winds whistling between the tired old buildings. He was cold, mindlessly cold, as he stood there in Stortorget trying to feel the wing beats of history.

I've no heart any longer, he thought, just a pump in there taking the blood round, keeping me alive. His feet took him towards Kornhamnstorg, where the cafés looked cheaper. He stood outside one, reading the menu in the window and calculating that he could afford two cheese sandwiches and hot cocoa for two kronor, twenty öre.

'Hey, my lad, you look pale,' the waitress called in a singing north-country voice, and Simon saw she looked like Mona, but older and even more motherly. He tried to smile, though not very successfully. The important thing was to be allowed to stay in the warmth for a few hours.

He took small mouthfuls of his sandwiches, sipped his cocoa and swallowed cautiously. Slowly, the warmth spread from his stomach down to his feet, where it turned round and made the long journey up to his head.

Once his brain began functioning again, the relief he had felt as he left Iza's bedroom vanished. God in heaven, what a bastard he was! For years he had fantasised about Iza, about how the evil in her would make him real. He would use her to participate in her essence, to make it comprehensible.

He remembered Mrs Ågren; how in his childhood he had been attracted to her and hated her; how he had wanted to cut off her breasts and gouge out her eyes. But only in his imagination. Always only in his imagination.

Simon's stomach turned over again. If he didn't relax a little he wouldn't be able to keep his food down.

Bylund. He and Bylund were really rather alike, he thought, but the sergeant was more honest. No, he wouldn't weep as the café was filling up with people. He would pay soon, and get up and go.

Bylund would have coped. Bylund with his quivering

nostrils would have been able to give Iza what she wanted. He could move from fantasy into action.

The memory that he had almost killed Bylund gave Simon a little strength. He managed to swallow the next mouthful of his sandwich and felt it settling in his stomach.

He tried to remember how his attraction to Iza had begun. He had been in the sanatorium, looking at this fat and ugly girl, and he had thought she was the first person he had met who was ruthlessly honest in everything she said and did. He recalled staring at the numbers on her arm and how time had stopped. He had thought at the time that she possessed an actuality like no one else.

I'll try to write to her, he decided. But what should he put in the letter?

Maybe I was wrong, he reflected. Perhaps it is the decent people who are palpable. Perhaps reality is to know you can trust each other. Like Karin and Erik. Like Ruben and Inga. Yes, she too knew what it was like to suffer.

But not that dreary musician who made love for a few weeks in the forest and then vanished, only to return a year later with a silly letter. A thousand kisses. God Almighty, how disgusting!

Simon gave a lot of thought to his dream about the fiddler heading towards his own destruction. Did he have the same attraction to evil as he did? Perhaps I have it in my genes, he thought. Inherited, like the music.

And death? I can walk to the station, slip out on to some track and throw myself in front of an express train. But he knew he wouldn't do it because of Karin.

He didn't want to die. The only thing he wanted to do was to go home to his mother, put his head in her lap and tell her everything. But he couldn't. He was alone in Stockholm.

For the first time, Simon realised he was now an adult and the thought was unbearable.

Chapter 28

'You're looking pretty awful.'

A man was sitting opposite him at the table, a middle-aged man with friendly, slightly slanting brown eyes. 'You ought to get some proper food inside you.'

'No money.'

'I can get you a plate of soup?'

The waitress had been keeping an eye on Simon and now rushed to bring him some hot soup.

Simon ate it gratefully, thinking that perhaps he'd met this man before.

'Name's Andersson.'

'Larsson.'

They shook hands, the man's broad, warm and dry.

'Have you deserted?'

'No, no. I'm due back in Göteborg. Been on leave.'

'And having a fling around Stockholm, I suppose?'

'Mm.' Simon grimaced, though he had to smile at the glint in those brown eyes. 'I've got a return ticket.'

'You can come with me if you like. I'm taking my truck to Göteborg tonight.'

Simon considered this was more than he deserved. 'My dad had a truck for years,' he said. 'Maybe that's why I recognise you?'

'You probably saw me when you were a child,' Andersson agreed. He paid for the sandwiches and the soup, and ordered ten more cheese sandwiches – no, five cheese and five with liver pâté, please.

'We'll need them.' He hauled two thermos flasks out of his bag and had them filled with coffee. 'Let's go, then.'

They walked up the hill towards the Slussen, turned off towards Södra Station where Andersson's truck was parked, loaded and ready. It was almost midnight, but the streets were still a restless and perpetual stream of people.

'Stockholm's becoming the kind of city that never sleeps at night,' Andersson commented.

Simon nodded. He was only interested in staying as close to this driver as possible. The man was unusually small, a whole head shorter than he was.

The green Dodge was heavily loaded and had tarpaulins roped over the back. There was a half-metre-wide ledge behind the driver's seat containing a thin mattress, a few old blankets and a large and surprisingly soft pillow.

Andersson jerked his stubby thumb at the bunk. 'You need some sleep, Larsson. I'll wake you at dawn somewhere in central Sweden.'

Simon slept like a child, enveloped in dreams, rustling grass and bright safety. He woke at dawn as they left the asphalted trunk route and drove on to a minor road. He lay there remembering where he was, sat up and met those slanting eyes in the rear mirror. He felt cared for and secure.

'Thought we'd take a turn towards Omberg and have some breakfast in the green up on the holy mountain,' Andersson said.

It was no longer green. A mild autumn sun was coming up over the Östagöta plain and the wheels were rustling through a carpet of reddish-yellow leaves.

'Beech,' Andersson said. 'Just fallen.'

Simon looked at the pillar-straight trunks along the

roadside. He had never seen beech trees before. 'What do you mean by the holy mountain?' he asked.

'Omberg,' said Andersson. 'One of the eight holy mountains of the world, mentioned in the secret scripts since time immemorial.'

'You're an Östagöta man.' Simon laughed.

'Maybe so,' Andersson replied and Simon reckoned they were probably even crazier than Göteborgians.

'I've lots of evidence,' Andersson insisted. 'Look over to the east, right out over the plain.'

Simon looked at the windows of red-painted cottages winking sleepily in the sun.

'That's where Queen Omma kept her marsh people once upon a time. They were magical people who knew the mystery of life and celebrated it with feasts every time the moon was on the wane.'

'You made that up,' Simon exclaimed. Then he remembered reading about the Dag moss excavations of a special Neolithic pile dwelling.

'They drove in over a thousand piles,' Andersson continued. 'Then put a floor on them. Not a very big job. Those were the days when giants still walked on earth.'

Simon envisaged the giants yanking Omberg's huge beeches straight out of the ground, snipping off the roots and slicing off branches, then running the trunks between thumb and forefinger.

'We'll take a piss with the old monks,' Andersson said, as the Alvastra ruin loomed up against the dawn light. He stopped the heavy truck, switched off the engine and put on the handbrake. 'You have to take her gently. She's not so young any longer and she has her whims – the truck, I mean.'

They walked towards the ruin and stood with their backs to a monument recalling Oskar II's and Gustaf V's

236

contribution to the history of the monastery. Simon watched the slanting rays of sun creeping through the arches in the nave of the church, and sensed the wing beats of history he had missed last night in the old city.

'Just think,' Andersson said. 'Imagine a long line of monks jogging through Europe, one after another as if on a string. With them they have all kinds of seeds of medicinal plants, cuttings for apple, pear and cherry trees, all to become the ancestors of this old heathen country's cultivations.

'Imagine them making their way through the primaeval forests of Småland, praying to their God every morning that this wilderness would come to an end before nightfall when the wolves start howling among the trees. Then one day they arrive here and begin building a church and a monastery.'

Simon glimpsed the grey Cistercians, the men of St Bernhard, among the ruins of the pillared hall.

'What courage!' Andersson exclaimed. 'All they had to put their hopes in was a letter from an old woman called Ulfhild. She'd killed off several husbands, married Sverker the Elder, and had set up here as queen of her royal demesne.'

'They probably put their trust in God too.'

'Yes. *Thy will be done.* That's the kind of thing called trust and it achieves miracles.'

'Overcomes matter and moves mountains,' Simon agreed.

Andersson laughed and said that quite a number of horses and men had probably been involved when the monks moved the mountain from the limestone quarry in Borghamn to build their church.

They washed in the rainwater in the piscina in the north cross-aisle where the monks had also washed their hands.

'I wonder,' mused Andersson, as he put his truck into first gear and they started crawling up the hill, past the elaborate woodwork of the tourist hotel, and Simon gasped at the view over Lake Vättern, 'I wonder if Ulfhild's guilty conscience was the reason for her bringing the monks here.'

'Politics may have had something to do with it too,' said Simon, memories of school coming back to him.

Andersson smiled, the kind of smile that showed he had more to say but was keeping it to himself.

He's like an old Chinese man, Simon thought.

'Anyhow,' Andersson went on. 'It wasn't long before church bells began to resound over the mountain and frightened away Queen Omma and the giants.'

'Where did they go?'

Simon was enjoying the moment, the man, the mountain, the view and their conversation. A kind of healing was spreading over the torments of the day before.

'They went to another reality where things were just as good.' Andersson's voice was so definite it was as if he could see them.

'That's a relief,' Simon said, and they both laughed.

'Down on your left is Rödgaveln's cave, the entrance to the mountain king's palace.' But Simon had no time to see the precipice before they were going downhill towards Stocklycke meadows, guarded by great oak trees. There were larches too, flaring against the sky. Then the truck swung sharply to the left and started to climb again, up Örnslid out to the precipice where you could see the Västra Väggar.

They stopped.

'Not afraid of heights, are you?' Andersson asked.

Simon shook his head, speechless at the magnificence before him. Just as the Rock of Gibralter meets the

Mediterranean, Omberg met Lake Vättern. The lake was a brilliant turquoise, the sun reflected in the water and enveloping the forested hills in a shimmering blue-green.

'What a light,' said Simon.

'No talking.' Andersson took his lunch box and blankets with him over to the very edge of the precipice.

I'll send him my poem about the sea, thought Simon as they ate the generous sandwiches and drank coffee.

'The water's green because the giants wash their filthy long johns in it,' Andersson said, swallowing his last piece of bread.

Simon exploded with laughter so loud it echoed in Omma's prehistoric fortress several kilometres away.

The sun was warm and Andersson smiled his secretive smile, stretched out on the blanket and pulled his cap over his eyes. 'Isn't it odd', he said, 'that all knowledge from outside has you believe that you're nothing but a fly spot in the universe? But what comes from inside insists that you're everything and have everything.'

Simon hadn't given that any thought. He pondered for a moment before answering. 'I suppose it's some instinct for survival persuading you that you're so damned important.'

Andersson knocked his cap off, propped himself up on his elbow and looked at Simon. 'Close your eyes, lad,' he said. 'Switch off your brain and go inwards, to the hall of the mountain king in your own heart. There you'll hear the truth about whether you were born in vain.'

Then he lay down and went to sleep. Simon did as he was told and closed his eyes. The second movement of the *Symphonie Fantastique* surrounded him and almost immediately he was beyond the images and out in the whiteness.

He was brought back to earth by Andersson putting

his hand gently on his shoulder. 'We must get on, lad. Did you hear the truth?'

'Not hear,' said Simon. 'More like feel.'

'Good, then let's go.'

From Borghamn, they made their way back to the main route, where the wheels quietened on the asphalt and Andersson began to whistle. Simon tensed, but not a note was off as Andersson piped the melody of the second movement of the Berlioz symphony.

It had been a morning of such wonder that he had ceased to be surprised.

Once they had left Jönköping behind them and started climbing into the Småland uplands, Simon told Andersson about Iza. 'Do you see what a bastard I am?'

'That's a bit much,' Andersson commented. 'I'd say you were one of those poor devils who go through life paying off old debts of guilt. You must stop that. There's no guilt except in your imagination.'

'So there's no point in trying to pay it off?'

'You can't. There's no valid currency. If the debt of guilt doesn't exist, there can't be anything to pay it off with.'

'I see what you mean,' Simon said. 'But—'

'If you don't stop, it will take you your whole life before you've paid off the instalments.'

Simon stared out over the mosses in Bottenaryd, thinking so hard his face was screwed up. So his internal burden, the pain of his guilt, didn't exist? 'Then I suppose it must be sorrow,' he said to himself.

'Sorrow', Andersson commented, 'is generally self-pity.'

'Now you're being stupid,' Simon exclaimed. But he had to laugh as well, for he realised suddenly that Andersson was right.

'It's only the moment that exists,' the long-distance truck driver told him.

'But, good God—'

'Exactly. God is the God of the present. He accepts you as he finds you. He doesn't ask what you've been, but what you're like at this moment.' He put the truck into neutral as they drove down the hill at Ulricehamn. 'You're probably also one of those idiots who think they can control life,' he went on. 'That's why you're drawn to what you call evil. You imagine that if you understand how it functions, then you'd be able to defend yourself against it and stop being afraid.'

Simon drew a deep breath. This was true too. It hurt him to admit it, yet it felt good at the same time.

Then Andersson's voice came again, gentler now. 'What are you afraid of, lad?'

'I don't know.' But at that moment he felt the terror moving deep down inside him. So he told Andersson about Inga, about being abandoned before Karin came.

Andersson nodded. 'The body has its memories.'

It was raining as usual as they approached Borås. Andersson wound up the window and after some jiggling managed to get the windscreen wipers going. 'There's something remarkable about infants,' he said. 'About their minds. Have you ever looked into the eyes of a new-born baby?'

No, Simon hadn't.

The rain stopped abruptly in Sjömarken. 'Have you any children?' he asked.

'A whole lot, scattered all over the world.'

'In America?'

'Yes, there and elsewhere.'

'So you've none left here at home?'

'Yes, I've a boy in Sweden,' Andersson said, his mysterious smile sunnier than ever. 'A bloody fine lad.'

According to the clock, six hours had gone by before they bowled down the Källebäck hills into Göteborg. But for Simon the journey had been short and he would have liked to stay in the truck with Andersson for ever.

'Here we are, then,' said the driver, braking in front of the Central Station in Drottningtorget. 'Off you get, now, quickly, as I'm a bit behind time.'

'Can I have your address?' Simon stammered as he stood on the pavement.

But Andersson was closing the door. 'See you some time, lad. We'll meet again, don't you worry.' He was taking his load to the England ship and it had to be stowed on board before five o'clock.

Simon watched the truck disappearing down towards the quays. He felt horribly lonely.

He went into the station, checked his money – still five kronor and seventy-five öre – and picked out some coins. Karin answered the phone.

'Hi, Mum, all's well with me. Is Isak there?'

'He's gone to the cinema with Mona.'

Simon tried to think. 'You all right?'

'Yes, fine.'

'Mum, can you tell Isak I managed all right, that it's over now.'

'What are you talking about, Simon?'

He could hear her ears flapping. 'A joke, Mum. A bet.'

'I see.' Her voice had a touch of acid in it. She didn't believe him.

'Mum!' he shouted. 'My money's running out, but I've never felt so well in all my life, do you hear!'

That she did believe and she laughed, and then they were cut off.

When Simon came into town the next Saturday he spent

hours in the central truck depot, going from driver to driver, asking after Andersson, a little guy with brown eyes who drove a green Dodge.

No, no one knew Andersson.

'Some cowboy, probably,' they said. 'Lots of them around in the trade.'

Chapter 29

Erik took Karin her coffee in bed in the mornings. At first this had embarrassed her, but it soon became a habit, a need, in fact, to be allowed to stay in the warmth of her bed with fresh coffee and the morning's thoughts.

This early spring, Karin's thoughts were mostly of Simon, at present happy and harmonious, despite the fact that the cold weather and winds out on the islands couldn't have been very cheering.

It was snowing one morning in February and Karin had switched off the bedside lamp to be able to see the snowflakes in the early light, when Mona knocked on the door.

Of course, Karin thought. It's Wednesday. Her day off.

'Can I come and sit with you for a while?' Mona crept on to the end of the bed and pulled a blanket round her.

'Would you like some coffee?'

'No, thanks. I've already had breakfast.'

Then, very quickly, as if she wanted to get it over and done with, she said, 'Karin, I'm pregnant.'

Karin felt her heart behaving oddly for a moment. Thoughts raced through her mind, contradictory emotions surged within her – fear of giving birth, tenderness towards Mona, anxiety and, most difficult of all, her old sorrow over her own childlessness. Envy, she thought. I'm envious.

Then she realised that she would have a grandchild. It wasn't strictly true of course, but this joy was the strongest of all. 'Heavens, how wonderful,' she cried, then laughed. 'I ought to have known, with so much love in such a cramped bed and only a little rubber thing to resist it.'

Mona had told her earlier about her cap. Karin had been astonished and had said that she would never have relied on such a thin, slippery rubber thing. Now Mona admitted that she hadn't used it for some time because she wanted a wedding, and children. Most of all, she wanted to leave the nursing school.

'You'll be a grandmother, Karin,' she said.

'Almost like one, anyway.'

They talked about whether Mona would have a boy or a girl.

'A girl,' Mona said. 'I'm almost certain it'll be a girl. We'll call her Malin.'

'Why?' Karin thought it an ugly name, smelling of poverty-stricken old Sweden.

'It was my mother's name,' Mona told her, so there was nothing more to add.

'Does Isak know?'

'Not yet.'

'You must get married.'

'Have you heard the hairdresser is moving into town? I suppose they can't stand the gossip about Dolly any longer. I thought we might be able to rent the three-roomed apartment above the Gustafssons.'

'That'd be good,' Karin said, thinking that life after all was kind. She would have Mona and Isak as neighbours.

And the girl. Karin had already begun to think of the unborn child as a girl.

'Maybe you would ring Gustafsson and ask?'

'Of course.'

Then they came to their concerns about Isak and Chalmers.

'We'll have to live on a student loan,' Mona said. 'Silly, when you think about Ruben. But, all the same, it'll have to work.'

Karin shook her head. Isak had become aware lately of the connection between money and self-esteem. He was careful to pay his way at Karin's and Erik's, and he had told Ruben he would pay Maria's fees. This was quite an expense especially as he realised he would need to go to her for many years. They had sometimes been so hard up that Mona had had to borrow her tram money from Karin.

Karin realised Isak's attitude was good, but she occasionally felt sorry for Ruben.

They sat there in bed listing their requirements in their heads: sheets and towels, duvets, covers, beds, furniture, saucepans, plates . . .

'The apartment will have to be as simple as possible,' Mona said.

Karin suggested they go and see what they had stored down in the basement and Mona had to look down to hide her annoyance.

'Pity about your training,' Karin remarked. She had been pleased when Mona had passed her nursing exams.

'Oh, well. I don't want to be a nurse.'

'But it's good to have a profession should anything go wrong,' Karin said, then realised there would never be any shortage of money in Ruben's family.

Before Lisa came, Karin rang Gustafsson and he said no, they hadn't promised the apartment to anyone. And yes, it would probably be all right if Isak and Mona took it on.

While Lisa was cleaning, Mona and Karin went for a walk along the shore. It had stopped snowing and a pale winter sun had emerged, painting the ice round the jetties a golden yellow.

'You must tell Isak,' Karin said.

Mona went into town that afternoon and stood on the quay, watching the barges coming across the river with the men from Götaverken.

Isak was in the first one and was pleased, though slightly worried to see her. 'Come and meet Onsala,' he said.

Mona shook the tall man by the hand, then the two of them were alone on the quay. She saw the question in his eyes. 'Let's go.'

Isak wheeled his bicycle while trying to put one arm round her shoulders. 'Nothing's happened, has it?'

'Yes,' she said. 'We're going to have a baby.'

Isak let her and the bicycle go, and it fell with a clatter on to the road. He stood still, letting his delight fill him. 'Heavens, how wonderful,' he exclaimed, just as Karin had.

He walked back to Sänkverket and locked up his bicycle for the night. Then he took Mona's hand. 'We must go and tell Dad first.'

They flew through town but as they approached the entrance to Ruben's apartment Mona stopped. 'What'll he say?'

'He'll be pleased.'

Even so, Isak was surprised at the extent of Ruben's delight as they stood in front of him, very young and rather scared, and Mona said, 'We're expecting a child.'

His joy had risen from great depths, from thousand-year-old sources, the joy of blood, the joy of the family.

Mona seemed to understand this. 'It'll be a Jewish child. We're going to be married in the synagogue and I'll convert,' she promised.

Then Ruben did something unexpected. He lit the seven-branched candlestick, put his arms round Mona and Isak as they faced the flames, and read a long prayer in Hebrew. The ancient prayer affected both them and the child listening. The words were incomprehensible but contained a peace that went beyond all reason.

A little later, Ruben phoned Karin and asked her whether they could come and have dinner with him that evening as he had something important to tell them. He could hear the laughter in Karin's voice as she accepted. She knows all right, his Wise Norn, Ruben thought.

'Dad, I think I'll stay on at Götaverken. Chalmers can go whistle as far as I'm concerned,' Isak said at dinner that night.

Mona looked down to hide what she was thinking, but Erik's eyes gleamed. Now they would see how deep Ruben's classlessness went. He wouldn't agree to his son becoming an ordinary worker.

'I've accepted that, Isak. You like it there so much.' Ruben turned to Erik. 'Isak is working his own lathe now, a tremendously intricate machine.'

Erik banged his fist on the table so hard, the glasses jumped. 'Well, damn me –'

'Don't swear,' Karin said, which startled him, as she wasn't that bad at it herself. But perhaps she was thinking about the baby.

'Isak,' Erik began again. 'You know nothing about what lies ahead, the way you get worn out, ruin your back. Rheumatism sets in, you damage your hearing, and then there's the wretched wages. I've worked on the shop floor and I know. In the long run, you can't stand the filth and the noise. And the lack of freedom,' he added. 'That's the worst.'

Isak was about to say that he'd seen quite a lot by now and he still preferred the hard work to becoming some fancy engineer.

'Isak needs practical experience.' Karin tried to change the subject. 'Even if he is to go to Chalmers, it won't do him any harm if he stays on at the yard for a few years so they have some order in their lives when the child is small.' She told them about the Gustafssons' apartment.

'Isn't it rather uncomfortable?' Ruben asked.

'No. They've put in central heating and a bathroom.'

Isak was thinking that God was good and he would go to see Gustafsson that evening. Mona and Karin were still pondering about sheets and linen, furniture and mattresses, plates and cups and other necessities. But no one said anything. When Ruben raised his glass to Karin, she could see in his eyes that he had had a good idea.

Mona told them she was going to convert to Judaism. Erik looked surprised but Karin nodded. She understood. No one gave a thought to Mona's father.

They broke up early so that Isak would have time to see Gustafsson. He came back half an hour later and said it was all arranged and he was to sign the rent agreement on Saturday. But it was going to be more expensive than he had reckoned and Karin gasped when she heard the sum.

'Gustafsson probably piled it on,' Erik said, when he and Karin were on their own. 'He must have reckoned rich Lentov's son could afford it.'

The next day Mona went to the superintendent of the nursing school with her resignation. She told her that she was pregnant. 'Well, Mona, you would have been expelled anyhow,' the stern lady said curtly.

As Mona filled in the necessary papers, the superintendent talked about how uncivilised the young were. 'Has the child a father? Oh, so there's to be a marriage, is there? May I ask who the lucky man is?'

Mona smiled gently. 'Ruben Lentov's son.'

'The woman looked as if she were about to choke,' Mona told Ruben later, who thought here, at least, was one child who was proud of him. They were having lunch at a restaurant.

He took out an envelope. 'This is a gift to my daughter-in-law.'

'But Isak?'

'Isak has nothing to do with *our* friendship,' he said, his eyes glittering.

Mona smiled as she put the envelope into her bag. On the tram journey out to Karin's she resisted the temptation to open it. It looked worryingly thin and they would need a lot more. Rugs, Ruben had said. He knew a place where they had wonderful rugs.

At Karin's, she took out the envelope, which appeared even thinner than she had remembered. 'You open it,' she said. 'I daren't.'

Karin took out a knife and slit open the envelope, which contained a piece of paper.

'A cheque, I think,' she said. Neither of them had ever seen one before. 'It says ten thousand.' And Mona had to sit down to stop herself fainting.

They collected their wits over a cup of coffee before going to look at the apartment where the hairdresser's wife had just started packing. So many roses, Mona thought. How ugly. But the rooms were lovely, large and light, and the kitchen was as spacious and pleasant as Karin's.

'You see,' said Mona, as they stood in the bedroom window overlooking the Larssons'. 'We can wave to each other.'

'It has awful furniture and terrible wallpaper,' she said when they got back. 'We'll paint every room white.'

Karin had never liked her neighbours, but she had always admired their home with its stylish furniture and crystal chandeliers, so she was surprised. 'What are you going to do?'

'White walls, white furniture, white curtains.'

'That sounds . . . light.'

'It will look like a country parsonage,' Mona announced. 'And the kitchen'll be like yours, with bright rag rugs on the floor. No chandeliers or stuff like that.'

Karin realised she was supposed to feel flattered, so said nothing about how she had always longed to have a crystal chandelier.

They heard Isak whistling in the drive, out of tune as usual, and Mona looked guilty.

He noticed at once. 'What have you gone and done?' He was joking, but was slightly scared when Mona said they'd better go upstairs and have a talk.

'If you need any help, give me a call.' Karin was also a little anxious now.

But a moment later, she heard Isak laughing. He came flying down the stairs, hugged Karin and, imitating Ruben's drawling voice with its slight accent, said, ' "Tell Isak he has nothing to do with our friendship." He's a cunning old Jew, Dad is.'

Isak seemed so relieved that Karin and Mona both realised that his head had been full of lists of sheets, linen, furniture and china as well.

Chapter 30

A few weeks later something occurred that was to go down in the family history as the Saturday everything happened.

For Ruben it did not start so well.

'Your niece is on the phone,' he was told.

Ruben hid a grimace. 'Not mine. My wife's niece,' he said wearily, though he knew he was being foolish.

The voice was as urgent and feverish as usual, and wanted more money. 'I'm starving,' Iza said.

But he had become hardened to her over the years and remembered Olof Hirtz saying he must limit the girl. 'You know you have to manage on your allowance.'

She was purring like a cat when she spoke again. 'Simon spent a week here, eating like a horse and living it up in town.'

Ruben's heart sank, but his voice was steady as he answered her. 'When was that?'

'A while ago,' Iza said evasively.

Ruben knew she was lying, but perhaps not about everything. 'I'll send you a hundred kroner. How are things going at college?'

'Fine,' she said. 'Thanks, Uncle dear.'

It was Saturday morning. He phoned Karin to ask whether Simon was coming on leave at the weekend.

'Yes, we're expecting him.'

'I'll pick him up.' Ruben was angry. Damn the boy, he thought.

Simon was waiting on the jetty for the boat to take him to the mainland. The wind was off the sea, north-westerly and cold as ice. But it didn't come from town, so carried no message of Ruben's fury.

He was in a good mood. He had been on guard duty

that night. It was monotonous and tough work but he was used to it now. At first he had almost wished for war, for hostile ships on the horizon, snipers on the skerries. Then you could fire and raise the alarm and make a hell of a noise. Some of the men had done that, been reprimanded by Sjövall, then teased for weeks afterwards by the men who had been dragged out of their beds by the alarm and had felt fear gripping at their entrails.

Simon had gazed at the skerries all that long night, thinking they knew he was there. They have their life in eternity, he could see, nothing had influenced them since the end of the Ice Age ten thousand years ago. But perhaps they had a different calculation of time. He recalled a conversation with an atomic scientist who had assured him that a dance went on inside the stone.

'I believe you,' Simon had said, trying to imagine the rhythm in the granite. Then he had been relieved and had managed a few hours' sleep before the time came for kit inspection and transport ashore.

Ruben watched the boy coming towards him, tall and happy, his big smile white in the weatherbeaten face. There was an intensity in his movements. He's an adult now and has a right to a private life, Ruben told himself. But it was already too late.

'You're angry with me,' Simon said.

'Iza phoned.' Ruben put the car into gear and eased his way out of the car park.

Simon flushed scarlet and nothing was said for a while. He felt exposed, as if Ruben had torn off his protective clothing to reveal his innermost secrets.

'Why did you go?'

'Because I was like a child, playing with emotions.'

Another long silence.

'I imagined she could make me feel real. But I failed. I just made it worse for her.' He tried to tell Ruben about the spiders, and realised how sick it sounded. 'I was full of guilt too,' he continued. 'Idiotic fantasies about participating in her destiny.' He searched for more words. 'I couldn't do anything for her.'

'Simon, no one can.'

'It was awful.'

'You're not going again?'

'Never.'

Ruben was greatly relieved. 'But you ate all her food and lived it up in town and spent all her money?'

'That's a lie.' Simon told Ruben how he had walked the streets with five kronor seventy-five öre in his pocket and had had to count the öre before daring to go into a café for a few sandwiches.

Ruben laughed.

'Can we stop for a while so I can tell you something else?'

Ruben manoeuvred the car into a parking slot. Then out came the story about Andersson, Omberg and Alvastra, and the giants washing their long johns in Lake Vättern. 'He said the most amazing things, you see. I've been happy ever since I met him.'

Ruben felt almost jealous, but he too was taken by the story of the mountain king's hall in people's hearts and how everyone knows that they haven't lived in vain.

'But best of all was what he told the about guilt,' Simon said. 'He said it doesn't exist, that it's about crimes that have never been committed, so can never be atoned for.'

'I've often thought that, too. But it's not true. People have always betrayed, hurt and neglected.'

'Not you?'

'Yes. I betrayed Isak when he was small. I hurt Olga by marrying her, although it wasn't her I wanted. And then there are my parents, whom I failed to persuade to come with me to Sweden.'

'How could you have made them?'

'I could have if I'd wanted to enough.'

'Andersson said that God is the God of the present and he only bothers about who one is now.'

'I can't make it that easy for me,' said Ruben.

But Simon was trying to remember other things that had been said in the truck. 'Anyhow, you can't settle things. There's no valid currency with which to pay off the debt of guilt.'

Ruben stared at Simon. That's true, he thought. It's horribly true. 'What else did he say?'

'That most people go on paying meaningless instalments throughout their lives, wondering why the debt never gets smaller.'

'I'd like to meet this Andersson,' Ruben said.

'You can't.' Simon told him how he had searched all over the depot for the driver. 'Absolutely no one knows him.'

They looked at each other, shook their heads and drove on into town.

'How's Mona?'

'She's well,' said Ruben, who then had to listen to how one should look into the eyes of new-born babies, for there was lots to learn there too.

As they turned off towards Långedrag, Ruben said, 'You haven't long to go before freedom now.'

'Six weeks,' Simon agreed. 'We're counting the days.'

'I'm going to America at the end of April, then back home via London and Paris. I thought I'd ask you to come with me, if it interests you?'

'If!' Simon cried. 'But why do you want me?'

'I thought it'd be fun.'

Simon laughed. It was true. They did have fun

together, he and Ruben. This wasn't about paying off some old debt to Karin. This was about him, Simon.

Ruben's face lit up. 'There's only one condition. And that is for you to stop calling me uncle. You're too old for that.'

'And you're too young, Ruben,' Simon said as they drove up to the house by the boatyard.

A large confused meal awaited them, breakfast, lunch and dinner all in one, Karin said, for no one had any time to cook more than once a day. The parlour had been turned into a sewing room, clouds of white muslin were heaped at one end round Karin's old sewing machine, and at the other end was a table laden with scale drawings, coloured cards, paper models of furniture and stacks of leaflets.

'A bridal dress?' asked Simon, looking at Mona with some surprise.

'No, silly. Curtains!'

Simon kneeled down before her. Then he put his head against her stomach, said hello in there, and looked up. 'A girl,' he announced.

'Yes,' Mona was sure. 'Of course it's a girl.'

'Those two are crazy,' Isak said.

'Pregnant women do go a little crazy,' Karin agreed.

'Yes, I've heard that. And Simon's always been crazy.'

They ate standing up and Simon told them that he was going to go to America with Ruben when he was demobbed.

Surprise and jubilation. But Karin said that this would kill her. Wasn't it enough with a wedding, setting up house and a birth without a trip to America in the middle of it all?

'Mum.' Simon felt anxious. 'You don't have to worry about my trip.'

'I know there's something magical about uniforms, that they grow apace with the boys inside them. But here at home, we don't know any conjuring tricks and I don't think you have a single garment you could get into.'

They laughed, as they had laughed every Saturday at Simon's attempts to get into his civilian clothes.

'We have a few days yet to arrange for something to wear,' Ruben said. 'But you must have your passport, Simon. Have you got one?'

Simon nodded. He had acquired one in his last year at school.

'That's good.' Ruben was thinking about the spirit of Senator McCarthy hovering over the passport authorities like everything else in the USA.

Simon and Isak were dispatched to the apartment next door to take some more measurements, in the kitchen this time. Simon stood looking out of Dolly's old room and Isak said you could see right into the top floor at home from there.

Simon nodded. He knew you could.

The room had been painted white as Mona had wanted. Simon joked that it was almost too dazzling.

They went back to the big living-room.

'Isak,' said Simon. 'There's something I want to tell you.'

'Something else?' Isak expressed mock horror. They had been discussing Iza and Simon's visit to Stockholm.

Simon lowered himself until he was sitting on the floor. Isak did the same.

'You know,' he began, 'I almost killed Bylund.'

Isak's eyes widened and he went hot all over. He wanted to know everything.

By the time Simon got to those front teeth in a pool of blood in the corridor, Isak could sit still no longer.

Staggering as if he were drunk, he got up and started dancing round the empty room.

'I've always been rather good at fighting,' Simon said with feigned modesty, and Isak stopped in the middle of his dance and remembered his first meeting with Simon, how, as a small boy, he had knocked down the tall son of a landowner in the school yard.

He wanted to say he loved Simon. Instead he had to make do with, 'I'll say.' His voice was full of admiration.

When they got back, Mona commented on what a long time it had taken. Karin told him that a letter from Stockholm had come in a brown envelope for Simon.

Simon was scared. 'Where is it?' he enquired, far too quickly.

'You may well ask,' said Karin. 'In all this muddle.'

They turned over white clouds of muslin, crawled under tables and sewing machine, but the letter had vanished.

'It'll turn up,' said Karin, and Simon groaned. Hell, he thought. Iza's on the warpath again.

He exchanged looks with Isak and saw that he was recalling what he'd said in the car. If she can get you to give her a kid . . .

Four months ago now, he thought. It can't be possible. But he was uneasy and slipped out to the boatyard, where he found Ruben and Erik in the partitioned-off room that still served as an office. Erik was looking worried. 'What is it, Dad?'

'Things are bad for Erik,' said Ruben. 'His yard's doing rather too well.'

Erik had to laugh. They counted up the timber stacked in high piles at the yard, which had long since grown out of the space available.

'I don't want to get any bigger,' Erik complained. 'There's something wrong about everything having to grow bigger. Why can't I be allowed to build three or four double-enders a year, just as I've always done?'

'Because your customers will go to a competitor who has larger capacity and shorter waiting times.' Ruben and his lawyer had said this to Erik many times during the winter and Erik had been equally angry each time.

'There's land going out at Önnered,' Simon said.

'Yes, I know, for Christ's sake. I've already got a sea site in Askim,' said Erik. 'But it'll all be such a bother, Simon. A lot of people, and keeping accounts and papers, and nothing but trouble.'

'You'll have to appoint a manager,' Ruben told him.

'Ruben Lentov,' said Erik. 'We've known each other—'

'Dad,' interrupted Simon. 'What about Isak? He's got Ruben's business sense in his bones.'

Erik stopped, and all three thought about how they had laughed over the years at Isak and his ability to buy cheap and sell dear, whether it was empty bottles or football stars in toffee papers.

'Do you think he'd want to?'

And Simon said, 'What about Chalmers? Your dream for Isak, never for me.'

Erik laughed again. 'You're a genius, Simon.'

'I know,' Simon admitted. 'I'm not without talent.'

Ruben was pleased. If all went well, as soon as Erik's pride would allow it, he could transfer his capital in the yard to Isak. Then the boy would be secure.

Then they thought about Götaverken, the basis of all Isak's pride.

'We must ask him,' Erik said.

'I'll go and get him,' Simon offered.

Isak was as surprised as he was interested. 'What an amazing day,' he said. 'Can I have time to think it over? I must ask Mona what she thinks.'

But he had already decided. 'How long is that business course?' he asked as he left.

It was late by the time Simon got up to his room and there was the letter, neatly placed on his desk, a large brown envelope, just as Karin had said.

He tore it open, then shouted aloud and raced downstairs like a madman. Ruben was still there, which was just as well, as Simon fell into his arms. 'They've taken it! They're going to publish it! My sea poem.'

Karin had to sit down. Her cheeks were scarlet and her eyes glowed. Her boy had become a writer. A book was going to be published with his name on the jacket. He had read the long poem to her and she knew it was beautiful, that it sang of the sea. Erik also beamed with pride.

But Ruben, who had had the poem typed up and had sent it to the publisher, was not so surprised. 'Let me see the agreement,' he asked.

Simon was to have four hundred kronor, the first money he had ever earned in his life. That should be enough for some clothes, he thought.

Part Four

Chapter 31

New York, New York beat the great heart of the city, and Simon enjoyed its sound. Everything was there in rapid succession: life and death, tears and laughter, fear and trust, cruelty and compassion. A melody freed itself from the rhythm, rose to the skies, took strength from the beating of that great heart and became obscene and arrogant, laughing over the roof-tops. A young song, full of hope, *New York, New York!*

There were moments when Simon, now twenty, felt old, a tired stranger from an ageing world. But mostly he felt in tune with this city that heightened his feeling for life. 'It's fantastic,' he said to Ruben over dinner at the hotel, and that applied to everything, even the food.

Ruben nodded, thinking how good his trip had been, thanks to Simon. Look, see that, have you ever seen, listen, taste – everything became new for Ruben too, a man of conservative habits who on his own would have visited the famous art galleries and possibly gone to the Met.

He had been there before the war and had been pained by the noise, the crowds, the shameless prostitution and wretched poverty. Now he was enjoying the contrasts, like Simon, and found he almost longed to leave his meetings, even those with old friends in the publishing world.

'It fits,' said Simon. 'And yet it doesn't. You see, I've been here before.' And he told Ruben about school and the boredom that used to come over him, and how he had learned to fly. He described in detail how he had trained himself to find the point of intersection between two lines in the right side of his brain, which enabled him to escape out into the world.

Ruben laughed.

'I often came here,' Simon continued. 'It looks just as it did then, more or less, but I missed the essence of it, the intensity, the rhythm.'

Ruben drank to him in the mellow Californian wine he found rather sweet, and resisted thanking him for making their trip such an experience.

They had crossed in the *Stockholm*, eight restful days in pleasant luxury for Ruben. But Simon found friends among the officers and crew, and disappeared down into the clattering bowels of the ship to plague machinists and engineers with his questions. Although a prohibited area for passengers, he had spent their last night on the bridge, looking out with tense expectation for the famous outline of the Statue of Liberty and the skyscrapers. At dawn he had woken Ruben and made him come and look. Ruben had said nothing about having seen it before, but went with the boy, only to realise that he hadn't seen it properly.

Their last days before departure had gone quickly. Simon was demobbed and had to equip himself for civilian life, so went from shop to shop with Mona trotting beside him, offering advice. But she was the one who decided and it was due to her that on the trip he always felt correctly dressed, just right. He himself would have bought clothes that were too ordinary or too showy.

Isak and Mona were married at a simple ceremony in the synagogue with a dinner at Henriksberg afterwards. None of Mona's relatives came to the synagogue, but at dinner Ruben escorted Mona's aunt to the table and as hostess, Karin looked after Mona's father. Neither couple found they had much in common.

Afterwards they all went to look at the apartment, now so pleasing that Simon stopped teasing Mona about her mania for interior decoration.

'I wouldn't be surprised if there weren't an artist hiding inside you, my dear,' Ruben told her.

On their last evening in New York, Simon and Ruben went up the Empire State Building and gazed out over the giant city with its thousand noises and tens of thousands of lights. Simon was sorry to be leaving, but found some consolation in that they were to fly across the Atlantic the next day.

But the flight was a disappointment and Simon had to admit Ruben had been right when he had said flying was a dull way of seeing the world. 'It's duller than walking,' Simon said, who loathed going for walks.

London received them with sunshine, a weary old lady, badly scarred by the war, but faithful and loyal. After catching up on sleep at a hotel on the Embankment, Ruben's and Simon's spirits rose again and they had a large lunch.

'I've got a lot to do here and not much time to spare,' Ruben said.

'I can manage on my own.'

'This city isn't as nice as it looks, Simon. It's larger and more dangerous.'

'I'll get a bus to the British Museum,' Simon said. From then on he saw very little of London. Over four days, he became a familiar figure to the attendants in the department of antiquities, the Swedish boy they had to go and look for when it was closing time. Ruben's evenings were taken up with Simon's descriptions of treasures, the incredible collections from Greece and Rome, Egypt and Mesopotamia.

'British imperialists were certainly not afraid to loot,' Ruben commented.

'There are differing opinions on that,' Simon said. 'But at the moment I'm just glad they're here, assembled in one place.'

They crossed the Channel, spring came and it was warm, almost hot on the train. Ruben's eyes glowed as they thundered into Paris, another elderly lady, more sensitive, elegant and sharper than London, but shabby and exhausted by the war too.

'This is the city of my youth,' Ruben told him. 'The city of my dreams, where I came across everything that was to prove decisive in my life, music, art, the great spirits.' And Rebecca, he was thinking. We met here one spring.

'Strindberg, too,' he continued. 'Not personally of course, but I found his books in German, cheap, on one of the stalls on the banks of the Seine.'

The next day Ruben had a meeting and Simon went to the Louvre. They agreed to meet in the entrance hall of the museum at three o'clock in the afternoon. Ruben was there on time, but not Simon. By four o'clock he was worried. He should have told Simon that this city was more dangerous than London.

Simon appeared and even from a distance Ruben could see something had happened. He was white in the face, as if he'd seen a ghost. 'Uncle Ruben,' he called. 'You must come with me.'

As Ruben hurried after him up the stairs and through the long galleries, he wondered why Simon had reverted to his old habit of calling him uncle, the first time on their trip.

In one of the galleries of antiquities, Simon stopped in front of a half-metre-high statue of a little man looking at them with centuries of inscrutable wisdom. Gudea,

Ruben read, Sumerian divine king, twenty-second century BC.

'It's him,' Simon said. 'The man I told you about, the man who was there all through my childhood and came back in the Berlioz symphony.'

Ruben could feel the hairs on his arm standing on end. He thought about Strindberg again, the writer who had given him an interest in Swedenborg and Sweden. But not even Swedenborg would have understood this.

Ruben looked from Simon to the statue, from the boy's scared eyes to the calm and superior oriental eyes of the sculpture. Finally he said in a voice not as steady as he would have wished, 'However unfathomable life may be, Simon, we are here now in these bodies which require food and rest.' To his relief, he saw that the boy was able to laugh.

They ate in silence, unable to appreciate the good food at this expensive restaurant on the Champs-Elysées. They had planned to do Paris by night, but agreed silently to return to their hotel room. Ruben was pleased he had booked a double room, not two singles. They showered, put on their pyjamas and Ruben drank a cognac. He hadn't managed to get his thoughts into any kind of order, or subdue his anxiety over Simon, who was still very pale.

But after they had lain in bed for an hour or so, gazing at the ceiling, Ruben's mind, the logical part of it, started to work again. 'I was thinking about a famous psycho-logical study I've read about,' he began. 'It proposed that people under hypnosis could remember what they thought was a previous life. Among many others, there was a man who spoke in fluent Latin.'

'Oh, yes?' Simon was interested. He sat up and switched on the lamp.

'Long strings of words, always the same. But it was remarkable, because the man was an American and lacked any education in the classics.'

'Yes.'

'Well, they tried to chart the man's life, everything he had been involved in, major and minor. Gradually, he remembered, in connection with a dramatic break-up with a woman he loved, sitting for hours in a library, utterly beside himself with despair. To be left in peace, he had borrowed a book, opened it and stared without seeing at two pages containing the particular text he had quoted by heart under hypnosis. It had passed his consciousness but become engraved on his subconscious.

'It strikes me,' said Ruben, his voice steadier now, more convinced, 'that this is what has happened to you. Some time when you were tired or so small you don't remember it, you saw a picture of that statue in the Louvre.'

'And the picture made a great impression on my subconscious. Is that what you mean?' Simon spoke in a voice full of doubt.

'Yes,' said Ruben. He told Simon he had recently seen a picture of Gudea in a German book on archaeology by someone called Ceram, which was being translated into Swedish.

'Have you got a copy?'

'In German. You can borrow it as soon as we get home. What I mean is that this is a famous figure, reproduced in a great many contexts. Have you the catalogue of the Louvre's prehistoric collections?'

Simon leaped out of bed and found it. In fumbling French, they read about Ernest de Sarzec, a French diplomat, who had excavated at the foothills in Lagash and found the statue, which was loaded on to a ship and sent to the Louvre. It had aroused tremendous attention in its day, because it confirmed that a culture had existed that was older than that of the Assyrians, even older than the Egyptians.

'When did de Sarzec live?' said Simon.

It didn't say in the brochure, but Ruben guessed the end of the nineteenth century. 'In the 1880s, I should think. If you would just calm down, I'll see if I can remember more from Ceram's book.'

Ruben had a good memory and, after a moment or two, he spoke again.

'For a long time in various scientific indices, largely linguistic, it was estimated that there had been an unknown people before the Semitic high cultures in Mesopotamia, before Sargon. The find of Gudea proved that they were right and the Sumerians entered history.'

Simon was interested. His colour had come back and he remembered that amazing day at school when war broke out and the young teacher had said, 'History begins with the Sumerians.'

'What I want to say,' Ruben went on, 'is that the statue is well known, and has probably appeared in Swedish newspapers in connection with some article on the arts pages or some report on archaeology. You have seen the picture and, being what you are, it has come to influence your imagination, your dreams and gradually your inner life.'

He was on safe ground now and his assurance calmed Simon. When they woke the next morning to make their way out to the airport and the plane to Copenhagen, the mystery had lost its hold on their minds.

Back at home, Simon found the time to read Ceram's book, which he found enormously interesting. Then Ruben invited him to dinner with Olof Hirtz. Simon had told him the story of how they had found the divine king of his dreams in a diorite statue in the Louvre.

Olof looked surprised at first. Ruben noticed, and told him his theory of the picture that had been stored in Simon's subconscious.

Olof nodded almost enthusiastically. 'Write about it, Simon. Write a poem, or a long short story about a day in childhood, a perfect day, as if created to form a lasting pattern in the child's emotional life. The sun is shining, there's a mildness in the mother's voice. She takes the child by the hand, strolls past the kiosk on the shore and buys a magazine. They sit in the sand and the tall grass on the edge of the shore sways in the wind and the shore meadow is endless. The mother is enjoying the warmth and leafs absently through the magazine, keeping an eye on the little boy digging canals in the sand and getting water to run from the sea into them.

'She is half asleep when the boy comes back, sees the magazine lying open beside her with an article on Mesopotamia. He can't read, but the pictures transfix him, the lion with a man's head, the canals, the temples and towers rising above the sea of grass. Most of all, the child sees the picture of the divine king with his strange round hat and gentle features which match the peaceful day. The boy is so small, he has still not yet begun to store away his memories, so everything is coloured by the beauty of the day, his mother's love and the warm light over the river, and goes into his subconscious.

Simon laughed. 'Write it yourself,' he said. 'You, who are so sure.'

'But I'm no writer.'

'Yes, you are. You've just proved it,' Ruben said and they all laughed.

But Simon reckoned he wouldn't write that story, even if the explanation was reasonable, credible, in fact.

My friend Andersson, the truck driver, would never swallow it, he thought.

Chapter 32

The professor was a small man with inquisitive eyes and a smile that flitted back and forth across his face. The Historical Institute in Göteborg was known for its vitality and it was said that students there became more gifted than they were by nature. Both intelligence and imagination were required of them, and most lived up to expectations. Students with a need to assert themselves soon disappeared to Nordic languages after a term or two where their chances of being in evidence were greater.

Simon had a brief talk with the professor and told him him that, after his first degree, he wished to specialise in hieroglyphics.

'That's good to hear,' the professor said, with a swift smile. 'Most students are fixated on the Æsir and the Vikings.' His smile came back again. 'Sweden is not a good field for Assyriologists,' he added. 'It'll have to be London perhaps, but all in good time.'

Apollo was dancing over the Elysian fields in Simon's dreams.

He was now sleeping at Ruben's in Isak's old room. There had been trouble at home over that, and about money.

'I'm getting a student loan, Dad.'

'No, you're bloody not. No child of mine is going to owe anyone money as long as I can afford to keep them.'

The temperature in the kitchen rose.

'It'll be much more expensive than school.'

But Erik had forgotten his complaints over school fees long ago.

'It's just as it's always been,' Simon grumbled to Karin when they were alone together.

'It's silly to get into debt unnecessarily,' she replied and Simon could see she was sad, so he said nothing more, particularly as Ruben had been drawn into the discussion and taken Erik's side.

'You can keep your independence in other ways apart from money,' he pointed out. He had accepted help from his family when he had started building up his business in Göteborg. But he realised this was a Jewish trait.

Simon asserted himself by saying he wanted to leave home.

Erik was furious. He had assumed that everything would be the same as before, now Simon was studying again. But Simon remembered only too well how you were made to eat Erik's bread twice when at his table, so he persisted, and received unexpected support from Karin.

'You seem to have forgotten what it was like being adult and having to live with your mother,' she said to Erik.

'Mothers are different,' Erik told her. 'And I was earning a living and contributing money that was damned well needed.'

'There you are,' Simon countered.

But Karin said that was enough and they both saw that she was near to tears. Erik disappeared with his tail between his legs and Simon stayed to console her. Nothing was sorted out.

There were no apartments to be had in Göteborg and the rooms to rent through college went to students whose parents didn't live in town. So Ruben had suggested that Simon should rent a room from him. 'That's no more than fair. You've had Isak living here for years,' he said when Erik flared up again.

For once Erik could find no reply.

Ruben had been impressed by Mona's efforts at interior decoration and had had his apartment redecorated too. The walls were painted white, the velvet and plush thrown out and the same kind of white curtains as Mona's hung at his windows. Even the old suite of leather sofas was carted off to the tip where they astonished a cleansing department employee whose wife was delighted with them. Ruben's apartment now had neat, pale-blue Carl Malmsten sofas, a white dinner table and graceful chairs.

'It looks like some manor house in Värmland,' said Karin.

Only the Chinese rugs had survived and glowed like jewels on the newly scraped parquet flooring. And Ruben's old glass-fronted bookcases stood where they always had.

'You'll soon be able to see how much good art you possess,' Simon said. After endless discussions, Ruben and Mona had rehung the colourful paintings on the new white walls. Simon told him how he had stood in front of the canvases as a child and tried to understand them. Now, he felt he could – at least some of the time.

When his radiogram arrived and was placed against the white wall in his large room which overlooked the courtyard, Mona said it was hideous. 'I've never noticed how ugly it was before.'

'I can forgive it.' Simon laughed. Secretly, he was pleased to be living with Ruben.

There was a reddish-yellow pony-tail in front of Simon at the lecture on scientific methodology. The sun was shining on it, making it sparkle. He couldn't remember seeing it before, so waited with some excitement for the girl to turn her head. When she did so, he was disappointed as he took in a long neck and an extremely high forehead in a narrow, pale, freckled face. He smiled slightly as they got up after the lecture and found she was almost as tall as he was, had a generous mouth and large grey-green eyes.

Klara Alm had noticed Simon's good looks on the first day of term. But there was something else about him: an unease that interested her. It was as if he were constantly preoccupied with the mysteries of life and was expecting fantastic answers to his questions. There goes the course's Don Juan, she thought. I don't expect he'll ever look in my direction.

She was wrong on the first score for, although girls flocked round Simon at first, he was friendly but no more. He hasn't even the sense to be flattered, Klara thought in surprise. But she was right on the second score. He hadn't noticed her.

Until now. Now he was smiling at her. How intense he is, she thought. And she wondered whether she was sweating, whether there were damp patches under her arms.

A few days later, Simon asked about Klara and was told she was going to be a doctor.

'She's already got her first degree,' he was informed. 'She's probably having a break with a little humanities.'

This surprised Simon. Klara must be older than she looked.

'She's very clever. She passed all her final school exams privately when she was sixteen. She's the intelligent, ice-cold kind, you know.'

Simon thought briefly that Klara Alm did not seem at all cold.

He forgot her until he saw her having coffee one day with Nordberg, the son of a wealthy businessman, who was holding court as usual about the necessity for a Marxist view of history.

Klara flushed scarlet with annoyance and got up so quickly the coffee splashed into the saucers. 'You're making things too easy for yourself,' she said. 'I think you should distinguish between private and political revolution, and settle your puberty argument with your father now rather than later.'

She left and there was a lot of laughter. Nordberg said furiously that she was a stupid, stuck-up bitch.

Simon followed her out. 'You're not stuck-up,' he said when he had caught up with her in the hall.

'No. But I'm stupid. They'll say I'm right wing now.'

'And you're not?'

'No. I largely agree with him. But he's so certain and his views are all second-hand, if you know what I mean. He quotes Marx without understanding the first thing about him.'

'"The new revolutionaries pick the bourgeoisie's fruits from the tree of knowledge and pay with money from capitalist fathers earned in a more or less honest way."' Simon laughed.

'So you are intelligent,' she said.

'Why shouldn't I be?'

'Well, you know. Good-looking boys . . .'

'You're wrong,' he said. 'There are plenty of pretty girls around who are clever.'

'Of course.' Klara smiled. 'As you may have gathered, I'm very intelligent.'

'Are you warning me?'

'Maybe.'

'Well, you needn't bother,' Simon said. 'You see, I'm a genius so you can't threaten me.'

Klara laughed to cover up how pleased she felt.

As they walked across to the cycle stand, Simon told her about his father. 'He was a truck driver, politically clear-sighted about everything except the Soviet Union. Now that you can't ignore the fact that the workers' paradise is a police state, he's lost interest in politics in general.'

'So you're working class?'

'Yes, to begin with at least,' Simon explained. 'Dad was unemployed when he came out of the army so he started building boats – sailing boats. Now he's got a yard of his own and stacks of problems and employees.'

'So he's gone from being a communist to becoming a capitalist?'

'Mmm. But he's a good man.'

'That's understandable,' Klara said, 'that you've got a great dad, I mean.'

'What do you mean, exactly?'

'Well, you seem to be the kind of guy who doesn't need to assert himself all the time, and that's unusual.'

Simon was surprised. 'I may be a genius,' he said. 'But I'm unfamiliar with psychological jargon. What about a beer and you could teach me?'

As they cycled down towards Rosenlund canal and the Fiske church where there was a pub, Klara decided to make a stupendous effort and be nice to him.

'Tell me about yourself,' Simon asked, once they had got their beers and were sitting facing each other across a table.

'My father owns a sawmill in Värmland,' Klara said, naming the place. 'My mother ran away with another man when I was eleven, and it still hurts. But I can understand her, because – well, he's difficult, you know, my father. He drinks.'

Simon tried to hold her gaze, but she held back, as if she were quite alone inside her grey-green eyes.

Simon understood a little what it was like to be abandoned when small, and he remembered how angry he had been with Karin when he and Erik thought she was dying. Then he realised there was no possible comparison.

Klara started to tell him about her studies, and her eyes lost their emptiness and met his again. When she wasn't angry, it occurred to Simon that she was beautiful.

'I thought of becoming a psychiatrist,' she said. 'But at the moment I'm obsessed with the ancient mythologies – that they have a psychological function, therapeutic even. Do you know what I mean?'

'Yes,' said Simon and she could see his interest was genuine.

'I'm interested in the popular sagas in particular,' Klara continued. 'The way they contain a lot of difficult emotions that children have, but mustn't have and must never talk about. You know – cruel fantasies, violence, that kind of thing.'

Simon's heart beat faster.

'I'd thought of concentrating on the Greek pantheon and of trying to find the connection between those gods and the forbidden fantasies of humans.'

Simon sat very still. This is my girl, he was thinking, and for a moment he could hear the truck driver's laugh echoing between the tiled walls of the pub.

Then Klara told him that a great many people had had the same ideas before her.

'Writers?'

'Yes, but scholars, too.' And she went on to talk about Carl Gustav Jung, his theories about the collective consciousness and the importance of archetypes: the hero, the wise old man, the great mother and the holy child. 'He studied the myths and found common foundations in all cultures. He taught that if you want to know something about mankind, you have to look at their myths.'

I've always known that, Simon thought.

'You can borrow some books,' she offered.

Somehow they made two beers last an hour, then they ordered two more then four sandwiches. When they eventually left, Simon remarked how strange it was that horrible fathers often had wonderful daughters. 'I know someone just like you. She's married to my best friend.'

Klara felt faint.

They parted company in the Avenue and cycled through the dark in different directions, both feeling that they had a secret in common.

Thoughts were racing through Simon's head, one after another. This wasn't love. It wasn't what had happened to Isak and Mona. There was no light round Klara. And she was not a nice person, she had said so herself. She was prickly when challenged. Plain, too. She was tall and flat as a board, with horrid freckles on her face and arms, and even on her hands, though they were lovely, secretive almost. She had long fingers with soft pads on the insides and the lifelines were deep crevices. And when she smiled . . .

No! He'd forget her. This was going to be easy as there was nothing to remember. Yet his last thought before falling asleep was that when he was with her it was as if he was with himself.

Simon dreamed he was walking along the shore and Life came towards him and had golden reddish hair and an apple in her long-fingered, freckled hand.

He sat beside Klara at a lecture the next day and asked whether she liked music.

'Yes,' she said.

'I've got two tickets for a concert on Saturday. They're playing Nystroem's *Sea Symphony*.' In fact, he had no tickets, but he would have time to get some. 'Would you like to come too?'

'Yes, please.' Klara closed her eyes so that he wouldn't see how pleased she was.

'I heard it at its première,' Simon told her. 'It made such an impression on me that I wrote a long poem.'

She looked at him in surprise and he couldn't resist the temptation. 'Bonniers are going to publish it.'

In her tiny apartment in Haga, in a block scheduled for demolition, Klara went through her clothes and decided nothing would do. But it was only Saturday morning, so she had time to nip down Linnégatan where there was a shop window she had often gazed into and fantasised about a different, more beautiful Klara.

She bought some stockings and the first high heels she'd ever owned, as he was taller than she was. Then she remembered a boy at an anatomy lecture telling her she had a delicious backside, so she tried on a very tight skirt.

'Fits as if welded to you,' the assistant declared. Next, she bought a green silk blouse with wide sleeves and a collar like a shawl round her neck.

'But I've no bosom.' Klara saw the way the silk clung to her. But the assistant smiled and said that was easy to fix, and before Klara could blink, she had bought a padded bra.

I must be crazy, she thought.

She washed her hair and rolled it in a towel to make it curl, then hoped she wouldn't come out in a cold sweat if she felt scared. 'Klara Alm,' she said aloud to herself. 'You won't be feeling scared tonight.'

Before dressing, she made the bed up with clean sheets. Last of all she darkened her fine long eyelashes.

When Simon arrived at half past six, he looked at her and beamed. 'You're awfully pretty,' he said.

Klara reckoned it would be good to die now, before everything was spoiled. 'You know, people at home say that I have the nastiest tongue in the village.'

'You're not plain any longer,' Simon insisted. 'So perhaps your tongue will be prettier too.' And he kissed her.

They were on time for the concert and the music worked its usual magic. Fortunately for Simon, Klara said nothing afterwards. As they walked back through town, Simon told her about the Indian women washing their children at the source of the river and about the wave wandering across the Atlantic, only to be smashed to pieces on the rocks of Bohus. 'When I heard the symphony for the first time, I thought the wave couldn't die because it never became personal. Do you understand what I mean?'

'Yes,' she said. 'I also think personality is largely a defence. That's why mine is strong and pronounced.'

He kissed her again on the mouth, slap in the middle of Östra Hamngatan.

Simon never dreamed that a girl could give herself to him with such trust, so willingly. She was so naked, so childishly open. But he took her with him and gave her enjoyment and satisfaction. She bled a little and he felt that this also was a gift.

At two in the morning she went into the kitchen to wash under the cold-water tap, then came back in a blue bathrobe. 'I'd quite like to die now,' she said. 'But before I do, I'll play to you.'

She got out her flute. Simon wanted to cry out no, please don't, Klara. Don't. But she sat at the end of the bed and played unaccompanied Carl Nielsen's flute solo from his concerto for that instrument, slightly tentatively at first as if she were out of practice, but soon increasingly surely, richly and warmly.

Afterwards, Simon lay still in bed.

'You didn't fall asleep?'

'Don't be . silly. You're no amateur, are you?' he added.

'I've had the best teaching you could get in Värmland,' she said, 'from a Jewish flautist in Karlstad. He had been in the Berlin Philharmonic Orchestra. He got out and earned his living teaching music. He was wonderful. Thanks to him, I survived when my mother left.'

'I was allowed to keep my mother,' Simon said. 'Perhaps that's why I never learned to play the violin.'

'Did you want to?'

'Klara, it's a long story and I haven't really understood it yet.' But what about Simon Haberman, he longed to ask, a violinist in the Berlin Philharmonic. 'Is he still alive, your teacher in Karlstad?' he asked instead.

'Yes.'

'Then one day we'll go to see him.' And they went to sleep.

They woke on Sunday at about twelve, feeling very hungry. They found a pub in the harbour which was open and ate herring and salt brisket. Simon ordered two schnapps, and as they toasted each other with the fiery spirit, Klara said she had never tasted anything so good before.

For a fortnight, they stayed in paradise. Then Simon remembered that he had a family plus Ruben and Isak, and asked her to meet his mother.

He saw Klara was scared, but he knew nothing of the demons in her heart which were now making their way to her head. But as he left, saying he would pick her up on Saturday and Karin would ask her to dinner, he could feel the wall growing between them.

Chapter 33

Simon should have rung Karin to tell her about Klara, but he delayed, blaming Klara and her reluctance. On Friday morning, between two lectures, he dialled the familiar numbers at last.

'It's a long time since we heard from you, Simon,' said Karin warmly. 'Where have you been?'

'Well, you see Mum, I've met a girl.'

'Oh yes.' The voice seemed distant suddenly and he wanted to explain that she was a strange girl, fragile and tough at the same time, plain and pretty, and I think I love her, whatever that means, but she's terrified of you. But he didn't, of course. 'I was thinking of bringing her out tomorrow so you can get to know her.'

'That'd be nice, dear.'

That wasn't what Karin had wanted to say either, but she was pleased she had said it and that she had sounded the same as usual.

'She's a doctor,' Simon continued. 'I mean, she'll soon be qualified.'

'Heavens!' There was a silence, then Karin added, 'We'll be having dinner at two as usual. I'll get some turbot and cook something really nice.'

'We'll be there. 'Bye for now.'

''Bye.' She wanted to say something more but couldn't think of anything. He wanted to say something else too but couldn't either.

Angry with himself, Simon went back to the lecture room. Karin replaced the receiver, leaned against the wall in the hall and thought about her heart. It was beating calmly and firmly.

She had known it would happen. Sooner or later, Simon would meet a girl, just as Isak had. She might be a girl like Mona, she thought. At this, Karin had to go back to the kitchen, sit down and speak seriously to her heart. 'There, there,' she said. 'There, there. Calm down and beat as you should, slowly and steadily.'

Her heart obeyed and Karin realised that if Mona had been Simon's girl she would have hated her.

She looked around the kitchen, at the security, remembering another kitchen, smaller and shabbier, with the smell of poverty in its walls, the nasty odour which came from pissing in the kitchen sink because the privy was three floors down in the courtyard. Another woman sat there, her hand on her heart to stop it breaking, and in front of her was Erik with his arm round the shoulders of a young girl, a lovely girl, her straight nose pointing up in the air and brown eyes flashing. 'That's the point. The old are to die out to make way for the young,' she had announced.

There's a price for everything, Karin thought. The memory of her mother-in-law helped her. She had her pride. She would never be like Erik's damned mother. No, she would be the best of mothers-in-law, just as she had been the best of mothers and no one would ever have the slightest idea what that had cost her.

Her heart thumped, ice in her breast. When Lisa arrived a moment later, Karin put on the coffee. 'Just think, Simon's got himself a girl,' she said.

'How nice.' Lisa's quick eyes, always on the look-out for dust and secrets, gleamed with excitement. 'Who is she?'

'A doctor.' She had said it and now could enjoy Lisa's surprise.

'Oh. my goodness. But then he's always been a bit superior, hasn't he?'

Karin realised there would be the usual talk among the neighbours about the Larssons and their rich Jewish friends, their boatyard and their son who'd gone to school and university to read ancient history. She could hear the snorts when they said that Simon was spoiled and thought life was nothing but a game.

'What's her name?'

'I forgot to ask! You see, I was so surprised.'

'Well, I suppose you thought you'd have him for the rest of your life.' Lisa smiled to take the edge off the malice.

Karin flushed and got up to go, reluctant to give Lisa the satisfaction of seeing her anger. She went to the boatyard, found Erik in the drawing office and gave him the news quickly. 'Simon's met a girl. She's a doctor. They're coming for dinner tomorrow.'

Erik dropped his pencil and compass, and took off his glasses. 'That's great news. God in heaven, Karin, what fun!' She could see his delight was genuine. 'Is he in love?'

'I assume so.' Her smile was wide, almost natural.

Erik went back with her for coffee. This had to be celebrated. He talked about the game of life when you were young and how he had always hoped Simon would fall in love. Then he laughed loudly. He had always longed for a doctor in the family, and 'Christ, yes, Erik Larsson always gets what he wants. When the boy doesn't want to be a doctor, then he gets hold of one. Smart!'

Karin joined in the laughter, but frozen angels went through the room when she saw his delight and thought about the girl he had once loved, the one his mother had frightened off. Erik had grieved so much, he had fallen ill with TB and been admitted to the sanatorium. Then she remembered her decision to be a good mother-in-law and considered it so intently that her face became still and cold.

'Goodness, how serious you look,' Erik said. 'You're not jealous, are you?'

'Of course not.' Karin's eyes flashed.

'I was only joking. You know that.'

Jealous. An ugly word, she thought as she went for her usual walk, not one suited to her sorrow which resembled another long ago. Petter, she thought. She had lost him when he died. But Simon was betraying her. She couldn't hate him, only the girl. Suddenly she thought about how she had always detested doctors, superior people with power over life and death.

She went to the fishmonger for her turbot and added half a kilo of shrimps for good measure. The girl was to have a welcoming dinner and no one was going to complain about that. She wanted no truths that day so she avoided the oak trees on her way home, and took the roundabout path across the wild old garden where she had played with Simon when he was small. No one would ever love him as she had then.

Over coffee that evening, Erik was nervous. Did Karin think the girl was upper class? Supposing she was snooty? Would they have to mix with a business family?

'I don't know,' said Karin. 'But Simon is usually a good judge.'

Erik almost snapped back. He could never stand not knowing so he rang Simon who wasn't there. Ruben answered the phone and knew a little more although he hadn't met the girl.

When Erik came back to Karin, he had calmed down.

'She's called Klara Alm, daughter of a sawmill worker who married money and took over the sawmill up there in Värmland.'

'Sounds good to me,' Karin said.

'Hmm. The father drank, apparently. There was a divorce. Klara's clever, but hasn't had an easy time.'

She was coming closer now, the girl, and Karin was not pleased, especially when Erik said that Ruben had reported that Simon was besotted with her and hadn't been home for two weeks.

Klara had fought her demons all night. And she had lost, she realised, when Simon came to pick her up and stood in the doorway filling the shabby apartment with his intensity. She agreed with the demons, with the one saying that she was silly to have anything to do with a man like this, and with the other who whispered, God how ashamed he will be of you.

Klara was in a black jumper, which made her look paler than usual, her freckles were standing out in her white face and she had rings round her eyes the same colour as the sweater. She could see he would have liked her to have worn something more cheerful, but she was grateful he didn't say so. It wouldn't show on black if she started to sweat.

They walked to Järntorget and took the tram to Långedrag. He attempted to talk to her about his school as they went past it, and anything else that was interesting on the route that had been his for so many years. But she wasn't as absorbed as she had been that first night when he had told her about his family and his wonderful mother, whom Klara disliked already. In the end he told her that she looked as if he were taking her to the slaughterhouse. She didn't reply. It's started, she thought. Now he's angry and will soon begin to hate me.

As they walked from the stop down to the river, Simon tried again, telling her about the time when Äppelgren had found him when he was small and had been lost.

This time there was some response. 'Why did you run away?'

'Run away? I suppose it was the need to go somewhere as inquisitive children sometimes do.'

But there was a question in his voice and she realised he had never really asked himself that before. She had knocked the first fragment out of his picture of his wonderful childhood, and she knew she ought to turn on her heel and go before she destroyed any more.

The afternoon went as badly as Klara had imagined. There she was, standing like a beanpole in the kitchen doorway while Simon greeted his mother. She could see the tie between mother and son was overwhelming. Then she looked at Karin and to her despair saw that she was not only good, but something much worse. She's beautiful, Klara thought. And intelligent. She could feel herself shaking as those wise eyes fell on her, saw straight through her and rejected her.

'Nice to meet you and welcome,' Karin said to this plain redheaded girl with clammy hands. Simon was looking frightened.

This is crazy, Karin said to herself. My boy and that —

Erik came in from the boatyard with rolls of drawings under his arm. 'My, what a tall, fine girl you are.' He looked brightly at her, and at last Klara was able to smile and be nice.

Simon hugged his father and laughed. 'She'll soon be a qualified doctor,' he boasted.

Things might have improved, but then the demons in Klara said that Simon was ashamed so he had to excuse her education.

The next moment Isak arrived. He was so frightened of her that he vanished into the boatyard with Erik's drawings, calling over his shoulder that he would make a start with the plans of what had to be done before they moved.

Erik looked surprised, but trotted after Isak and the three of them were left alone in the kitchen, with Karin laying the table with a newly ironed cloth and their best china.

The turbot and shrimps were as good as always, but Klara ate her food as if it were cardboard and found it hard to swallow. The sweat poured off her.

Isak told Mona that Simon had brought a peculiar bird back, as tall as a crane, plain and stiff, and snooty as hell. So Mona went over to Karin's to borrow some sugar. She was more lovely and pear-shaped than ever and could easily have stepped out of a Renaissance painting as the expectant Virgin Mary.

Klara distrusted her immediately because of her gentle maternalism and because she was so friendly and natural. But Mona went home to Isak, saying that Klara wasn't arrogant. 'She's just frightened. You must see that.'

No, Isak couldn't see it. And anyhow it was stupid – there was nothing to be afraid of at Karin's house.

'Well, I'd be dead scared if I were Simon's girl and was to meet Karin for the first time,' Mona told him.

After dinner, Klara went with Erik to the yard and that helped a little. It was draughty and cold so she stopped sweating. Erik was proud of his boatyard and Klara thought the two double-enders which were almost finished and were to be launched that autumn very handsome.

In the kitchen, Simon appealed to Karin. 'She's scared, Mum. Can't you see?'

'Yes, but what can I do?'

'Take her with you up the mountain, Mum. Look at the view and talk, as you usually do.'

'Would you like to go out for a while?' Karin asked when Klara came back from the yard.

Klara nodded, but she felt as though she was going before a court of law that had already decided on their verdict.

They sat on the mountain and Karin showed her the fortress, talked about the sea, and said that there were good and bad points about living so close to it.

In the end, Klara couldn't stand it any longer. 'Why are you going on like this? Why don't you say it at once? You think I'm horrible and should leave Simon alone.'

'What are you saying?' Karin asked.

'I agree with you. I don't think I'm worthy of him and I know I'll ruin his life.'

Karin felt jubilant. 'I can't dislike anyone I've never met before.'

'Nicely put, but you've probably seen enough of me,' Klara said hopelessly.

'Klara, dear,' Karin said. 'Perhaps you could begin by telling me a little about yourself?'

'Me?' said Klara. 'I'm the plain daughter from the sawmill with the nastiest tongue in all Värmland.'

'How did you become that?'

'Perhaps when my mother disappeared with another man when I was small. But I don't know. I'm probably nasty by nature.'

'Did you never hear from her again?' Karin found it difficult to hide the satisfaction in her voice. She was not very successful and both of them sensed it.

Klara laughed scornfully. 'No, not even she was able to love me.'

'You'll have to go and find her now you're grown

up,' Karin said as if that were the simplest thing in the world.

Klara thought about her mother's phone number in her diary and how she had been trying to call her for three years. 'That's good advice.'

'You must dislike yourself a lot to be so angry with other people.'

'It's called projection in medical jargon.'

'Are you trying to impress me?'

'No. I know that wouldn't work.'

'I find it difficult to be with people who don't like themselves,' said Karin. 'They let other people pay such a high price for it.'

'I understand perfectly well that you hoped for a better girl for Simon. We are agreed on that. Rely on me, Karin. It'll soon be over, our brief love story.'

Klara was as still as a statue as she gazed out to sea.

Realising that this was her way of holding back her tears, Karin felt guilty. 'Are you trying to blame me?'

'No,' Klara said. 'You are a good mother and good mothers are always blameless. You have to be to survive.'

That hurt, but Karin managed to keep her voice steady. 'You are probably the nastiest person I've ever met,' she said.

'I told you this would happen.' But Klara looked frightened when she saw that Karin was pale and was clutching her heart. Simon had told her about her weakness.

As they walked down the mountain, Klara knew she had to leave quickly. As soon as they got into the kitchen, which was full of people, she went round saying goodbye, thanking Karin for the meal and apologising that she had to go home and work for her exams. 'You can rely on me,' she repeated quietly to Karin.

Ruben Lentov was there and she held out a clammy hand.

Simon went with her to the tram. 'I'll come up to your place for dinner at five tomorrow,' he said when it arrived. 'Perhaps both of us will have calmed down by then.'

All Sunday, Klara walked round her gloomy apartment in Haga thinking about the promise she had made Karin. She was as miserable as anyone could be. At half past four, she opened a tin of mushroom soup and made some sandwiches.

Simon arrived on the dot of five, tried to smile, to take her in his arms, but she pushed him away.

'Was it that awful?' he asked.

'Of course not,' she replied. 'They were exactly as you described. Erik is nice, Isak pleasant, Mona terribly sweet, and your mother – the Great Mother who allows herself to be worshipped in her temple which is turned modestly into a kitchen – is fantastic.'

'Shut up,' Simon said, but Klara couldn't stop herself.

'Even the rich man was there, prepared to kiss the ground the Great Mother walks on.'

'Who are you talking about?'

'Ruben Lentov, that typical representative of the cultured Jewish capitalist class.'

Simon was sitting very still, but his eyes were burning. 'I've never understood how anyone like you could be a psychiatrist,' he said. 'I knew you hadn't the slightest sense when it comes to people, but I didn't know you were anti-Semitic.'

There was something in her face – an appeal for mercy – but it was too late.

'Let's take one thing at a time,' Simon continued. 'Karin is no Great Mother, because she's never been able to have children. That's the sorrow of her life. I am adopted – a Jewish child. My father was a typical representative of the Jews who were gassed at Auschwitz. You would have done well there – among the executioners.' As he left, he slammed the door behind him so hard that the old building shook.

That night, Klara took four sleeping pills.

Chapter 34

The next morning Klara woke feeling sick, with a thumping headache. She rang the Historical Institute and told them she was giving up the course. They reprimanded her and informed her that the term's fees would not be refunded.

Then she dialled the hospital and asked her supervisor if she could start her houseman duty now.

'You've a month to make good,' he said curtly, but he liked her for her quick intelligence, so he added that it would probably be all right. 'I'm glad to hear you've got rid of all that psychological nonsense.'

Klara spent all Monday writing a letter. *Simon, I'm a horrible person and you should be glad things between us are over. But I am not anti-Semitic and I don't think I would have been among the executioners in Auschwitz, where your father died. That is, I hope not . . .*

She got in a muddle again, but it didn't matter as she never sent the letter. On Tuesday morning she was at the back of the crowd of medical students on the ward rounds, her gaze more distant than ever. But she was listening and the fact was, the more she closed her heart,

the clearer her mind became. Her demons were quiet
again.

Simon had never believed it could hurt so much. There
was a sheer physical pain in his chest. The air was clear,
the September sun shining mildly over town, but his
world was grey. It wasn't guilt this time, he told himself.
He didn't regret a word he had said. On the contrary, the
only thing that gave him any comfort was finding nastier
things he should have said. Fascist bitch!

Sometimes he thought there was something wrong
with him, with his relationships with women. First there
had been Iza and now this cow who was even worse. He
remembered his fantasies about the evil that was to make
him real, but now life had never been so unreal. Ruben
spoke to him, but Simon didn't listen. It was the same at
lectures, the damned pain inside his chest meant he
couldn't hear.

He kept trying not to think about Klara.

Ruben phoned Erik to say he was worried.

'You can't die of a broken heart,' Erik said. 'But it can
make you ill.'

'We must do something, Erik.'

'No one can do anything. But it's a damned shame.
She was a nice girl – unusual.'

A fortnight later, Simon developed a temperature.
Nothing could be hidden from Karin. She arrived at
almost the same moment as the doctor Ruben had sent
for, who told them Simon had pneumonia.

'It's no longer dangerous,' the doctor said, giving
Simon antibiotics. But to be sure, he wanted the boy
admitted to hospital. Karin went in the ambulance with
him.

Simon lay in the Sahlgrenska Hospital, dreaming again
that he was running after a girl in a sea of grass. She was

long-legged and slim, elusive as a ray of sunlight, and he caught her, knowing it was Klara, but when she turned round it was Iza, laughing at him. Then he heard a flute and saw the mist was lifting from the river, but he didn't want to go there, didn't want to see that it was Iza playing and laughing in his face.

Karin sat with him throughout the night and, for the first time in her life, prayed for forgiveness. The doctor on duty had examined him and said he would soon recover, she told herself. They trusted this new drug and no doubt it was more reliable than her own whimpering to a God she didn't believe in.

Karin was given coffee. The girl had been insane and would have destroyed Simon's life, she thought. So what had happened was probably just as well.

Then Simon started to call out in his sleep. Karin thought he had stopped breathing and her fear was terrible. She heard her mother saying *poor me, poor me*, and she saw herself in her mother-in-law's kitchen saying the old have to die to make room for the young. She realised that with these words she had made a pact with the devil and now he had come to demand his own. But he hadn't come himself. He'd sent a girl, a witch who had crushed her self-esteem, which was what her son lived off. So he had to die.

Karin wept in despair. Erik was there, and Ruben, saying she had to be careful of herself. Then her old cardiac specialist came, summoned by Ruben. He examined Simon and said he would soon be back on his feet, the drug had worked, his temperature was down. He gave Karin an injection and she was never to remember how she got home. Fourteen hours later she woke in her own bedroom as Erik brought her coffee in bed and told her Simon had slept well all night and his temperature was now normal.

She dozed all morning and thought about the God she didn't believe in and how all-encompassing his power was. As far as the devil was concerned, she had met him in her own heart. He was within her as he was in everyone else.

She remembered how she ill she had been when peace came, ill from all the evil that had been revealed that terrible spring four years ago.

She also recalled the dreams she had had at the cardiac unit, and she dwelled for a long time on the memory of Petter and the night he had come to her in her sleep, wanting to say something to her, but she had been too tired to listen. Perhaps I didn't want to, she thought. She knew now that what Petter had said was that evil exists within everyone, and that not until that is accepted can it be understood and fought against.

Karin got out of bed, looked up Klara's number in the directory and phoned her.

Klara's voice rose with surprise and with something else as well. Joy, Karin thought.

'I know you two have broken up, but I've mulled over what you said to me about good mothers and I think you might be right,' Karin said incoherently. 'But the thing is, Simon is so terribly ill and I thought you, as a doctor, might be able to—'

'Simon's ill?' Klara's voice was shrill.

'He's in the Sahlgrenska.'

'I'll go at once. And I'll phone you back.'

Klara took a taxi, then regretted it as it would have been quicker to cycle, but she got there in the end. White coat, right expression. The Ward Sister was polite, but kept her distance when, looking as if about to cry, Klara said she wanted to be told about Simon's prognosis for private reasons.

She's in love, poor creature, thought the nurse, taking

out the case sheet. He had lobate pneumonia. Antibiotics had been prescribed, he had been X-rayed after a drop in his temperature. There were no remaining patches on the lung.

'You can look in on him if you want to.'

Klara felt braver as the nurse added that he would be asleep and she was sure Klara realised he shouldn't be woken.

He was in a ward on his own, and he was asleep as the sister had said. And goodness, how handsome he was.

Klara stood and looked at him for a while and, as if he felt her presence, he opened his eyes. 'Go to hell, you fascist beast,' he whispered.

As she turned round to go, she bumped into Ruben, who had been there for some time. He must have been watching her, she realised, and had heard what Simon said.

Klara stood quite still, but it was no use this time as the tears poured down her face. She was scarcely aware of the big handkerchief Ruben produced, but she felt his warmth as he wiped her face. 'There, there, Klara dear. There, there,' he said.

She pulled herself together and tried to speak, tried again, then finally succeeded. 'Would you tell Simon that the only person I loved when my mother left was a Jew who played the flute.'

'I'll remember that,' Ruben promised.

When Klara got home, she phoned Karin. 'I've been to see him,' she said, feeling calmer now. 'I saw his case notes. He's in no danger and he'll be discharged in a few days.'

'Thank you,' Karin said. 'Thank you, my dear.'

'I'm very sorry.' Klara's voice was unsteady. 'I hope

you'll forgive me for what I said – about good mothers . . . for making you so miserable.'

'Don't take it back. I understand why you said it. But mothers are necessary all the same, aren't they?'

'Karin, I'll phone her.'

'Do that and ring me if you want to talk.'

'But Simon . . .'

'This has nothing to do with him, Simon is a difficult creature and always has been,' Karin continued in a rush as if she was afraid of changing her mind. 'He'll never find a nice pretty girl, the kind mothers dream of.'

'Then I might be suitable, after all?'

'I think so.'

Klara could hear Karin's voice shaking. 'I know this isn't easy for you,' she said.

'No,' Karin agreed. 'Life is difficult to understand in general. And Klara, there's something else you don't know about Simon. He never gives up.'

'He's probably given me up,' Klara replied. 'You didn't hear what he said to me in the hospital.'

Karin put the receiver down. She still disliked Klara but the girl had an honesty about her which appealed. She was the only person she had met who had confronted her demons. I'll never be able to deceive her, she realised.

Klara wasted no time. She didn't even take off her coat. She booked a call to Oslo. 'May I speak to Mrs Kersti Sörensen?'

'Speaking.'

'This is Klara.'

It was as quiet as if the earth had stopped in its orbit. God has made time cease, Klara thought. Then she heard her mother crying.

'I hoped you would make contact. I've dreamed of it all these years.'

'But why didn't you telephone?'

The world stood still again until her mother's voice came back down the line. 'I didn't dare. But I know you're reading medicine at Göteborg. I'm so proud of you.'

'But why did you never contact me when I was small and needed . . .'

'I wrote, Klara. I've piles of letters your father sent back unopened. I contested custody and spent all the money I inherited from my mother on lawyers. But it was hard in those days. I hadn't a chance. I'd been unfaithful, you see.'

'Oh, Mother . . .'

'In the end, your father transferred my share in the sawmill to you in exchange for a promise that I would never get in touch with you again.'

Klara was crying now.

'You were so intelligent, Klara. I wanted to ensure your education and I knew how mean he was.'

'But I've had to beg for every penny. And I took out a student loan.'

'Phone Mr Bertilsson, the lawyer in Karlstad. Do that, Klara. If you give me your address, I'll send you those letters.'

'Have you saved them?'

'Yes. I thought . . . They'll give you some idea of what things were like, how I felt.'

The telephonist interrupted to say their time was nearly up. Klara gave her mother her address. 'I'll be seeing you, Mother. I'll come at Christmas.'

'That'll be heaven.'

It was lucky for Klara that she still had some anger left over the next few hours. She contacted the lawyer at his home in Karlstad, and he confirmed that there was an account in her name and that it had been there since the divorce. He sounded quite surprised.

'How much is there?' Klara asked.

'About twenty-five thousand kronor,' he said. 'It will have accumulated of course, so there should be thirty by now.'

She phoned the sawmill and could hear that her father was drunk. 'You're a bastard!' she shouted and slammed down the receiver.

But after a while she forgot the money because of her mother, because of the voice she recognised, because she could hear for herself the pain and love within it.

I have a mother, she thought. I too, Simon, have a mother who cares for me.

Two days later the letters arrived from Oslo. Klara phoned the hospital to say that she had an autumn cold.

She read the letters and wept, then read them again until she knew them by heart.

She phoned Karin and told her what had happened.

'That's wonderful,' said Karin. And Klara could hear that she too had her old strength back.

Chapter 35

Sprawling in an armchair at Ruben's, Simon considered how his broken heart and pneumonia had both healed. But he would never be really happy again.

Then, one evening, Ruben told him that he had heard what he had said to Klara that afternoon at the hospital.

'I was dreaming,' Simon protested.

'You weren't.'

'I was delirious.'

'You called her a fascist. After everything that's happened it is unforgivable to hurl words like that about. This is about decency, Simon, and respect for the dead.'

Simon drew in a sharp breath as he saw the anger in Ruben's eyes. 'You don't even know what she said, for Christ's sake.'

'I know what she told me after you'd gone back to sleep, and that was enough. She asked me to tell you, and it was so important that I wrote it down, word for word.' He took out his wallet, found the note and read it out. ' "The only person I loved when my mother left was a Jew who played the flute." '

There was a long silence.

'That man knew my father,' Simon said.

'Simon Haberman?'

'Yes.'

Perhaps I was wrong about Klara, Simon thought. Perhaps the pain inside me was guilt after all. 'I'll write and ask her to forgive me.'

'You do that.'

He spent two days on the letter, filling a waste-paper basket with his attempts.

Klara, ran the letter he finally sent. *Please forgive me for the hideous things I said to you. Naturally I know you're not a fascist. Simon.*

Simon, was her reply. *Thank you for your letter. I can understand your reaction because I was so damned awful myself. Klara.*

They struggled on apart all that autumn, determined and industrious as they had always been. Simon began to take an interest in politics and had endless discussions with Ruben's friends about the emerging state of Israel. Occasionally he thought he would go there. But he wasn't a Jew on paper, and his skills would be no use in a country fighting for survival.

Over the Christmas holidays, Mona gave birth to a daughter and, for the first time for many months, Simon sensed what happiness was. He looked into the baby's eyes, as Andersson had instructed him, and they were as deep and as unfathomable as his own. He realised that he had acquired a sister.

The day before Christmas Eve, Klara flew to Oslo, her suitcase full of presents for her mother and the young brothers and sisters she had never met. But Christmas turned out to be less perfect than she had hoped. Her mother met her at Fornebu airport and they couldn't find the words for the things they wanted to say to each other. For days, they got no further than chat about the occupation, how much more plentiful food had become and so on.

Her half-siblings spoke fluent Norwegian, and said that they had always heard about how amazing she was. Klara realised she had not come up to their expectations. Worst of all, Kersti's new husband was another alcoholic, but he was kinder, not so destructive as Klara's father had been. Even so, Klara could see that things were still difficult for her mother.

Kersti suggested that Klara should do something with her hair and they went to an elegant salon in the city centre where Klara had her hair styled and permed.

'I hardly recognise you,' Kersti said.

Klara kept looking into shop windows where she could see her reflection and admire her face with the fringe she had always longed for.

They met Kersti's friends. 'This is my daughter. She's studying medicine in Göteborg,' her mother told everyone. She was proud and this was good for Klara.

The day before New Year's Eve she flew back to Sweden and, on the plane, realised that she hadn't given Simon a thought for a whole week. She was on duty at the hospital on New Year's Day, and this was a relief. But returning was difficult. Klara found she hated her dirty old apartment, now icy cold and dark. It was such a rat's nest!

There was a parcel waiting for her and at once she recognised the handwriting. *Dr Klara Alm*. She opened the package and there was Simon's book. *To My Love* had been inscribed on the flyleaf.

Klara sat on her bed with the book in her hands. Perhaps she had known all along that there was no way out and she had had to go to Norway to make her peace with her mother because of Simon.

She was so cold by now that she was shaking so she lit the kitchen stove. Then she unpacked, went down to the corner shop and bought bread, butter and coffee. She avoided the fish which looked at her with eyes that had been dead for far too long, and bought pork chops so that she had some food over the New Year.

He shouldn't have used that word, she thought. It was wrong. They had never talked about love. Now it had been said, the word stood there like a house, making their relationship painfully real. Demanding, even.

It took Klara almost two hours to get her apartment warm enough for her to crawl into bed. Still wearing her woolly mittens, she lay reading the sea poem. Just before she fell asleep, she realised that it was the sort of poem which she might have written herself. She and Simon were so much alike . . .

She slept all night and when she lit the stove the next morning she was aware that what she was feeling was happiness, just that and nothing else.

This must be what people call serenity, Klara thought, remembering how suspicious she had always been of the word. She had never understood it, although she recognised the feeling. Perhaps she had experienced it as a child, before her mother had left home. And in music, in the life inside the notes when you allowed the flute to play by itself.

She phoned Ruben's apartment and he answered. She gave her name and asked to speak to Simon. She could tell he was pleased to hear her. Simon was not at home, he said. He was with his parents preparing to celebrate the New Year.

'Oh.' Klara was disappointed. She did not want to phone them.

'You wouldn't like to have lunch with me, I suppose? I've wanted to talk to you for some time.' Ruben sounded slightly shy.

'I'd love to,' she said, although she didn't think they would have much in common.

'Can I come and pick you up?'

Klara felt slightly faint at the thought of Lentov in her scruffy apartment. 'I'll come to your place.'

'Take a taxi. Then we'll go and find somewhere that's open.'

'Food's not all that important as far as I'm concerned,' Klara said.

'Nor me. I'll see what I can find here.'

Klara brushed her newly curled hair so that it crackled, and found the skirt and green silk blouse she'd worn to the concert with Simon. As she was putting on mascara she told herself there would be no crying today. Nor any sweating either, she thought in the taxi when she remembered she had forgotten her deoderant.

Ruben let her in. She recalled how kind he had been at the hospital and thanked him for the handkerchief. He smiled, said how furious he had been with Simon and that he had passed on her message.

'I knew that when I got his letter,' she said.

At first they were rather stiff and silent.

'I've read the sea poem,' Klara said after a while. 'Now I know we're very alike, Simon and I.'

He nodded. 'That was what I wanted to talk about. And of course, about this peculiar but difficult thing called love.'

'That word scares me.'

'Let's talk instead about how unusual it is, and how most people confuse it with their unsatisfied needs.'

'Not me.' Klara saw Ruben's mouth twitching. 'I mean, if I were able to confuse my dissatisfaction with love, I'd be in love all the time.'

They both laughed at that and Ruben agreed with Erik's remark that here was an unusual girl. Klara thought how wonderful Ruben was and whether she would have the nerve to tell him so. She took a deep breath. 'You are a wonderful person, Mr Lentov.'

He blushed like a schoolboy and asked her to call him Ruben, so that he could continue to call her Klara.

He offered her some sherry and went out into the kitchen to look for something to eat. 'I want to tell you something I've never told anyone else,' he said decisively when he returned. And he searched for words to describe Rebecca, the girl he had loved and whose sister he had married.

'Rebecca and I were made for each other,' he began. 'Maybe I'm romanticising. No, I'm not. I know we were meant for each other. But she wanted to escape from the Jewish faith, and I understood how strong her longing for freedom was and let her go to a German officer with an aristocratic name which I hoped would guarantee her a place among the Aryan race.'

304

He paused. 'I was wrong on both counts. The grand German name was no help when the Gestapo came. She died in a concentration camp with two of her children.'

Klara realised she had been mistaken about not crying, but the mess the mascara made on her cheeks couldn't have mattered less.

Ruben told her how they had met in secret at a restaurant in Paris, the city he loved.

'I had such noble ideals,' he said. 'But, God, how much harm those ideals caused. How could I have given her up, gone against the will of God and my nature, and chosen her sister instead, whom I brought here with me and who went mad with fear and lack of love?'

Klara went to the bathroom to splash cold water over her face. She felt calmer when she came back.

'Please don't let this go any further,' Ruben said. 'Not even to Simon.'

'I promise.'

They had another glass of sherry before he spoke again. 'I have to be at the Larssons' by five. Will you come with me?'

'Yes,' she answered.

In the car, he told her about becoming a grandfather, about the child just born. 'They say she's like me,' he added.

'Here I am,' he called when they arrived. 'And I've brought a surprise with me.'

Karin stared at Klara, and Klara watched as expressions of joy, despair, anger, then happiness crossed her face.

'Perhaps we shouldn't expose you to such shocks,' Ruben said.

'Happiness can't be harmful.' Erik, hugged Klara so hard it hurt. I must find out what's wrong with Karin's heart, Klara thought.

Simon was learning to drive Erik's car with Isak.

Mona was cooking, laying the table and watching over the turkey in the oven. The smell was delicious.

'Take the baby away so that I can organise things,' she instructed, and Klara found herself with a new-born infant in her arms.

She gazed at the tiny face, then at Ruben. 'Yes, it's true. She does look like you,' she said solemnly.

'The doctor says so, so it must be true,' Mona joked.

Karin and Klara took the child into the old parlour. The walls and curtains were now white, but the old oak furniture was still there, looking slightly shamefaced among the brightness.

Klara told Karin about her mother and the new husband, another alcoholic.

'I can't believe it,' Karin exclaimed. 'Why is life so difficult?'

Both of them gazed at the baby lying there, so simple and good. Then they heard the car and Karin looked nervous.

'You might give Simon a shock. Run upstairs and we can prepare him a bit.'

Klara handed over the child, her heart beating so fast it hurt, but there were no demons in her fear as she went upstairs.

'The door on the right,' Karin called.

She went into Simon's old room and her knees felt so weak that she had to sit down on the bed.

When Simon came into the kitchen, Karin saw only his thin face and anguished eyes, and she wondered what on earth to say.

Happily, Erik found the words. 'That amazing Ruben Lentov has brought you another Christmas present, Simon. It's up in your room. Prepare for the worst for it's even better-looking than the radiogram.'

Simon laughed. Ruben should stop giving him

presents, he said. And anyway, he'd already had one from him.

He started off towards the stairs, but Karin stopped him. 'A drink, Simon?' she said. 'That's soothing.'

Ruben didn't know whether to laugh or cry. Mona chose to laugh.

'Mum, you're off your head,' Simon said.

He went upstairs and the house held its breath, but despite the quiet, no one could hear a word. Only a door closing.

'Let's forget about them until dinner's ready.' Mona began clattering about with pans again.

Simon stood by the door, staring at the girl on his bed. He went over to her and without a word started to undress her, the silk blouse, the tight skirt, the nylon stockings, finally her bra. He lay down beside her and made love to her as he had done in a thousand dreams over the last six months, fiercely and silently.

'Thank you,' she said afterwards, but he put a finger over her mouth.

'Have you brought your flute with you?'

'No.'

'Tomorrow,' he said. 'You're to play for me.'

When Mona knocked on the door to say that no one could live on love and they had been waiting almost two hours for dinner, it seemed to them both that only a moment had gone by.

Simon laughed.

I'd forgotten what a big laugh he has, Klara thought as she dressed.

They came downstairs hand in hand and said practically nothing all evening. It was difficult to look at them, they seemed so naked somehow, stripped to their very souls. Only Karin dared gaze at Simon, and this told her what she already knew: that she had lost him and that he was happy.

As midnight struck, they raised their glasses.

'To your love,' said Erik. 'Cherish it, for God's sake.'

Chapter 36

At six the next morning, Klara woke the sleeping household. 'Simon, I'm on duty! I have to be at the hospital before seven and I've no comfortable shoes. Are there any trams?'

'You were going to play the flute for me,' Simon groaned. Then he saw the seriousness of the situation and woke Erik, who pulled on his trousers over his pyjamas with a grunt and went to get the car out. Karin found her a pair of shoes, thankful that they took the same size.

Klara was embarrassed about the fuss she was making. 'I'm so sorry, Karin. You're angry and think I'm careless, forgetting the hospital and work and everything.'

'I just wonder how long you're going to go on deciding what other people think,' Karin told her. 'I might possibly think you're silly for not understanding that anyone can lose their head after an evening like yesterday's.'

'I'm not sure I've found it yet,' Klara muttered.

'I pity your poor patients,' Erik said, as he drove the car round to the front of the house.

The following week, Klara moved out of her shabby apartment into Simon's room at Ruben's. They talked and talked, and by Twelfth Night they had said so much that they both recognised it was enough for a lifetime.

At Easter Simon went with her to Oslo to visit her

mother. I'm not scared at all, Klara realised, sure that he would take Kersti by storm, which indeed he did.

When spring finally came, they paid a quick visit to the sawmill, largely so that Klara could show Simon off to the neighbours. He understood this and stopped to kiss her here and there, wherever houses and windows were close together.

Her father was worse than Simon had imagined. His language was crude, and he rejected all attempts at friendliness. He scared Simon, who recognised his anger and hatred.

Now that Simon had a driving licence, they could borrow Erik's car. 'You're like your father when your demons get at you,' he said to her on the way to Karlstad.

They were about to visit Joachim Goldberg, Klara's old flute teacher, having written first to ask if he remembered Simon Haberman.

'I'm the nervous one this time,' Simon confessed as they climbed the stairs of the apartment block, where Mrs Goldberg was waiting for them with coffee and cakes, and the old man received Klara with great warmth.

'I'm afraid I have to disappoint you,' he said to Simon. There had been over thirty Jewish musicians in the Berlin Philharmonic and Goldberg could only vaguely remember a shy violinist called Haberman. 'He was one of the faithful few who stayed behind, refusing to believe that what was happening all around us was going to happen to him.'

On their way home, they stopped at Trollhättan to look at the waterfalls, and were soon quarrelling furiously about everything and nothing. They were silent all the rest of the way home.

They married on Midsummer Eve in 1949, in Oslo,

where Kersti arranged a wedding that grew larger and more elaborate than any of them had wished for. Karin liked Klara's mother from the first moment and stayed on for a few days in Oslo to visit the cousins she had sent food parcels to throughout the war. She soon realised that they disliked her: the rich relative from the protected neighbouring country.

'You couldn't carry on a conversation without the German trains being rammed down your throat,' she complained to Mona when she got home.

Part Five

Chapter 37

Karin was sitting in the kitchen with an old pan on her lap. It had never been up to much, and it was now bent and buckled after many years of use, and one handle was loose.

She looked at it with some surprise, remembering how pleased she had been when she had seen it in a shop and dreamed of all the good soups she would make. She must have done so over the years, but once dreams are fulfilled, she thought, they are seldom revisited. 'Out with you,' she said, heaving it into the large rubbish bag in front of her.

It was 1955, a summer so hot it was impossible to go outside. The kitchen was cooler than the shade under the trees, as there was a slight cross-draught but, even so, Karin was finding it hard to breathe.

She and Lisa had decided to use the hot afternoon to clear out the cupboards. In the past, Karin had always found it difficult to throw things away, but now it was almost a pleasure. Old black-handled cutlery, the metal soup ladles she had always disliked, the flowery coffee set her brother had given her when she had married – they were all thrown into the sack in the middle of the floor.

Lisa sighed, objecting now and again, and she cried out when the coffee service and cream jug was put into the bag.

'Take them if you like.' Karin stopped for a moment. But then they both sighed again because they knew how full Lisa's cupboards were too.

On Thursday afternoon the sky grew dark, clouds massed, thunder rolled, lightning flashed and the rain poured down over sea and land. The soil drank it up thirstily but without gratitude, the sky thought sulkily, and it turned grey and cold without producing any more water.

The evening after the downpour, Karin didn't feel like going to bed, so she stayed in the garden breathing in the cool air until she found she was cold. Now that she was sufficiently cool, she would sleep well, she realised.

The next day the sky was grey again, but Karin was pleased, as she could go out for her walk as usual. She slipped slightly guiltily up the path at the back of the house, afraid someone would see her and want to follow her. She wanted to be alone with the hills and the sea, the river and the yellow meadows. She headed for the old bathing place and stood thinking it wasn't all that long ago that Simon had taught her to dive there. Time runs through your fingers and it gets faster the older you become, she thought sadly.

No one could bathe there any longer, however, for the water was brown and oily. Karin looked at the new houses – boxes perched on the hillside – which a few years earlier had ruined the lines of landscape that the sea, the river and the hills had spent centuries shaping. She had never imagined prosperity could become so ugly. She had thought that when the welfare state was complete, people would escape the oppression that follows poverty. Now it was here, everyone was better off. Worries over survival no longer weighed heavily on the working classes. Instead, people were plagued by desires for material objects, desires that could be satisfied only in this new and ugly abundance.

I'm an old reactionary, Karin scolded herself. In these boxes people have good housing, hot water and proper drains which run into the sea to mix with the effluent from the great industries along the river.

She turned away, and took the path across meadows marked with the foundations for yet more new houses. Well, she thought, I won't be seeing these anyway. Just what she meant by that she didn't know, but when she got to the oak trees and sat down to rest she felt she wanted to tell them about the old pan.

'You see,' she said to the trees, 'it was such an old pan and had served its purpose. It used a lot of electricity to heat it and it wouldn't stand flat properly on the stove any longer.'

The oaks listened and understood. But when she went on to tell them how ugly the pan had become, buckled and crooked, the handle loose, they didn't agree with her. It had had a faithful old beauty, the oaks thought, and Karin agreed that they had a point.

Then she told them about Simon, as she usually did, and about Isak and Mona, and their children. Things were going well for all of them and she had to be grateful.

For the fourth year running, Simon was at University College, London. He must be doing something important, Karin said to the oaks, because he had been awarded a government grant. Year after year, money came in which enabled him to return to those strange signs on the old clay tablets from Mesopotamia. Karin didn't know what was so important about them, or why people struggled to understand a language that no one had spoken for thousands of years. It was all a mystery, like prosperity and ugliness.

I must be getting old, she admitted, and the oaks laughed at her. Well, perhaps that wasn't right either, for she was only fifty and that was no age to worry about.

The oak trees suggested she think about things she understood, so Karin thought about Simon and Klara. Klara was now in Switzerland and would soon have finished her training. She and Simon didn't see all that much of each other, but that was probably good for them and their relationship.

Karin's thoughts dwelled for a while on Klara, the girl

who knew more than anyone else did about her, but who would never be close to her. Respect, mutual respect, was what existed between them. She had stopped being ashamed of what had happened when Klara had first come to meet them. That had been a difficult time and, as Karin walked alone in the hills that summer, she had accepted that she was not all that different from her own mother-in-law.

Most important of all in Karin's life, even more important than Simon, was her image of herself as a good, wise woman – the Great Mother, as Klara had called her. Karin could laugh a little at this now. Whatever happens, she thought, you strive to make the image you choose of yourself into reality, and the good, wise Karin had been the right one for the children. What it had been like for herself was something that she was only now coming to terms with for she had worked hard and had, over the years, become rather worn and buckled like the pan she had thrown out.

Klara had a profession. She had what Karin had always wanted. She wasn't dependent on a man for survival. And yet, Karin reflected, she was more dependent on Simon than Karin had ever been on Erik.

This was surprising, yet it was the same for Mona and Isak. Their marriage too, was full of demands. They felt they had to share everything with each other, understand everything about each other and this inevitably led to disappointments. She could see clearly how Isak's and Mona's despair grew on both sides until they renewed their efforts, and their quarrels, to be even closer. Some things should be left alone, Karin thought. She could never be persuaded that a man and a woman should be able to understand one another at a deeper level.

Malin came running up the slope from the house – the

blessed child, Karin thought, as she always did when she saw Isak's and Mona's daughter.

Simon called her his little sister, but that wasn't because they were alike. Whereas he was as eager as fire, she was as calm as the trees, and whereas he was bursting with questions, she was rich with knowing.

Karin sat down and took the girl in her arms. 'Malin, six years old and light of my heart,' she said in an almost formal greeting. She ran her fingers through her granddaughter's thick hair and kissed the back of her neck, smelling her special fragrance. 'You smell as if you've come from the sky.'

'I saw you leaving and was going to run after you,' Malin told her. 'But then I thought you might want to be alone.'

'You were right. But now I don't want to be alone any longer. Now I want to be with you.'

'What was it you had to think about?'

Karin considered for a moment then, rather to her surprise, said, 'It was that old pan I threw out yesterday. I was feeling sad about it.'

Malin shared Karin's sense of loss. 'Couldn't you have given it to me? I could have played with it in the sandpit.'

'But you've got so many smart new buckets.'

'But I love old pans,' Malin cried and Karin smiled at her.

They walked hand in hand down the hill and into the big new garden. Despite the grey sky, it spread its magnificence before them, the morello cherry tree, the strawberry beds now picked clean for the year, the soft lawn which crept up to the trees, the aspens by the hill towards the river and the spruce hedges which weren't up to much yet, but would provide shelter from the north-east wind in a few years' time.

Karin sat down on the old deck-chair on the wooden jetty by the pond. She looked at the Turk's cap lilies curling their dark purple perianths in and out, their fiery red leaves sprawling insolently. They were about to go to seed and, later in the year, Karin would put their elegant seed cases into vases indoors.

Malin sat quietly by her feet, feeding ladybirds with greenfly.

'I don't like captured animals,' Karin said. 'Put them on the roses, dear.'

'I will soon.' Malin looked at the heavy roses by the pond, now badly affected by the heat and the downpour.

When Karin leaned back, she could see the apple trees on the edge of the old garden, the garden she and Erik had laid out at the beginning of their time together. They were Åkerö apples, gnarled old things, but they would provide a good crop in the autumn. I won't bother to bottle them this year, she decided. Mona can have what she wants and the birds the rest.

Malin seemed to sense that Karin wanted to be alone with her thoughts again – happy thoughts now, about the garden and everything it had given her. Her joy had been secret at first. Then, when the boatyard had moved, Mona and she had had an idea. All that early spring, when Malin was a baby and was handed from one pair of arms to another, or slept on a cushion on the kitchen sofa, they had drawn up plans for the boatyard land. Mona had dreamed of a wild meadow of ox-eye daisies and columbines, cornflowers and poppies in the south-facing corner. Karin had wanted a kitchen garden with strawberry and rasp-berry beds. They were to have creeping plants and primulas in the rock garden for pleasure in spring, and brilliant blue gentians for the autumn.

'Sedums,' Karin had said solemnly.

'You know,' Mona had told her, 'there are twenty different species of wood anemones, purple and yellow. White ones, too, but double like little roses.'

Karin hadn't known that, and she had thought that anemones should be white and ordinary for the short time that was theirs.

They had begged gardening books off Ruben and soon their dreams began to assume a rather frightening reality. They had had difficulty persuading Erik. 'You'll work yourself into the grave,' he had said. 'Anyhow, I'd need to get something from the land.'

'You talk like a capitalist, you bloodsucker,' Karin had shouted at him. She had wanted to call him an exploiter, but had been so angry that she couldn't find the right words.

He had been furious too, but since her heart trouble their quarrels had never really amounted to anything and, as usual, he had taken his rage with him to the workshop.

Only Isak supported them at first, agreeing that it would be marvellous to have a garden right down to the river. Ruben had shaken his head and been inclined to agree with Erik. How would she and Mona be able to look after such a large patch? He had also been thinking about ownership and that Isak and Mona only rented their apartment from Gustafsson.

No one knew what would have happened if the Gustafssons hadn't died so conveniently, the old man first, then a few months later his equally old wife, who had complained about her husband for sixty years but had never been able to live without him. Their heirs hadn't wanted to live in the big house with its awkward angles and leaded windows. It would cost a fortune to modernise, they declared. So they were only too pleased when Isak put in a reasonable bid. Mona was overjoyed and Karin was happy too, but held it quietly in her heart.

That summer, people came with machines to clear and level out the boatyard land and they had load after load of manure spread over the flower beds before the frosts came.

The winter was spent on alterations to the Gustafssons' house. There had been eight rooms and two kitchens but now there were only six rooms for Mona was not afraid of pulling down walls to create light and air. The old kitchen on the upper floor became a work room for Mona who had been on a course and learned to weave while Karin looked after Malin.

By the time the garden had been laid out, Mona was pregnant again and had sat, large and clumsy, in the rock garden, her stomach getting in the way of her trowel. Erik employed an old gardener, who came once a week and did the heavy work.

The twins arrived the following winter – two boys who were totally unalike, one dark as night, Jewish, introverted and thoughtful, the other fair, happy and apparently uncomplicated.

'Like my father,' Mona commented.

'Hush!' Karin had been appalled, but Mona had laughed, hugged her blond baby and said that she loved her father. That things had gone wrong for him was due to his upbringing and his heritage. 'You know,' she had said. 'My grandmother was an absolute devil.'

'Like my mother-in-law,' Karin replied. 'I wonder how they came to be like that.'

Golden years, Karin thought, heavy with sweetness and the same kind of security as when Simon was little.

She took Malin with her back to the house. Lisa had gone for the day and Karin and the child decided to make a cream cake to go with coffee in the evening. They beat the eggs and sugar, spilling flour over the kitchen floor as they whipped the cream and had fun. They put the cake into the oven and forgot it, so it was slightly burned.

'Never mind,' Karin said to Malin. 'We can trim off the burned bits and it will still taste nice. But you'll have to sweep the floor. I'm a bit tired.'

As she left, Malin said, 'You're not miserable about your old pan any longer, are you?'

'No,' Karin replied. 'Probably not.'

By Sunday, the wind had swept away all the clouds, and the sun was playing freely with the trees and people. As usual, Ruben came to dinner with Isak and Mona. They sat in the garden and chatted, he and Karin, and she told him about the pan she had thrown out. She couldn't get it out of her mind.

'It's strange,' she said. 'I hadn't seen it for years, so I can't be missing it.'

Ruben told her about the rabbi who said you should live every day as if you were saying farewell to everything, all your possessions and all the people you loved. If you managed to do that, the rabbi had maintained, then life would be real.

Karin gazed at Ruben, much taken with his story. A shadow flitted through him and he regretted what he had said without really knowing why.

Just before she fell asleep that night, Karin thought she was probably beginning to learn at last to free herself of people and things. The pan was only a beginning. That was why it had been troubling her.

Karin slept like a child, more soundly than for a long time. Her walks in the hills became freer, she had fewer memories and found more pleasure in observing things.

'I think I'm beginning to stop thinking,' she said to Malin a few days later.

'That's good, isn't it?' Malin replied. 'Thinking just muddles things.'

'You may be right there.' Karin looked at this new person who had only recently started to think.

Karin sat beneath her oak trees, wishing that she had not

321

always hurried so, done everything in her life quickly to get it over and done with. What had she done with the time when she hadn't been working? She couldn't remember.

As usual, the oaks comforted her. They knew, as she did, that it was silly to grieve over things that can never be undone. Walking back, she had no memories and was feeling strangely free.

'You're very quiet,' Erik said. 'You're feeling all right, are you?'

'Oh yes. I've never felt better. The thing is, you see, I've stopped worrying.'

'Then there's nothing to talk about. Is that what you mean?'

'And not much to think about either.'

'Well, it's about time you stopped worrying.'

Karin could see there were suspicions in Erik's eyes. But this didn't bother her.

He and Isak were to go to America at the end of November to look at yards for small boats. They were both worried about the trip, Erik most of all because he couldn't speak the language and couldn't stand being at a disadvantage. But he didn't like to admit it, not even to himself.

He wanted Karin to go too, but she had said that she hadn't the energy for such a long journey. You can't keep hanging on to my skirts all your life, Erik Larsson, she thought. The time is coming when you'll have to stand on your own two feet.

It rained in September, but at the beginning of October an Indian summer dawned, mild and golden. Karin found a place along the shore where the reeds were so high that they hid everything except the sky and the river. She took to sitting there for hours and just looking.

She had never been so clear-sighted as she was now that

she had freed herself from her ideas about what life should be like.

That day, Tuesday, the waxwings came, a flock of them on their way south. They landed around her and she looked at the orange stripes on their wings and their funny heads with their defiant crests, and she heard their song once more, that strange song halfway between joy and dark sorrow.

All the same, she was surprised, when she realised that this was what all the signs had been preparing her for, that a new and greater freedom lay ahead.

Trying not to disturb the birds, she lay down calmly and quietly, paying careful attention to the way her heart was slowing down, until gradually it stopped beating completely.

Chapter 38

Mona threw out the tea that had been drawing for too long and was now cold. 'It's stupid to worry,' she said, aloud this time.

Malin came in crying. She had been on the hill a hundred times at least to meet Karin, she told her mother. 'Why isn't she here?'

Mona phoned Lisa and asked her if she could look after Malin and the twins for an hour or two. Then she took to the paths she'd come to know so well. She's probably sitting somewhere, even fallen asleep, so I mustn't give her a fright, she said to herself.

Then all reason left her and Mona ran beneath the oaks, over the hills, across the meadows, along the shore, calling her name. She searched for an hour, then another, but there was no trace of Karin. As she turned towards home, she still had a small hope that Karin would be in the garden with Malin as usual. But, in her heart, she had begun to prepare herself for the worst.

Fortunately, Isak was at home. Mona asked Lisa to stay a bit longer and she and Isak hurried towards the shore.

'I've looked everywhere,' she panted. 'Perhaps she's fallen into the water.'

Isak's eyes darkened with fear. Together, they hunted along the river bank, then turned in among the reeds. And there she was, lying peacefully, as if she were asleep.

'Karin,' Isak shouted, relief in voice. When she didn't answer, he looked at Mona, grabbed her shoulders and shook her. 'Mona, it can't be true. Tell me it's not true?'

But it was. They stood among the reeds holding hands like children.

Mona freed herself at last and picked a few late summer flowers and put them in Karin's hands. Both of them could see that she had begun to go rigid. Isak cried out in horror.

Her lips white, Mona told him they had to keep calm. One of them should keep guard while the other went home to phone for a doctor.

'I'll stay,' Isak said. He realised he wanted to be alone with Karin for a while, to talk to her as he'd always done when things were difficult.

'When will Erik be back from the yard?' Mona asked.

'He was working on a blueprint. He needed to get it done.'

Mona ran to Lisa to ask her to put the children to bed.

Malin looked wide-eyed at her. 'She's gone, Mamma. She has, hasn't she?'

'Yes,' Mona replied. 'Malin, darling, you must be a brave girl now.'

'I will.'

Mona rushed to the Larssons' house and found to her dismay that Erik's car was in the drive.

'I was worried when Karin didn't answer the phone.' But Erik didn't look worried, just happy as usual.

What shall I say? What in heaven's name shall I say? Help me, God, Mona thought.

'Karin's . . . ill. We must phone the doctor.' She rang the old doctor who had looked after them over the years, holding firmly on to Erik's hand as she told him that he must come at once, that they would wait on the road outside the house and show him where Karin was.

'Let go, Mona!' Erik shouted angrily.

Without releasing his hand, she eased him on to the kitchen sofa and kneeled down beside him. 'She's dead, Erik.'

But she could see he didn't believe her. 'The doctor'll be here soon, won't he, with his injections?' he begged.

At last the doctor arrived, Erik leaped into the car, shouting to get the syringes ready, and when they came to the end of the road, Mona ran ahead along the path. The doctor could see at once that it was too late. But not Erik.

He threw himself at Karin and shook her furiously. 'Wake up woman. Wake up!'

It was terrible. Isak had to use all his strength to pull Erik off and take him to the car, where the doctor gave him an injection. At last Erik's rage was obliterated by darkness.

'We'll take her home,' Mona said. 'We'll hold a wake over her until Simon comes back from England.'

And this was what happened. With shaking hands, Mona made up the bed with Karin's best linen. Isak saw to Erik and the telephone.

He called Ruben first. Isak could hear him shrinking at the other end of the phone, as his voice cracked, then disappeared. 'Dad!' he yelled. 'Dad, we mustn't give way now. You must get hold of Simon!'

Ruben's voice came back from nowhereland, brittle at first. 'I'll do that. Then I'll come on out.'

Ruben set to work. Simon shouldn't be told over the phone, he decided. So he booked a call to Zurich, and at last heard Klara's calm voice.

Klara turned cold with the effort of not showing she was upset and said she would catch the evening plane to London. She and Simon would take the first flight from there to Torslanda the next morning.

'Take care of him,' Ruben said.

'How in heaven's name am I to do that?' she cried.

She managed to get a seat on a plane and sent a telegram to Simon from Zurich airport. *Meet me at Heathrow this evening at eleven o'clock. Your Klara.*

When Simon got the telegram, he was pleased. Then it struck him that this was not like Klara. Something must have happened.

The moment she appeared, running towards him in the Arrivals hall, he saw that her eyes were distant in that way she had when things were difficult.

'Look out for my case, will you? The ordinary red one, you know. I'll go and fix tickets for tomorrow.' Her voice was calm.

'Are you really going back tomorrow?'

She didn't answer. On the way in to London, she sat very close to him and Simon knew they were heading towards something serious. He felt frightened. 'Klara, can't you tell me what this is about?'

'Not here, Simon.'

'Karin died this afternoon,' she told him at last when they got back to his room.

She saw him die too as he stood in front of her, growing more and more stiff by the minute. After a while, he began to shudder, so she got him into bed and lay down beside him. He said nothing, but occasionally in the night she could feel him crying and the tension in her gave way a little.

In the morning, he got dressed mechanically and went with her to the taxi and the plane. As they fastened their seat-belts, he opened his mouth for the first time since the evening before. 'I hope we crash.'

'We'll probably make it,' Klara said. 'We have to, for Erik's sake.'

The plane landed neatly at Torslanda where Ruben's car was waiting for them, one of his employees at the wheel.

Göteborg was shamelessly the same as ever. But in the garden by the river, Erik was going crazy, his fury such that it could move trees and shift boulders. It wasn't possible. No one could bloody well treat him like this, he raged.

Isak had been with him all night, trying to hold him when things were at their worst. At dawn the doctor had returned and given him some tablets.

Ruben and Mona had sat with Karin. Malin, too. She had appeared in her white nightie at three in the morning, sat down beside them and looked at Karin.

Karin had been on her way ever since she had thrown out the old pan before the rain. She spoke the words Ruben and Mona recognised as being true. 'She wanted to be on her own.'

Lisa arrived and made coffee and breakfast, saying they had to eat. Mona found it hard to swallow, but Ruben drank cup after cup of black coffee and was unusually alert. This only increased his torment.

Mona went back to the children for a while and told them that Lisa was going to spend the day with them. She spoke so seriously that they made no protest. Then she went back to the Larssons' house. Fortunately Erik was sleeping. The doctor had told Isak that he would be more resigned to Karin's death when he woke. He'll never be resigned, Mona said to herself. Not deep down, anyway.

At last Simon appeared with Klara. Thank goodness, another adult, Mona thought, as she hugged Klara. She whispered that they had all gone mad here, Erik most of all. His mind seemed to have gone.

Simon went straight in to see his mother. He sat with her as the candle burned down and no one ever knew what he was thinking or what he said.

Erik was calmer when he woke, his rage returning only when he saw Simon. 'It's so unfair! No one should treat us like this,' he shouted again.

'You're bloody well right!' Simon shouted back and Klara sighed with relief.

Towards midday the undertakers came and, as the hearse containing Karin's body moved away, the road was lined with weeping neighbours and silent children. Not wanting to watch the hearse leaving, Ruben went into the garden. She's dead too, he thought. The second woman I've ever loved, and I've no right to mourn this time either. He decided to go home, for there he would be able to shout like Erik.

Klara saw him walking slowly towards his car and she sensed his great sadness. She hesitated, then phoned Olof Hirtz at the hospital. He was also shaken by Karin's death, and worried about Ruben. He said he would go and see him as soon as he was finished for the day.

'Jews seldom take their own lives,' he said, though if that was meant as some consolation to Klara, it failed. She put down the receiver and made a supreme effort not to scream as well.

Things settled down gradually as they spent the week doing what had to be done for the funeral. As she worked, Klara kept hearing the hopeless words, 'Ashes to ashes, dust to dust'. Karin would never have agreed with this, she thought.

It isn't true. This is all one big lie. Life is much, much more than a spadeful of soil, Simon raged.

Inga was among the family mourners.

'Could you stay with Erik for a while, until he's over the worst?' Klara asked her when they were alone.

Inga said she would.

Mona insisted Isak and Erik should go to America as had been arranged. When Erik came back, Inga had moved into the house by the river and locked up her own by the lake. They were cousins and had always liked each other. She became his housekeeper, keeping the place clean and tidy, and Erik away from the drink. She was kinder than Karin, more compliant. Through her, Erik gradually regained his equilibrium and was able to take control of his life. But he was never happy again. That joy that had once been Erik's gift from the gods had been lost one Tuesday in October down by the river.

Chapter 39

They could see the coast of Norway outlined against the blue sea from the air.

'It's strange, but there is strength in the midst of chaos,' Simon said.

All Klara could think of was how tired she was. 'Does that surprise you?'

'I've always believed that if she didn't exist, I wouldn't either. But perhaps "believe" is the wrong word.' He fell silent.

'If Karin died, then Simon would too?'

'Something like that. I didn't think it through. It just felt obvious, like the ground or the night.'

'But it didn't happen. You didn't die.'

'At first, when you came and told me, I thought I might. But not any longer.'

Klara stayed with Simon at the student hostel for a week while he began work on his thesis again. She sat next to him in the British Museum Reading Room and thought about Karl Marx sitting there too, day after day, doing his research. Did he ever consider the wretched state of his finances, his deceived wife and poor children while he wrote *Das Kapital*, she wondered? She looked at Simon, envying men their ability to do one thing at a time and be totally absorbed by it.

They were having a meal at an Indian restaurant in Bloomsbury one evening, when Simon turned to Klara. 'It's like being born again in great pain.'

Klara drew in her breath sharply and took a mouthful from her glass of water. There were tears in her eyes from the spicy chicken.

'I realise that what makes it different is that you are here now,' he said. 'I won't be abandoned this time.'

Klara gazed into the distance.

'Hello there. Come on out,' Simon said gently.

She looked at him. This time the tears in her eyes couldn't be blamed on the spicy food. 'I've had an idea,' she said. 'But I'm scared to talk about it.'

'Try me anyway.'

Klara told him about the little Volkswagen she had seen – red with a canvas hood. She had been to see it that afternoon while Simon was at a lecture. 'It's second-hand and not very expensive. And we've got the money.'

'I'd never dare to drive in London.'

'Let's try it tomorrow.'

The next day they took the red Volkswagen for a test

drive. Simon found he had to have his wits about him as he negotiated the city's traffic. It was fun.

'Well?' Klara asked, as they parked the car outside the showroom and he wiped his brow.

'Yes,' Simon decided and she saw he was pleased.

'You need a car. Everything here is so far away.'

'I think about going to the country occasionally,' he said. 'Trees in London parks are not the same thing.'

The car brought excitement to the days they had left before Klara returned to Zurich. 'This is crazy,' he said. 'I ought to be ashamed of having such a good time.'

Klara refrained from saying she knew that it wasn't the car that was freeing his emotions, but the driving and the demands it made on his concentration.

She left and Simon was unprepared for the loneliness waiting for him in his hostel room.

Why wasn't I at home? he thought guiltily. I could have walked along the shore with Karin and helped her keep her hold on life. Last time I was there she wanted to live for my sake. But his reason told him that what the doctor had said was correct. If a heart was worn out then it could function no longer.

'Anyway,' he said aloud. 'I couldn't make her take pleasure in life, not always. Not even often. She pretended most of the time to be happy and I know it.'

But perhaps it was my fault she wasn't happy, Simon thought suddenly. A chasm opened and his fear was so great that his mouth became dry. Sweat poured off him and his heart thumped so loudly that it seemed to reverberate against the walls.

There was half a bottle of whisky on the bookshelf and he drank it quickly. He remembered Klara saying that she had left a box of tablets in his desk drawer. 'Only if things are unbearable,' she had instructed.

Well, they were now. He took two pills and fell asleep immediately.

When he awoke the next morning he realised that there was something much more important waiting for him than his headache. His tutor, Professor J. P. Armstrong, was giving a lecture. 'I was sorry to hear about your mother,' he said as Simon came into the hall.

It was a very English admission of his loss and Simon was almost able to smile as he thanked him.

Klara rang that evening and realised at once what had occurred. 'You mustn't take those pills every day, Simon. Do you hear?'

'You've no idea what it's like.'

'I'll come back.'

'No!' Simon shouted, flinging down the receiver. He hated her, just as he hated Karin, both being women who had mothered, then abandoned him.

An hour later he booked another call. 'Forgive me,' he managed to say.

'Promise me you'll phone before you take any more?' Klara begged.

'They'll be very expensive pills.' They both laughed.

You mustn't do that, he thought as he went back to his room. You mustn't behave badly to Klara.

But he was frightened as he lay on his bed and remembered his sudden feelings of hatred. Black hatred had always existed within him. Had Karin seen it? Of course she had. Guilt twisted the knife and placed it right in his heart.

Simon didn't sleep at all that night, but some sense returned in the morning. He sat at his desk and took out his notes. Hieroglyphics: a vanished language to be resurrected? How stupid! How completely idiotic. That a grown man could occupy himself with such nonsense –

why, that was insane. He started to laugh, and soon found he was crying and had to lie down again.

Why hadn't he been trained to do something sensible with his life? I could have been a doctor by now, Mum, he thought. How proud you would have been if I had been a surgeon saving lives at a hospital. I could have saved you. Perhaps you wanted to go on living?

When Klara rang, he told her about his fear and his terrible feelings of guilt.

She sighed. 'Oh Simon,' she said. 'Your responses are so total.'

He didn't understand what she meant, but assured her that he was feeling more positive now.

He returned to the casts of clay tablets on his desk: fragments from the great Gilgamesh epoch that would show what had been borrowed by Babylon during Sumerian times. It was difficult work but, as he translated the hieroglyphics, he began to be charmed by the story of the huluppi tree by the Euphrates that saved the goddess Innana from drowning in the river. She took a shoot to her garden and tended it carefully, for when it grew, she intended to make a bed from its timbers. But when the huluppi tree grew to its full height, it couldn't be felled. The serpent, whom no one could tame, had built its nest at its foot and, in the tree-top, the demon Lilith lived, whom Simon also recognised as the evil woman in Jewish legends.

Simon read on as Innana shed bitter tears over her huluppi tree, and eventually enlisted help from Gilgamesh who killed the serpent and drove Lilith away. It was a strange and comforting story.

Simon thought about Samuel Noah Kramer, the American who had come to lecture in London and hunted out his notes. Early Sumerian scripts consisted of lists, long repetitions of birds and animals, plants and trees, types of stone, stars, all of which were distinguished by their visible characteristics. There was order in the Sumerian universe and the gods had definite tasks.

All transcendental qualities were lacking, Kramer had said. It was a fact-defined culture and the most religious that the world knew. The old people, who called themselves the dark ones, had thought the only way of controlling the world and its unfathomable forces was to name everything it contained.

In the beginning was the word, Simon recalled. It created the world and overcame fear.

That evening he wrote a long letter to Klara telling her about his fear that he had betrayed Karin and his inability to make her happy. He wrote like a child, not bothering about how he phrased things, nor about her eventual reply. But his heart thumped when her letter came through the post.

Simon, as I said on the phone, you are so total in your responses to everything, particularly when it involves Karin. But you have an adult mind. Can't you see how childish and egocentric your relations to her were? A Freudian would call it an unresolved Oedipus conflict. Can't you see that you weren't everything in her life, perhaps not even the most important thing? As far as her sorrow is concerned, that was there long before you came into the world . . .

For once his anger came immediately, rising like white-hot iron through his body, exploding in fury in his head. He hadn't asked for a diagnosis, and had long distrusted psychology, even if he had always been fascinated by its interpretations. What did Klara know, what *could* she know, feel, understand about his relationship with Karin? She did what people generally do when faced with the incomprehensible. She had found a few phrases, choice bits of jargon, and distanced herself from him and his feelings. How could Klara have any idea about the network of sorrow and guilt, love and intimacy, that had existed between him and his mother? It always had, Simon said to himself. It was primaeval, decreed by fate, woven together through the centuries.

He flung the letter down on his desk, heard the telephone ringing in the hall and thought, there she goes, phoning again. God, how I hate her! He had to get out of the building before she caught him – that marvellous psychoanalyst who understood nothing.

He ran towards New Oxford Street, caught a bus in Tottenham Court Road and, as dusk fell, gazed out of the upstairs window at the city and the people moving about.

Outside Harrods in the Brompton Road, an Asian man in a grey jacket was staring into a shop window displaying kitchenware, saucepans, cutting boards, knives and toasters. He was totally absorbed. Perhaps he thought that the objects in the window spoke a secret language, a European language he did not understand. Simon wanted to shake him and tell him there was nothing to understand. Everything was superficial. Have you ever heard of an unresolved Oedipus conflict, he wanted to ask? And you didn't understand? Well, I can tell you that there is nothing to understand. It's as meaningless as the kitchenware in that window.

He was attracted by some black youths queueing outside a cinema. Simon joined them, keeping as close as he could, wishing some of their strength would rub off on to him. These men with their flashing laughter knew more about life than any damned psychologist. Simon turned away from the ticket office and set off again.

He was as real as Karin had always been, he thought. Her sorrow had defined her. She was courageous enough never to have to look for words that would free her. She had always known that life shouldn't be explained, only lived. Endured.

He bumped into a prostitute, and looked into her white face and red mouth which was painted like a wound of despair.

'What a nice boy,' she whispered. There was no mistaking her surprise when he took her arm. But he was determined. This evening he was going to sink with her into the depths of her shame.

He shut out the details of her dirty room, the slack fleshiness of her body, the absurdity of their situation. He wanted to touch her despair and be scorched by it. Naturally he did not succeed. He smiled, she smiled, they made love. He paid, left, wanting to wash but rejecting the idea. After all he wanted to be defined by her essence.

Afterwards he went to the nearest pub and got so drunk he had no idea how he got back home. When he woke in his own bed the next morning, he found two notes saying that Zürich had phoned at seven o'clock and half past nine.

Klara was probably worried by now. Serve her right, he thought.

He felt ill in the library and telephoned after his last lecture. 'Thanks for your letter,' he said coldly, savagely.

'Simon, please be sensible. You must –'

'I must nothing,' he shouted and hung up.

I regret I opened up to you [he wrote later that day]. *I think you should take all those grand words about Oedipus and stuff them up your arse. You've understood nothing, neither about me nor the myth . . .*

It was crude, but he thought it funny at the time and posted it. He regretted it the next day, however, and phoned her to ask her to tear it up without reading it.

She wouldn't, she said. They talked about minor matters

in tones of voice that would assure each other that all was well between them.

That night he dreamed he was lying in bed. He had become weightless and was rising, floating up to the ceiling and through it, through the dirty grey fog over London and up into the blue sky.

In the daytime, he was absorbed by the origins of the Sumerian culture, a mystery that could only be solved through an understanding of their language. But the language was like no other, being neither Indo-European nor Semitic. He was fascinated by the Hittite scripts he was also studying, the first Indo-European scripts in the Middle East. Although the words were long and incomprehensible, the clay tablets were beginning to assume a familiar resonance. There was something about them, a rhythm, an inkling of a tune that related to himself.

At the beginning of December, Ruben came to a book fair in London. He stayed the weekend and they drove out into the country and found a coaching inn with a long history and a warm interior. On Sunday they roamed around the countryside, across fields and through clumps of bare trees. It was misty.

'I'd like to talk about Karin, about what she was like at the end,' Ruben told him.

It was hard going, but Simon needed to know as much as possible about what she had thought and how she had felt.

Ruben told Simon of their conversation about the old pan. 'I quoted an old rabbi, who used to preach that one should live every day as if saying goodbye to everything, even people. It seemed to make a big impression on her.'

Simon looked at Ruben in surprise.

'Then Mona told me Karin's walks were getting longer and longer,' Ruben went on. 'I was rather worried and one day I asked her what she thought about on her long walks.

She said that she had stopped thinking, that she was now free of emotions and thoughts.'

Simon stopped on the path as he took in what Ruben was saying.

'There was something strange about her, something new,' Ruben continued. 'When I got home that evening I tried to work it out, to make out the expression in her eyes.'

'And?'

'I came to the conclusion that Karin was happy. What was new about her was this happiness. For the first time since I met her she was without sorrow.'

'Do you think she knew she was going to die?'

'I don't know. Perhaps she did, but not consciously. I don't think she really considered it.'

Simon wept, but it didn't matter in the mist.

'I've thought a lot about it since,' Ruben said. 'That there is a deeper meaning in death, that it's not merely physical. Everything I have lived through, all my knowledge, my happiness and my suffering, all my memories and endeavours, these will come to an end. But the familiar, the family, children, home – all that I have identified most closely with – will be left behind.'

Simon remembered how his wave was dashed against the Bohus rocks and how it gave back its experience to the sea before it could be born again.

'It seems to me that this is what death is,' Ruben concluded. 'It's a relinquishing of life. And I guess that's what we all fear so much, don't you think?'

'I suppose so.'

'I wanted you to know that Karin died free. She left everything and was happy before she passed away.'

When Ruben had gone back to Sweden, Simon felt a great

sadness. But he didn't feel guilty any longer. It was as if he hadn't room for both emotions.

In the end, he decided he had inherited Karin's sorrow. This is where she lived and worked. It is a large and lonely place, he thought, but not unbearable. I can live here and do my work as long as I take care.

Chapter 40

Klara and Simon flew home for Christmas, meeting at Kastrup airport, then taking the train from Malmö.

Things weren't easy. The days went by as heavy as lead, as long as Karl Johansgatan. They got through them as best they could – for the sake of the children, as they kept saying.

Simon had his old room back at Erik's house. Erik's rebellion against fate was over. He had shrunk in stature and grown milder. Simon thought this very sad – his dad had always been a big and angry man.

Klara had completed her studies and been given a post at the psychiatric clinic at the Sahlgrenska Hospital. Simon had only two exams left to do and would be home from London in March when he would complete his thesis. They were in a queue for housing, but Ruben had his eye on a ninety-year-old widow who had a three-room apartment in Majorna.

One wet day at the end of February Simon's tutor, Professor J. P. Armstrong, asked to speak to him. Simon sat in his handsome office surrounded by the professor's books and papers, and his casts of Assyrian lions. Although he was a specialist on the Assyrian period, Professor Armstrong had taken part in his youth in Sir Leonard Woolley's famous excavations of the royal tombs at Ur.

'Pennsylvania University have a dig in progress at Girsu – the Eninnu temple.' He smiled when he saw Simon's interest. 'One of their men has fallen ill – the script expert. They've asked us if we can send a replacement quickly. I thought I'd ask whether you would be available?'

If the Sumerian sun god had stepped down from the sky and spoken to him, Simon couldn't have been more surprised. And if Innana herself had invited him to her love nest, he couldn't have been more pleased.

'You've practically finished here and congratulations, by the way, on your findings. Perhaps it might amuse you to see the culture from a slightly more down-to-earth viewpoint?'

'Amuse', Simon thought. He was being given the chance to see Gudea's temple outside Lagash at close quarters. 'Amuse' was a very English word to describe the jubilation he felt. 'I'm really very grateful, sir,' he stammered.

Professor Armstrong smiled graciously at him.

After that, everything happened quickly: visa, money, tickets. Simon managed to pack up his thesis and send it to Sweden. He rang Ruben who was genuinely pleased. Even Erik said he realised you couldn't refuse such an adventure. Only Klara was miserable.

'It'll be only for a few months. They stop when the hot weather comes,' Simon told her.

'Look after yourself,' Klara said.

She's getting more like Karin every day, he thought angrily. 'You must see I have to take a chance of this kind.'

'Of course I do. It's just that I feel a little envious.'

They both laughed.

'Look after yourself,' she said again, as he put down the telephone.

340

Simon flew to Basra. With stop-overs, the flight took thirteen hours, so he was almost asleep when he registered at the English colonial hotel that looked like a stage set at the back of the airport. There was a park on the other side of the building and he could hear the rustling of the wind through the palms outside his window.

At eight the next morning, David Moore burst into his bedroom. 'Hey, man, life's serious now and waiting for you outside in the form of an old jeep.' He was so American that he could have stepped out of a Western.

'Have I time for a shower?'

Simon realised he sounded rather English and he noticed David's eyes narrowing with dislike. God knows how Queen Victoria's plumbers had managed in this mausoleum, but he was sure a shower could be produced from a rusty pipe somewhere, David said.

Simon laughed, got out of bed and held out his hand. 'Larsson. I'm Swedish, so I have had nothing to do with imperialism, colonial hotels, gentlemen or anything British. I'm innocent. OK?'

David laughed heartily and threw himself into an old wicker chair which groaned and creaked. 'A Swede? From University College, London? Couldn't they send anyone else?'

They had a large English breakfast, then Simon and his case were packed into the jeep. Carefully, David fastened the hood and taped over a crack by Simon's door.

'Will it be cold?'

'You'll soon find out.'

Within half an hour they were out of town and taking the road north. Simon remembered Grimberg's words: 'Mesopotamia is a land of death and great silence over which the Lord's hand weighs heavily.'

Desert stretched as far as the eye could see, sand in treacherous dunes. Here and there, the road disappeared under flying drifts, but they drove round for a while and soon found their route again.

'Not all that unlike snow-drifts,' David remarked. 'I suppose you're used to that?'

Simon laughed and swallowed a mouthful of sand. The hot wind blew it into the vehicle, into his eyes and mouth, under his collar, down his back and round his stomach where it mixed with sweat and itched.

They stopped at a bar on the banks of the marsh town of al-Shubaish and rinsed the sand off their faces with filthy water.

'I don't think you can get a beer here' David said. 'The prophet Mohammed dictates the drinking habits. Don't rinse your mouth out with water, for Christ's sake. You'll have to buy a Coca-Cola.'

So Coca-Cola had arrived even at this hovel of reeds which looked as though it was about to collapse. The drink cooled him and banished the grittiness between his teeth.

'I usually bring young, rosy-cheeked students here,' David said. 'It's a useful place for romantic fools. You can still see how people lived in the days of the ancient Sumerians.'

He waved a hand along the jetty and Simon gazed at the Marsh Arabs' pointed canoes. They were the same as the famous silver canoe discovered in Meskalamdig's tomb in Ur.

But mostly he watched the men poling and the emaciated children, their eyes covered with flies.

'There's everything here,' Moore told him. 'Malaria, leprosy, tuberculosis, bilharzia. Take your pick. Living conditions comprise oppression of women, cruelties of various kinds, vendettas and the charming practice of female circumcision.'

This was Simon's first encounter with destitution and he was unprepared for the shame he felt, a burning sense of how tall and well-fed, white and educated he was.

'The Garden of Eden is supposed to be located not far from here,' David continued. 'Nothing surprises me any longer except man's ability to lie.'

Simon looked away from the woman passing them. She was as timid as an animal and so thin that her pregnancy looked grotesque.

'Are you a Christian?' said Moore.

'Officially I'm Lutheran,' said Simon. 'But Scandinavia is fairly secular.'

'The British have been here for years and years. But they have done little else but mix quinine in their drinks and guard the oil route to the sea.'

They hired a canoe. Simon was ashamed when a green dollar bill changed hands and it was clear this was a big thing for the Marsh Arab who smiled a strangely gentle smile.

'Apropos quinine,' said David. 'There's quite a few of the delightful Anopheles here.'

'What's that?'

'The malarial mosquito.'

It was a distinctive world they poled their way through, a world built by people thousands of years ago from the clay of the delta. Here and there were houses of the same kind as those on ancient Sumerian reliefs, bundles of reeds bent into curved arches.

'They should bring in bulldozers and drain it, spray everything with DDT, send the kids to school, build a hospital and take the veils off their women,' Moore declared. 'Then we'd be doing something useful instead of digging about in piles of ruins in the desert.'

'Why did you become an archaeologist?'

'Because I was a fool, like you.'

They got back into the jeep. Unable to speak because of the sand, Simon tried to suppress the images of the children

343

in his mind. He remembered David's questions about religion. Had he seen that he was Jewish? 'What religion are you?' he asked.

'Me? I'm an orthodox Jew.'

'The old man's got great expectations of you,' David said as they crossed the main road and the Euphrates to continue north towards Tello. 'His name's Philip Peterson and he believes every damned shard we've found is going to reveal important secrets.'

'What?' Simon was appalled.

'Yeah. For instance, he wants to ascertain where the capital of Akkad – the much-lauded and vanished Agade – was situated. There's a chance our friend Gudea was involved in levelling it to the ground.'

'Hardly,' Simon said. 'The mountain people, the Gutiers, did that.'

'When it comes to Mesopotamia you can never be sure. Someone sticks a spade in the ground somewhere and the course of history is changed.'

When they arrived at the dig, David introduced him to his colleagues. 'To avoid any misunderstandings, this is Simon Larsson, a Viking from Sweden. He has only been honouring London for a few years with his presence.'

They all laughed. Peterson, a man of about fifty, was also in the group and Simon liked him from the start.

They were exposing the scribes' district and it looked as if a mad giant had thrown smashed walls at the moon. A large tent had been erected for sorting through the shards that had been found.

'I hope you won't be disappointed, sir,' Simon said to Professor Peterson.

'For God's sake, the name's Philip,' the professor exclaimed. 'You're a Sumerologist, aren't you? A script expert?'

'Yes.'

He was given a mug of canned American soup, then went straight into the tent where the fragments had been arranged in orderly rows.

'Get going, son,' Peterson said, smiling. So Simon had time only to glance at the ruins of the Eninnu temple before sitting down in the tent. It couldn't be this hot even in hell, he thought.

They didn't stop until darkness fell so swiftly that it was as if someone had turned out a light. Peterson looked hopefully at Simon who shook his head.

'Haven't seen anything except the usual so far.'

A man whom he hadn't met came up to him. 'Thackeray,' he said. 'English. Grandson of the writer. I'm the doctor at this cowboy camp. You didn't let that damned Moore drag you round the marshes, did you?'

'Had I any choice?'

Thackeray groaned. 'I hope you're a man with luck. If not, you've got about ten days.'

'What are you talking about?'

'Malaria.'

There was a box of quinine tablets on his table. 'Dissolve four tablets in boiled water every morning and evening,' Thackeray told him and left.

'It's not a dangerous illness,' a man from New York with a mop of bleached hair said. Another man disagreed. Five people had caught it recently and been flown home with high temperatures.

'But that's crazy,' Simon exclaimed.

The man opposite him laughed and told him that this was the sort of place where survivors should envy the dead. After several days in the heat and sand, Simon knew what he meant.

Day after day, Simon was aware that he was disappointing Peterson. But their mood lightened when Simon was given some new fragments a few days later. He saw at once that they were different and much more interesting. His heart thumping, he translated them, Peterson leaning over his shoulder:

> He cut the thongs of whips and switches and put pieces of the wool from a ewe on to them. The mother did not scold her child, no one opposed Gudea, the good shepherd, who built up Eninnu.

Almost simultaneously they recognised the text from Gudea's famous cylinders in the Louvre. What they had found were copies. Peterson was inconsolable.

Twice Simon climbed the vast walls of the ruined temple. There was no sign of life, not even a whisper of Gudea. He had no idea what he was expecting, but his disappointment was as great as Peterson's.

Late in the evening of the tenth day, when he was alone in his tent, Simon felt the first shivers. He knew that he had only an hour before the fever took him over. He ran over to the ruins and climbed to the top.

The moon was out.

'Gudea,' he shouted. 'For the sake of the merciful god, come to me.'

He was so cold his teeth were chattering. But he got what he wanted. A man was also standing on the wall, waiting for him.

Chapter 41

He could just make out Gudea's mysterious smile and the gentle wisdom in his half-moon-shaped eyes.

When Simon asked the question that had been burning

within him ever since childhood – what are you doing in my life? – the smile grew broader and became a laugh ringing round the walls. He could feel the fever raging through his body and he wanted to scream with rage and despair. He was so close now to the answer to the mystery of his life. But this damned malaria would soon take over his mind.

He could feel himself falling from the wall and hitting rock as he landed on a ledge. The desert wind cooled his fever but increased the pain in his leg unbearably.

The next moment Gudea held out his hand and Simon took it. It was a small hand and there was a strange firmness in its grip. Light as a feather, the hand lifted him over the top of the wall and he saw that the temple had been resurrected: golden bulls decorated the walls between the pillars in the market square and the ziggurat rose to the sky, solid yet airy, a testimony to man's unity with God.

It was light. The sun blazed over the temple city, reflecting the magnificent azure, dark diorite and white alabaster stonework. Most of all, it lit up the gold covering the ceiling and walls, until it shimmered and glowed.

Simon was dimly aware that outside the walls, the night and the desert were as before, that Steven Thackeray had found him, got hold of helpers and a stretcher, and splinted his broken leg. But Simon forgot the darkness around him as he marvelled at the stunning interior of the temple.

'What did it sound like, the language you brought back to life?' he asked the man who had always been present in his dreams and now filled his mind.

This time Simon thought there was a touch of sorrow in Gudea's smile. 'It's not as you think,' he said. 'It was greater than the Sumerian language, an ancient tongue, the oldest in mankind, a language that could be spoken to animals and trees, the sky and water.'

He sighed. 'I thought I had the key, that I would be able

to resurrect the connection between the new and ancient tongues. But it was too late. The way to a greater reality was closed and our songs could not open it. It was perhaps the last attempt made on earth to enable man to participate fully with the natural world again.

'But now the great God is making a new effort, an attempt to establish a wholeness, with every child that is born. At the beginning of life, children are able to communicate with everything that lives, with the rivers and the skies.'

Gudea pointed his finger, and oak trees grew in the market square, Simon's oaks from the land of his childhood. Before them was a little boy with anger burning in his eyes, calling out his separation, measuring, judging, evaluating and finally rejecting the trees.

Simon screamed with pain and someone somewhere stuck a needle into his arm and the torment receded.

Gudea took Simon's hand again. 'We must start our journey by going to see the God who lives in our hearts and who strives to resurrect the pact between ourselves and the world around us.'

Simon saw the sorrow had gone from Gudea's face and his half-moon eyes were full of confidence. They went into the temple at the bottom of the tower and he was astonished by the size of the hall.

But when he turned to the God awaiting them at the end of the hall, Gudea stopped him. 'No one may look at him without being destroyed. You may look at him only with your heart, in the temple where he always waits for you and which knows no limits.'

Side by side, they fell to their knees, and the great desert and the golden temple in the sun vanished.

Gudea put his hand on Simon's shoulder, a light touch full of tenderness which he recognised. 'Now you will meet Ur–Babar's daughter, Nin–alla, the high priestess of the moon god and my wife.'

Simon followed Gudea, who was a head shorter than he was, up the ziggurat staircase until they came to the temple of the moon god at the top.

'The priestess is asleep and may not be woken until the next new moon,' Gudea told him. 'She needs all her strength to guide the silver ship across the skies.'

Simon bowed to the sleeper whom he knew well, and whose red hair was plaited into a fine wreath round the high white forehead.

On the way down the staircase he heard a violin playing a tune of wild beauty.

'Yes,' said Gudea, 'you may listen to our violinist, the one you chase like the wind, but can never find.'

Simon knew it was Haberman playing and he ran after the sound, but it mocked him as it disappeared among the pillars in the great palace. Only once, for a brief moment, did he catch a glimpse of the back of the player, and he was as he remembered him in his dream: timid, fleeing.

I'm lost, Simon thought. I'll never find my way out of this palace. He cried out in fear, and tall Aron Äppelgren leaned over and lifted him up on to his bicycle. They walked home as usual across the meadows and Aron imitated all the birds and teased the gulls, and Simon laughed just as he had as a child, and wet himself just as he had also done when he was little.

Then he remembered where he was. 'Gudea,' he shouted.

'I'm always here.' The gentle voice was close to him and Simon knew there was nothing to be afraid of.

They were standing in a bedouin tent, the dark cloth cloaking the light. It took a while before Simon's eyes adjusted. Then he saw a woman bowing to them in the middle of the tent.

'I was childless,' she told him. 'It is a fate worse than death in our people. So you can understand my joy when Ke-Ba, the priestess, came one night and asked me to look after the boy she had given birth to. But I knew that Gatumdus's priestess could not be with child for her seed belongs to the goddess and cannot grow in the womb of her priestess. So when Ke-Ba became pregnant, she knew the child was the god's own and dared not talk about it to the priests of Akkad who would have destroyed the holy child.'

Simon nodded.

'So Gudea grew up here with me and he gave my life value and became a blessing to all his people.'

For a long time Simon looked at the woman for there was something about her he recognised. But it was not until they bade her farewell and he saw the great Nordic forest behind the walls of the tent, that he realised it was Inga speaking to him and that the long lake was there, blue and cool in the endless desert.

Then Gudea said he wanted him to meet his mother, the great Ke-Ba. He took Simon to another room with glowing blue walls and a ceiling covered with gold.

A woman was waiting in the centre of the room.

'I'll leave you alone,' Gudea said.

And Ke-Ba, who had given birth to the child but had not been allowed to keep it, turned slowly round and her warm brown eyes met his.

'Mother,' Simon said. 'Karin, my darling mother.'

She smiled her old wide smile and he thought, God, good God, I'd forgotten how beautiful she was, and he recognised every note in her firm voice as she said, 'Simon, my boy.'

They stood there holding hands and the joy between them was so great that it split the walls of the room.

'I don't like this guilt you torment yourself with,' she

said to him. 'You were a joy every single day in the house by the river. Nothing you did, do you hear, could have been different.'

Simon could hear the force, the challenge in her words. 'Mother,' he said. 'Why did you die?'

'I chose to go when I thought I had done what I could, Simon. I had had a good life and I didn't want to hang around getting old.'

He opened his mouth to protest, but stopped when he saw her smiling.

'I'm joking, Simon. There was something you didn't know about.' And she told him about Petter and the waxwings, and at last he understood the source of the sorrow in her heart.

'Life is great, Simon. Much greater than we imagine.'

He looked round and the infinity of the plain met that of the sea. Behind Karin were the forests, the deep forests, and above them the sky without end.

Then Karin looked uneasy. 'Simon, we're wasting time. You must hurry!' She said, as she always had done. 'Run,' she urged, hanging his satchel of school books over his shoulder. 'You'll be on time if you hurry. Put your best foot forward now.'

He nodded. He was safe. She cared for him as she had always done. He would be there on time.

He turned round at the kitchen door and there she was, standing as usual by the stove, laughing.

'Hurry, boy. Hurry now,' she called after him.

Chapter 42

Simon opened his eyes to a grey room one ordinary Swedish afternoon and heard voices outside the door, Swedish voices. I'm home, he thought. He wasn't that surprised for he had been aware of injections and stretchers, planes and white coats, Klara's face leaning over him, cool hands turning his pillow and wiping his forehead, Ruben's eyes anxious and Erik's fearful.

He felt sad, unsure whether he wanted to return to the reality so many people thought was the only one.

It soon became clear to Simon that the people outside the door were talking about him.

'We can't let it go on like this. He seems to be in a state of confusion that has nothing to do with malaria,' a young voice was saying.

'Concussion and fever, that's a good enough explanation,' an older one replied. 'His relatives have assured us that he's stable. And his wife is a psychiatrist and she's not worried.'

'But he's been hallucinating for two weeks between attacks of fever when he should be calm.'

The young voice was raised again and Simon wasn't sure that he liked the sound of it. I must make a stand against my visions, he thought, and not give way any longer.

Put your best foot forward. Then he realised that his other foot and leg were in plaster and he remembered dimly breaking it when he fell off the temple walls.

He tried to sleep. Images appeared and he drove them away. At last he rang the bell by his bed and the night sister came. 'Could I have a sleeping pill?' he asked.

He could see she was surprised that he was awake.

A harassed doctor appeared, took his pulse and told the nurse to take the drip out of his arm and give Simon a cup of gruel. 'Welcome back to the real world,' he said as he left the room.

Simon smiled, ate the gruel, took the pill and had a dreamless night.

The next morning, the ward doctor came into the room, the owner of the young voice, and Simon found they knew each other from student days.

'Hello there. How are you feeling?'

'All right, thanks. A bit tired.'

Per Jansson looked at Simon's temperature chart, now going down nicely, took his pulse and listened to his heart. Simon realised that this was to conceal the fact that he was curious. He talked about malaria for a while, told Simon that his recovery would be straight forward, and that his leg was healing well.

He turned to go, but when he reached the doorway, he stopped. 'Who is Gudea?' he asked.

'A Sumerian king, one of the last.'

'What was so special about him?'

'Well, he built a great temple and tried to blow life into the Sumerian language which had become almost extinct. His name means "Called". Why the hell are you interested in him?'

'You've been raving about him for nearly two weeks now.'

'Have I?' Simon said, feigning surprise. 'It's not that strange, I suppose. My thesis is on him and I've had a high temperature.'

'We thought it peculiar. Lasting hallucinations aren't part of the picture.'

'Really?'

'For a while I thought you were almost possessed.'

'Possessed?' Simon's surprise was now genuine. 'Does the medical world believe in that kind of thing?'

'"There are more things in heaven and earth . . ." ' His friend shrugged his shoulders and left.

Simon lay back in bed. He had coped, he thought, and would probably do so again. But he felt no satisfaction in his victory.

Klara came in and yes, he was pleased to see her.

'You can be frightening, Simon,' she said quietly.

'I didn't mean to be.'

'Did you meet Gudea?'

'Yes, at least in my dreams,' said Simon worried she would start talking about Jungian prototypes. But she merely sat and held his hand until he fell asleep.

'He didn't take away your will to live, did he, Simon?' Klara asked on the third day.

She saw he'd been weeping, but he couldn't tell her that it wasn't for Gudea, but for Karin and it was because she had told him to run away from her kitchen.

Erik came for a while, but he could see Simon was tired so he just sat there, his eyes glistening. 'I've been so bloody worried about you.'

'You needn't have, Dad. After all, you taught me to fight.'

They managed to laugh.

Ruben came with flowers and books for him. He brought Malin and it was good to see her.

A little later, he heard the doctors talking in the corridor about giving him anti-depressants.

Klara objected. 'He'll pull through,' she told them. 'All he needs is time.' But Simon knew she was worried.

A few days later, Per Jansson appeared again. 'We've got an Englishman here,' he said. 'He's a bit of an expert on malaria.'

There were more doctors than usual on the ward round the next day. There were white coats everywhere, including one worn by a small man who spoke meticulous English.

Per stammered out the details of Simon's condition in his clumsy English. 'We were worried about the patient for a while, as he hallucinated almost continuously for several days.'

'That happens occasionally,' said the Englishman. 'Excuse me.' He pulled back Simon's eyelids with a practised hand and shone a light into his eyes.

'There's no sign of any lasting damage.' He looked at the case sheet. 'He's had a fall too, so there's probably concussion in addition to his fever.'

A jolt went through Simon's body. He recognised the hand, the touch. He stared at the stubby fingers, raised his eyes to the face above him and saw into eyes smiling a secretive smile. I am mad, he thought.

Warning bells rang. *Watch out! Watch out, for God's sake.*

But as the doctors left his need to know for certain overcame his fear. 'Forgive me, sir, but haven't we met before?' he asked.

The Englishman turned round and came back to the bed. He looked first at Simon, then at the chart with his name on it. 'Simon Larsson, of course. I remember that morning at Omberg very well,' he said almost cheerfully.

Everyone looked surprised and the consultant said, as people do, that the world was a small place.

Simon could feel laughter rising in him. 'Do you think the giants still wash their long johns in the Vättern, sir?'

'Of course,' the man said, his eyes glinting, Simon's laughter leaped from him and exploded round the room. It was probably echoing in Queen Omma's fortress as it had once before, he thought.

All the doctors laughed then, most of them uncertainly, some thinking that English humour was rather trying when it was as obscure as this.

The Englishman turned to his colleagues and explained in an apologetic voice that he had spent a day with this young archaeologist when he had made it clear that he was to search for the hall of the mountain king. 'And do you think he listened to me?' he continued. 'No. He went straight to the malarial marshes of Iraq and the ruins in Lagash.'

The doctors nodded, not understanding, their smiles becoming more and more strained.

'How are your children, sir?' Simon persisted.

'I've had some trouble with my son, but he's better now,' he replied. 'And now I have a little daughter.'

'Congratulations.'

'Thank you.'

He put his hand on Simon's shoulder, and Simon could feel his power. 'We'll meet again, Simon Larsson.' And he was gone.

But he left behind him a joy and a sense of security which took root in Simon's heart, right into the hall of the mountain king.

Simon recovered quickly. He ate like a horse, slept like an innocent child and had gentle, friendly dreams.

Klara came to fetch him the day he was discharged. 'I've got a surprise for you downstairs,' she told him.

And there was his car, the red Volkswagen that had been shipped over from London.

'I can drive if your leg is not strong enough yet?' she offered.

'You do that.'

It was good to see the world again. The rest of Simon's family were waiting for him in the house by the river mouth.

He took Malin in his arms. 'Karin sends her love,' he whispered.

She nodded, not at all surprised.

The table was laid at Mona's and Isak's house, so Simon limped through the big garden, noting that spring had begun her work, that the blue anemones were out and vying with the blue of the scillas under the aspen trees.

They sat down for dinner and raised their glasses. 'Here's to Karin, to her memory,' Simon said.

They drank to her and for the first time Simon felt her sorrow had lost its impact, for him and for the others.

At dusk, he made his way slowly up the hill, across the meadows, towards the oak trees in the land of his childhood. It was time, he felt, to renew his friendship with them.